NO LONGER PROPERTY OF
SEATTLE PUBLIC LIBRARY

AUG 18 2022

THE LION

A Novel of Ancient Athens

CONN IGGULDEN

PEGASUS BOOKS

NEW YORK LONDON

THE LION

Pegasus Books, Ltd.
148 West 37th Street, 13th Floor
New York, NY 10018

Copyright © 2022 by Conn Iggulden

First Pegasus Books cloth edition May 2022

All rights reserved. No part of this book may be reproduced in whole or in part
without written permission from the publisher, except by reviewers who may
quote brief excerpts in connection with a review in a newspaper, magazine, or
electronic publication; nor may any part of this book be reproduced, stored in a
retrieval system, or transmitted in any form or by any means electronic, mechanical,
photocopying, recording, or other, without written permission from the publisher.

ISBN: 978-1-63936-222-6

10 9 8 7 6 5 4 3 2 1

Printed in the United States of America
Distributed by Simon & Schuster
www.pegasusbooks.com

To Michelle Whitehead.

'What remains of us is love.'

– Philip Larkin

THE LION

Locations

Agora	Ἀγορά	ag-or-a	ag-<u>or</u>-a	Open place, market.
Areopagus	Ἄρειος πάγος	a-ray-oss pag-oss	a-ree-<u>op</u>-ag-ous (as in danger-ous)	Rock of Ares. Hill in Athens used as a court.
Cypros	Κύπρος	cou-pros	<u>sigh</u>-prous	Island of Cyprus.
Plataea	Πλάταια	plat-eye-a	pla-<u>tee</u>-a	Greek town in Boeotia.
Pnyx	Πνύξ	p-nooks	p-<u>niks</u>	'Packed in'. Hill. Meeting place of the Assembly in Athens.
Scyros	Σκῦρος	skoo-ros	<u>ski</u>-ros	Island where bones of Theseus were found.

Pronunciation

Military terms

	Ancient Greek	Ancient Greek Pronunciation	English Pronunciation	Meaning
archon	ἄρχων	ark-own	<u>ark</u>-on	Ruler, leader.
epistates	ἐπιστάτης	ep-ist-at-airs	ep-<u>ist</u>-at-eez	Chairman in the Athenian Assembly.
keleustes	κελευστής	kel-eu-stairs	kel-<u>you</u>-steez	Trireme officer.
lochagos	λοχαγός	lock-a-goss	<u>lock</u>-a-goss	Rank equivalent to captain.
phalanx	Φάλαγξ	fal-anks	<u>fal</u>-anks	Body of heavily armed infantry.
strategos	στρατηγός	strat-air-goss	<u>strat</u>-egg-oss	General, commander.
trierarch	τριήραρχος	tree-air-ark-oss	<u>try</u>-err-ark	Commander of a trireme.

Underlining indicates stressed syllables.

Characters

Agariste	Ἀγαρίστη	ag-a-rist-air	ag-a-<u>rist</u>-ee	Wife of Xanthippus.
Anaxagoras	Ἀναξαγόρας	an-ax-ag-or-as	an-ax-<u>ag</u>-or-as	Friend of Pericles, natural philosopher.
Aristides	Ἀριστείδης	a-ris-tay-dairs	a-<u>rist</u>-id-eez	Strategos, eponymous archon 489 BC.
Cimon	Κίμων	kim-own	<u>ky</u>-mon	Son of Miltiades.
Eleni (Helen)	Ἑλένη	hell-en-air	e-<u>lay</u>-nee	Daughter of Xanthippus and Agariste.
Ephialtes	Ἐφιάλτης	eff-ee-al-tairs	eff-ee-<u>al</u>-teez	Athenian politican.
Epikleos	Ἐπικλέος	ep-i-kle-oss	ep-i-<u>klay</u>-oss	Friend of Xanthippus.
Leotychides	Λεωτυχίδας	lair-oh-took-i-das	lee-oh-<u>tick</u>-i-dees	Spartan king.
Pericles	Περικλῆς	per-ik-lairs	<u>per</u>-ik-leez	Son of Xanthippus and Agariste.
Tisamenus	Τισαμενός	tiss-am-en-oss	tiss-a-<u>meen</u>-ous	Soothsayer.
Xanthippus	Ξάνθιππος	ksan-thip-oss	<u>zan</u>-thip-ous	Strategos, leader.
Xerxes	Ξέρξης	kserk-seez	<u>zerk</u>-seez	King of Persia.
Zeno	Ζήνων	zairn-own	<u>zee</u>-no	Friend of Pericles, natural philosopher.

Prologue

Pausanias took a deep breath, feeling calm spread through him. He exchanged a glance with his soothsayer, then rose from kneeling to walk the length of the hall, for once completely alone. The royal chamber of Sparta was cool after the heat of the morning. His armour clinked and rattled as he strode down the central aisle. He was unwounded, thanks to Ares and Apollo, his patron gods. He would endure no crippling disfigurement, no fever to steal away his wits. In the prime of his youth, he had already recovered from the hardships of the campaign. Of course, victory had a way of reducing aches and hungers. Only those who lost a great battle had to endure exhaustion. Those who won often discovered they could dance and drink enough for two.

Pausanias was pleased he had managed to bathe before the summons. His hair was damp and he felt cool despite the heat. Yet he had not been long back in Sparta. His personal helots had still been cleaning his cloak when the runner came. Most of the dried blood and dust had been brushed out, as well as lines of salt his sweat had left behind. It would do. He draped a length of it over his shoulder as he walked, held with an iron clasp.

When he had first immersed himself in the cold pool, Pausanias had watched a skin of oily filth moving away from him over the water. He still hoped it was a good omen. He had looked up from strange patterns and suddenly seen the red eyes of his helots, their trembling hands. He understood then, as he had not before. They grieved.

He might have dismissed them for intruding on his thoughts; he had not. They too had fought at Plataea, losing thousands of their number against Persian infantry. It had been a kind of madness and he still blamed the Athenians for inspiring them. Pausanias had warned Aristides not to let slaves think they were men!

As he walked down the long nave, he thought the helots would not need to be culled that year. In normal times, when they grew too numerous, young Spartans would hunt them through the streets and into the hills, competing for kills and trophies. Yet as he had leaned back in the pool, he thought he'd seen something new in their eyes, something troubling. For just a moment, he thought they looked on him as wild dogs might look on an injured deer.

He shook his head. Perhaps he would order a cull after all, to remind them of their place. Curse Aristides! Helots were too numerous ever to be free. It was a knife-edge Sparta chose to walk – the constant threat that kept them strong.

He caught himself in his thoughts. *He* would not order any cull. His authority had ended the moment he crossed back into Spartan territory. No, it would be the man who had summoned him who would make decisions of that sort.

When he reached the end of the hall, Pausanias dropped to one knee, staring at polished stone. He was somehow not surprised when silence stretched. The younger man wished him to understand which of them held power in that place. Pausanias told himself to be cautious. There was more than one kind of battlefield.

'Stand, Pausanias,' Pleistarchus said at last.

The young king was still a month from his eighteenth birthday, but the fact that he was a son of Leonidas could be seen in the massive forearms, thick with black hair. Pleistarchus had wanted desperately to command at Plataea, but the ephors of Sparta had forbidden it. They had already lost their battle king at Thermopylae. His son was the most precious resource Sparta had.

Instead, it had been Pausanias who led the army of Sparta, standing in as the king's regent. It had been he who won an extraordinary, impossible victory, ending the great invasion and breaking at last the dreams of Persian kings.

Pausanias swallowed, suddenly weary. His triumph had earned him no goodwill, he could see that. He raised his head and met the cold gaze of the king. At least whatever was coming would be quick. Athenians seemed to be three-quarters wind for all the talking they did. His own people spent words with more care.

'You have done your duty,' Pleistarchus said. Pausanias bowed his head in response. It was enough, and still more than the young king wanted to say.

Two of the ephors nodded, expressing their support. It mattered more that three did not. They only watched the man who had led every Spartiate and helot to victory.

'I will present the names of the honoured dead,' Pausanias said into the silence. The helots would not be listed, of course, only Spartan warriors who had fallen. With the blessing of Apollo and Ares, they at least were few.

Pausanias tried to resist the fierce pride that rose in him then, despite the formal words. He had been part of that extraordinary day! He had held back men in dust and chaos, until it had been time to put them in, as a golden stone in the flood, to stand against the Persian generals. The ephors had not been there then. The son of Leonidas had not been there!

Pausanias felt a weight settle upon his shoulders. That was exactly the problem they faced, the reason they stared as if they wished to open him up like a fruit and examine his entrails. The ephors had forbidden Pleistarchus from leaving

Sparta – and in doing so, denied him the greatest victory in the history of the city-state. The young king must hate them for it, or perhaps . . . Pausanias felt his mouth grow dry. He had been called alone to that place. Only because the sooth-sayer had been with him had the other man come. Would either of them be allowed to leave alive? He tried to swallow. The heart of Sparta was in *peitharchia* – total obedience. This son of Leonidas had endured utter misery, watching his father's army taken to war by someone else. He had not made a word of complaint, Pausanias recalled. It spoke rather well for the sort of king he would be.

'I have been deciding what to do with you,' Pleistarchus said.

Pausanias felt cold steal into him. If the young king or-dered his death, he would not leave that room. By his own hand or another's, his life was in the hands of a youth who resented him, in the hands of ephors who regretted the bat-tle that had saved them all. Win or lose, it seemed there had been no way back. Sensing his life hung in the balance, Pau-sanias spoke quickly.

'Majesty, ephors, I would like to visit the oracle at Delphi, to learn what lies ahead.'

It was well judged. Even the ephors of Sparta would not ignore a request to speak to Apollo's own representative. The Pythian priestess sat above steam from the underworld and spoke with the voice of the god. Pausanias felt his heart leap as two of the ephors exchanged a glance.

King Pleistarchus shook his head, frowning.

'Perhaps you will, when duty allows. Until then, I called you here this evening to give you command of the fleet, Pau-sanias. King Leotychides and I are in agreement. You will take our authority amongst the cities and their ships. There are Persian strongholds still. They cannot be allowed to rebuild or grow strong once again. Sparta leads, general. So lead – far from here.'

The message behind the last was clear enough. Pausanias felt relief flood through him. He had swung from pride to dread and back, and he felt himself flush as his heart thumped. It was a fine solution. The victor of Plataea would go far away from the young king who actually ruled the armed forces of Sparta. There would be no awkward clash of loyalties, no chance of civil war. Men revered those who led them, Pausanias knew very well. In that moment, he might have flung the entire army against the ephors. They had to fear him. He thought he saw it in their eyes, in the way they watched. Yet he was obedient.

He knelt once more.

'You honour me, Majesty,' he said. He was pleased to see Pleistarchus smile. He must have been worried about his battle-hardened general returning with victory under his belt.

'It is more than a reward for service, Pausanias,' the young king said. 'Athens seeks to rule at sea, as we rule on land. They have been gathering at Delos, but I do not want them leading our allies. Sparta is first among the Hellenes and always will be. You will take six ships to them, with a full complement of Spartiates and helot rowers. Your authority is given by my hand to remind them of that. You will lead the allied fleet, do you understand?'

'I do, Majesty,' Pausanias said. He could feel his skin twitch, hairs rising. He wondered how the Athenians would feel about that.

He rose to his feet and was pleased when the young king held him by both shoulders, then kissed him on each cheek. It was a mark of royal approval and it meant he would survive. He felt himself tremble in reaction, sweat making his skin shine.

'Your ships are in port by Argos, Pausanias. Summon whomever you wish as your officers. I leave that to your discretion.'

Pausanias bowed in reply. Of course. The young king sought to rid himself of anyone else who might support Pausanias over his own right to rule. Pausanias forced himself into cool *praotes* – the perfect calm of Spartan men. He took the king's hand in his own and raised it over his head.

'You have served Sparta well,' an ephor said.

It was not one of those who had shown any support for him, Pausanias noted. Even so, he bowed deeper. The five old men spoke for the gods and kings of Sparta, after all.

Pausanias strode back down the long nave, his head high. He saw Tisamenus waiting for him there, both eyebrows raised in question. The soothsayer was not sure what mood Pausanias was in after whatever he had been told.

Pausanias clapped him on the shoulder as he passed, allowing himself a tight smile.

'Come on, my friend, we have a lot to do.'

'You're pleased, then?' Tisamenus asked.

Pausanias thought for a moment and nodded.

'Yes. It's good news. They have given me the fleet!'

PART ONE

'In great good fortune, men never think
they might yet stumble.'

– Aeschylus

I

In darkness, the trireme struck the beach at the speed of a running man, knifing through shingle in a hissing roar. A second followed, almost the shadow of the first. One after the other, they came to a halt, and leaned.

On the third ship, helmsmen threw their weight against twin steering bars, aiming for clear beach. Below their feet, oarsmen beat waves to a froth, ninety to a side. They had scouted that coast as best they could, but in the night, none of the three ships carried lamps. Those who laboured on the benches could see nothing at all. A hoplite leaned far out at the prow, ready to call a warning, ignoring the sea spray crashing over him.

When the third keel struck, it sliced through shining banks, peeling them back. The first jolt of contact threw men down, tumbling them where they knelt on deck. One went over the side with a stifled cry, landing in shallows and then rolling clear in panic. Shingle lifted under him like a bow wave, pressing him aside. He was left behind, blowing in relief at stars overhead.

The Athenian warship ground on, cutting higher and higher up the shore until the vast weight and speed suddenly fell away. Wooden beams ticked and croaked and the trireme stopped. It was out of its element: clumsy where it had been quick, dead where it had been alive.

The deck tilted slowly on its keel, bowing to the land. Ropes and ladders unfurled like festival ribbons and men leaped down. The rowers on both sides had been quick to pull their precious charges in, rather than see oars snapped to kindling. They too spilled out, crunching over sand and stones. The slope into the sea was gentle there, which was why Cimon had chosen that place. On another day, their task would have been to put small boats into the water, to carry ropes to whichever galleys were still afloat. They would have heaved the ships down the trench again, into the shallows, until the moment of joy when the sea claimed her own. Not this time.

Cimon had sent his three ships like spears against the shore. All the Athenians had learned to row, taking turns like the crew of the *Argos* centuries before. On land, they took up weapons and shields, gripping them tightly, murmuring thanks to the gods. Cimon had seen the strength of rowers, the powerful shoulders and legs that meant they walked like cats and climbed like Barbary apes. He had insisted on his hoplites taking full days at the oars, building fitness. In return, he had trained the rowers with spear and shield. They had all rowed; they had all fought.

The hoplites gathered a little way from the dark hulls. Their kit cost a small fortune, so they carried a part of any family's wealth with them. A good shield could be three months' salary, saved up for a year – the bowl measured and fitted, then painted with a personal crest. Greaves too had to be shaped by a master, held to the shins by the spring of metal. Crested helmets cost as much again. Some wore swords on their belts, but the main weapon was always the long dory spear.

Each set was a treasure of Athens, marked with family names, guarded and oiled, brought home from every battle. For those who fell, the bronze pieces were collected. In time, they would be handed to an eldest son, or sold so a widow could live.

As Cimon dropped to the shingle, he saw only good order under the stars. His men stood in ranks, exchanging greetings and comments in quiet voices, ready to march. He nodded, satisfied. The hoplites moved well with spears, as befitted ones who had practised since childhood. Each of the fearsome things was topped with a leaf blade of iron, thick as armour. Those were balanced by a heavy point at the other end. In the hands of a competent man, those spears were destroyers of cavalry, breakers of Immortals, the bristling spines of the hoplite shield line. At Plataea and Marathon, they had shown their worth. At Eion too, where they had sacked a Persian fortress.

Pericles watched Cimon stand apart from them, dark and very still in the starlight, though his cloak twitched in the breeze. Pericles himself stood with Attikos, a man at least twice his age but who was of his tribe and deme in Athens. Attikos shivered in the breeze off the sea, his teeth clattering so that he began to hum through the noise. Much shorter than Pericles, he sometimes appeared more ape than man, breathing always through his nose. Attikos would not admit his age, but he knew his trade and he revered Pericles' father. There were times when Pericles wondered if the man had been sent by Xanthippus to keep him safe.

'Waste of time standing here, freezing my balls off,' Attikos grumbled to himself, his voice barely audible. 'Hear that sound? Balls landing on shingle. I'd look for them if it wasn't so dark. I'll have to leave them for when we come back. If I can even find them. Then there is my back, which is a red-hot iron at the moment, from jumping down. It was the same at Eion. *That* will only get worse . . .'

Pericles shook his head. Attikos muttered when he was nervous. Telling him to stop worked for a while, but then he began again, unknowing, like a child talking in his sleep.

Pericles preferred silence. He knew he was ready for this. He would march with the others when Cimon gave the order. He felt the heft of his shield and spear and it was a good weight. He would not turn from the fight, though his bowels ached and his bladder wanted to empty down his leg. Until the moment came to move, he would endure a feeling of sickness, a gripe in his gut. Attikos muttering about his endless physical ailments did not help at all. The man had fought at both Marathon and Plataea, picking up new scars to add to his collection. For a bronze obol coin, he would show them to anyone who asked.

A shudder went through Pericles, roughening the skin on his arms and bare legs, making hairs rise like insect wings. He told himself it was just the sea breeze, the damp. In truth, it was more because he wore his brother's armour. He had seen Ariphron killed wearing it, not far from a shore like this one, on the same sea. Pericles had tried to hold his brother's wound closed, but his fingers had slipped on pale lips. The blood had stolen his brother away from him. While Attikos muttered on, Pericles flexed his grip on his spear. His fingers felt wet. It had to be sea spray or perspiration. It could not be his brother's life gumming his fingers together, it could not. Even so, he did not lift his hands to peer at them.

They had trained for this, he reminded himself. The order had come down from the Assembly of Athens – to find and destroy every Persian fortress and garrison in the Aegean. The entire fleet had gone out in threes and dozens, hunting the enemy, making sure he would never know peace. Persia ended before the sea. They would have no more footholds there – not the islands, not even the coast of Thrace.

Cimon had gathered some six hundred men to his name and rank of strategos, earned at Salamis. Ninety of them were experienced hoplites and the rest better trained than any oarsmen had ever been. A month before, they had landed on part of the Thracian coast held by Persians for a century. Cimon had chosen it, a stronghold and a symbol of their influence. There had been walls there, with a river running by. Pericles remembered Cimon peering into the distance, judging the land around the city.

The governor had refused to surrender, of course. In reply, the Athenians had killed the messengers he sent out, then blocked all roads around his walled fortress. Cimon had told them his plan that night. Pericles could still see his gaze as it rested on him, weighing him.

'Achilles knew,' Cimon had said, 'when he stood before Troy. A man should run *towards* death, not just accept it. He should seek it out, shake blood from his beard into its face and laugh! Only in that way can he win whatever glory makes us more than sailors or farmers or makers of pots. Only then can we earn true fame – *kleos*, where men and gods meet.'

Pericles swallowed. He wanted Cimon to know he was one to trust. He was nineteen years old. He knew he could run all day, then drink or fight or make love all night. He found himself grinning at the last. Chance would be a fine thing. He hadn't even seen a woman for a month. Yet he *was* strong and fit – and the son of a great hero. He was an Athenian. He was made for this.

Somehow, reality threatened to unman him, like some terrible dream so real he could feel sand crunch under his sandals. He had not found *kleos* in the Persian fortress. He and the others had settled in for a long siege, waiting for starvation to wear down the inhabitants. Weeks had passed in boredom and sword drills. Cimon had spoken to all the carpenters and shipwrights, scouting the land around the stronghold. The task of war had turned into something else as he crept up each night to examine the walls. Pericles shivered in memory, recalling his terror they would be spotted.

The Persians had used poor mortar to lay their stones. Over three days and nights, Cimon's people dammed the river and turned it onto a new course, sending it against the Persian foundations. In just hours, an entire section had crumbled, the walls collapsing like ramparts of sand.

Pericles had cheered with all the others, racing forward to meet the enemy. What they had found had stilled both voices and laughter. Inside the fortress of Eion, the Persians had chosen to die rather than be captured. The commander had killed his family in the last moments, then turned the knife to his own throat. Pericles swallowed at the memory of blood splashed on marble, brighter as he looked back than it could possibly have been. He had not drawn his sword in anger since.

They had found riches in Eion – and that too was a victory, like pulling a gem from a knife's hilt. More importantly, Persia would no longer have safe haven there, nor be able to dominate the land around. Yet Pericles did not feel he had proven himself. He still feared some weakness lay within, like a crack in a shield.

Neither Cimon nor Attikos seemed to be nervous, not in the way he was. He clenched his fists, telling himself the choice was made. Shingle shifted under his feet and he took a step, changing his stance. He would go in with the rest and if necessary, he would die. It was simple. He could throw his life away, for *kleos* and his father's name. No son of Xanthippus could bring shame on the family.

He felt relief flood him. He might die, but what was death, really? Nothing at all. He had found the body of his father's dog on the shore at Salamis. Its eyes had been white, he remembered, stained by the moon or sea salt. It was the same for men. When the gods took back their part, what was left was just flesh.

CONN IGGULDEN

2

Pericles loped up dunes with only the panting breath of those about him and the jingle of metal to break the quiet dark. At first the going was easy, over loose stones and scrub grass. Some of the men stumbled when they crossed patches of sage or thorn bushes, leading into the hills. Compared to them, Pericles touched the ground only lightly, as if mere roots could not claim him. He was determined not to let anyone else down. His father had stood at Marathon and he had won. Reputation stayed with a man, like a scar. Pericles was determined to choose death over scorn. That was a certainty. His mother may have named him 'Famous', but there were different kinds of fame. He would not live in shame. He reminded himself of that as he scrambled with the others over unseen ground.

Attikos cursed suddenly behind him, though Cimon had given an order for silence. None of them truly knew what to expect on Scyros. Over time, the island had become known as a dangerous place, even cursed. Fishing boats never dropped their nets there, though the waters teemed with anchovy and squid. There were rumours of lone men sighted by passing ships – shepherds or deserters, perhaps. Stories drifted in from traders, of merchant vessels seen burned to the sealine. Of raiders out of Scyros, of coastal villages made charred timbers, with all the women taken. The reputation protected the island. Most gave it a wide berth, rather than risk small boats stealing out to board and set ablaze.

Thieves, pirates and murderers had made Scyros their

refuge. Yet it was not for them that Cimon had brought crews to that place. Not that he would refuse to dig them out if the chance came. Pericles had seen a zeal in him, a desire to use the strength he had been given. Cimon would never be satisfied with a life of quiet duty. He was one who wanted glory, however it came to his hand. Pericles felt the honour of being one of his chosen, almost like pain. He would not let him down. Cimon would learn he could rely on him, like a good blade.

The three hoplite ranks tramped over the first hill and down the other side, so that the glitter of stars on the sea slowly vanished behind. Two hundred rowers went with them, with the rest left to guard the precious ships. Triremes burned only too well, but Cimon left nothing to chance. Like Pericles, he took his responsibilities seriously.

Scyros was all hills, with very little water and wild hares bolting away. No one would choose such a desolate place to eke out a living, Pericles thought, not unless the rest of the world was barred to them. Or because they could live without laws on Scyros, he did not know. His father said some men were too weak to live within bounds. Pericles shook his head. When he was younger, he'd thought Xanthippus knew all there was to know. He had been wrong.

There was no sign of either homes or inhabitants as he craned his neck in the darkness, turning this way and that. Pericles was shifting his spear in his hand when it was jolted from behind. Attikos told him loudly to watch where he put that thing, then threatened to stick it somewhere darker. Pericles clenched his jaw, staying silent as he had been ordered. Hundreds of men made noises as they moved; it was unavoidable. There was no reason to make it worse with idle talk.

It was late in the night by then, with a sliver of moon dipping down and dawn just a few hours away. The sea-scavengers

CONN IGGULDEN

had to sleep somewhere on the island. On foot, in the dark, Scyros seemed much larger than it had by day. If Cimon had to search for long, the sun would rise and all their surprise would have been wasted.

A couple of younger lads had gone ahead without armour or weapons to slow them down. Like long-legged hares themselves, they'd vanished through undergrowth, barely rustling fennel and sage as they passed. Pericles watched for them to return as he climbed another hill, beginning to sweat despite the night's cold.

Somewhere in the distance, he thought he heard a whinnying sound, a cry of warning. Were there ponies on the island? He supposed raiders and savages would value the animals as much as anyone else. It was hard to build anything without horses or wild asses broken to harness. Athens still had only a few, having lost them all to hungry Persian soldiers. If there was a decent breeding herd on Scyros . . . He put the thought aside for later on.

In the deep shadow of the valley, Pericles could no longer see the faces of those around him. Attikos had come alongside and they climbed for a while in silent companionship, placing each step and grip as the slope grew steeper. Both he and Attikos wore their helmets high, resting on a club of hair. Attikos had his shield on his left arm and leaned on the edge, almost like an armoured limb as he clambered up. Pericles' shield still lay across his shoulders. It made him feel invulnerable with it there.

They leaned into the climb as the ground roughened, small stones scattering and falling. In daylight, they would have chosen the best path, but at night, all the men could do was remain together, no matter how hard the going became.

Pericles was panting and trying to control the sound of it

by the time the ground flattened onto a wide crest. Attikos was not breathing half as hard, he noticed in irritation. The older man seemed to take physical exertion in his stride, as if he could march or climb for ever. Or he hurt as much but showed it less. Either way, Pericles tried to match him, though sweat fell in fat drops.

There were still no crags there, only rolling hills where lizards or nesting birds scurried away from the presence of hoplites. The entire front line halted when a shadow startled, breaking into sudden life. A few even lowered spears as the unmistakable sound of hooves came to them. Some sleeping horse went racing off down the hill, kicking its heels and whinnying in outrage. That sound carried far and Pericles could only shake his head. Like barking dogs, the horse would surely alert anyone else to the presence of strangers on the island.

Halfway down the other side, Pericles suddenly resolved the shadows, understanding what he could still only barely make out. He dropped to one knee, Attikos beside him. The rest of Cimon's hoplites did the same and the rowers all halted behind. They were looking down into a much wider valley than before. There were no lights down there, but Pericles thought he could make out the shapes of houses, even the lighter strip of some sort of road that caught the moonlight. It looked more like an actual town than a rough camp for killers and exiles.

Pericles could hear murmured questions from the men. He had not been wrong, thank the gods. Halting them on a false alarm would have been humiliating. Pericles realised he could hear running water somewhere in the distance. A stream then, or some ancient spring. There had to be a reason for the inhabitants of Scyros to have chosen this spot. He turned his head slowly, seeing the bowl of hills around them.

CONN IGGULDEN

Perhaps the smoke from their fires was hidden from passing ships. Or perhaps they lived cold; he had no way of knowing.

From over on the right, Cimon strolled the length of the line, passing three ranks of thirty hoplites. They had kept their sense of separate ship crews, though they were all his in the end. He favoured no particular ship, knowing how jealous men could get. He could be found sleeping on the open deck of any one of them. Pericles was in awe of him – and of the things Cimon had seen. While Pericles had been forced to sit with his evacuated family on the island of Salamis, Cimon had been out commanding squadrons of ships, burning and boarding Persian enemies. It was in his eyes, his voice. He had surely known *kleos* then. In his presence, Pericles was reminded he had yet to earn his own.

Cimon stopped by him. The strategos wore helmet, greaves and breastplate over a thick linen tunic that left his legs bare. He carried a shield as if it weighed nothing. The crest of his helmet was black and white, but he looked like any of the others. Pericles knew him, however.

'What can you see?' Cimon said softly, peering into the night.

Pericles blinked, understanding his eyes were better than those of the man he revered.

'There are houses down there – a hundred perhaps, or a little more. A path and a crossroads, some sort of running water.'

'I can hear it,' Cimon replied.

He shook his head as if in irritation. He had not had any trouble in the daylight, Pericles recalled. Some men saw better in the night than others, that was all. It made him feel useful and his chest swelled.

'We've found them, then,' Cimon murmured.

Pericles nodded.

'I can't see any movement,' he said softly.

He saw Cimon rub the back of his hand along the bristles of his chin. This was the moment that would decide lives – those of his own hoplites and the scavengers of Scyros.

'I don't think I can leave them in peace,' Cimon said. 'They know this island better than we do. I don't want them arming themselves tomorrow to come at us while we are looking for the tomb.'

Pericles was pleased to be included in the conversation. He was not sure Cimon would take his advice, but the opportunity was there.

'We have a duty to the towns and islands they prey upon,' he said. 'We cannot leave them alive.'

The helmet turned to regard him for a moment of stillness and silence, then Cimon clapped him on the shoulder.

'I agree,' he said. 'We'll go in – with caution. Even rats bite when they are threatened. You have command of the left wing, Pericles. Take three ranks of fifteen and . . . half the rowers. Allow no wildness in your men. Whatever we find below, if we come through without a single wound, I will be content. Treat the enemy with the caution you would bring to a battle line. Keep shields high – and close together. Use spears if you can. Strike with the shield boss as you draw your sword, to knock them back.'

It was basic instruction, of the sort any strategos might tell new recruits. Yet Pericles was grateful. He rose slowly to stand under the stars, feeling suddenly ill. He understood he was about to fight men, to their death or his. It felt right to go over the simplest things when his mind had gone blank. This was why they trained so hard, until sweat poured from them. Because killing was difficult and brutal work. Only a few took well to it – and they either became heroes or were hunted like lions.

'I won't let you down,' he said to Cimon.

'Nor I, strategos,' Attikos muttered at his shoulder.

Pericles felt his pride tinged with irritation at having Attikos intrude just as he was showing his worth to Cimon. He rolled his eyes, but Cimon had already turned away, jogging back to his own position.

'Pass the word – but quietly,' Pericles said to the men behind him. 'We're going in as the left wing – quick and silent.'

He cleared his throat, remembering how his father addressed men older and more experienced than he was. Sternness was the key. He hoped they could not hear the quaver in his voice, but somehow he could not rid himself of it.

'I will stripe the back of any man who gives out a battle cry,' Pericles told them. They were grinning, one or two of them. He hoped it was out of nervousness and not in amusement at a young officer telling them their business.

'Pay attention, you shit-trench cockerels,' Attikos said clearly. 'Or I will speak to you myself, after.'

Pericles closed his eyes. Attikos had undermined him at a crucial moment. It could not go unanswered. He felt his cheeks flame in a great heat, but Cimon was already moving and they were being left behind.

'*Thank* you, Attikos,' he snapped, meaning it as a rebuke.

'You're welcome, kurios,' Attikos replied. 'I'll bring you through safe, don't worry.'

3

A dog barked, a series of deep sounds that turned into a frenzy of howling. As Pericles reached the valley floor, a blur sprang from between the buildings, all shadows and scrambling paws. One of the hoplites swore as it came at him, more afraid of its teeth than any man he might face. The howl strangled as someone jabbed a spear at it. Snapping rage turned to screeching and Pericles winced. The whole island had to have heard that.

'Keep good order,' he growled. 'Steady pace.'

They all knew the work better than he did, but at least he had given them no cause to doubt him. Pericles heard the scrape of shields coming together, overlapping like scales so they advanced as a battle line. It would last about as long as it took to reach the shacks of thieves and pirates, but neither would they be caught in a sudden ambush. Fighting was already a dangerous business, his father always said. There was no point making it harder by being careless.

More dogs took up the barks and howls of the first. Another of them attacked and was cut down as it broke its teeth on the edge of a shield. Still, there was no sign of defenders. Pericles peered and squinted, straining to see. The houses were all dark. Was the place deserted? The dogs might have been part of a wild pack. It would be a fine joke if they found the entire place abandoned after all the caution of the approach.

Pericles called an order to halt. Cimon was out of sight, but still trusting him, relying on him. There would be no mistakes, not while he commanded. Pericles could not control a great part of his life, but for one night, for this advance and these men – well, they were his and he would not let them down.

'In threes,' he snapped. 'Lay down your spears on the right side – they're no use indoors. Spears down, I said. Draw swords. Quickly now! On my order, go in fast. Search every room – and watch for attacks. There is something wrong here. They . . .'

Pericles stopped the string of instructions, turning sharply. A woman's voice had cried out, or a child's. It had sounded above the noise of soldiers and he waited. Over there, he was almost certain. He pointed to a building, then to the closest pair.

'You two. Go with Attikos. Find whoever made that sound and bring them to me. The rest of you, what are you waiting for? In threes – advance.'

If he had called fours or sixes, the hoplites could have formed just as quickly. They all knew their groups and they could arrange themselves a dozen different ways, even in the middle of a battle. It meant the lochagoi or the strategos could adjust attacking lines as they saw fit, choosing where to bring the greatest strength. Only the full phalanx worked as a single formation, pressing forward against an enemy.

As the first doors were kicked in, Pericles found himself grinning, as much from nerves as excitement. Yet it was a grand scene as it played out in his imagination. Athenian hoplites in helmet and armour would be like Achilles reborn in a small home – untouchable, fast and deadly. If there *were* scavengers hiding in the houses, they would surely be slaughtered. Yet it nagged at him, making his heart thump and flutter in his chest. These people knew this place. It was their home, and he wondered if something had been missed.

THE LION

A shriek sounded away on his right. Pericles turned his head, listening, trying to understand. The rowers still stood at his back. They were in no great hurry to go in, he could sense that much. Most men would prefer to stand without an order to move, at least when the alternative was walking through doorways in complete darkness, never knowing who waited behind each one. Pericles could not send them after the hoplites, not until he had a better sense of what lay ahead – or until they had sprung an ambush. Only forty-five hoplites had gone crashing through the street of shacks. Further away, he could hear shouts and metal on wood as Cimon brought in the second wing. Whoever they caught in the middle would surely be helpless, but still the sense of wrongness nagged. Pericles needed to see, but it would draw enemies like crane flies if he sparked a lamp. If they were there.

He heard Attikos returning before he could see him.

'Bite me again. I'll knock you out,' Attikos snarled.

He and another man held some writhing figure between them. She must have ignored the order as Pericles heard Attikos hiss in pain. The older man raised his arm in reply, but Pericles gripped his wrist, catching it.

'We need to question her,' he said.

Attikos shook himself free. The man muttered something that made her try to kick him, so that he had to jerk back, swearing and laughing.

One of the other hoplites still had the woman's long hair in his grip, a great hank of it wrapped around his fist. Pericles waved him off and he released her with great caution, standing away before she could lunge at him. Pericles rather admired her spitting rage, though she was about as helpless as a cat and in more danger. They would cut her throat in an instant if he gave the word. Judging by the way he sucked his fingers and glared, Attikos might do it anyway.

CONN IGGULDEN

'How many men live here?' Pericles said.

The woman ignored the question, looking around, clearly judging if she could make a break for freedom. With three men blocking any way out, she slumped.

'Do you speak Greek?' Pericles demanded. 'You're no use to me if you don't.'

'I am of Thebes,' she said. 'You? I hear the accent of Athens.'

'Good,' he replied in relief. 'If you are a prisoner here, can you tell me how many men there are? We can take you away, as far as Athens, if you help us.'

'Why would I help *you*?' she said. Without warning, she raised her voice to a great shout into the darkness. 'If my *husband has any sense*, he will stay . . .'

Attikos stepped in and smashed a blow across her face, knocking her to the ground.

'We didn't tell you to shout, love, did we?' he said.

Pericles was furious. He hadn't forbidden Attikos from touching her, but he'd thought the older man had understood. It felt like disobedience.

Pericles could hear other groups returning. They were herding what sounded like women and children, some of them already wailing. He shook his head, unnerved by the strangeness of it. He could hardly see his captive in the darkness. As she fell, her hair had been flung loose, hanging over her face like a curtain. He saw something pale shift under that hair as her arm twitched at her belt. Then she launched, coming up on strong legs, straight at Attikos. He roared in pain as she stuck him. His wild blow in return caught her on the side of the head and she fell dazed, leaving him to yank her knife from his thigh.

'That bitch!' he shouted, lifting the blade to strike.

Pericles stepped across him.

'Is mine to question. Stand back, Attikos – and put that down.'

Attikos was breathing hard, more in anger than pain. He was close to cutting loose, Pericles could feel it. The young man returned the gaze, his confidence total. If Attikos disobeyed, Pericles knew he would kill him. He was nineteen, trained and fast. He did not doubt himself. Some of that certainty seeped through at last to the man he faced. Attikos dipped his head, giving way. Pericles watched him even so, in case he changed his mind. He'd fought his brother too many times to be fooled by some trick or false surrender. In that moment, he missed Ariphron with a fresh pang. Still teaching lessons, though he lay cold in a tomb.

'In fact, Attikos – go in again and find me anyone else alive in this place.'

Attikos turned on his heel and vanished before Pericles had even finished speaking, leaving him with a hundred oarsmen at his back, waiting for orders – and an unconscious prisoner at his feet. A crowd of women and children was being assembled on the road around them, with hoplites prodding at the edges.

'Tie her hands,' Pericles ordered one of the rowers. 'She is a Greek – though of Thebes. Be gentle with her. She is one of ours and perhaps has been treated cruelly.'

It was a noble sentiment and he was proud of the delivery. He had to ignore the crude comment another of the men made. If he reacted to every one, he'd never get anything done.

'Where are your men?' Pericles said, raising his head and addressing the crowd of captives.

Some of them had begun to weep and the rower at his back murmured something else that made him flush. Pericles smothered his irritation. He saw hoplites as decent men who might fight for the city, then sit as a juror. Honest, even noble, they were part of the dream of Athens. The rowers did not seem quite the same sort. He clenched one fist. He'd inspire the bastards, or put an iron edge against each throat. There would be no bothering these women, not while he stood as officer over them.

'Ladies! You are not here alone!' he called again. 'Where are your men?'

He could smell them, he realised, a scent of herbs and unwashed flesh. Dawn was not far off. If there had been more light, he thought their poverty and filth would have been even clearer. Even as he looked across them, there was the first hint of grey in the dark. There couldn't have been more than eighty or so. He imagined each one had been snatched from somewhere else. There would always be men cast out from their towns for some crime, driven into exile like a dog. They might find their way to Scyros, without a doubt, but not the women. The women had to have been taken, or been born there.

A number walked with small children or carried them on a hip, snivelling and owl-eyed. They were no threat, but there was still the mystery of their menfolk.

'Leave us alone!' one of them shouted. The voice of a crone.

Pericles hesitated, suddenly fearing Athena stood in the shadowy crowd. There were perils in dealing with women when the goddess could walk amongst them. He swallowed. It sounded weak, but he repeated himself once more.

'I will not ask you again,' he said. 'Where are your men?'

'They're out hunting, but they'll be back,' one of them shouted. 'They'll kill you all if you touch any one of us!'

He could hear fear in her voice. Attikos had returned to stand at his side, limping badly. Pericles realised he could see the man. Dawn was upon them at last, in all its grey glory.

THE LION

'Gone hunting in the dark?' he heard Attikos mutter. 'I don't think so. Nothing much to hunt anyway, not in this place. Unless she means those ponies . . .'

The older man trailed off and Pericles felt his own eyes widen. The men were not hunting the land. They were out at sea, either looking for fish or a different kind of prey.

Pericles looked up as Cimon approached. He stood a little straighter and saw that Attikos did the same.

'I can't find anyone except women and children. You?'

Pericles shook his head.

'Same on this side. I think the men are out looking for ships to attack.'

Cimon nodded.

'They might not be back for days, then. It doesn't matter. Leave a few guards on these . . . men you can trust.'

He said the last with a peculiar emphasis that made Pericles flush.

'I can stay, kurios,' Attikos said. He addressed himself to Cimon, but it was Pericles who answered.

'No, I need you with me, Attikos. I'll choose the ones we must leave behind.'

He felt rather than saw the man's suppressed fury as Pericles turned back to Cimon.

'You're going to search for the tomb?'

Cimon had not missed the strange tension between the two men. He actually missed very little, but he saw no weakness in Pericles, so trusted him to handle his own problems. After just a beat, he dipped his head.

'It's why we came. Not for ragged pirates or their women. Theseus died on Scyros. If there really is a tomb here, it could be his. If it *is* his, I want to bring the bones back to Athens, for a proper burial. He was an Athenian king. His father named the Aegean!'

The woman at their feet stirred then, struggling when she realised she had been bound. In the dawn light, Pericles saw she was a little older than him, with hair that had never been cut and hung in a mass to her waist. She was filthy, but he felt a strange sensation when her eyes met his. Her face was already swelling, with a great bruise on one side that reached right to her eye.

'The lads will kill you when they come home,' she said.

Cimon chuckled.

'You are Greek? Then look around you. Go on, it's not just shadows now. Do you see my hoplites and rowers? You think your men will take us on? I don't think they will. If they have any sense at all, they'll stay out of sight until we have gone. We have no interest in any of you, not really.'

'They'll kill you,' she said again and spat on the ground at his feet. Even in her anger, she was careful not to let the spittle touch his sandal, Pericles noticed.

Overcome at her insolence, Attikos stepped forward, his hand raised.

'Get *back*, Attikos!' Pericles growled. 'I swear, if you strike this woman again, I will strap you to the prow for a week at sea.'

'Kurios, she . . .'

'Not another word!' Pericles snapped.

He turned to the woman then as if the matter was settled and beyond any further dispute. The corners of her mouth twitched at seeing Attikos reined in, which she tried to hide under the curtain of her hair.

'What *do* you want?' she asked Cimon, her curiosity showing.

'First tell me your name.'

'Thetis,' she said with a shrug.

'Like the mother of Achilles?' She nodded and Cimon

smiled. 'That is an old name – a name of power. Well, Thetis, we are looking for a tomb . . . perhaps a temple. Old and lost and probably overgrown. Somewhere on the island. My father said he'd heard of one here.'

He waited while the woman considered. Her eyes had flickered at his description and Cimon found he was holding his breath, excitement catching in his throat.

'You've seen something like that?' he said.

She shrugged.

'Perhaps. There is an old grave on the north side, high in the hills over there. Some of the children play around it.'

'Can you tell me how to get there?' Cimon asked. 'That's what we came for. Nothing else matters to me.'

His voice was suddenly gentler, as if he soothed a wild deer. She could not seem to look away and, to his surprise, Pericles felt a pang of jealousy. *He* was the one who had saved her from Attikos! He was the one without ties, while Cimon had a young wife back in Athens, already pregnant with his first child. Yet the woman's dark gaze lingered only on his friend.

'I can show it to you,' she said.

4

With the sun rising, the young woman led the Greeks up the other side of the valley. Cimon had ordered a still-limping Attikos to keep hold of her. He pinched her arm cruelly in his spite. Pericles saw pale marks from his fingers, but said nothing, not while there was a chance Thetis might bolt and leave them far from the others. Attikos seemed to be suffering from the wound in his leg, though he had bound it. The man muttered threats and promises to Thetis as they went, making her lean away from him.

The going was hard, with thick undergrowth and olive trees about as old as the island. Twice more, they saw one of the wiry little ponies startle and go cantering off at the sight of armed men. It might almost have been pleasant, if their purpose had not been so serious. They hurried along, watching the sun.

Cimon had leaped at the chance to see the tomb, leaving behind the bulk of his force. Pericles bit his lip at the thought. Cimon had almost a dozen years on him, but it was still a young man's error. They had taken only six hoplites along with them. The rest waited in the valley or were back guarding the ships.

On a goat path barely more than a thread along the ground, Thetis reached the crest. She didn't hesitate, going straight over, stretching out her free hand for balance on a steep slope. With his injured leg buckling, Attikos yanked savagely at her, making her cry out. Pericles watched in sullen anger as she swung to slap him. Once more Attikos pulled back a fist.

'Attikos!' Pericles roared at him.

He used his voice as a weapon, forgetting they were in a hostile place. The crack of sound echoed back from the hills, so that a couple of the hoplites turned their heads, following it. The rest stood like statues, stunned for an instant, then grinning. Pericles had always had a good voice for a battlefield.

Pericles heard Attikos swear in disbelief. Another young man's error, this time his own. His irritation only increased as he felt his face grow hot. It had been Attikos who'd pushed him to it, embarrassing them both in front of Cimon.

In silence, Pericles strode forward, feeling the stares of the others. He waved Attikos off and took Thetis by the arm. She watched him from underneath the mass of brown hair and seemed to be smiling. He wondered when she had last bathed.

'He won't hurt you again, you have my word,' Pericles said.

He ignored Attikos standing just a couple of paces away. In response to her quick and nervous glance, the man snorted, but had the sense to stalk off and leave Pericles alone with her.

'You won't kill me when we reach the tomb?' she said.

Pericles looked at her in surprise.

'No. I have a sister and a mother who would never forgive me. You won't be harmed.'

'Your friend said he was going to have me . . . like a husband and wife . . .' she said.

Even beneath the protection of her hair, he could see her flush a deep red. He assumed it was a mirror of his own face in that moment.

'He is not my friend, s-so, I think . . . no it doesn't matter. Come on, is it this way?'

She began to head down the slope once more, with the

hoplites falling in behind. Pericles saw her hesitate on a section where rocks protruded through the earth. She needed both hands to climb down and he released her arm, ready to throw himself after her if she ran. She shook her head, reading his thoughts as he scrambled closer.

'I'll show you the tomb,' she said. 'Then you'll leave. That's what he said.'

'We'll want to see who lies within, if it is a tomb,' he replied. 'But yes, after that, we have no more interest in this place. A great man died here once, long ago. That's all Scyros is to us.'

She led them on through a hillside of bracken, with strange black flies that seemed to seek out exposed flesh. Pericles rubbed at a spot of blood on his forearm where one had bitten him.

'Will you stay here, on the island, when we go?' Pericles said.

Attikos had come closer, so that he was just a few paces behind, chatting to one of the other men. Cimon brought up the rear, so he did not hear Attikos suggest 'the young kurios' had been 'caught by her parts, like fishhooks'. It was as perfectly audible and yet as under the breath as any soldier could manage. Pericles felt his fist close and made himself open it. He had to ignore mere insults, for all they were meant to hurt or mock. He put it all aside, like salt, for later on. If his father had told Attikos to watch his back, perhaps it was time to remove that protection and fend for himself. The price of having him close was just too high. Pericles glanced over the shield on his shoulder, finding Attikos watching him with a crooked grin.

'Are you all right back there?' Pericles asked.

'Yes, kurios. All fine and alert,' Attikos replied, with perfect insolence. He was still angry at being roared at in front of them all, that was clear enough.

THE LION

Pericles smiled back, as easily as he could. He could not undo his mistake, not then. Perhaps he owed the man an apology – before knocking him out. He wondered if he could beat Attikos in a fair fight. The man had an indifference to pain that made him a hard prospect. Pericles could imagine battering at him and just making the nasty old bastard laugh.

The sun pulled free of the hills as the morning wore on. The distance they covered was not that great, but they never found a clear path. Pericles endured a marsh of black muck that threatened to keep one of his sandals and reeked like struck flint or sulphur. He and the others climbed over fallen trees, under broken branches and past thorns like a wall, so that they had to be hacked apart. There were times when he began to wonder if Thetis was deliberately leading them through the worst obstacles she knew.

Coming out onto bare cliffs where seabirds wheeled was a blessed relief. After so long in green shadows, Pericles felt like an explorer sighting the sea for the first time. It lifted his spirits for as long as it took to spot eight longboats full of men, rowing fast around the island. He looked at Thetis and she grinned at him.

'The lads are back, then,' she said. 'And you are here. You won't get down to them before they've killed all your people.'

'You planned this?' Pericles said in disbelief.

He could see only triumph in her expression, as if she wanted to dance. She expected them to kill her, he could see that. Somehow, she didn't seem to care. She had found her *kleos* as she laughed at him.

Cimon came through the others, making Attikos stand back rather than be shoved aside. He did that respectfully enough, Pericles noted.

'Why have we stopped . . .'

Cimon trailed off as he caught sight of the boats down below. They were close enough to see it was a lot of men, but still a world away over rough country. Cimon rubbed the bristles on his face as he understood the wild look in Thetis' eye. She was trembling, Pericles saw, expecting death.

'Clever girl,' Cimon said. 'Was there ever a tomb?'

Her eyes flickered east for a moment before she shrugged and shook her head. Pericles tightened his grip on her arm once more, making her wince. Cimon too had noticed the slight betrayal. He pointed.

'Over there? Or is this another ruse?'

'They're landing down below,' Pericles said. 'We can't get back in time, even if we set off now.'

Cimon looked at him and nodded. He was about as calm as the breeze, Pericles noted in surprise.

'Then we might as well explore a little,' Cimon said. 'In case our guide here really did see a tomb.'

The little group broke up and spread out in all directions. Cimon looked at the woman Pericles held. His hand tapped his sword hilt and she drew in a long breath, waiting for his decision.

'I'll see to her, kurios,' Attikos offered. He had remained. 'She stuck me with a knife, after all. I don't mind wasting a little time on her in return.'

'Just make it quick,' Cimon snapped. He too was angry at the woman who had led them away from his men, perhaps getting them all killed.

Without thought or time to reflect, Pericles released her arm. He felt Thetis look at him in a moment of confusion – and then she was off, sprinting like a deer along the bare cliffs.

Attikos shouted a curse and went after her. On another day, he might have been fast enough, Pericles thought. The man was the sort of hound who could follow a trail. The wound in his leg gave her a fair chance – as good as she deserved and no more. The pair of them vanished from sight behind an outcropping of rock. Her fate was with the gods.

In the other direction, one of the hoplites suddenly shouted and held up his hand. The rest converged on that spot like golden sparks dragged through the green furze. Cimon closed his mouth on whatever comment or rebuke he had been about to make.

'Is it the tomb?' he called.

Pericles was already moving.

'Let's find out.'

They began to run, their weariness vanishing.

Cimon used his sword to hack through vines and roots, spread like a lattice over a huge stone.

'Help me with it,' he ordered, so that the others did the same, working hands or blades into whatever lay beneath. It had not been disturbed for a very long time, that was clear. Cimon gasped when he peeled back an entire section of white rootlets, like a rug.

'What is it?' Pericles asked him.

'Look at that edge. Dressed stone, with sharp lines. Why would there be such a thing high on a hillside in Scyros? It is the work of master masons, Pericles. By Athena, we'd never have found it without that woman! Even now, it is almost invisible. Come on, we have no hammers to break it. We'll have to turn this stone over if we're to see what lies beneath!'

Pericles glanced back to where he had seen Attikos stumbling after her. Cimon was already working a knife under the stone, trying to find its lower edge.

'She's not your concern now, Pericles. This is. Get your hands dirty. Now.'

Pericles nodded, feeling the sting of a rebuke. He knelt in

CONN IGGULDEN

the bracken and drew his eating knife. The stone was a massive thing, as thick as a tomb marker at home, twice as deep as a clenched fist. He could make out more and more of the hidden lower edge, but it would be a beast to lift, even with so many hands. Six men scraped and heaved at the great flat block, while only a couple more stood guard. Cimon was lost in silent concentration as they ripped and pulled and hacked at it, revealing the shape to the open air.

'All onto one side now,' Cimon said suddenly. 'Let's see if we can get it over.'

They scrambled across, jamming fingertips under the lip they'd cleared and getting ready.

Pericles turned at a thin cry in the distance, almost like a gull.

'I need you here, Pericles,' Cimon growled at him. 'Lay hold.'

Pericles gripped the stone alongside Cimon. Part of one hand vanished underneath, so that he could feel the underside. Strange things crept across his skin and he shuddered.

'On my mark,' Cimon said. 'Ready? Lift.'

The stone rose, the men shifting their holds and grunting under a vast weight. It was limestone, as old as the world. The ground beneath seemed to hiss as relentless pressure broke the grip of a thousand roots. Beetles and many-legged things curled at the first light they had ever known. It continued to rise even so, further and further as they pushed, lost in the effort until it was suddenly leaning away, crashing down and splitting in half on the other side. Pericles felt a pang of regret. It could not be undone now, put back. As with his brother, as with everything that mattered, he could not make whole what had been broken.

On hands and knees, they looked into what was clearly a burial plot. A huge man had been laid there in death, in a shallow cavity hacked from the earth. Roots and grasses had grown through the space, white threads filling every part of it, like a nest. Yet a bronze helmet was visible still, over a skull wound about by roots. Thigh bones and ribs could be made out, along with a breastplate and greaves, the bronze dark green after so long under the stone. There was no shield.

'My father told me Theseus was killed on Scyros,' Cimon murmured in awe. 'That if he was anywhere, he would be here . . . I never thought we might actually find his tomb. I really didn't. I knew the odds were good I had the wrong island, or that wherever he died, he might have been robbed or eaten by wild animals, his bones scattered. All I had was the story of an old king, killed by a traitor. Yet I had to search. I couldn't just tell myself there was no chance . . . when there was.'

He shook his head in silent awe. As Pericles watched, Cimon reached down, pushing past the web that covered the bones and armour. He touched the finger bones.

'This is Theseus, who called Heracles a friend. This right hand struck the Minotaur and held Helen of Troy. Our greatest Athenian king! Come, help me clear away this foul growth. We are taking every bone and piece back to the ships.'

'Are you sure it's him?' one of the men asked.

Cimon did not look away from the object of his reverent gaze.

'Who else could it be, on Scyros, in the middle of nowhere? This man wears hoplite armour, aged by centuries. And look at the *size* of him, the length of those bones! If he rose up now, he would be the tallest among us. Who else but Theseus would merit a stone of this weight, that all of us together could barely lift? He was a great warrior, even as an old man. Whoever carried him to this place wanted to be sure he would not rise up. That speaks for him.'

Cimon began to clear the roots away, gashing at the thick mat of yellow strands. Each handful revealed more and the other men worked hard and fast, so that the full figure was revealed in just a short time.

Cimon leaned into the tomb, black to the elbows with mud and filth. Pericles thought he might kiss the skull of the fallen king, but instead he lifted out a black spearhead. Cimon scrubbed flakes from it with his thumbs, then laughed.

'Hand me a spear, lads,' he commanded, holding out a hand.

As one of them passed a dory spear to him, he held the heads together to compare them, ancient and new. Any wood in the grave had rotted away, leaving just the spike of crumbling iron. The owl symbol of Athena could just be made out. The hoplites looked in awe as Cimon turned it in the light, showing them. It was already breaking apart, staining his palm dark red, leaves of rust slipping as he disturbed them.

'Fetch a cloak, to carry it all – bones and armour,' Cimon said. 'Theseus waited a long time for this – for us. We'll bring him home.'

They began to cheer then, giving thanks. It was a moment of pure wonder, loud enough to startle the gulls along the cliffs. Pericles felt his heart racing. He helped with the collection of bones and armour, holding each piece with reverence. Only when it was all tied in a bundle and completely secure did he trot back to where he had seen Attikos vanish. While Cimon readied the men to return to the other side of the island, Pericles reached the same spot and called aloud. He did not want to leave Attikos behind, despite his anger.

'Attikos! We are leaving now!' he roared, cupping his hands. This time, it did not matter if his voice echoed back, though the sea stole half his power.

He could hear gulls call, then, at the very edge of hearing, the same faint cry he had heard before. Without a thought, Pericles went forward, pressing his back to a spire of rock to get round it. The drop at his feet was so great he didn't dare look down.

Behind him, he heard Cimon call his name, but Pericles went on. He had to be sure.

It wasn't far. As he came around the column of grey rock, the ground dropped away. Part of it followed a narrow ridge like a path of stone, worn by sea storms and centuries to a thread. The rest yawned in space, a drop to jagged rocks. Pericles felt his stomach constrict as he leaned over, peering down. There.

Attikos had fallen badly, he could see that. The man's leg lay at a horrid angle, making Pericles wince to see it. There was no chance of Attikos climbing back up, not with that injury – and the wound in his other leg. There was no sign of Thetis. No doubt she had made her way along the path in perfect safety, while the Athenian fell.

'Pericles! Thank the gods. Help me!' Attikos called. The relief was clear in his voice. He must have worried no one would come, that he would die alone in that place.

Pericles looked down at him, while gulls shrieked and beat against the breeze.

5

When Pericles made it back to the tomb, Cimon and the others had gone. He didn't know whether to take that as criticism, or perhaps its opposite – that Cimon trusted him to do whatever he had to do and get down to the ships. The grave was utterly empty – only the broken capstone and trampled scrub were proof they had been there at all. Unfortunately, it meant there was also no one there to help him. He stood for a time, thinking. He could not blame Cimon for leaving, not while his men were being attacked. There was no choice, he realised with a grimace. If he left Attikos to die, he'd have to live with it. He had to try, even if it was just to be sure he could not save him. Pericles shuddered, sensing eyes on him. There was no one watching, though the tomb gaped like an accusation. He turned back to the spire of rock that led away.

By the time he put his head over the edge once more, Attikos lay in a slightly different position, the broken leg dragged close to the other. He saw Pericles immediately and waved.

'Get a rope,' he shouted. 'I can tie it on. Have a few of the lads pull me up.'

'They're gone,' Pericles called to him. 'It's just me.'

He saw Attikos' expression grow bleak. Attikos had survived a fall that could easily have killed him, crashing onto a ledge a dozen or so paces below. If he'd rolled even once, he would have fallen much further into the sea. It seemed he had used up all his luck.

Attikos was close enough for Pericles to see grim resignation, but it was still a daunting drop. He feared if he climbed down, he too might be unable to get back out. The cliff was sheer and pitted with gull nests. Pericles had climbed a few trees as a boy; this was very different. He felt fresh sweat start at the thought of just falling and falling. The cliffs blurred as he blinked at Attikos. Slowly, he dropped to his stomach and leaned out as far as he dared, gripping grass in both hands while gulls screamed and threatened him, trying to see a way.

There had been not much honour in the thought of abandoning Attikos, but neither the gods nor his duty demanded the impossible. Pericles took a deep breath to ask if there was any message Attikos wanted taken back. As he did, he saw a cleft in the rock, a seam by a long crack that might provide handholds for part of the way. That was the route he would take, of a certainty, if he was fool enough to go down . . .

He swung a leg over, trying not to think. His heart thumped and hammered, making him light-headed as he lowered himself, pressing as close as he could to cold stone. This was insanity! He could feel his arms trembling, but he was moving, his grip like iron. He could not look down to see his feet! How would he find a place to stand? He prayed to Athena to keep him safe, while one sandal twisted to fit some small crack, barely holding his weight.

Little by little, he lowered himself. Attikos said nothing below. The figure of the fallen man swam in and out of sharpness as Pericles searched for grips. The muscles in his forearms protested and his legs began to shake as if he had a fever. He was young, he told himself – young and strong.

'I will not fall,' he whispered, over and over.

He almost made himself a liar when one foot slipped and he had to cling like a crab with two hands and one toe,

CONN IGGULDEN

scrabbling for the lost hold. He had torn a nail off his left hand. Oddly, it didn't seem to hurt, but it bled freely in drops that streaked the cliff. His fingertips were numb, he realised.

When Pericles reached the ledge where Attikos lay, he slumped down with his back to the cliff. The sea was a vast and cruel drop, while Attikos watched in something like disbelief.

'You don't have a rope?' Attikos asked.

Pericles shook his head, bringing his breathing under control. It was as much fear as exertion, but he was recovering quickly.

'Just . . . me,' Pericles replied.

'Then you should have gone with the others,' Attikos said. 'I'm not going to be climbing out, not with both legs done. And now you're stuck here as well. You might as well jump off. It will be a lot quicker than dying of thirst.'

Pericles looked up at the slope he had negotiated to get down. He had never climbed anything like it before, but he had learned with every grunting step. He winced as he peered at the finger where the nail had ripped free. Climbing was hard – and it hurt – but he had enjoyed something about the challenge. He thought he could make it back to the top.

'It's just sea below,' he said. 'You think you could survive the fall?'

Attikos gave a weary snort.

'With one leg broken and the other stabbed? No.' He fell silent for a time. 'I suppose . . . that bitch got away?'

Pericles shrugged.

'I haven't seen her,' he said. He felt Attikos' stare. 'I haven't!'

'I was thinking if you'd just kept a better hold on her, I wouldn't be here with my leg smashed, waiting to roll off when I can't bear it any more. That's all.'

Pericles considered, then shook his head.

'You'd still have one good leg if you hadn't attacked her,' he said. 'You did this to yourself.'

He looked up at the cliff face as he spoke. He'd had an idea before, but what had seemed possible at the top looked a lot harder from below. More importantly, he knew he had to rest before trying it. It would probably still be impossible, but he was nineteen. Nothing is impossible at nineteen.

'Did my father put you in Cimon's crew?' Pericles asked suddenly. 'To keep an eye on me?'

Attikos was prodding his broken leg and wincing at pain that had to be almost overwhelming. It was a reminder of what a gnarled old whoreson he actually was, that he had not once cried out.

'To *protect* you,' Attikos corrected. He shrugged at Pericles' surprise. 'Not much point in hiding it now, is there? I'm not going anywhere.'

'I can carry you,' Pericles said. 'On my back.'

Attikos paled further as he looked up and up.

'No,' he said at last. 'I have been stabbed and battered today, with bones broken and more skin lost on that damned cliff than I care to look at. I've had about enough, son. I told your father I'd keep you safe, so . . . that's it. You climb back up if you can. Leave me and tell your father I did my duty.'

Pericles chuckled. Dramatic old sod. Cimon would expect them both back. Unless the attackers overwhelmed armoured Greek hoplites, he would eventually send someone to check on his missing officers. He bit his lip. Of course . . . if Cimon was killed, it might be a few days before anyone else even noticed they were gone. There was a chance no one would come for them.

'I don't think I will,' Pericles said just as firmly. Slowly, he pushed himself to his feet. 'Take off your clothes, Attikos.'

'Not while I have my strength you won't,' Attikos said.

Pericles was in no mood for humour.

'To cut the weight down. It's going to matter. You can wrap your arms around my neck, and under one armpit. I think . . . if you can keep your grip, I can get you up. I'll go back for your kit then.'

Attikos swore with surprising energy, but the young man looming over him looked ready to batter him if he refused. Grumbling, Attikos unbuckled a breastplate of leather and Pericles helped him pull the tunic underneath over his head. The man's chest was much paler than his arms and legs, so that he seemed strangely shrunken. The broken leg was still swelling and marbled with streaks of blood, already more meat and bone than a working limb. Pericles didn't look at it as he took Attikos by the arms and heaved him up, ignoring the man's growl of pain in his ear as he latched on.

'I can do this,' Pericles said, to himself as much as the one who clung to him.

The broken leg hung loose, while Attikos managed to tuck the other around him as best he could. His forearm passed under Pericles' throat, a hairy bar that rasped against his skin. It was awkward and ungainly, but it left Pericles free to climb.

As he reached up, Attikos began to murmur behind him.

'Athena and Apollo, my patrons, keep us both safe in our trial. Forgive this boy his youth and his arrogance. Look after us both, if it is your will.'

Pericles nodded and took a grip with each hand, raising one foot to a good spot. He straightened his leg, lifting both Attikos and himself with a grunt of effort. The top was a long way off, but the sun shone on him and his strange passenger. He smiled as he heaved them slowly upwards, hold by hold.

'Lean in *close*,' Pericles hissed in sudden fear.

Attikos had shifted his weight, easing some cramp or weariness. The man had begun to groan at intervals, pitiful sounds wrenched from him as his leg knocked and swung. In turn, Pericles gasped for air, feeling heat and sweat spring from his skin. His torn finger chose that moment to feel pain again, throbbing in time with his racing heart. He was barely halfway up as he looked for another good foothold, but he could feel his muscles already shaking like a horse beset by flies. No. He was strong enough. He had not been certain until he'd straightened his legs the first time with Attikos on his back. He could carry another man up a cliff. He could.

He dared not look at anything else but where he would put his next grip. He went fast because he felt strength draining with every moment. Soon it would be gone, and they would fall and be smashed on the rocks, or in the sea below.

Attikos stayed very quiet, understanding it was better not to distract a man who literally held his life in his hands. Only when he saw Pericles scrambling with splayed fingers for a hold did he use his better view to call 'up a little with your left hand' or 'raise that foot a finger-width higher'. He too was sweating, so that his bare arm slid across Pericles' neck in a slippery intimacy neither of them wanted.

To see the fringe of grass just above was an agony. Pericles had climbed mindlessly, his concentration total. Even the cries of gulls had been muffled. It all flooded back in as he shook stinging sweat from his eyes. He knew he could fall, that it had been a terrible mistake. His arms shook and he could not see a way to heave himself over the edge, not with Attikos making him feel he was made of lead.

'Attikos, I can't . . . I can't get us over.'

'*What* then?' Attikos snapped into his ear. 'What can *I* do?'

'You need . . . quickly now, Attikos . . . you need to reach

CONN IGGULDEN

out and take a grip before I fall. If you can . . . take your weight on your arms, I can get over the last bit.'

'Just hold on,' Attikos said. 'I'll try.'

He had heard the desperation. If Pericles fell, they were both dead, so he didn't argue. He grasped Pericles around the throat with one hand like a strangler, making lights flash across Pericles' vision. The other gripped an open seam and Pericles gasped as the weight lifted across. In moments, Attikos hung helplessly on the cliff face, one leg scrabbling for a toehold to support him further. His broken leg swung limply and the pain must have been extraordinary, but he said nothing about that. The older man watched in grim silence as Pericles heaved himself over the edge.

Panting madly, Pericles skittered straight round and lowered his arms. One by one, Attikos took his hands and they heaved and grunted in a messy tangle of limbs until both of them lay on the scrub grass, utterly beyond speech.

The gulls hovered over them for a time, indignant at the men who had dared to interfere with their nests. Pericles could only breathe and stare at them.

'That was . . . harder . . . than I thought,' he said.

Attikos sat up. Though his injuries had made him drawn and cold, he had not driven himself to collapse as Pericles had. Naked, he shivered in the sea breeze.

'I don't think you can go back for my kit,' he said.

Pericles shook his head, beginning to laugh to himself.

'I don't think I can, no.'

'And you still have to carry me down to the ships,' Attikos observed after another pause.

Pericles shook his head. His joints hurt and every muscle ached. Just the thought of carrying this naked ape across hills and marshes was enough to make him groan.

'We'd better get going,' Attikos said. 'I don't want to be

left to the mercy of the women here if Cimon decides we're not coming. How long will he wait, do you think?'

Pericles swallowed nervously. That was not a pleasant thought. He rolled over to his hands and knees and then stood. Attikos scrambled up on one leg, hopping and hissing to himself.

'Is it bad?' Pericles asked as the other man took a grip around his neck and armpit.

'My shinbone is broken, so yes, I'd say so,' Attikos replied. 'It needs two splints and a few thongs of leather to tie it all to me. Unless you have those things hidden about your person, we should get going.'

Pericles set his jaw in irritation, remembering how much he had grown to dislike the man.

'Come on,' he said.

Attikos said nothing more as Pericles took his weight and trudged off with his unwanted burden.

After a time, Pericles began to laugh as he marched along, bowed down.

'What is it?' Attikos demanded. His leg was being jostled with every step and pain was making him weak and light-headed.

'I was thinking how much like Aeneas I am today,' Pericles said, chuckling. 'He carried his father to safety on his shoulders when Troy fell.'

'I see. Did this Aeneas make his father listen to idle talk as well?'

'No,' Pericles replied, glowering. He did not speak again for a long time.

6

Pericles slumped against a bank of wet moss, near a stream. Water seeped out and dribbled down his arm, cold enough to startle him. Attikos mumbled something, but he hardly heard. Pericles just breathed and leaned, so exhausted he thought sleep or death might take him by force. Over the course of a long day, he had gone through old pains to entirely new ones, to skin rubbed away and muscles that fluttered and grew fat with blood. He had fallen many times, but not once laid Attikos down by choice. No, he had gone on, reduced to a single spot of thought as he clambered over fallen trees and pushed through thorn bushes, leaving stripes on his thighs where they tore at him. Biting flies swarmed around them both, feasting on sweat and salt and anywhere skin had been scraped off. Pericles hardly felt them any more. He had no wood to make a fire, no food to restore his strength. All he could do was close his eyes and drift. He would recover, he told himself. He always did, just as long as he could drop out of the world for a little while . . .

Attikos tapped him on the shoulder, silently, trying to bring him back from his stupor. With a silent struggle, the older man took his weight on his unbroken leg. The stab wound had allowed some foulness into it, of course. That was no surprise in the green shadows and muck they'd laboured through. That leg was both hot and oddly swollen, so that Attikos felt fever grow in him. Yet he forced himself to stand like a hoplite and tapped Pericles again, rousing him to alertness.

Ahead of them, not half a dozen paces from where they had come to rest, a pale grey pony dipped its head to drink. Attikos and Pericles both watched as the throat flexed, the animal gulping the freezing water.

'Can you see it?' Attikos whispered.

The animal's ears pricked up and rotated, but it did not stop drinking. Pericles felt some of the fog of pain and weariness lift in sheer irritation as Attikos tapped him on the shoulder again, like a child getting the attention of its parent.

'Go on! Run!' Pericles shouted without warning, waving his arms. The pony practically fell as it reared up, whinnying, then turned and galloped off, splashing through the shallow stream bed.

'What did you do *that* for?' Attikos asked. He looked as if he wanted to strike Pericles and raised a fist to him, shaking it in his face.

'It was a wild horse!' Pericles replied. 'Did you think it would let us ride it down or something? In the state you're in, it would have killed you. They're strong, Attikos. Too strong for us, right now.'

Attikos lowered his fist, blushing.

'I don't know anything about horses.' He paused only for a moment before speaking with more of an edge. 'I didn't grow up with them, you see.'

Pericles closed his eyes for a moment, focusing his will. He had carried Attikos as far as he could, beyond anything anyone had asked of him before. It would all be wasted if he beat him to death with a stone from the stream.

'Well, I did – so I know. Now, if you're thirsty, I can help you to drink . . .'

He stopped when he saw a thick trail of smoke appear over the hill. They were near the coast, he knew that already.

Pericles was no tracker, but it had been hard to miss the marks of Cimon's group once they'd come across them. He'd been following in their footsteps for hours, while the day wasted. He nodded, understanding they were almost back at the beach.

With a wince, he reached behind him and crouched.

'Come on. Nearly there.'

Attikos was parched, but he had a fear of being left behind. It was one thing to die fighting, quite another to imagine being discovered by vengeful women after the Athenians had gone. Women could be cruel, he knew very well. Worse than men, in all honesty. At least when no one was watching. They reminded him of dolphins in that way . . .

He shook his head, understanding that he was close to delirium. He clasped Pericles around the neck, ignoring the sick ache from the leg that dangled.

'Come on then, pony,' Attikos muttered, making a clicking sound in his cheek. 'On you go.'

Pericles swore as he took the weight, but he did not falter. It was just a little further.

The two men staggered over the dunes and halted. Attikos let himself slide off so that he stood on one leg, the sea breeze drying his sweat. With a groan, he used both hands to ease himself onto a clump of grass, sprawling gracelessly.

'I would prefer not to let the lads see me like this,' he said gruffly.

Pericles blinked.

'What, naked?' he asked.

Attikos looked at him.

'Who cares about that? They can see my white arse any time they want to run with me. No, I mean like this . . . *wounded*.' He gritted his teeth as if sand had made its way in, 'Carried like a child. If you fetch me wood for splints and a spear to lean on, I'll make my own way down.' He thought for a moment. The wind had strengthened and he was shivering. 'And a cloak as well. If you find one. Don't go looking for it, just if you happen to see one.'

Pericles waited for anything more, but Attikos was peering at bodies lying on the sands and in the surf, trying to read the battle that had been fought there. The pirate boats had clearly come in fast, beaching high on the shore. Pericles wished he'd seen that first clash, when they suddenly understood they were outmatched.

Two of those boats had been set on fire, lifting plumes of smoke into the clear air. A third began to burn even as Attikos and Pericles watched. Attikos grinned to himself. Raiders and thieves would have been helpless against trained hoplites. He turned to say as much to Pericles, but the young man suddenly walked on, stiff as any wounded woman, just about. Should he have thanked him for carrying him all day? He suspected Pericles thought he should. Yet what choice had the boy had, really? Fate had put them in their roles when the ground had given way and pitched Attikos down a cliff. If it had been the other way around, Attikos thought he would have carried Pericles across the entire island. That was duty, right there – and youth, of course. Good bloodline, as well, he thought, remembering the young pup's father. No, you didn't have to thank a man when he had no choice. That was just sense.

Pericles returned with a spare cloak and one of their own ship's carpenters. The man opened a roll of tools and splinted the broken shin with quiet patience, breathing through his nose in a soft hiss like waves breaking on the beach. When Attikos was ready, Pericles helped him to rise and the three of them hobbled down to where Cimon stood, directing the aftermath.

CONN IGGULDEN

His eyebrows lifted when he saw Attikos, but it was followed by a smile and not a rebuke, for which they were both grateful.

'We killed around half of them,' Cimon said. 'The rest escaped back into the hills.'

He looked quietly satisfied, standing easily as his men swept the beach for anything of value. Their own ships were further off, a distance Attikos eyed with resignation.

Cimon saw the disappointment in Pericles and understood immediately. The younger man was scuffed and filthy. One leg was black to the knee from where it had sunk into mud and his skin was marked like a map of insect bites and thorns. He had not been part of the battle. Instead, he'd had a miserable time bringing just one man out. Cimon grinned. This was a good day.

'It doesn't matter,' he said to them. 'We have Theseus himself on board. That is why we came to Scyros! Your father would understand, Pericles. You brought Attikos all the way back from the tomb?' He shook his head in wonder, giving the young man praise. 'That was well done.'

Pericles flushed and dipped his head. Attikos raised his eyes for a moment. His story was less heroic, having been carried across an island. Yet he was pleased to be back in the world he knew and not the endless journey with his leg jarring at every step. He was exhausted and in pain, and he showed none of it to men half his age. This was Cimon's victory, his expedition.

'If you can make something into a crutch,' Attikos muttered to the carpenter, 'there's a drachm in it for you.'

The man eyed him, judging his height. There was a broken oar on the sand nearby and he picked it up and handed it over without a word. Attikos was about to tell him any fool could have done that, but the thing was a good length and he could lean on the blade without too much discomfort. Reluctantly, Attikos fished a coin from his cheek with one finger and tossed it over. The carpenter caught it easily and grinned, trotting back to the ships. They were growing busier as the crews concentrated on getting just one into the water, where it could tow out the rest.

'Can you walk?' Cimon asked.

Attikos nodded.

'Come on. There's nothing else for us here.'

Attikos managed to hobble along, with Pericles standing close by like a nursemaid, still protective of his charge.

'It's all right, kurios,' Attikos said. He had meant it to be sharp, but it came out as thanks, embarrassing him. He was pleased to be among friends again. He told himself not to be such an old woman, and keep up.

The air was clean and fresh off the sea. The three men passed a few more bodies on the sand. Pericles looked on them as he drew close, seeing the deep tan of fishing folk, as well as thin arms and legs. The pirates did not look much like soldiers, he realised. The hoplites would have cut them down about as fast as they could land. With lochagoi on hand to keep them from any wild rush or charge, it would have been butchery. He found himself wondering if Thetis' husband had survived and whether she would welcome him back. Had it been his imagination that she was attractive? Her eyes had certainly been striking, more grey than brown. He shook his head as he walked, amused at himself. Cimon looked pleased and so his own spirits rose. They had Theseus!

It took six rowers to fashion a chair out of ropes to raise Attikos back on board. He yelped when his leg cracked against the hull on the inward swing, making everyone who saw it wince. They all knew him and there was more than a little pleasure in some of the men's expressions as they heaved him in.

Launching a trireme from a high beach was no easy task. The crushing weight of the ships had settled the keels. Cimon had just two small boats between the three ships, towed behind on normal days. The little craft took ropes out and began to sweep, raising the lines tight so they fell in and out of the water. Cimon set some twenty crewmen to press on the hull, as many as could find a place, feet slipping in the sand. The day was ending and he lost his good mood as the sun set and he was still stuck on the island. He just needed to get one ship back in, to pull the others. A night spent there came with a risk of attack, perhaps as the pirates grew bold once more. He could think of half a dozen ways to cause him grief – with fire arrows high on the list. His beloved warships were beached and helpless and he fretted for them as the sun turned the hills gold and red.

Pericles was pressing his back to hull strakes and calling the heave when he paused and waved a hand, giving the men around him a chance to rest. He could feel drops of sweat itching his nose as they dripped. He looked up and saw the pirate boats were still burning. Three had been torched to black ribs, with another smouldering. Yet there were still a few beyond that, ignored by the Greeks. He clapped a hand to his forehead.

'Lochagoi here, to me,' he called. Two of the closest captains came trotting up, as worried as he and Cimon were at the exposed position. Pericles pointed.

'However many rowers you can get into those boats. Tie on new ropes and row with the other two. Pray to Poseidon it will be enough to drag us off this beach.'

They wasted no time, whistling up the rowers who stood in dark groups, nervously watching the hills. Some sixty of them went off, racing the failing light. They left weapons and armour behind, pushing the raiders' boats into the shallows and then jumping in. The dark shapes seemed to grow spidery legs as they swept the sea, skimming away from shore. This was work they knew. Others on board threw down ropes from the stern as they came round, watching as loops vanished in the gloom and the boats dwindled to the end of the length. Little by little, those lines stretched and grew taut. Helmsmen signalled those on the sand and men raced the length of the ship to hang over the prow, looking down on those ready to push. With furious shouts, they were sent away to the stern, where their weight might do more good.

'*Now*, lads!' Pericles called to those around him, pressing his weight and strength against the keel. 'One, two and *three* . . . one, two and *three*!'

They worked together and the grip on the hull suddenly broke, the ship sliding down the shingle, splashing hard into the water and rocking madly. Alive, where it had been dead. The gathered men cheered at the sight, echoed by boat crews already coming back. The sun had set and it was dark, but they were no longer trapped. If it took all night to tow off the rest, it did not matter. They were men of the sea, and the sea had reclaimed them.

When the last of the three ships was afloat, with oars out, Cimon set fire to the final pirate boats. The survivors would make new ones over time, but they would not be racing out meanwhile to attack passing ships or raid islands for women and slaves, not for some time. He waited until the fires had taken hold, pride filling him. He wished his father could have lived to see the bones of Theseus found.

His flagship wallowed in barely enough water for the keel not to touch. There were no rocks on that sandy shore, but Cimon knew he'd be pleased to have deep sea under him once more. He climbed on board up a ladder of steps set into the side for that purpose. His two rowers caught a rope flung to them and tied on. Cimon stood still as a voice called in the distance, high and desperate.

'What was that?' Cimon said, peering into the darkness. There was light from the burning boats, but his eyes were weak in the night and he could see nothing. He was relieved when Pericles came to the edge of the deck and pointed.

'There. Someone running . . .'

There was a pale figure on the beach, sprinting towards them.

'Anyone else?' Cimon asked, turning his head this way and that as he squinted.

'No. Just the one,' Pericles said. He made a surprised sound as the running figure hit the water with a smack they could all hear, arms flailing in a white froth.

'Throw a rope, then,' Cimon said. 'Is it one of ours?'

Pericles shook his head.

'I don't . . .' he said. 'No, it's not.'

They all watched Thetis grab the rope thrown to meet her, hanging on clumsily, so that she seemed to walk up the side of the ship. Her feet slipped and she dangled, calling out in fear. Cimon gestured and a couple of burly rowers heaved her the rest of the way, laying hold and depositing her on the deck.

'Sanctuary!' she said, half-choking on seawater and fear. 'I am a Greek, of Thebes. I beg sanctuary.'

'Isn't that . . . ?' Cimon asked.

Pericles nodded.

'The one who led us to the tomb.'

'You've made a strange choice, coming back to us,' Cimon said to her.

'They think I betrayed the men,' she said. 'My husband is

dead and there's nothing for me here, not any more. So, I am a free Greek – a captive here. If you are the senior officer, your duty is to return me untouched and unharmed to the mainland. That's all I ask. I will find my way home then.'

She was shivering, Pericles could see. Her hair hung in a thick rope and her dress was torn and filthy, as dark as the deck she stood on. Yet she waited for an answer with some courage. He admired her for that and opened his mouth to speak in her defence.

'Very well,' Cimon said before he could. 'You came out of the sea and I will not risk Poseidon's anger by sending you back . . .'

'Kurios, am I under your protection?' she asked.

It was no small thing and desperation showed in her steady gaze. If he refused, she had no more status than a prisoner. At his word, she could have been made a slave in recompense for the costs of the expedition. Cimon made a decision in his quick way. He inclined his head.

'You have my oath. Now, I'll put you ashore in Athens, or . . .'

'Strategos! Ships!' a voice roared.

The woman was forgotten in an instant. All three of Cimon's ships were close to shore, with no room to manoeuvre. More cries went up and two of them began to turn to face the threat even so, oars already in the water. It was too late. Pericles looked out into a night where the moon was low and fat on the horizon. He swallowed at the sight of at least six warships that had crept up on them, trapping them while they were distracted. He wondered if the smoke of the burning boats had drawn them to that place.

'We'll have to beach the ships,' Cimon said grimly. 'They have us cold here. We'll have a better chance on land.'

'Wait . . .' Pericles muttered. 'Just a moment, please . . .'

CONN IGGULDEN

He was watching the sweep of oars, recalling the sea battle of Salamis. They were not Persian ships, he was certain. They could have been the twins of the great vessel under his feet, the product of Athenian shipyards.

'They're Greek, I think,' he said. 'I'm sure of it. Main fleet.'

Cimon clenched and unclenched his hands, hating to rely on the eyes of other men. Pericles swallowed when he saw the newcomers were putting down boats. Enemies would have tried to shear their oars or ram them from deep water, racing in while they were helpless. Perhaps Cimon should have kept his own boats out, to signal, Pericles thought. They were still learning the ways of the sea. It seemed another young man's error to have been surprised against the shore.

'Take us out a little way,' Cimon ordered. 'Just until there is deep water under us. Drop anchor there.'

Even as he spoke, someone on the closest approaching boat hailed them, calling cheerful greeting in the language of home. The men around Cimon lost their frozen tension in chuckles and muttered comments.

Cimon's gaze remained cold as it passed over the half-drowned young woman, still watching him. He did not smile. Even if the strange ships were from the main fleet, they would surely take his command. For just a short time, he had known the freedom of Perseus or Jason, or Theseus himself as a young man. He glowered.

'Just stay out of our way,' he said to her.

Thetis nodded, her eyes large and dark in the night.

The boat that bumped alongside brought three men climbing up. Two of them made it look easy, despite the sway and snub of the ship at anchor. The third went slowly, placing each hand and foot with the care of one who has fallen before and does not want to do so again.

The younger pair were armed as hoplites, though they kept their swords sheathed on Cimon's deck. They said nothing and all heads turned as the last one clambered up, pausing on the threshold and holding out an arm.

'A hand here,' Aristides said.

Pericles stepped forward and helped the older man to his feet. Aristides was panting lightly, shaking his head as he looked around him.

Cimon dropped to one knee and then rose. It was the bare minimum of courtesy to an archon of Athens, one whose name had graced years in the calendar.

'It is my honour to have you as a guest, Archon Aristides,' Cimon said.

'I imagine so,' Aristides replied. He grinned under the moonlight. 'It is good to see you well, Cimon. We have half the fleet out looking for you. I'm so pleased to be the one to bring you in.'

'Bring me where?' Cimon asked.

There was a tension in him and Pericles looked from one to the other.

'To the island of Delos,' Aristides said, 'two or three days south of here. We have called all our allies to one place. Honestly, I think you will be about the last, now I've found you. We could not leave you out, Cimon, not after all you've done.'

Aristides frowned slightly as he looked at the dark island, where boats still burned like campfires in the night.

'Why *are* you here, though? I have ships searching as far north as Thrace. I'd almost given up on ever finding you. If I hadn't seen the smoke, I'd have gone straight past.'

Cimon touched his forehead in thought. When he looked up, Pericles had to grin at his expression, where modesty and pride struggled together.

'We found the bones of Theseus,' Cimon said.

It was gratifying to see the old man's expression change.

'That is . . . by the gods! That is *great* news. A good omen for the talks on Delos!'

'What talks are those?' Pericles asked.

Aristides turned to face his questioner.

'You've been away too long. The ones for Hellenes, for the future – for the fleet that came together to defeat Persia at sea. It is a great undertaking and your father has done much to bring it about, Pericles. Though he has . . . suffered and suffers still. He lives to see this done. Oh, I'll let him tell you the rest himself. Xanthippus will be pleased to see you, I know that. Come, gentlemen. Rest tonight and row south with me in the morning. With the blessing of Athena and Poseidon, I think you will see something new in the world.'

He put out his hand and Cimon took it in a firm grip. Aristides did not let him go as he spoke again.

'May I see the king's bones?'

Cimon smiled and nodded.

'My father Miltiades always spoke well of you, Aristides,' Cimon said. 'Thank you for searching for us. Whatever is happening at Delos is something I would see.' He gripped the older man by the shoulder. 'Bring a lamp!' he called.

7

Nine warships held formation as they rowed south to Delos. Though it was not said aloud, Cimon's crews put their backs into it, beating the waves white to stay ahead. They carried the bones of a great Athenian king, after all. They were Argonauts reborn. They were the fleet of Odysseus, part of history. Either way, whatever they were, they would not allow Aristides and all the old men to lead them into port.

The second afternoon had grown overcast, with rain threatening. They had come south under sail the day before, but the wind had backed against them and the great sheets had been folded and stowed. The masts were left up, with a boy at each top, clinging on in wind and rain to get the first glimpse of their destination. Those lads could grin at one another for the sheer wonder of skimming south at speed. Even without that silent competition, they would all have been racing for the sacred harbour of Delos, seeking shelter before dark as the wind became a cold gale.

On the flagship, Cimon looked to the rear, where six captains under Aristides kept pace, never quite letting him pull away. The wind was dangerous to ships like theirs. Already the rowers on the lowest banks were being drenched as rogue waves smashed past leather oar-gaskets. Aristides was an archon of Athens and a veteran, Cimon reminded himself. He and his generation had stood with Cimon's father at Marathon! Aristides had commanded hoplites in the great war, beating back a Persian host more like swarming cicadas than men. Aristides was of his father's generation, one who

CONN IGGULDEN

had grown old in defence of Athens. It meant Cimon could look on him with awe and not a little envy. It did not mean he liked the man, nor being shepherded back to the fold like a naughty child.

Pericles came up from below with a bowl of bean stew and a spoon, sprinkling a little salt on it as he reached the deck. Though he also held a clay cup in the crook of his elbow, he moved with good balance. The deck trembled under them both, the keel striking the waves.

'Here, it'll keep you warm,' Pericles said, passing the food over.

'Are you not having any?' Cimon asked. He cradled the bowl in both hands and said a prayer of thanks before he ate.

Pericles shook his head, raising his cup to show the mush within. It was as red as blood.

'Just this – wine, barley, a little grated cheese. I asked for honey in it, but the cook just laughed.'

Cimon chuckled.

'It isn't . . . pangs of love stealing your appetite?'

Pericles blinked and shook his head.

'Do you mean the woman?'

'Are you pretending you don't know her name?'

The younger man flushed.

'I know it. Thetis. I think she has eyes for you, though. If I think of her at all, it's to make sure she does not stand too near the edge of the deck while Attikos is close by.'

Cimon frowned. He scraped up the last of the stew, though it had been more gristle and burned vegetables than anything satisfying. The running joke amongst the men was that it was terrible muck – and there was never enough.

'He is . . . still angry about her,' Cimon replied after a time. 'Attikos came to me formally. He says it's bad luck to have a woman on board.'

Pericles tapped his groin and spat over the side, warding off the evil eye.

'She made him look a fool, that's what matters to him. Even so, we could not leave her. Set her down on Delos if you wish, kurios. It'll be a while before Attikos can do more than threaten, anyway.'

Cimon scratched the back of one ear as he thought. He took the responsibility of being in command seriously and he had given his word. Pericles knew he would try to protect their passenger. Yet there was spite enough in Attikos to drown them all.

As if summoned by their quiet conversation, Attikos appeared, making heavy weather of climbing the steps from the lowest hold. His splinted leg had swollen to the point where men winced just to see it. The Athenian warships had few spaces below where an injured man could lie down, but those storerooms were both tight and always damp. Attikos preferred the sea air. His crutch was one the carpenter had whittled for him, sitting more snugly under his armpit than the broken oar. Cimon had lent him one of the rowers to help him get about. That burly young man waited nervously in case he fell, darting glances at the strategos.

Attikos nodded to both Cimon and Pericles as he reached the deck. He was sweating, his skin clammy with it. The man had endured brutal pain, yet he hadn't complained, at least until he'd been safe in the hold. Even then it had been more cursing than anything. Pericles wrinkled his nose when he realised he could smell the man, despite the breeze. He moved a step to put himself upwind, watched suspiciously by Attikos as he moved. Despite that sour gaze, Pericles felt his spirits rise. Eight ships rowed behind or alongside, a fleet of enormous power in itself. Commanded by Athenians, his people.

CONN IGGULDEN

At the mast top, the carpenter's boy suddenly howled like a wolf and pointed, making Pericles grin. Delos was there on the horizon, a low, flat island in the middle of the sea. Both the god Apollo and his twin sister Artemis had been born on that shore. Temples and gardens flourished there – and a great port. Only caretakers and priests actually lived on Delos, beyond the major festivals. It was neutral ground to all Greeks, though Athens had paid for the marble temples, the port, the stipends for the men and women who kept lamps burning day and night. Pericles smiled wryly at the thought. Ships brought trade, and trade brought wealth . . . and wealth, well, wealth was simply power.

'Are you looking forward to seeing your father?' Cimon asked, breaking his reverie.

Pericles felt his expression tighten as Attikos turned to hear his answer.

'Of course,' he said.

His eyes remained cold, however. His father had been changed by time and grief since they had last stood together on a Persian shore. After the loss of his oldest son, Xanthippus had run mad for a time, committing atrocities against the innocent. Pericles had not seen him for months and the thought of meeting that searching gaze once again was hard. He could not be his brother. He could not be anything but a disappointment to the man who clearly wished Pericles had been the son to fall – not Ariphron.

The port at Delos was as busy that year as the great Piraeus at Athens. The sight of so many ships brought back painful memories for Cimon – and anyone else who had been at Salamis. No one had believed they could beat the Persian fleet. They had chosen to stand even so – and thousands of his people had drowned or been cut down. Those who remembered that day had all lost friends or brothers or sons. They were sombre as they eased into the port.

At least a hundred warships had already been beached or filled the quays. For those coming late, there was little shelter to be had. In places, a man might almost have walked ashore across the decks. Even with experienced officers, finding a spot to anchor required delicate judgement, ignoring angry shouts. Cimon brought his three ships as close as he dared before leaving the rest to his captains. A small boat was made ready to take him ashore.

Attikos would not be coming with them, not with a broken leg. Pericles was halfway down the ladder in the side when he realised he should not leave Thetis to the man's mercies.

'One moment, kurios,' he said to Cimon, scrambling back up.

Cimon raised his eyebrows, but when he saw Pericles return with her, guiding her feet to the wooden steps, he seemed to understand well enough.

The long summer evening was easing into grey gloom as two small boats took Cimon and his officers past the prow of his flagship. Ahead, he saw Aristides standing in a sturdy little craft, rowed by four men and making good speed.

Cimon and Pericles exchanged a glance. The water was chaotic around them, with small boats everywhere, ropes flung and anchor cables drawn tight enough to become a hazard for everyone else. The coast was barely two hundred paces away.

'A tetradrachm to each of you if I put my foot ashore before Aristides,' Cimon said to his own rowers.

It was two days' wages and they leaned into the very next stroke, making the sea hiss under the strakes. Cimon kept his face impassive as they hauled Aristides in and passed him. Pericles was careful not to look back, but he was grinning as the little boat reached the docks and Cimon stepped onto an iron ladder, running up the last few steps to stand on stone. True to his word, he tossed a heavy silver coin to each of his men, marked with the head of Heracles. Pericles clambered out after him, then Thetis. Out of place, she stood nervously at their side, her head bowed.

Cimon regarded the woman while he waited for Aristides to reach the dock. His own boat was already heading back to the ships at anchor, though he heard the rowers offer to take others in as they passed ships of Eretria and Mycenae.

'If you wish to go your own way, I will not stop you,' Cimon said to Thetis. 'Nor will I abandon you here, if you'd rather stay with us until we reach Athens. You'll need new clothes, food and somewhere to stay while we are on the island. I can arrange for those. It's no more than a tithe to the gods for our safe passage – and for helping us find the tomb of Theseus.'

Pericles smiled. In Athens, Cimon had made his friends wear thick cloaks – then insisted they give them to anyone who asked. His generosity was famous, though it seemed word of it had not reached Scyros. Thetis looked at him with more than a little suspicion.

'Am I still under your protection, Athenian?'

'If you wish to be,' Cimon said with a shrug. 'I have learned to keep my word. In fact . . .'

She stepped forward suddenly and slapped him across the face. He looked at her in astonishment.

'Why would you do that?' he said. There was a dangerous air to his stillness in that moment, though she did not seem to sense it.

'You killed my husband, Athenian. Or the man I called husband. He may not have been much, but he was mine – and you took him from me, though he'd done nothing to you.'

Pericles moved to take her by the arm, his own face flaming. To his surprise, Cimon raised a hand, halting him. He had recovered his calm.

'I see,' Cimon said. 'So, are you satisfied? Or must I watch my back whenever you are close enough to attack me?'

Thetis blinked. The Athenian strategos gleamed with health and strength. He was the son of a senior archon of Athens and he had grown up with a thousand buffets and scrapes in training and in war. His face showed the mark of where she had hit him, but he seemed utterly unmoved by it. There was even humour in his eyes and the tilt of his mouth. She found herself trembling.

'I am . . .' she said.

'Be *certain*,' Cimon added with a little more force. 'I expect you to keep your word, just as I keep mine. There are some who believe women have no honour, that they will always break their word. My mother and my wife would call them liars. So . . . give me your word, Thetis, your oath of good behaviour. I will accept it. No one will lay hands on you, or treat you roughly. I will set you down wherever you wish to go.'

It was her turn to grow red as she stood on the docks. Aristides had been brought to the ladder by then and was climbing up. He looked at the strange scene with interest.

'I give you my word,' Thetis said.

Cimon nodded and turned to greet Aristides.

'Archon, I am pleased to see you safe. I was worried about the wind swamping us all for a time.'

Aristides looked both Athenians over. Oil lamps were being lit against the gloom, all along the docks there. He could see Cimon and Pericles were involved in something he did not care enough about to winkle out. Perhaps it was just their youth, or the presence of the striking young woman

CONN IGGULDEN

who stared at her feet in his presence. For some reason, or because Cimon had made his rowers work like madmen to reach the docks first, Aristides found himself irritated with all of them.

'As I said, we are almost the last ones in. Pericles? Your father will be hoping to see you before the meeting tomorrow. Shall I say you will attend on him?'

'Of course,' Pericles replied. He felt Thetis studying him with new interest and was pleased.

Cimon gestured to the mass of ships filling the bay and port, more than the island of Delos had ever known.

'You didn't say why we were called, Archon Aristides.'

'Really? I thought I had,' Aristides replied. He rubbed his jaw for a moment, choosing his words. 'We are here to take an oath, as allies – so that if any of us is attacked, the rest will go to war. That is the heart of it. We learned that much at Salamis and Plataea. Alone, even Athens is not strong enough to stand. Together, though . . . we defeated an ancient empire. This alliance, this league, will be a formal oath, set in iron. One language, one people.'

Pericles looked out on the ships of thirty or forty cities and regions. He squinted as far as he could, but there was no sign of one in particular among them. He had seen them at Salamis when he'd stood on the dunes and watched carnage unfold. They had worn red cloaks that day, as they stood on the deck.

'Where is Sparta?' he asked.

Aristides' mouth twisted, as if he sucked a shred of gristle from between two front teeth.

'Their ephors refused, though your father went in person to describe the idea. The journey exhausted him . . .' Aristides waved a hand. 'Oh, they are such an arrogant race – with some right to be. Yet this is too important. I have had my fill of persuading Spartans to the cause. We'll go on without them.'

Cimon shook his head. He admired the Spartans more than most, indeed had modelled himself on some of their practices, establishing a discipline over his life it had once lacked. He wore a Spartan knife in his belt, the famed kopis that was as useful for chopping down a small tree as killing men.

'Sparta has earned the right to lead in war,' Cimon said with a frown. 'You were at Plataea, kurios. You know.'

Aristides looked at him, judging the serious young man Cimon had become. He had been a drunk once, wild and uncaring. Cimon had spent money on fools and women to surround him. There was no sign of that in him then and Aristides took the comment seriously.

'I was there – and I do know. Plataea was a wonder, like Marathon before it. Yet you will recall Salamis, Cimon, with the fleet – with Xanthippus and Themistocles. Where was Sparta then?' As Cimon began to reply, Aristides went on. 'This is not their domain, Cimon. Athens is the great power at sea . . . and we choose to lead this alliance, with or without Sparta. Men of Thrace and Chalcis are here, with Lemnos, Corcyra – dozens more. Every island and kingdom and city where Greek is spoken, just about. Sparta cannot expect to remain apart, not now. We are making something . . .' Aristides made himself stop, though his enthusiasm was still rising. 'You'll see, I think.'

'Without Sparta, this is a dangerous game,' Cimon said flatly, unmoved. 'It will be a challenge to them.' He inclined his head to Pericles. 'I'm sorry, I know your father for an honourable man, but this is a bad path to go down.'

Aristides shook his head.

'While you have been seeking out old kings, Xanthippus

CONN IGGULDEN

and I have put together a league of friends, a brotherhood. He and I were witness to its birth, Cimon. Your father commanded only men of Athens at Marathon, but at sea? The fleet that went north against the Persians was thirty states and polities, all risking life and limb together. Those of us with eyes saw something . . . worth preserving.'

Cimon chose not to reply and merely stared out to sea rather than argue. He had made his point and, in that moment, he was more Spartan than Athenian. Aristides seemed to understand, though it saddened him.

'Come, bring your slave,' Aristides said. 'Perhaps Xanthippus can explain it to you. It is his idea, after all.'

'I am not . . .' Thetis began.

Pericles shook his head and she bit her lip, following them to the road that led inland. It was lined with points of flame, stretching away. A stream of men and some women were making their way in from the port. The great temple of Apollo was their destination, god of oracles, of poetry and the sun. The healer – and the bringer of plagues.

8

The temple of Apollo was surprisingly modest for the birth-place of a god. Pericles had expected at least a town, or something to rival the great temples that had graced the Acropolis before the Persians came. Instead, a simple build-ing of white stone was lit by torches. Long and low, it was roofed in tile and had no separate wings. He wondered where the priests lived for the rest of the year, if they stayed on Delos at all.

Under the portico roof, he gave both Cimon's name and his own to a hoplite standing guard. The young man was a stranger, but he seemed to think it was his role to take them further in and gestured for them to follow. Cimon gave the tiniest of shrugs. He had been called and he had come. What-ever Xanthippus and Aristides had created that year was not his responsibility. He only feared they had overreached. Old men often relived the glories of their youth – and sometimes they sought to keep the flame alive too long. He revered both Xanthippus and Aristides, but he feared their plans and ambitions, at least while they failed to understand Sparta.

Pericles hesitated as he considered the woman they had brought to that place.

'You can wait here, if you wish,' he said to Thetis.

The hoplite was watching impatiently, shifting his weight from foot to foot.

'You want to be rid of me,' she said.

Pericles nodded with only half his attention, already look-ing past her to the inner sanctum of the temple. Charcoal

CONN IGGULDEN

burned there in a huge copper bowl. In the flickering light, he could make out groups talking and drinking in a fine panoply of colour. He did not respond, until Thetis leaned across to interrupt his gaze.

'What? No, I have no interest in you at all,' he said curtly. 'Cimon has given his word to see you to a safe harbour. I acknowledge my part in it.' He waved a hand. 'Beyond that, my concern is not with you. Wait here.'

'Alone? I would not be safe.'

Pericles looked at her in frustration. Thetis was not exactly wrong, though he could hardly imagine any of the delegates or their guards taking an interest in a lone woman while great affairs of state were going on. He could hear the accents of a dozen regions from where he stood. If Aristides was right, this was a moment of awe and wonder – and he needed to see his father. As he hesitated, the hoplite cleared his throat.

'Very well,' Pericles said. 'Stay at my side and do not say a word. Can you manage that?'

Thetis nodded and smiled. It changed her so completely he paused a beat, distracted as he turned. The hoplite had been staring at the ceiling, waiting for them. He led them in, down the long central aisle.

Pericles passed a dozen groups of men and a few senior women. One or two were certainly priestesses of Artemis, in delicate robes. He heard Thetis take a sharp breath as they passed one of surpassing beauty, speaking in low tones to what looked like a wealthy nobleman of Thrace. The lady held a fawn on a leash. She wrapped and unwrapped the leather strap around her wrist as she talked, while the deer sat like a little dog at her feet. It should not have been surprising for a devotee of the goddess, but it added to a sense of unreality in that place. Lit by torches and crackling oil lamps, all was gold and shadows – and at the heart of it, by the eternal flame, stood his father, Xanthippus. The archon of Athens was more bent than Pericles remembered, leaning heavily on a cane of iron and olive wood.

The hoplite from the outer precinct bowed deeply, interrupting the conversation. Pericles had the sense it had been an argument, with both his father and another man looking beady-eyed and angry. Xanthippus almost waved the hoplite away, but then saw his son and Cimon, with Thetis a step behind, trying hard to be invisible.

There was a moment of silence as his father stared. Pericles felt his judgement like a weight.

'Pericles,' Xanthippus said coldly. 'Cimon. You've cut it very fine. I've spent a week thinking you would not make it back.'

'It is good to see you too, father,' Pericles said.

Xanthippus ignored the response, turning once more to his companion.

'Cepherus, this is Cimon, son of the late Archon Miltiades, who commanded at Marathon. His companion is my youngest son, Pericles.'

He did not seem to feel a need to introduce his companion in turn. It suggested Cepherus was someone of great status, or simply that Xanthippus had not yet learned to treat his son as a man. Pericles had not missed that they had both been described as the sons of others. He was used to it from his father, but he prickled with indignation on behalf of Cimon. Cimon had commanded part of the fleet at Salamis. He was owed respect.

The stranger nodded to the two young men. He seemed content to put aside whatever he and Xanthippus had been discussing, at least for the moment. His eyes passed over Thetis, but he did not ask about her, drawing his own conclusions.

'I hear you have brought something back with you,' Cepherus said. Pericles felt his eyebrows rise and the older man laughed. 'News spreads quicker than fire, quicker than you could run from the port. Is it true, then? It is Theseus?'

Xanthippus turned his head in sharp interest and Pericles realised there was at least one who had not heard. No doubt his father had been too busy for idle gossip. He looked weary enough.

'It is,' Cimon answered, choosing to be part of the conversation. 'He lay beneath dressed stone on a hill overlooking the sea coast, a warrior of extraordinary size, in Athenian armour.'

He raised his hand and Pericles blinked at a thick gold ring he had not noticed before. Cimon had to have taken it from the bones while he had been rescuing Attikos.

'This was his,' Cimon said.

Xanthippus tapped his stick on the stone floor as he came forward. Cepherus leaned in with him, so that both of them peered at the gold.

'An owl crest,' Xanthippus said. 'The signet of a king of Athens.'

There was surprise in his voice and Pericles basked in it.

'Though you have no right to wear it, Cimon,' Xanthippus added.

Their smiles froze as Xanthippus held out his hand.

'Father, I don't think . . .' Pericles began.

Cimon had adopted the mask that hid all emotion once more. He shook his head.

'No, Pericles. Archon Xanthippus is correct, of course. I do not own it merely because I found it. It belongs to Athens. Here, kurios.'

He handed it over, watched by many eyes around them.

The little scene had not gone unnoticed and they had become the centre of a fascinated group.

Xanthippus made the ring vanish into a pouch and inclined his head. Cimon had clearly impressed him.

'Thank you,' he said. 'You remind me of my son Ariphron. The same sense of duty.' He paused just a beat, then went on. 'When we return home, I'll ask the Assembly to vote funds to a new temple, with a statue to Theseus on the Acropolis. It means more than I can say.'

He stared for a moment, his eyes unfocused. With a frown, Pericles saw again how much his father had aged. The stick was new. His father's hand trembled on it, swept through by pain.

Xanthippus shook off whatever moved him.

'You are welcome at the ceremony tomorrow. The oath will be made on land, but it will be sealed aboard ships. It will be something to see, I think. Something to tell your own children about.'

'I am glad of it,' Cimon replied, 'though without Sparta, can any alliance be truly legitimate?'

Silence seemed to fall across the temple. Even the echoes of footsteps stopped. Only the charcoal huffed and crackled. Pericles swallowed. Cimon returned his father's cold gaze with no sign of weakness, a reminder that he had not given him the ring of Theseus out of fear, but because he had chosen to. Cimon was neither moved nor cowed by the august authorities in that room. Not even by Xanthippus, first in Athens.

'We are free men, Cimon,' Xanthippus said. 'I remind you that I asked Sparta to join with us, alongside the other states of the Peloponnese. They chose to look away. It does not make our oath less, nor our purpose. We will make something new in the world tomorrow. You'll see then, I think.'

CONN IGGULDEN

The crowd resumed their talk amidst the clinking of cups and quiet laughter. Xanthippus turned his shoulder just a fraction, shutting the two young men out as he bent his head and resumed whatever discussion they had interrupted. Cimon grew still, as if at an insult. He opened his mouth once more, but then shut it and walked away. Pericles was left with Thetis. He accepted a cup of wine from a server and drank it to the dregs. Thetis looked at him in silent question as he moved her out of his father's hearing.

'What a stern man,' she said.

Pericles turned on her. He looked hurt, or offended.

'He was not . . . You didn't know him when I was growing up. He was exiled by Athens, do you understand that? I was just a child when they sent him away. A weak man would have scorned them all, let it fester . . . but not him. He put his pride aside when he was called back – because they needed him. Because no one else could take charge of the fleet.'

'He is a hero to you,' she said.

She was standing closer to him and he could smell roses, as if the heat of her made the scent rise. He wondered how she had found rose oil in the time since they had landed.

'He is a great man, regardless of what I think. No matter what he thinks of me.'

A line appeared between her eyes as she thought through what he had said. She began to speak, but then stopped with a visible effort of will. He frowned at her.

'What is it?'

Thetis sighed.

'The man I called my husband . . . used to bring problems to me, his pains and worries. I would discuss them with him in the quiet and the dark. It is an old habit and I almost did the same with you. I'm sorry.'

'Was he not truly your husband, then?' he asked.

She shook her head.

'More the man who took me in a raid, when I was young and foolish. I was out collecting shells along the shore while my father traded – and Hipponicus came and snapped me up, like a little fish in his nets. There was a ceremony . . . I called him husband in the end. He was not completely without kindness.'

She was looking into memory and Pericles wondered if he would find her so interesting if she had not been attractive. It was the curse of men to see beauty as more than it was. If she had been taken young, he wondered if she even knew.

'You are sorry he is dead . . .' Pericles murmured.

Thetis gave a brittle laugh.

'He was my protection on the island. I learned to make him happy, so that he would not hurt me. Do you understand? No, of course you don't. If I had not been his, there were a dozen other men who might have forced me. I was safer with him, that's all. I am still . . . understanding that he is truly gone. I wish I'd known you would take me on board. I might not have run from you then.'

Pericles recalled the spite in Attikos. The man's blood had been up and there was less kindness in him than the one she'd called husband. Cimon too could be ruthless, which she seemed to have forgotten. No, her instincts were good, he thought. She'd been right to run.

Cimon came back at that moment, looking wry at finding them standing so close to one another. He was accompanied by a temple acolyte, a young boy carrying a candle behind a curve of beaten bronze. It cast a pool of light across all three of them.

'There is some sort of priest cell we can have, apparently. One between the three of us, and that the last available. I'll sleep on the floor. Come on. Whatever your father has planned, it will begin early tomorrow.'

Pericles followed Cimon and Thetis, suddenly very aware of the prospect of spending a night crammed into a small room with her. He wondered if he would get any sleep at all.

In darkness, Pericles awoke, confused for a moment as to why he was on a tiny pallet bunk and not the rocking deck of a warship, wrapped in a cloak. The room seemed to shift under him after months at sea. He blinked, then lay very still, understanding the soft and rhythmic noises that had woken him. He clenched his jaw, outraged almost to the point of jumping up and startling them. The window to the tiny cell was high and small, but there was enough starlight once his eyes had adjusted to make out the two figures moving together under a blanket. Pericles felt jealousy stab through him. As silently as he could, he turned to face the wall, furious with both of them and himself. It was a long time before a soft cry sounded, quickly stifled. They grew still after that, though he remained awake.

9

When Pericles opened his eyes, the room was empty. He cursed, filled with fear he was late. He emptied his bladder into a tall pot and was heading out when footsteps sounded and the door opened. Using one foot to hold it back, Thetis brought in a bowl of steaming water.

'Sit,' she said. 'There is still time.'

She carried a flask of oil in the crook of her arm and a razor in her teeth. When the bowl was safe on a side table, she gestured to a chair. Cimon entered at that moment, rubbing his face and neck with a cloth and looking both refreshed and cheerful. Pericles stared ahead as the two of them pretended everything was as it had been.

He sat still as Thetis leaned close to oil his skin. Cimon's cheeks and jaw were freshly shaved, he noted. The strategos was unusual in going without a beard. For most Athenians, it was the sign they had reached maturity and were responsible. They cherished their beards for all it said about them. Pericles was tempted to grow out his own, the visible sign he was a man and no longer a downy-cheeked youth. The only difficulty was that it would not come through.

He held very still while Thetis dragged the blade across his upper lip. The razor looked a little like an axe head, with a long curved tang so she could grip it securely even when slippery with oil.

'You've done this before,' Pericles murmured as she paused to wipe the edge on a cloth lying over one shoulder.

'My husband,' she said. 'He was a poor man, I think you

would say, but he found having a beard was too hot in summer. Shaving was a luxury and he missed it. When we finally got a razor like this one, I did this every day.'

She worked the blade against the sides of his cheeks and around his chin. There was a space between those spots that had never needed to be shaved. Her fingers were firm and strong and he felt a mixture of longing, jealousy and simple irritation with them both. Cimon had clearly not forced her. Why then had she chosen the older man over him? Pericles had thought there was something between Thetis and himself, but that had clearly been wrong. The revelation of the night before made him feel like a fool, or a child excluded from a more adult world. One thing was certain, speaking about it would steal what little dignity he had left.

'There's no time to eat,' Cimon said. 'Your father is up and about already, if he slept at all. The whole island is heading down to the port to seal this alliance, this league of theirs.'

'Of ours,' Pericles corrected. As much as he revered Cimon, he was in no mood that morning to agree with him.

'I suppose so . . . though I fear they push Sparta too far.'

'Well, perhaps it is no business of Sparta's what we do here,' Pericles said.

Cimon looked at him in surprise. Pericles shrugged and then hissed in pain as Thetis cut him. A trickle of blood ran down his cheek. She dabbed at it with the cloth Cimon put into her hand without a word.

'This is an alliance for war as much as trade,' Cimon said. Though he spoke gently, it was still in reproof. 'And Sparta commands in war. How do you think they will react when they hear of this great oath – excluding them? At the very least, it is an insult to their honour. We could not have won at Plataea without them. We would have lost and been conquered,

Pericles. That is a simple truth, not a boast. Aristides should know better. Your father . . .'

'My father knows very well who his allies are — and his enemies. Sparta fought alongside hoplites of Athens and a dozen others. Yes, they won! I thank the gods for it. They came out from behind their wall because Athens threatened to go over to Persia rather than let our city be burned a *third* time. We shamed the Spartans into war, Cimon. Don't forget that. They cared enough to move only when they feared our fleet in the hands of a Persian king! That was not the action of a friend and ally. Not then. Not now, either, if they try to deny us this. My father is gathering a great alliance for the benefit of us all. I see that now.'

'What's got into you this morning?' Cimon said.

Pericles said nothing, rather than have his objections made petty through jealousy. He was right. The fact that he was furious with them both for other reasons did not make him less right!

'Nothing at all,' Pericles said. He rubbed his chin and murmured thanks to Thetis, not quite meeting her eye. 'Come on, then. Whether Sparta approves or not, I would like to see this Athenian league begun.'

He saw Thetis had brought in a tooth stick with the hot water and took it up, rubbing his teeth clean and using the sharpened end to remove a piece of gristle that had been bothering him. Pericles passed it to Cimon to use in turn, filled a cup with still-steaming water, swilled it around his mouth and swallowed. He dipped both hands in the bowl and ran them through his hair, keeping it out of his eyes.

'Ready?' he said curtly to them.

Cimon nodded and Thetis bit the inside of her lip, wondering at his change in mood.

Pericles went out, leaving the little room and the pair of

them behind. The sun barely showed on the horizon, but the island streets were heaving with people. Many more than he had realised had come to Delos. Kings, queens and noble councils had all come with their servants and slaves. Men and women walked in crowds or were carried on litters as befitted their customs. Just one had summoned them, Pericles reminded himself. Not Cimon, or Aristides or any of them. His father, Xanthippus. As he walked, he thought he heard Thetis call his name, but he did not turn round.

On the docks, Pericles saw his father standing with Aristides and a dozen priests. The followers of Apollo and Ares were first amongst them, but he saw too a priest of Hades and one of Athena, a matronly woman who wore a warrior's helmet high on her head, as well as a white robe. Pericles was in such a foul mood he didn't hesitate, approaching the group to stand with his father. He saw Xanthippus glance at him as he came close, but the old man said nothing. At least he did not send Pericles away.

Every moment brought more and more senior men and women down to that place. The tail of them tapered off until it seemed every officer and crewman, every noble and archon, was present. Out at sea, revealed in the first glimpse of gold, crews stood at respectful attention on the decks, solemn in the morning light.

The priests of Apollo began the dawn chant, the welcome to the day that was the gift of their patron. The crowd stood with heads bowed, enjoying the prospect of warmth after the night's chill. Pericles looked a few rows behind him and saw Cimon had stopped there, brows drawn together as he too understood what a great undertaking he was witnessing.

A bull lowed in mournful confusion as the dawn chant came to an end. Brought forward by sweating priests, it was strong, a massive animal. Its ribs showed, though, making it look a little thin. Pericles wondered if it had been brought by ship to the island. Animals often fared badly in the hold, whereas men seemed to thrive on deprivation and strangeness.

Fires were lit on bronze stands, then wine spilled across the animal's head, along with grains of barley. The gods were watching and it was well done, Pericles saw, in solemnity and ritual. Prayers were said to the entire pantheon of gods as priests asked for blessing and wisdom on all those gathered in that place, on that sacred coast.

When Xanthippus stepped forward, Pericles saw Aristides going with him. They both looked tired but somehow satisfied as they faced the crowd and bowed their heads. One by one, priests and priestesses came to bless the two men, anointing them with oil or drops of water flung from fennel and sage. Pericles was suddenly aware he had missed all the meetings and discussion over the previous months. He had not known his father's plans. In that, like Cimon at his back, he was a stranger in that crowd. Whether king or slave, those present were from a hundred different places, yet they all looked to the two Athenian archons with something approaching reverence. Pericles could see it in them. He hoped Cimon and Thetis could as well, as he felt a fierce pride. It was his father commanding the crowd in that place. Though Xanthippus had aged since he'd last seen him, there was strength in him still.

Xanthippus raised his left hand while his right gripped a stick of olive wood and silver.

'Some of us walked decks or land when Persia came to make us slaves,' Xanthippus began.

His voice had once blasted across the battlefield at Marathon and it had not become an old man's quavering pipe, not then. Whatever it took to hold a crowd rapt, Xanthippus had it. Pericles felt time grow still as a breeze blew. He was glad he had come back.

'We stood together then, because alone, we could not stand. Together, we put a fleet to sea, greater than any of us had seen before. Three hundred ships by my reckoning. Those of you who had no ships to send, know your people sat on the benches or fought alongside Athens. If you were not there, you sent food and willing hands when we called. Make no mistake! We asked for good men because we had no choice. My city had been burned by a king of Persia. Not once, but twice. My people were taken as refugees to a tiny island not much bigger than this one, there to learn their fate and simply. . . hope. Not once, but twice. My own wife, my sons . . .'

Perhaps only Pericles and a few of the Athenian contingent knew why his voice caught then, but Xanthippus barely missed a beat before he went on.

'My family waited on the dunes of Salamis and they did not know if the men landing there would be ours or Persian soldiers, come to rape, come to own.'

He looked across them all and no one moved. Only the bull lowed, a pitiful sound against the noise of waves lapping the shore.

'If you were not at Salamis, perhaps you came to us in Athens, where we gathered an army and took the war to Persia. Perhaps you provided food, or silver or wine. All of you played a part – none of you looked away. I will never know a brotherhood like this again. Persia came to destroy – and instead . . . bound us together, stronger than we have ever been. I call you brothers because we know the same gods, the same language. Because we have the same ancestors. From this day, I call myself Athenian – and Hellene. I will be brother and husband and son to all our people.'

He smiled and Pericles felt his heart lift. It had been a long time since he'd seen anything but simmering anger or disappointment in his father. To see joy in him almost brought tears to the eyes, for all that had been lost.

'I call you now,' Xanthippus said, making his voice ring. 'In the living presence of the gods and their priests. As we have agreed. Speak now a sacred and eternal oath, to bind our threads into one golden rope, until the end of the world. To create and support an alliance of Hellenes. To pay the shares we have allotted according to our strength, to ask for aid according to our need. As one.'

From the deck of a ship tied to the dock, a dozen hoplites in highly polished armour tramped down across a trembling wooden bridge. They carried a huge clay urn, of the sort used to exile men in Athens, or even larger. Even empty, it took six men to carry it, bearing the weight on long poles through handles of iron. They deposited it on the docks and Pericles saw his father nod to Aristides. He gestured to an officer on board and another troop of men came out. This time, they bore sacks that jingled and revealed their contents even before they poured a silver stream into the pot. Pericles looked back and saw Cimon was as astonished as he was.

The Athenians poured at least thirty sacks of coins before the hoplites stood back. Others came forward then, bearing fortunes. Each one was marked on a record sheet of papyrus, against the name of a city-state. Some poured in a dozen sacks, some only four or five, or even fewer. Aristides stood by the great urn and exchanged a few words with each group, thanking them. They seemed pleased and proud to be part of it and Pericles could see no resentment in them. None had brought as many as the Athenians, he noted with pride.

'This is our treasury,' Xanthippus said to the crowd. 'A

CONN IGGULDEN

sum vast enough to tempt thieves and enemies, I have no doubt. It will remain in the temple of Apollo on Delos when we leave. As we have agreed, ten men of Athens will administer this great fund, while ships of Athens patrol these waters and keep them safe. No one will land without the permission of this brotherhood. No one will take a single silver drachm unless it has been agreed he is right to do so. Each year, we will return with the same tithes, next year and a thousand years from today. This is our oath, spoken in silver, in the birthplace of Apollo, before all the gods. On the honour of your noble houses, your cities, your kingdoms and your souls, repeat these words.'

He paused and Pericles could only stare at the man his father was. Gnarled and bent by years, Xanthippus stood tall even so, raising his stick high so that it no longer touched the ground.

'We are one brotherhood, one league of men,' he called.

They repeated it and one or two had tears in their eyes. Pericles bowed his head and said the words with the rest.

'We offer our most sacred oath, in this most sacred place, to stand as one, in peace and in war . . .'

He paused again to let them repeat his words. The breeze was a warm breath on their skin as the sun continued to rise.

'To return to this place, this day each year, there to deposit our contribution – from each according to his strength, to maintain peace and the fleet.'

Pericles turned his head when he realised Thetis was speaking the words with him. He frowned at that. She was no representative of a city or a people. She had no right to be part of it. Though there were other women in the crowd, they were queens or priestesses, far above petty restrictions of custom. For Thetis to join them might even have been considered mockery. Pericles felt himself tense. He glared at her, willing her to stop. He could not say anything, not as his father went on.

'We give this oath freely . . . to Zeus and Hera, to Apollo and his sister Artemis. We give this oath to Athena, Poseidon, to Ares and Demeter, to the smith, Hephaestus. We give it to Aphrodite and the messenger, Hermes. We give it to Dionysus and Hestia – to wine and the hearth. We swear this oath on our shades, on the Fates, eternal, to the end of all things, and the last day.'

Each line was repeated and silence fell. Pericles swallowed. Such words were never said lightly. One of his own mother's ancestors had broken an oath a dozen generations before. That had still not been forgotten. Those present were chaining not just themselves but their descendants, with no respite, no chance to undo a single word. The gods could be spiteful to those who broke an oath made in their name. Whatever restraint held back their wrath in normal years, they threw it aside then. Cities could be lost to fire, their lands salted. Wars could be brought about, with entire peoples made bones or slaves. It was no small thing to stand on Delos and speak those words on a gentle morning.

'We came here as a hundred separate peoples; we will leave as one,' Xanthippus said.

His words were repeated by the crowd. He took a physical step to one side then, lowering his staff, signalling that the oath-taking was over as he spoke again.

'Bring forth the iron,' he said.

Of course there were a few voices who repeated that as well, too slow to realise the shift. It made others laugh and suddenly they were all smiling, the fear and awe of the terrible binding oath making a strange lightness in them.

Pericles recognised the iron blocks that were brought through the crowd. They had been taken from the deepest holds, brought up to the light for the first time since the dockyard. With dozens more, the slabs balanced warships, allowing them to lean under sail. Pericles could see they had been wrapped around with ropes in the form of a cradle. When a pair of hoplites put one down to shift or ease a grip, their hands looked like dead flesh, crumpled and pale.

Pericles glanced across as Cimon and Thetis came to stand with him, easing up through the crowd. Cimon raised his eyebrows in silent question. There had to be seventy ballast blocks resting on the quayside.

'I don't know,' Pericles murmured. He saw Thetis was leaning in to hear his answer and was suddenly irritated. He kept his voice at a breath, barely a whisper. 'Though I know you should not have spoken that oath . . .'

'I do not see Thebes here,' she hissed back. 'Perhaps I spoke for Thebes.'

The sheer effrontery of that robbed him of words for a moment. He could see his father was readying himself to complete the oath and he did not want to be drawn into a furious argument, but what she had said was unforgivable. It was also true, he realised. Not only was Thebes missing, more importantly, he had not seen anyone of Corinth or Argos there. With Sparta absent, it meant the main powers of the Peloponnese were all excluded. It meant it was first and foremost a brotherhood of the sea – of cities on the Aegean coast. He scowled at Thetis, annoyed with her for seeing something he had not.

'You do not speak for anyone,' he whispered furiously. 'You don't even speak for Scyros.'

She folded her lips in and clenched her jaw, looking like a rebellious child.

On the docks, Xanthippus raised his hands and the crowd quieted. He nodded to a great burly figure who had come to stand by him. The man responded by placing what looked like a metal peg on the surface of one of the ingots. A second man raised a hammer and they all watched as it was brought down without a flinch.

When the peg was removed, a circle had been stamped into the metal. The pair moved immediately to the next, so that dulled notes rang out at intervals.

'When you take back your ballast,' Xanthippus said, 'you will bear the symbol of this alliance in your holds – and you will know we do the same. Yet we agreed one last thing as a sign of our oath. As you return to your ships, each of you will leave one of these iron blocks on the sea floor, by Delos. As we agreed, they are the symbol of our faith. Until they rust to nothing, we stand as one.'

They cheered that, the crowd breaking up as at the end of a great festival. They clapped one another on the back and hundreds went to thank Xanthippus and Aristides. Hoplites drifted to the iron blocks, collecting them in pairs – each one marked with a circle. They staggered and grinned as they took them back to ships along the quays or stood by them, waiting for their turn. It would be dark by the time the last of them was safely off, Pericles thought. Those ingots would sink a small boat.

Cimon had the same thought.

'I'll have to lay hold of a couple of those until I can bring my own in,' he said. 'Will you stand over them with me? I imagine there are enough.'

Pericles nodded, though he glanced at Thetis from under lowered brows. Cimon had said the oath – with every right to, as a strategos of Athens.

'I didn't ...' Pericles began. He saw Cimon had paled, looking out to sea. Pericles spun round. Some of the other men on the docks were calling out and pointing by then.

The ships that came into view were not Persian. The crews on Delos would have gone out with savage smiles if Persia had sent warships against them. No, it was worse than that. A dozen ships came round the coast, with sails billowing in the morning sun. Six of them had red sails. The fleets of Sparta and Corinth had come.

Cimon chuckled, though it was a bitter sound.

'I suppose we'll see now,' he said. He looked across at Pericles. 'I hope your father knows what he is doing. Look at those hoplites on the shore! Lions made lambs.'

He gestured to the crowd on the quayside. Where they had been joyous and proud before, they were suddenly afraid. It showed in the way they stood, the way they hurried. They still took the ingots, Pericles saw. No matter what Sparta thought or did then, the oath had been sworn.

IO

For Pausanias of Sparta to summon all the captains gathered at Delos was no small undertaking. The sheer number of them made any conclave on a single flagship impossible. Negotiations took the best part of the day and it was dark by the time two Spartan vessels had been anchored and lashed together in what Pericles privately called 'the other dance floor of Ares'. The rest of the ships with Pausanias took station around that double deck. Trierarchs from as far away as Thrace and the coast of Ionia mingled in boats with men of Athens, Eretria and Leuctra.

Pausanias himself stood on the prow of his flagship, one foot on a step, in case he chose to raise himself further. The soothsayer Tisamenus waited with him, looking every inch the Olympian pentathlete he had once been. Most of those gathered there knew Tisamenus had been promised success in five contests by the oracle at Delphi. The triumph at Plataea had been his first – and his presence was a good omen for those who knew his story. Such a man, touched by prophecy, would be a fortunate choice for any undertaking. Apollo himself had marked him for glory.

The decks creaked as Pericles climbed aboard, taking the grip of a Spartan soldier rather than risk falling back into the arms of Cimon. He grimaced at a rasp of callus on a palm more like an old glove than anything of man. The Spartan heaved him up, then extended his hand to the next Athenian.

Behind Cimon, Thetis climbed. She wore the loose robe

CONN IGGULDEN

of a priestess of Artemis, having begged for something clean from the temple on Delos. It meant if she fell into the sea, the weight of cloth would surely drown her. She was wide-eyed as the Spartan almost flung her on deck, misjudging her weight so that she staggered two steps. Pericles raised his eyes to the stars above, but they couldn't have left her on board with Attikos. He'd been eyeing the woman from Scyros with sullen and unmistakable intent – and he had friends and favours owed in that fleet. Pericles did not trust the man not to take a small boat to whichever ship they left her on. Of course, with his broken leg, she'd have more than a fair chance. The problem was, if she managed to pitch him overboard, Cimon would be forced to have her hanged. The belief that women were bad luck on a ship sprang from exactly that sort of situation. Either way, it meant Thetis remained with them.

Pericles had not said a word about his memory of the night before. There was no sign of any new affection between Cimon and Thetis, at least as far as he could tell. Yet it had been real, he was certain. He could not understand why he still looked on Thetis with longing. As a man, he told himself he should have been able to close the door on anything like that. She was not his.

He realised he was staring. Pericles could have sworn he looked at her no more often than his gaze fell naturally on Cimon, but Thetis simply drew his eye somehow, again and again. He hoped she had not noticed.

'Pericles? Are you with us?' Cimon reached out and tapped him on the shoulder, breaking his reverie. 'Come on, before this deck gets any more crowded. If a Persian ship came by now, it could sink a dozen small kings and noble archons.'

Cimon seemed amused by the strangeness of the situation. Pericles followed the two of them as they moved forward to the prow, trying not to see how Thetis swayed in that dress. He needed to put such things out of his mind!

Aristides and Xanthippus stood close by Pausanias, attending on the Spartan in respectful dignity. The entire league of Delos stood on those twin decks. Pericles wondered if Pausanias and his captains had even come to join them in their alliance.

Pausanias was an impressive figure in the torchlight. An iron lattice had been raised at the prow, on a wand of the same metal. It gleamed with coals, leaning out over the waters. The light it cast must have looked like a pool of gold in the dark sea, spreading into shadows as crowned kings waited for a Spartan to speak. With the light above and slightly behind, there were shadows on Pausanias' face, even as he nodded to Aristides and those he knew. Tisamenus too raised a hand in greeting to some in that crowd. Perhaps it was artifice, to remind them of their ties, or perhaps it was simply that many of those present had stood at Plataea and faced the Persian host. They had survived when they'd thought they would die. That was its own bond, as great as the oath of Delos in some ways.

Pausanias had to be a little nervous. The Spartan had been regent for the son of Leonidas. At Plataea, he had acknowledged no other authority beyond his own. Yet that night he faced the leaders of Athens and seventy cities or kingdoms. How far would his Spartan certainty take him? Pericles did not know.

'By the gods, I give thanks to see so many friends here, alive and in good health,' Pausanias began.

His voice was made to speak to crowds, Pericles thought. It was strange to witness one of his own best qualities in another and he felt a touch of resentment spring in him. Pausanias had proven his courage in war. He had led men,

CONN IGGULDEN

just as Cimon had. It seemed at times as if Pericles would never have the chance to prove himself to Thetis . . . He stopped, aware that his thoughts had taken a strange turn. She stood directly in front of him and the light of the torch at the prow revealed an outline inside the white robe. He cupped one hand down by his waist and imagined touching her, drawing her to him. His entire body was giving off heat in that moment. He felt a line of sweat trickle down his cheek, almost like a tear.

'Some of you will know me from the field of Plataea,' Pausanias went on. 'Those who were there that day, who stood with me against the Persians, will know I am not a rash man. Ask any of the council of Athens, where I marched in their defence, with every Spartan warrior at my back. They will confirm. I choose my time to move – and when to wait. So you will know, when I speak, that I follow the will of the gods. Sparta commands in war – and I am Sparta's son, here among you. I see the faces and garb of many ports and you all know me, by reputation or by the bonds of arms.'

Pericles glowered at the high tone. Pausanias spoke as if *he* had brought them together in that place, not Xanthippus! As if they would have gathered to hear a Spartan speak! Yet it was effective, Pericles could see that. Pausanias included them all in the fates of great men. He spoke to them, not as equals – Pericles knew the arrogance of Spartans too well for that – but as colleagues, as brothers setting out on a great enterprise. It was the very spirit of the alliance at Delos, and Pericles could only wonder if the Spartan had chanced upon the right note, sensing the mood of the crowd, or whether he had been blessed by Apollo and Ares to speak the right words at the right time. No one could deny the impossible victory at Plataea. It had been Pausanias who sowed the seed of it, who first brought Tisamenus to his side, interpreting the words of the oracle to suit them both. Perhaps of the two of them, it was Pausanias whom the gods truly loved. Both captains and kings smiled in his presence.

'I see some of you from the coast of Ionia,' Pausanias went on, looking across them. 'You can tell the rest how Persia creeps back, in its trade and officials, in petty laws and in the mouths of men who take Persian gold to speak for the empire and against freedom.'

Some of the heads nodded in the crowd and Pausanias copied them, magnifying the response.

'Persia was beaten at Plataea – and at Salamis, where men like Themistocles and Xanthippus and Cimon worked with Eurybiades of Sparta to beat back an enemy more like a swarm than a fleet. We triumphed against them, at sea and on land, yet Persia remains – and there are some of us who fear letting them grow strong once again, strong enough to venture forth once more. It must not be our curse, that we beat them back, only to fall asleep! They came to the fennel field at Marathon, where Aristides and Xanthippus did such wonders as to be told for a thousand years. Yet that great victory won Athens just a decade of peace – until they came again.'

'What can we do?' someone called.

Pericles wondered if it had been one of the Spartan soldiers on board. Pausanias waited a beat, as if in thought.

'If a viper makes its nest under the floor of a house, we do not ignore it, or strike back only when its children crawl into our rooms at night. No, we dig right down – and we burn it out, until there is nothing left.'

He looked around them, seeing concentration and purpose in many of the faces he knew. With a sweep of his arm, he gestured past the fluttering torch, over dark, still waters.

'This is *our* sea, eternal. It is named for the father of

Theseus, Aegeus – and we row and sail its length, from Crete to Thrace, from Athens and Argos to the coast of Ionia. We have earned that freedom, that right, with blood and sweat. At Marathon, at Plataea and at Salamis. To the east, I am told the Persian empire is vast – beyond my imagining. Yet this sea is where Odysseus sailed home, where Jason sought the fleece. It is *ours*.'

He paused and no one called out as he reached for the right words. His hand gestured as if he snatched them from the evening air.

'I am a Spartan. I know there are no true rights, no laws, beyond respect for the gods and what we can hold as our own. All that is good must be won by those like us, torn from the hands of enemies . . . or given up. Life owes us *nothing* else.'

It was the speech of one who had been regent in Sparta, who had known all the powers of a king for a single summer. Pericles could only stand in awe as he listened. Pausanias was a better speaker than he had known. No one broke the silence. Even his friend Tisamenus stood with his head bowed, as if in the presence of the sacred.

Pausanias smiled, one eyebrow raised as if in astonishment.

'Tonight, you represent a great fleet,' he told them, 'with the strength to burn out the last Persian strongholds in our sea. That is my purpose in coming to you here, in joining my strength to yours. I will not lead you against mere villages or crumbling fortresses. No, Persia has only one great stronghold left in our sea. We have the ships and the men to drive them out of it – this year, in this place.'

The name was whispered like a breeze by those who knew it.

'Cypros,' they said. The isle of flowers and copper. Pericles heard it over and over. Cypros lay to the east, beyond the Aegean, off the coast of Phoenicia. The Persians had built a fortress city there fifty years before, massacring local people. The stronghold was said to be impregnable, with high walls and gates and soldiers of the empire. Persia may have retreated after the losses at Plataea and Salamis – back and back, right across the Aegean, but not from Cypros. On that double deck, on that dance floor rocking in the swell, Pericles could imagine the great fleet taking it on. He felt his heart racing at the daring of it. He would see fighting at last. He would prove his worth. Thetis would come to him and realise that she had made a terrible mistake choosing Cimon, who was married anyway, when she could wrap her long legs around him instead . . .

'That is why I have come,' Pausanias went on.

He smiled more widely, reflecting their expressions once again as their mood rose with his. Pericles could only stand still as impure thoughts surged in him. His father, Xanthippus, was nodding, he could see. Did he have a choice?

'I will speak to individual commanders and discuss formations,' Pausanias said. 'As I told you, I am not rash. I choose my moment – and this summer is the time to pluck that peach.'

The boat back to their ships was manned by four rowers. Pericles, Cimon and Thetis went to one end, but then Xanthippus too had clambered down, wrapped in a massive fur cloak against the cold. Rather than wait for his own boat, he chose to impose on them. He was helped by Epikleos, who knew Pericles from his youngest days.

'Epikleos! I didn't know you were here!' Pericles said in genuine pleasure.

Much younger than Xanthippus, Epikleos was still older than either Pericles or Cimon. There was grey in his hair and yet he was still handsome. He and Pericles embraced in the centre of the boat, making it rock alarmingly.

CONN IGGULDEN

'Where else would I be but at your father's side?' Epikleos said. 'You have grown, Peri. It's good to see you so strong. The last I heard, you were hunting Persians in Thrace.'

'With some success! Cimon, this is Epikleos, my father's oldest friend – and a second father to me.'

Pericles glanced at Xanthippus to see how he had taken that, but the older man was lost in thought, digesting all he had heard. Above them, Aristides was being helped down in turn. He was still the wiry, small-framed man who had run every day around the city of Athens, at times in full armour to build strength. The archon of Athens took a seat by Xanthippus at the far end of the boat. They bent their heads together in muttered communication as the boat moved away to let another come alongside the Spartan flagship. The moon had risen, casting a pale line on the sea that moved with them as they were rowed back.

'What do you think of all this? Of Cypros?' Pericles said.

Epikleos looked past him to the rowers. Pericles shook his head.

'They are all loyal. Cimon's men. Athenians.'

'And the young lady?' Epikleos asked.

'Just a stray,' Pericles said.

It was a foolish thing to say, but he was enjoying seeing Epikleos again. Thetis' expression was winter-cold when he looked back at her. The rowers swept the sea, taking them over black waters. The sound was peaceful and rhythmic. For just a brief respite, they were all able to relax, away from the clamour. Pericles seated himself on a bench midway down the boat, one leg on either side. Epikleos took a place across from him and reached over to pat his knee.

'Is it true you found Theseus?'

'It is – on Scyros,' Pericles said proudly. 'His tomb was in the hills there, with marks of Athens. You should see the size of the bones. He must have been a giant of a man.'

'It has to be a good omen – the great king of Athens returned to us. Perhaps this plan of Pausanias has come at the right moment.'

'Does he . . .' Pericles began. He hesitated, unsure how to say it. 'Do you think he knows about the league, the brother-hood? The oath that was sworn?'

'Oh, he knows,' Xanthippus said gruffly, before Epikleos could reply. 'I would imagine the rumours of that are what brought him to these waters. I have been putting this alliance together for months. I would be astonished if Sparta and Corinth hadn't heard every detail. Yet his plan is sound enough . . . I've heard rumours about Persian forces digging in on Cypros. It is a target I might even have chosen myself. It would certainly be a fine demonstration of the sea power we have gathered at Delos. And yet . . . if Sparta leads us, I wonder if all we have done will be for nothing.'

'We don't *need* their ships, do we?' Pericles asked. 'What if we refuse his right to lead? I spoke the oath at Delos. We stand together, as one. Sparta can't take us all.'

Aristides cleared his throat. He shook his head ruefully.

'I was at Plataea, son,' he said. 'The truth is, Sparta can. If we refuse Pausanias and war comes of it, there isn't a force on earth that can stop them on the battlefield. Believe me. I saw the hosts of Persia break against them like sea crashing over a rock – and the rock remained.'

'The oath we swore is eternal,' Xanthippus said quietly, his voice almost a growl. Pericles leaned to hear his father speak, though the old man did not look at him. 'It will last beyond me, beyond us all. Perhaps it will take a generation for Sparta to understand what we did here – or two, or a dozen life-times. It doesn't matter.'

CONN IGGULDEN

Xanthippus looked up, meeting his eyes, his expression fierce.

'Today we made a nation, Pericles. I'm glad you were there to see it.'

He seemed to slump then, smaller, wrapping his shaggy coat around him as if he suddenly felt the sea breeze. Epikleos went to him and fussed with the furs, more to give comfort than out of any real need.

The Athenian flagship loomed, large enough to crush a small boat coming alongside. Pericles stood with Epikleos and Aristides to help his father up the steps, ready to catch him if he fell. Xanthippus was breathing hard, in pain or weariness, Pericles did not know. As his father vanished above, Pericles reached out and touched Epikleos on the arm.

'Is he all right?' he asked.

Epikleos hesitated, long enough for Pericles to feel his stomach drop away.

'He is ill, Pericles. I hope he will recover, but he has driven himself to exhaustion for months and he was not well at the beginning.'

Pericles stared for a beat. Epikleos too had been present when his brother had died. They had that shared grief in common, and he knew Epikleos was not a man who would speak lightly of such things, not to him.

'I'll come over in the morning,' he said.

Epikleos clapped him on the arm and climbed the wooden steps to the deck above. Aristides had already gone ahead and only Cimon's people remained. Pericles said nothing as the rowers took them out once more.

Thetis woke in darkness. She did not like the tiny cramped cabin below decks, with a moving rudder bar that stank of seaweed and released gusts of foetid air whenever it moved.

She was always afraid that she would be dragged into it and crushed. She kept as far away as she could against the wooden wall. She lay still, listening to the sounds of the ship, understanding that dawn was coming. The rudder bar let a little light through from above as it moved with the swell of the sea. The creaking had not woken her, she thought. The waters around Delos were still calm. She wondered . . . Her thoughts choked off as the door opened and darkness entered. There was barely room for her on her own in that tiny space. Two men coming in meant they already leaned over her. She took a breath to scream and felt a rough hand grab her by the throat, stifling all sound.

'Hold her tight, son. She's a fierce one. Hello, dear,' Attikos whispered in the gloom.

She kicked out, aiming where she thought his broken leg had to be. He rewarded her with a gasp of pain, but then he chuckled.

'You owe me, love, don't you? For the leg, for all my trouble.'

She could see the gleam in his eyes as he looked her over. Dawn was coming. The crew would be rising from their places on the deck above. Yet Attikos had not been on board the night before, she was certain of that. He'd come somehow like a ghost in the night and she was terrified. She could taste salt – blood on her lips or on the fingers preventing her from crying out. The other man was a stranger, though as the light grew, she saw his expression was much the same. He ran his other hand down her leg with obvious intent. She felt herself trembling.

'The strategos said I was not to harm you,' Attikos said. 'Well, as far as I know, this doesn't harm a woman. Hold her still, son! You can go after.'

CONN IGGULDEN

I I

The fleet that had come to Delos had eased apart a little in the night, selecting new anchor points, shifting amongst themselves as lambs might ease away from the presence of a dog. The Athenian warships had not moved. Pericles had slept for just a couple of hours, tossing and turning on deck, wrapped in a cloak. There were two cramped rooms in every warship, far to the stern and cut through with the rudder bars. Cimon usually used them to store food and wine, but Thetis had been given one, to keep her safe until they could set her down. Attikos had been sent to another of the three ships for a while. Neither Cimon nor Pericles believed he had given up on the object of his hatred. It was a problem they had handled quietly, without being forced to stripe the back of a loyal Athenian, on top of his wounds.

As the sun showed in the east, Pericles rose from his spot on the deck, seeing an outline of himself in the morning dew. He emptied his bladder over the side and considered hanging his buttocks over the stern. Yawning, he nudged a few younger hoplites, rousing them. They began to bring in the boat that bobbed behind the galley, heaving it in, hand over hand. Pericles yawned again as he stared out, then frowned. There was a second small boat with the first, bobbing along empty. Had it been there the night before? In all the movement to and from the Spartan ships, he could not recall. Around him, the rest of the crew were coming awake, shivering and coughing in the cold air.

Pericles heard his name and saw Cimon emptying his

bladder over the side. He felt his stomach grumble and wondered if he could wait until he'd eaten before heading over to see his father. It would be a while before there was anything like stew or soup ready – and he had promised Epikleos he would come.

'I'd like to take a boat to the flagship,' he said.

Cimon nodded, making a quick decision.

'I'll come with you.'

Pericles felt himself moved, so that he smiled. Cimon was a good leader. His crews all knew it.

'The old men will be discussing the Spartan offer, I don't doubt,' Cimon said.

Pericles blinked, hiding his disappointment. It had not been concern for Xanthippus, then, but cold assessment. The Athenian flagship was where decisions would be made. Cimon expected to be part of it.

A cry sounded beneath them, muffled, but high in pitch. Cimon and Pericles shared a glance of sudden suspicion.

'Where is Attikos?' Cimon said immediately.

Pericles swore. The second boat. Attikos had been on another ship, but he'd had someone row him across in darkness. Pericles was already heading for the central trench that led to the rowing benches below. He swung down into a hold that reeked of sweat, rancid oil and other things less pleasant.

The keel beam was barely a pace across, a narrow walkway in the gloom as he ran down it. Cimon was just a step behind, his reactions as fast as any hoplite. They both heard the cry again, a woman's voice. A man growled in response and the shout was cut short. Pericles reached the tiny cabin and followed the sounds, kicking the door hard enough to break it down.

Thetis was there, struggling with two men. Her legs flashed in the gloom as she kicked. Attikos froze at the crash and she took the opportunity to hack her nails across his face, making him yelp.

Pericles grabbed Attikos by the neck of his tunic. With a single heave, he yanked the smaller man entirely into the air, flinging him aside. Attikos struck the rudder bar with a crack, leaning like a drunk as he recovered his wits and understood who had laid hands on him. Panting, he lowered fists he had raised to return the attack. The sight of Cimon in the doorway stilled whatever reply was on his lips, so that he stood in sudden dread, head bowed and trembling.

It was Pericles who helped Thetis to her feet. Her cheeks were flaming in humiliation.

'Did I not make it clear you were not to have any contact with this lady?' Cimon said softly to Attikos.

The man had gone ashen and his mouth opened and closed.

'You said I was not to harm her,' Attikos murmured. 'And I haven't, either.'

Thetis moved suddenly, kicking his leg as hard as she could. They all heard the bone give way with the splints. Attikos shrieked and fell, all colour draining from him, so he looked like pale wax. Cimon put out his arm as she moved again. He thought she might go on to stamp on the leg, but his authority held her back.

'Go up to the deck, please, Thetis,' Cimon said. 'Pericles and I are heading over to the flagship. I'll leave you there.'

The look she cast on him was one of utter betrayal.

'I see. What about him?' she demanded. Tears spilled from her like water over the lip of a cup. Her voice choked as she went on, jabbing the air with her hand. 'I am a free woman of Thebes, Cimon. What about the one who wanted to do this, while his friend held me down? What about them?'

Cimon did not flinch from the entreaty.

'I'll have these men bound and I will make a decision about them when I return. For now, I must leave, I'm sorry.'

The keleustes officer stuck his head in the broken doorway to see what all the noise was about. Cimon gestured.

'Take these two into your custody, Nico, would you? Bind them to wait on my judgement when I get back from the flagship.' He turned to Thetis, wincing at the bedraggled state of her. 'Can you . . .' He waved a hand, suddenly awkward. 'Can you . . . be calm, when I am on the other ship? You can stay in the small boat if you wish, but I really should go now.'

Thetis flashed a look of grief at Pericles, as if Cimon too had humiliated her. She wore her hurt openly and could not seem to shutter it away.

'I can be calm,' she replied.

Attikos moaned as he moved on the floor. A tear leaked from under one eye though both were screwed shut. Thetis looked on him with no sympathy. Attikos swore weakly as the keleustes lifted him up, his leg hanging limp, with the foot at a strange angle. Thetis went out with Cimon and Pericles, without looking at any of them.

The boat journey to the Athenian flagship was spent in pained silence. Thetis accepted a cloak from Pericles, wrapping herself like a cocoon against the sea breeze and then saying nothing. Both Cimon and Pericles were lost in thought, shocked at what they had seen. There would have to be a punishment. Attikos had disobeyed a clear order from Cimon, his strategos, his trierarch.

When they pulled oars in alongside the flagship, the rowers held ropes thrown down to them, keeping the boat steady by main strength. Cimon rose and held a hand out to Thetis.

'Come if you wish. Or wait here, but you must decide.'

She hesitated, but had no desire to remain in a boat with burly strangers. Cimon and Pericles were men she knew. She climbed easily enough after him, with Pericles bringing up the rear.

On deck, they were greeted by hoplites in polished armour, standing to attention. Pericles and Cimon were treated with great respect, but still surrounded by armed Athenians as they were taken below decks. Thetis found herself swallowing in nervousness. She was out of place there, but she still trusted the young men. Of course, Pericles had rescued Attikos on the island, as she'd heard it. He had given her a chance to run before that, though. Her feelings were confusing, but she did not think she could fully trust him. More, Cimon was a man in a way that Pericles was not, quite, for all his fine features and the flashing gaze that seemed to follow her whenever she moved.

The Athenian flagship had been refitted since Cimon had seen it last. He looked around a long room towards the stern, formed by walls knocked into place with hammers. The space was low-ceilinged, but just large enough to hold a table. Sheets of papyrus covered its surface, with the images of coastlines visible on them.

Aristides was there, as well as Xanthippus. Four senior trierarchs stood around the table, deep in discussion. The two archons looked up as Cimon stepped through a door held for him, Pericles on his heels. Aristides nodded once, while Xanthippus seemed to weigh his son, his eyes looking for something, anything. His expression suggested the search had been fruitless. He barely dipped his head before pointing to something else on the chart.

When Thetis followed them in, the room went quiet.

Aristides was first to respond.

'Unless your companion is captain of one of our galleys, Cimon, I'm afraid she must wait outside.'

'I'll vouch for her,' Cimon said.

Aristides shook his head.

'Not today. She will be safe, Cimon. You have my word.'

No one else spoke and yet Cimon did not reply, unwilling to give way. Aristides raised one eyebrow in silent question. He knew Cimon better than most, but they could not have a stranger listening, no matter who stood for her name and honour.

'I'll go up,' Thetis said, unable to bear it any longer. She turned on her heel and vanished, breaking into a run as she reached the steps to the open air above. Pericles and Cimon exchanged a glance of quiet communication as Pericles closed the door.

'As I was saying,' Aristides said with wry emphasis, 'there is nothing actually wrong with the plan Pausanias brought to us. Cypros is the sort of target we might easily have chosen ourselves – there is little point assembling a fleet of this size and then bringing the hammer down on a single nut. We swore our eternal oath to reduce Persian strength in the Aegean. Cypros is easily the strongest of those spots.'

'Trust a Spartan to plan a war,' one of the other captains said. It had the sound of an old saying or a proverb.

Aristides frowned at him.

'Well, exactly. Yet we did not go through those oaths on Delos to be led by men of the Peloponnese! Our alliance did not include Sparta or Corinth or Argos. I see no ships from the third, but Sparta and Corinth sail out their little fleet to us and just expect to lead? I only wish we could tell them to go to hell with their offer.'

'But we cannot,' Xanthippus said.

His voice was hoarse, Pericles realised, as if he had been

shouting. Perhaps he had, in private. He certainly seemed angry enough. Xanthippus still wore the cloak of furs though it was warm down in the hold. It added a breadth to his shoulders as he looked around at faces in that small room, confirming they were loyal men.

'If we let Sparta command here, our alliance will lose its foundation. Yet we cannot refuse without risking those red-cloaked soldiers marching on our home cities. Persia could not stand against them. Perhaps Athens could, but I doubt it. No, we are in a vice, caught.'

He looked around once more, as if he could see right through to their souls.

'I have spent the night discussing it with Aristides,' Xan-thippus said. 'We cannot refuse Pausanias. However, neither can we simply accept his plan and let Sparta use our strength as their own.' He was breathing hard and he glared as if chal-lenging them to dispute his assessment.

Aristides spoke into the silence, letting Xanthippus rest.

'The Spartans have a young battle king – a son of Leoni-das. They have a second king in Leotychides, a man of good character who prefers not to go to war. Our Pausanias led at Plataea and after that extraordinary victory, the ephors of his people could not just send him into retirement or exile. In-stead, they gave him their fleet – a stroke of genius, I think. Yet if he fails here, it will be a long time before they have anyone else with the authority or experience to replace him.'

'You said he had a fair chance of taking Cypros,' one of the other captains said. 'And there is that soothsayer, whatever his name is, the one who brought him victory at Plataea.'

'Yes,' Xanthippus replied.

He had recovered, Pericles saw. Aristides knew him well enough to have stepped in, giving him time. Xanthippus still gasped like a crow, as if just drawing breath took effort.

'We will accept Pausanias in command,' Xanthippus went on, his hand cutting the air. 'And Cypros as the target. I will decide . . . responsibilities when we assemble for the assault. Now, gentlemen, those of you below the rank of strategos should leave. With my thanks. You are dismissed.'

One by one, the trierarchs bowed and left the room without a word. Cimon remained and it was his sharp gaze that made Pericles realise he too had been told to leave. As he began to move, Xanthippus shook his head.

'Not you, Pericles. You should hear this.'

The four of them were alone, shifting their weights with the ship as it moved in the swell.

'This much I could not say in front of the others,' Xanthippus added, his voice a soft growl. 'We have to bring him down. I say this to loyal Athenians alone. No one else. Pausanias cannot survive the assault on Cypros.'

'That is madness,' Cimon said. His voice hardened as he spoke. 'I don't want to hear this.'

'You are an Athenian, Cimon,' Xanthippus snapped back. He was reddening, struggling to breathe once more. 'Or would you . . . violate the oath you took at Delos?'

'What does that have to do with it?'

'You swore to all the gods, an eternal oath . . . of alliance. Sparta was not there, but you'd have Sparta lead us? You skirt your oath, Cimon. You risk the wrath of the gods falling on us all.'

'That's not what I meant . . .' Cimon said. He raised his hands, wanting peace. 'I might hope for Pausanias to fall in battle, but that is a long way from whatever you are suggesting.'

'That sounds like cowardice,' Aristides said suddenly. The archon felt all eyes turn to him and looked around with a shrug. 'What? I agree with Xanthippus. I saw something great at Delos. Sparta was not part of it – by their own choice. Corinth and Argos too, preferred to take their lead over ours. Well, they cannot have it all. They cannot remain apart from us, scorn us, and then expect to lead as well! No, this is an Athenian fleet. We lead it, no one else. Just as Themistocles once had to put that pompous fool Eurybiades in his place. That was right and so is this.'

Cimon rapped his knuckles twice on the table, in frustration as much as to demand their attention.

'Even if you are correct – and I have not said the principle is wrong – we cannot try and fail.' His voice fell to a harsh whisper. 'If one word of killing Pausanias gets out, Sparta *will* march in anger. Not just a king's guard either, or a thousand men, but all of them, as we saw at Plataea. You know then that Athens would be destroyed. So, if you gentlemen can spare a moment, perhaps we could discuss other ways to untie this particular knot. Ideas come from discussion, my father used to say. You both knew him. Honour him with that much.'

Xanthippus and Aristides exchanged a glance, but both of them had known Cimon since his youth and they were impressed by him. Pericles felt a longing grow that they would look on him in the same way. How was respect won if not in battle? That was Cimon's great advantage, of course, as well as the passage of years.

By the time the meeting ended, the tension had gone from that cramped room in the heart of the Athenian flagship. Even Xanthippus had lost his scowl and settled his breathing. Cimon knew Spartans rather better than the others, it seemed. Not only had he visited many times and lived among them, he had been the representative of Sparta in Athens for a year. He understood how they thought, and both Xanthippus and Aristides had nodded grudging acceptance as he laid out plans and possibilities. Pericles saw his father in particular give up some of the burden, almost as if he had been waiting for one capable of taking the weight for him.

In the end, the discussion turned to lighter matters. Cimon left in cheerful conversation with Aristides, the archon's arm about his shoulders. It took only a quick gesture for Pericles to signal he would stay and speak to his father. The two men were suddenly alone in that false and creaking room, with the noise of waves slapping the hull outside.

Pericles looked at his father with fresh eyes, seeing how time or illness or worry had worn him away. Only the furs gave him bulk. As Xanthippus returned his gaze, Pericles felt as if words stuck in his throat.

'Father, I know Attikos is your man,' Pericles said awkwardly. 'He tried to rape the woman you saw.'

'Discipline on your ship is no business of mine,' Xanthippus said after a moment. 'There are always troubles of that sort. Few men of quality on a warship, Pericles. Have him flogged.'

His eyes were steady, confirming nothing.

'Cimon may have him killed,' Pericles replied. 'But . . . Attikos says he is one of yours, father. If that's true, if you really set him to watch over me, you could ask for him to be returned to you. Just say the word.'

His father stared, his eyes cold, almost contemptuous.

'I don't know the man. Do as you please with him,' he said, going to stand. As he rose, something griped at him. One eye closed and he held his side for a moment, digging his fingers under a rib as if to ease a stitch.

'Are you unwell?' Pericles asked, reaching out to him. 'Epikleos said you had been driving yourself to exhaustion.'

His father shrugged off his hand.

'He had no right to say anything like that. Damn that old

CONN IGGULDEN

woman with his worrying! He's worse than your mother. Duty and this alliance, this *symmachia*, keep me at sea, Pericles. As long as it takes. As it should for you.'

Pericles watched his father leave, a shambling figure wrapped in furs, where once he had been sword-thin and fit as a leopard.

That evening, Pausanias sent word to every member of the fleet. To reach so far around the coast of Persia would take a month of sailing and a supply chain capable of feeding forty thousand men. Delos was the heart of the Aegean – central in all directions. Pausanias ordered them to return to the island two months from that day, at the end of summer, with food and water, with new weapons and armour – whatever they needed to take the war to the great Persian stronghold of the east.

Cimon had returned with Thetis and Pericles to the foremost of his three ships. He'd said nothing as they'd crossed back and Thetis had chosen to remain silent as well. Pericles was grim with memories of his father and no one to talk to about it.

The following morning, before the sun rose, one small boat returned, a groaning figure lying across the thwarts. With the aid of ropes and two men on deck, Attikos was heaved on board the Athenian flagship. The crewmen looked down at him, whistling at the new stripes on his back, the still-raw scratch lines down his face and the freshly splinted leg.

'Looks like you've been in the wars,' one of them said.

Attikos nodded, raising his hand to be helped to his feet. He made no sound, though everything hurt.

'There was a woman on board my last ship,' he said. 'Always trouble when that's allowed. Always.'

One of the men clapped him on the shoulder.

'I'll let Archon Xanthippus know you're here. Is it to visit, or as permanent crew?'

Attikos looked across the waters, to where three ships were raising sail. He scowled at the sight.

'Permanent,' he said and spat over the side.

12

The port of Piraeus was busy, with every stone quay and repair berth filled. As well as the business of bringing in food and goods for the people of Athens, the main fleet was in dock, preparing to go out. Pericles and Cimon had matched each other for lack of sleep and sheer labour over the course of three weeks. It had begun as something like chaos, then settled into checking accounts and tallying up resources. Each ship had to have enough fresh water, grain, dried meat and cheese to keep two hundred souls at sea, a vast undertaking on its own. Adding in a store of weapons, helmets and shields was just the start of it. Sailcloth, oars, nails, tools, bronze blanks and wood for repairs made each trireme its own workshop and storehouse.

There had been no shortage of replacement crew members, at least. Both rowers and hoplites took injuries in training. An arm crushed in an oarlock or a bad blow to the head meant a man might have to be turned out onto the streets. Others grew too old, or the sailor's gripe became so painful in their joints that they could not go on. A man's mates would raise a cup to him then and spit against bad luck, but his seat or place on deck had to be filled one way or the other. Young lads from the city came trooping up to the signing table each morning, ready to train or take up an oar. One or two were followed by an angry mother or father to drag them back to a family shop or business, but most were accepted and given the first part of their pay. There were no slaves working for free in the Athenian fleet.

The flood of silver drachms going out each week in dock made even Cimon sweat. With a group of senior trierarchs, he'd gone to the council in the Agora to ask for funds. Though they could see the fleet patrolling the waters of the strait by Salamis, it had still been a struggle to get his own people to release what was needed. The mines at Laurium were working night and day, producing much more for the city's coffers than when Themistocles had been in charge. There was still a difference between agreeing something was good and right – and actually handing over talents of silver and seeing them walk away. For once though, they were not the only source. The treasury on Delos had come to four hundred and sixty talents in all, a hundred and twenty of those from Athens alone – a vast war chest. Given the constant demand for stone, iron and wood, the seams at Laurium could not have met demand. It was fortunate that a merchant fleet now bought and sold goods all over the Aegean. With Persia cut out of commerce, a single ship's captain could make a fast fortune trading food or pots of red and black. The Assembly took a fifth tithe – and no captain dared complain. Only one had his licence revoked and his ship taken against debts. The rest accepted the cost of using the port and reaching the great market of Athens. The flood of wealth showed even in the new theatre, with row upon row of seats made from timbers taken from the Persian fleet. The great tent that had once sheltered King Xerxes on the shore now formed part of the back stage. It was true, tickets cost twice what they had before the war, but every space had been filled, first to see a comedy, then a work by Phrynichus that had men weeping in the street as they walked home.

Cimon yawned as he stood on the dock. It was almost noon and his stomach was making odd noises, reminding him he had not eaten since the night before. He'd lost weight, he realised, just through physical work and ignoring his hunger. He usually slept on sacks of grain at the port and ate with the dockers there.

He caught sight of Pericles in patient conversation with one of the shipwrights employed by Aristides to oversee the port accounts. Cimon had been plagued by the fellow until he'd made Pericles his official contact and left them to it. The result had been a week of sweet peace, though Pericles claimed he had come close to strangling the man at least twice.

Cimon frowned at the sight of Thetis walking just a pace behind the pair. She carried a leather bag over one shoulder and a rolled scroll under each armpit. She looked as if she'd picked up everything Pericles had forgotten, which made Cimon smile, though warily. He saw the little group would pass by and he prepared himself for awkwardness. His wife and child were in Athens. Having Thetis still around as the fleet prepared to leave meant they met at intervals. Pericles was his second in that port, or had made himself so with labour and intelligence. They met and consulted many times a day – and Thetis was always there.

Cimon made a 'hmm' sound at the back of his throat. It was not uncommon for Athenian men to take a mistress, or for that matter to while away a night with a stranger. He was not expected to bring them home, however. Cimon breathed through his nose, thinking to himself. He had been more than generous with the woman from Scyros. His particular difficulty of imagining how his mother would want him to treat her had kicked in at the moment of parting. Thetis had cost him already in food and trouble – not least in forcing him to give up a competent man to Xanthippus. Cimon knew he could easily have turned her out on the docks without a drachm to her name, but he had not. Instead, he had given

Thetis enough to keep her while she looked for work – and even arranged an offer from a laundry and seamstress. Her home city of Thebes was a long way off and no friend of Athens that year. He had no further responsibility, and that might have been the last he'd seen of her if Pericles hadn't interfered. Somehow, the young idiot had offered her a tour of the city – of all the temples and landmarks. That had turned into ... Cimon looked up as the three of them reached him. He was not completely sure what it had turned into.

'Ah, Pericles!' he said. 'I was just thinking about you. I don't know why everything always comes down to a frenzy at the last minute. To leave tomorrow, we'll be working through the night, I don't doubt it. Yet if I took another week, it would be exactly the same.'

They smiled, as he expected them to. Cimon spoke without much thought, giving Pericles honour by taking the time. That was the power of status, of being a strategos. The third member of the little group, Aristides' man . . . No, the name would not come. Cimon bowed his head, including him in the gesture. Thetis was watching, Cimon thought. Had she ensnared Pericles to remain close to the one she wanted? Cimon hoped not, for Pericles' sake as much as his own. He had known women of that sort before, with their large eyes and haunted expressions. Once the obsession began, it never ended well for anyone.

Not for the first time, the thought of just rowing away from port and leaving everything behind was Cimon's private joy. His ships. Oh, perhaps Athens had paid for most of them, perhaps Aristides and Xanthippus were in formal command, but still, when the oars bit, and the waves crashed, all his troubles could be left like a pile of clothes on the shore.

'How is your father, Pericles?' Cimon asked. He saw the quick grimace before the reply and understood it.

'Not very well,' Pericles said.

Despite the tone, he spoke unaware, a form of confidence Cimon could barely remember. Pericles knew the forms – the correct response. His father lay hunting for breath in rooms by the port. His son would show all the proper dignity and restraint, but he did not truly believe Xanthippus might actually die, that he might not get better as he always had before. Pericles had never known a day of his life without Xanthippus in the world. The possibility of going on without him was not real. Cimon had seen that in a dozen conversations, as he'd tried to make the younger man visit the archon, just so he could say he had done all he could and said the right words.

Cimon's own father had died when he was just a boy. He remembered the triumph of Marathon and the disgrace of the failed expedition after it. His poor father had come home a broken man, hot with fever and tormented by a trial. Xanthippus had played a part in the accusations then – and Cimon had begun to drink enough for three men. He'd lost himself in grief and pain and anger . . . and Pericles was oblivious, trying to look stern and full of grief, while it was all just a counterfeit. Cimon saw Thetis touch his arm in comfort and raised his eyes to heaven. He could not make the younger man understand, though he would soon enough.

'You should see him,' Cimon said gently. 'We'll be heading out tomorrow . . . you should say your goodbyes.'

'Of course I will,' Pericles said.

He knew he was being pressed and he didn't like it. Thetis seemed to understand better than he did. Yet her eyes remained on Cimon as he turned to the sea, wanting to be out there, wanting to be away.

*

The lamps were low when Pericles entered the house, close by the docks. His father owned property at the heart of the city as well as an estate outside it, but the journey into Athens had become difficult for him. He had rented a few rooms in the port, where he could still walk down to the ships each morning.

Pericles raised his eyebrows in surprise to see his mother, Agariste, with his sister Eleni at her side in a dark veil. Already married, Eleni had grown into a beautiful young woman, with one daughter and another child swelling her womb. Eleni had been marked by time or loss, with deep lines showing around her mouth. In quiet dignity, she came over to greet her brother, pressing her head into the nape of his neck as she embraced him. It was hard to see the girl with scabby knees who had taught him to ride in the back field, but Pericles knew women gave up such things.

Eleni's eyes widened a touch as she saw Thetis at his back. Thetis had come because Pericles had asked her to, but it felt wrong for her to be there in that moment. Under the piercing gaze of two women, Thetis felt herself flush and kept her head bowed. She mumbled a greeting to Eleni and Pericles' mother – women who would wonder what she wanted with the younger son of their house. At times, Thetis was not even sure herself.

She stood to one side with Eleni then as Pericles went further in, responding to his mother's quick gesture. The man on the pallet did not seem aware of them. He lay breathing lightly, lit by a low flame burning. Under that soft gleam, Xanthippus was burnished, his flesh a dull gold. Pericles reached out and took hold of his father's hand. It was uncomfortably warm.

The eyes opened and Xanthippus turned to see him. The man immediately began to struggle up and wife and daughter stepped around Pericles to help him, moving cushions under his back. Eleni pressed a cloth to his forehead, mopping away sweat. The noise of Xanthippus' breathing seemed to fill the little room, louder than it should have been.

'There you are at last,' Xanthippus said. 'I thought you would not come. How is . . . the fleet?'

He turned his head back and forth like a blind man, working his tongue over dry gums and teeth. Pericles saw he was panting, his mouth remaining open between breaths. The skin was more yellow than gold, he realised.

'Did the new oak come in?' Xanthippus went on. 'I don't trust those Macedonian suppliers . . . someone has to go through every part of the tally and make sure the wood is sound.'

'Yes, I'll do it, father,' Pericles said. 'Don't worry.'

He felt the hand tighten on his fingers in response and Xanthippus nodded, slumping against the cushions. Just his word, his promise, had been enough – and pride suffused him as he understood that. Pericles felt the hair on the back of his neck stand up as he looked again at Xanthippus. His father was not old, but something terrible had him in its grip. Something that might not let him go.

'Will you be coming out with the fleet tomorrow?' Pericles asked. It was a child's question. Pericles thought Xanthippus would not respond, but the eyes opened and he smiled.

'I don't think so. I need to rest for a while, to recover my strength. Your mother just wants to fuss, you know that. You'll go to Cypros without me. Trust Aristides. He is a good man.'

The eyes closed and he turned his head, breathing gently.

'Is he sleeping?' Pericles asked. 'Good. He looks exhausted.'

His mother said nothing for a time, busying herself straightening the pallet and the cushions Xanthippus lay upon.

When Pericles rose and stretched his back, his mother looked up.

'*Must* you leave, Pericles? The estate – your father's concerns. He is in no condition . . . They need a man to run them, to make certain we are not beset by thieves.'

Pericles felt anger rise. It was wrong for her to speak in that way while Xanthippus slept, as if he no longer mattered.

'I think . . .' Pericles said, choosing his words carefully. 'I think you and Eleni will survive, mother. My duty is with the fleet.'

It sounded a little pompous even to his own ear. As he turned away, he saw Thetis still there in the doorway, wide-eyed. His heart lurched as he saw how beautiful she was.

'Come,' he said to her. 'There's nothing more to do here.'

On the docks outside, the air smelled of salt, fish and oil. With the Athenian fleet ready to set sail the following morning, it was a world away from sickness, a place of bustle and healthy noise, with shouts and calls from men carrying sacks or beams. Pericles thought of the last shipment of oak and the fact that it had to be checked. He waved a hand at the thought. He didn't care.

He looked at Thetis, seeing she still wore the leather satchel stuffed with plans and accounts. She held another scroll in one hand, forgotten. The kohl around her eyes had been smeared in a streak, he saw.

'I should . . . er . . . take those tallies to Aristides, Thetis,' he said. 'I'll be leaving tomorrow, with Cimon. It should all be . . .'

It was suddenly too much. Something in the way she looked at him made him trail off. She dropped the satchel and gathered him in. He was awkward then, unsure if he wanted to be held or not.

'He could recover,' she murmured.

CONN IGGULDEN

He could smell her hair, an odour of flowers.

'He will!' he said. 'You don't know him. He is so strong . . .'

'And he loves you,' she said, almost in wonder.

Pericles broke for air, shaking his head.

'He loved my brother Ariphron, not me.'

He looked into her eyes, suddenly very aware that he was holding her, standing breath to breath, her body pressed against him.

'What about you?' he asked. 'When I leave tomorrow, what will you do? This is not a safe city for a woman alone.'

'I have a room,' Thetis replied. She bit her lip as she considered it, looking worried. 'There is work enough. In time, I'll save to return to Thebes. Perhaps my parents still live, I don't know. I will be fine.'

The thought of losing her was suddenly unbearable. Time ran out and Pericles spoke.

'Why don't you marry me?' he said. 'I think you know how I feel about you.'

Thetis stood very still.

'You are . . . upset about your father – and about to leave, Pericles. Don't say something you will regret.'

'I have never been more certain of anything in my life,' he said. 'As my wife, you could stay with my mother. You'd be safe then, with my family around you.'

'I am older than you,' she whispered.

She did not love him, she knew that. She loved Cimon, her rescuer, who would hardly look at her since he had come home. Yet the thought of being abandoned in a city she did not know was terrifying. She knew the docks, a thought that made her skin roughen. Athens had only one use for foreign women there. Life was harder than Pericles knew. She had been taken as a child and made to live with men little better than wolves. Yet she had survived amongst them.

'Say yes and nothing else matters,' Pericles said. 'I'll fetch a priest and we'll complete the ceremony on these docks, with Cimon as witness. My mother and sister are right here, Thetis! Let them welcome you to the family. Say yes.'

'Then . . . yes,' she said. She found herself weeping as he pressed his lips on hers for the longest time, hard enough to hurt.

The priests of Hera and Apollo were on hand, ready to bless the ships. Pericles sent one of the rowers to fetch them, and slowly all work on that part of the docks came to a halt as the sun set and torches were lit. Cimon came out of the flagship hold, looking in wonder on Pericles as he drew him aside. That searching gaze was difficult to meet and yet Pericles did so.

'I heard your father is ailing,' Cimon said. He embraced the younger man. 'I'm sorry. I know a little of how that feels. Now, I would counsel you not to do anything rash, Pericles, at least for a time. Perhaps it feels as if you have to make a decision before we leave on the dawn, but Thetis will still be here when we return, I'm sure. It might be better to wait till then to marry her.'

'No, this is right. And my father will be fine – he's strong. Look, Cimon . . .' He hesitated, blushing. 'I know you and Thetis . . .'

Pericles broke off and it was Cimon's turn to look embarrassed. He hadn't known Pericles had been awake that night.

'I . . . hope that won't cause trouble between us.'

'No, not at all. She loves me, Cimon. And I love her.'

'Then you are a lucky man. Though she has no father to give her away.'

'Her previous husband is dead and she has no relatives here. You can act as her guardian, Cimon, if you would.'

CONN IGGULDEN

'Of course. If you are sure.'

Pericles felt irritation grow like a weed in him, hearing only criticism.

'I am sure, yes.'

'Then I am pleased for you both.'

Cimon took position alongside Thetis, facing the priest of Hera as the man began to intone the words of a marriage ceremony, dedicating the joining of two young people to his goddess. Of necessity, the union would be as brief as possible, with the whole fleet waiting to leave the following dawn. The crowd around them were all from the ships, delighted to see the son of Xanthippus taking a wife. It was a good omen for all that lay ahead.

Little of that showed in his mother's furious visage. She had been called from her husband's sickbed with a damp cloth draped over one shoulder and tendrils of hair waving in the breeze. She was not dressed for a celebration in her dark skirts, but at least the colour suited her expression. Pericles' sister had come and kissed him, whispering in his ear that it would be all right.

Cimon felt Thetis' eyes on him for a long time as he took her arm. Pericles stood just ahead, waiting for the woman who would be his wife to step forward.

When the priest beckoned, Cimon turned to the woman who would marry his friend. Their eyes met and his stomach sank at what he saw there. He stepped forward with her, then back alone as Thetis took her place beside Pericles.

When it was done and they kissed, the crowd cheered wildly, raising the happy couple on their shoulders and marching them to a tavern. The sky was clear and the evening was still light, despite the late hour.

PART TWO

'Experience is the beginning of learning.'

– The Spartan poet, Alcman

13

Artabazus leaned on a balcony of polished stone, looking out into a star-filled night. He could hear waves washing against the shore, a restful sound. As he breathed salt air, he rolled a sticky black ball between his fingers, feeling very much at peace with the world. The moon was just a sliver, but achingly clear. He could see the coast of Persia across the strait. Cypros was a beautiful island, a great jewel of the sea. He nodded to himself, wondering if he had a poem in him that evening. He waved a hand, knowing he was too full of wine and food. Poets needed hunger, not good things. His verse had always suffered as a result.

He had already put one of the little balls on his tongue, a mixture of opium and hashish resin. He knew a second would bring dreams so vivid he might wake gasping, but at the same time, the world would dissolve. On such a night, after red wine and good company, it would make his bathing slaves into nymphs and angels. Perhaps the experience would be gilded, not truly real, but what *was* beauty, if not its impact on his senses?

He might not remember the details in the morning, he reminded himself. In truth, the feast had been a little excessive and he knew he'd be ruined if he stayed up much longer. Twenty years before, he would have taken that second ball and drowned it in Persian red, then danced or made love until the sun rose. He belched softly into his fist.

He deserved a little pleasure – and better dreams than remembering Plataea and the Greeks. He could still recall the confidence he'd felt in the Great King's presence at Salamis, before Xerxes had taken part of their army and fleet and just gone home. His poor generals had been lost after that, unable to decide whether to offer the Greeks freedom or burn all their cities to ashes.

Artabazus sighed. The night air was sweet with the scent of flowers. On his arrival, he had been astonished to see the sheer abundance of them, the array of bright colours on the hills. Cypros was a far cry from the dry land of the Greeks, or even his own home. He didn't know the names of the red blooms that grew in such profusion, nor the vast bushes of pink and purple buds that lined the road to the port, making the breeze redolent of perfumed oils. He smiled – he did not need to know. He was a soldier, or at least he had been.

At Plataea, Artabazus had watched a great and noble army break against a Spartan square. He had advanced with the left as General Mardonius went in. He had seen Persians and Medes slaughter snarling Greeks in dogskin caps. It had begun so well! He belched again, against all the bitterness that rose in his throat.

For an age, a Persian host had flung themselves against the red-cloaks. Artabazus had howled with all the rest, waiting for the enemy to be routed, for the great rush forward that would be the sign of their victory. It had come at Thermopylae, in the end. It had not come at Plataea. Instead, Mardonius had been brought down by a thrown spear and the cry that went up had been one of despair.

There had been horses everywhere, Artabazus recalled, running madly without riders. It had been the action of an instant to grab the reins of one, using the animal's speed to swing up to the saddle like a tumbler. Artabazus frowned at the memory. Perhaps he had intended to rally the army then, to gather in cavalry who seemed so lost without their commander Masistius. He too had fallen and in that moment, as Artabazus had gained the means to escape, he'd felt his own death coming like a shadow. It had not seemed so strange to wheel that mount and withdraw a few hundred paces.

Some scouts had gone with him, heads down and ashamed. When he'd made himself turn back, it had been to look across a scene of utter devastation. The Persian heart had been ripped out, but the Spartans still stood, surrounded by the dead. Athenian hoplites had made their own square and they were another stone, ruining the scythes of better men . . . Artabazus found himself weeping in memory. He rubbed his eyes. Opium had that effect sometimes, though he had always been a man of passions. His girth was proof of that. He saw too much, he thought ruefully – felt too deeply. Men like Mardonius were mere blocks in comparison, while Artabazus could wrestle threads and wisps of memory for decades after, reliving moments of pain, even in the midst of joy.

On impulse, Artabazus put the second resin ball between his lips, splitting it between his teeth, then swallowing it whole. That was how life should be lived, he told himself – gulped down! Let the wild dreams come! The satrap of Cypros had promised all the pleasures of the world to his guests that night. If his hospitality to that point was anything to go by, the bathing slaves would surely be a delight. Artabazus looked up at the moon, surprised to see how much of the night had already gone. There was always a place for new things, he thought. They banished old pain.

Plataea was behind, he reminded himself, memories of a distant land, in another year. Artabazus gave thanks to Ahura Mazda and his guardian angels for escaping the horrors of that defeat. The bones of Mardonius would remain for ever on the battlefield, with Masistius and Hydarnes of the Immortals. Of all the commanders of the Persian side, Artabazus was the only one who had made it home. He touched his lips and heart in thanks for that.

Perhaps twenty thousand had ridden with him from the battlefield, lost in the dust as they rode north into Thessaly. He'd survived the suspicions of allies there and in Macedonia, saying he rode on a private mission for the Great King. In Thrace, he'd almost been killed in an ambush, but ridden clear. It had taken him the best part of a year to get home, but King Xerxes had welcomed him with open arms and kisses on his lips, over and over. Artabazus wondered if he would have received Mardonius as warmly. There were benefits to being a cousin of the Great King, it seemed.

Xerxes had promised him a satrapy of his own, by the Hellespont. He was to build a new bridge, apparently. Artabazus felt his senses swim as threads of opium spread through his veins. He could feel the cold itching of the tendrils and he sighed, resting his head on his arms as he looked out to sea. His cousin was a good man. Xerxes valued Artabazus as family, but also because he knew the land of the Hellenes. When it came time to return, by sea and by land, Artabazus knew he would be in command. He would not make the mistakes Mardonius had made, not with all his experience. No. He had plans enough to shake the world . . .

His thoughts slid away, made glass somehow, so that he could not hold them. He blinked at the sea, where the moon's silver stretched like a fishing line right to the shore. There was something out there, he thought. Something that moved. He blinked, feeling his heart beat faster, burning in his chest. Fear bloomed and yet he couldn't speak.

They had come for him, he was certain. Serpents that slid through the waters. They knew he had escaped them and

CONN IGGULDEN

they had come. The Greeks, the Greeks, the Greeks. He began to cry out in fear, his voice splitting the silence of the night.

Aristides heard his order to hold repeated on the deck below. The rowers beneath his feet backed oars for a single sweep, halting forward motion. He shook his head in something like wonder as the rest of the fleet went in. Only four ships remained around him, three Athenians and a Spartan trierarch. To see two hundred ships – more – going hard against that shore, spilling men onto the beaches, well, it filled his heart. Aristides had stood at Marathon against a Persian army two or three times as many. He had seen greater numbers still at Plataea, a host to fill the world. For the first time in his life, his people were not outnumbered. They were the iron hammer coming down on a sleeper's hand. He exulted at the thought.

On the shore, Aristides watched under starlight as officers took charge and marched hoplites inland. Squares of silver moved free of the ships like beetles, scuttling off, looking for an enemy. Cimon and Pericles would be among them, Aristides thought. The two friends kept their own counsel, or so it seemed to him. There was certainly a thoughtful caution in Pericles since they had left Athens. Aristides had tried to speak to him as they'd set sail for Cypros with the main fleet. The young man had waved off his advice, saying he knew, he knew.

The illness of Xanthippus went unspoken, though Aristides felt his absence every day. Xanthippus intimidated even senior commanders, so that they lost their train of thought in his presence. It was a gift and Aristides wished they still had him.

With a smile, he recalled the hastily arranged marriage on

the docks of Athens. Grinning oarsmen and hoplites had lined the quays and called suggestions when they thought they were not seen. It had been a ribald event that raised the spirits of all those about to head out the following morning. They had carried Pericles on their shoulders with his new wife, right to a tavern, the best room given over for their marriage night.

Aristides had wanted to warn Pericles about acting rashly. Young men made mistakes of that sort all the time, rarely as soon ended as they were begun. He had stayed his hand, knowing it would earn him only sharp words or a rebuke. The woman – Thetis – had looked beautiful. Whatever her odd history and first marriage, she was still young enough to produce children. Aristides hoped he was wrong, but he preferred a marriage to be a solemn affair between great families, not a show. It had been theatre of a sort, he realised, though whether a comedy or a tragedy was not yet possible to say.

Xanthippus deserved grandsons, at least. Aristides wondered if there was a chance he would live to see them. Life went on, it had to.

The ships on the beach were under guard and in good order. Others held position in the shallow bay, ready to tow them off. Pausanias was quite capable of planning a campaign; that had never been in doubt. Cimon too was a trusted man and Aristides made himself relax as his ship rocked in the swell. His own task was less violent, less chaotic, perhaps for nothing, he did not know. The island of Cypros had many bays and inlets. The Greeks had scouted it from a fishing boat during the day, but there were still a dozen places where a fast ship could be hidden, perhaps to get word back to the Persian king.

That was the role Aristides had chosen for himself. Pausanias would lead the hoplites in, but if some warship or messenger sprang out, Aristides would be there, ready to break its oars, ram it and send it to the bottom.

As he watched the shore, Aristides thought he saw a paler shape, set back in a stand of trees. Could it be a mast, or just some dead oak, its bark all gone? He turned his head back and forth, but he could not be sure. No one else seemed to have spotted it.

'Put a boat down and take word to the others. I'm heading in to look at something. Tell the rest to hold position and remain alert.'

Another three ships had been sent to the far side of Cypros, though he thought that was probably a waste of their strength. The Persian stronghold was on the eastern coast, closest to the mainland. There were mountains between their garrison and the other side. Yet Pausanias had warned of bonfire signals and Aristides could hardly fault the Spartan for being thorough. There would be no word of this raid in Persia until it was long over.

He waited while his little boat went from ship to ship, then returned. Xanthippus had always loved the rituals of the sea, especially in war. Yet Aristides found it all unbearably slow compared to battle on land. In command of ships, it seemed he could not even make a decision without informing others. Admittedly, they had flag signals for the day, but at night, each ship was just a shadow, forbidden even lamps on deck during the actual assault. He waited while the moon crept overhead, leaning on the prow and watching the island.

One of his own hoplites was first back, bowing to the Athenian archon, awed to be speaking to him.

'The Spartan said our orders are to hold position, not go chasing every shadow. He says to wait.'

The officer spoke to the night air rather than look directly at Aristides. The older man could understand his embarrassment.

Spartans never seemed to know or care how their words were received. Aristides sighed to himself.

'I understand. Return to your post.'

Aristides waited for the man to join the silent force of deck soldiers before giving his orders in a slightly louder voice.

'Keleustes – quarter speed ahead. Helmsmen – aim for that dark place on the shore. We will "hold position" there, as ordered. Once we have scouted the inlet, we will hold position further out.'

It might have been foolish pride, or petty resistance all for nothing, but Aristides felt his heart thump faster. He had followed orders from Pausanias well enough at Plataea, but the sea could not be Spartan. The sea was for men like Themistocles and Xanthippus and Cimon – and Aristides. He thought back to what Cimon had said about Spartans and accusations. If a chance came, Aristides knew he would not hesitate. The sea was Athenian.

Below his feet, oars rattled out once more, then bit in unison, easing the ship forward. In the quiet dark, he could hear the beat called by the keleustes. The oarsmen rowed blind, trusting him. Aristides whistled up the carpenter's boy and had him hold the prow and look for white waters breaking. They eased forward, slow and steady. With an effort, Aristides stood confidently, showing no sign of nerves. If he stranded them in shallows or holed the hull, he knew he'd never hear the end of it.

14

Pericles rushed down a gloomy corridor, Cimon on his left. The shields they held before them were designed for a battle-field, each protecting the next in line. In a narrow space, he and Cimon blocked the corridor completely. Those behind kicked in doors as they went, searching each room, killing anyone they found. They had no idea yet of the size of the Persian garrison, only that surprise was their chief advantage – surprise that drained away, moment by moment.

The main gates had been open for whatever celebration had been occurring on Cypros. Plans had changed as Pericles and hundreds of hoplites had gone through at a run, seeing men and women standing in shock. Greek landing crews had poured past the curtain wall and into the inner compounds in the midst of a party. When the Persian guests saw bronze helmets or the red cloaks of sprinting men, they threw down cups of wine and scrambled to get away.

On the high walls, a few arrows had been shot, but that only drew the attention of the Greeks below, so that they sent pursuers up the inner steps. A dozen things had gone wrong for the Persian garrison, but war was never fair. They had thought themselves safe on Cypros, far from the Aegean fleet. That had been a terrible mistake.

As Pericles raced to the end of the corridor, a troop of Persians raised shields there, light but sturdy things of wicker. They did not seem disposed to run. Pericles hardly had time to understand what was going on before he was crashing his own shield against them, protecting Cimon on his left. With his right arm, he hacked down, his sword catching in a beam overhead. He wrenched at it and only the narrow corridor and confusion saved his life. A Persian guard flinched from a blow that didn't come, then recovered, trying to jab his sword past the wide hoplite shield. There was the disadvantage of fighting in a confined space! Pericles felt panic as he wrenched at the hilt and lost his grip. The enemy seemed slow in that moment, so that he was able to leave the blade where it had wedged and reach across to the kopis in Cimon's belt, drawing it clear.

The short Spartan blade was a far better weapon in that place. Pericles felt the weight in his hand as if he had come home. He lashed out with the thing and caught a man on the jaw, chopping part of it away. Blood sprayed across them both and the Persian fell with a shriek. Two more guards darted spears at them, cutting curls of bronze from his shield as Pericles blocked and saved Cimon. He restricted himself to blows around the edge, finding shins, feet, hands, anything he could reach. The Persians were brave, but they were outmatched. They dropped or staggered away as wounds stole will and strength.

Cimon and Pericles edged forward. At their backs, the next pair had retained the enormous dory spears, against all sense in that place. Yet they were experienced men and used the leaf-head points to stab and withdraw, as if they were epistatai following the first rank. It meant the team of four became a wall of moving points, advancing steadily. The Persians could not defend against one without being hit by another.

Pericles was not sure if he and Cimon had grown faster or whether the firing of his senses just made it seem so. For a time, it felt as if they could not be touched. He hacked his kopis into another man's neck and yanked it back, the man's expression as much surprise as fear or pain. It felt more like butchery than battle. In that moment, Pericles felt a blade catch him in the chest, grinding on bone, then skidding away through flesh. Pain flashed like a burn, vanishing as quickly as it came. The answering blow was quick and ruthless, taking the hand of the one who stabbed at him. The kopis was a butcher's cleaver, needing strength and speed more than skill. With it, Pericles moved like a wolf snapping. He and Cimon trampled Persians, trusting those behind to cut throats and be certain they would not rise.

Pericles kept his shield high as more guards came scrambling out of the room beyond. The bronze disc itself was a weapon, pressing into faces as they tried to attack, cracking against hands and shaking their grip. With the edge or the main shield boss, he punched with it. For the first time, Pericles understood why Athenian training involved so much boxing. Cimon was panting hard. Yet Pericles still breathed well – a son trained by Xanthippus. His shield was light on an arm that had thrown jabs for a thousand hours.

Pericles felt heat coming off him in waves. The air seemed to sparkle, to writhe with moving threads of light across his vision. He knew he had been cut. There was no time to examine the wound, but he could feel nausea and something cold sheeting down the front of his tunic. The Persians wore dark, panelled armour with strips of enamel bound to cloth. He found the kopis would not break through, though he made men wince at each impact.

Something hit him in the leg. When he glanced down, he saw blood pouring from a gash across his calf, as if spilling over the edge of a cup. The leg felt suddenly weak and drops spattered with every movement. There was no pain, though, for which he was grateful. Cimon seemed to be shouting and pulling at him. The floor was polished wood, he noticed.

One of the Persians crashed against his shield, knocking it into his face. That stung worse than more serious wounds for some reason, sharpening his anger. Pericles chopped the kopis against a man's hilt and was rewarded with a cry and fingers spinning through the air. The weapon fell and Pericles grinned through freshly bloody teeth.

It felt like a dream to be fighting inside a house instead of in the open air. The entire plan had changed when they'd found the gates just open. Pausanias and his Spartans had led the charge against what guards there had been, cutting them down before they even knew what was happening. Shock had held the Persians still, and hoplites had gone through that crowd, hardly slowing as they crossed courtyards and climbed stairs. The fortress was a city in itself, a place with more rooms and halls and cloisters than they could believe. Pericles had no idea where in the collection of buildings and palaces he was, nor the part he was playing in the overall assault. He only hoped the entire force wasn't locked in small-scale actions while the main garrison assembled, ready to fall on them like a winter storm.

He did not tire, as those who stood against him tired. The guards he faced were the last in that part of the fortress, presumably the most senior. He could see grey in their beards and gold on their wrists and at their necks. As their arms grew weary, Pericles brought the kopis against flesh and bone in ceaseless attack. He cut one man's ankle when he had to duck under his shield to protect himself. The Persian went down with a scream that was somehow more terrible for all the shock in it. Pericles dropped to one knee to kill him, while another scrambled across his shield above. Pericles stood despite the weight, borne up on youth and strength and will.

Cimon grunted as he barely slipped a killing blow. The

Persian he faced next had enough calm to hook the Greek shield and wrench it aside. It was neatly done and the following lunge caught Cimon along the ribs as he turned desperately. The wound stung like fire, though it was better than being impaled. He killed its owner with a straight blow, extending his right leg. The action stopped in that moment, a strange stillness that had them all crouching and wary, ready for another attack.

The last of the guards lay unmoving as Cimon and Pericles pushed through to the rooms beyond. They were both panting, filthy with dust and oil and blood, but they stood with blades raised and shields ready.

There were two women and a man in the room. The man wore fine silks and a cloak rather than armour, though he stood in front of those he protected with a jewelled sword ready. There was fury in his expression, but also a certain calculation as he took in their wounds and battered state. He would not surrender, that was clear.

Cimon glanced at Pericles and his eyes widened at the blood trail the young Athenian was leaving. Pericles was badly wounded, though he did not seem to know it. Behind them, two more hoplites entered the room. Without orders, they fanned out, swords braced over the curve of their shields, facing the only enemy. Out in the corridor, some keleustes or trierarch was waving another group down the corridor. He stuck his head in for a moment in silent question.

'We have this,' Cimon said.

The face vanished and a great rush and clatter of running men and metal went past, seeking out more of the enemy.

'Put up your sword or be killed,' Cimon said, his voice clear and loud, as if speaking to a child.

The Persian showed only confusion. It was unlikely he

spoke Greek, Pericles realised. Yet there were some words they had learned in Persian.

'*Teshlam?*' Cimon asked, trying out the strange word. It hardly sounded like a command to surrender.

The man frowned, but did not lower his blade. Pericles felt a wave of dizziness wash through him. He took a step to catch himself, as if he had been pushed from behind. The Persian shouted a stream of words then – and Cimon stepped forward with sword and shield, ready to cut him down.

One of the women raised her hands, holding out her palms.

'Please . . . stop,' she said in broken Greek. 'My brother does not speak. We submit.'

She followed the words with a stream of Persian and the man looked back over his shoulder, snapping an angry response. She only waited and he threw down his sword in disgust. It clanged on the tiles and skidded towards Cimon.

'Royal household . . . Achaemenid,' the woman continued. Her accent was strange, but Pericles found he could understand. 'You reward . . . if no harm.'

Pericles looked her over. The room seemed to be getting brighter. It was true a window faced east on the other side, with curtains billowing in the breeze. He'd lost track of both time and direction and the room clashed somehow with memories of blood and the dead. He shuddered, feeling ill. The floor was of polished tiles, with a large bed, dressing tables, even a polished silver mirror that caught the light. He could see movement in it, he realised, waving a hand back and forth and seeing a reflection. The surface was incredibly fine. Was the sun rising? It was.

Pericles had not truly looked at the woman before, but the reality was startling. Her eyes were huge and dark and they watched him. Her mouth . . . He reminded himself he was a newly married man. She wore some sort of pale blue gauze in layers that hid whatever lay beneath, but her youth and beauty were still obvious. The air itself was perfumed, unless it was flowers opening in the sun. He staggered another step.

'Your friend is to fall, I think,' the woman said. 'Please do not kill . . . if he does. We are prisoners. I give word . . . oath as a daughter of the Achaemenid.'

Cimon looked across at Pericles.

'Are you all right?' he said.

The Persian who had thrown down the sword said something else in a tone just as angry as before. Cimon regarded him for a moment, before tilting his head and addressing the woman.

'Tell your brother to remain silent, or I will kill him,' he said.

She repeated his order immediately. The brother glared and ran a hand through his hair, but he did not speak again.

'Tie them up,' Cimon said to the two hoplites at his back.

As he spoke, Pericles fell with a crash, measuring his length on the polished floor.

Aristides felt a quiet satisfaction as his warship entered the inlet. A vessel was indeed anchored there, tied up on a stone quay. There was a bustle visible on its deck. Even as his rowers eased his ship across the entrance, they cast off. Ropes were flung back to shore and their own oars rattled out, pushing them away from the dock.

Something changed from one moment to the next, no doubt as they sighted the Greek craft blocking their escape. Aristides smiled at the thought, thinking of the Spartan. He would be sure to tell him his error when they next met. Lessons were never wasted, he believed.

For moments of cheerful silence, Aristides considered his

next move. There was not sea room enough for the enemy to get around him, or to escape. They were trapped, just as surely as if he had tow ropes on them. He heard orders called in Persian and frowned as the ship began to ease back to the dock. Whoever commanded had seen the position was hopeless. Perhaps they still intended to run. Dawn would make that harder, but Cypros was a huge island. Someone who knew it well might yet lose himself.

'Helmsmen!' Aristides called back. 'Put us between the dock and that ship.'

It was a delicate manoeuvre, but they had forward speed and the water was like glass. Before the Persian could do much more than dip oars and begin to scull back, the Athenian trireme was slipping and scraping alongside. Oars were pulled in as if stung, before they could be broken. It was well judged, the grinding ships easing to a halt. Those few still on the docks could be seen haring away.

'Boarders!' Aristides called.

He had twenty hoplites ready to step across. His men were bustling forward as the other crew showed themselves, hands raised.

'Artabazus of the Achaemenids surrenders to you,' a voice called in Greek, 'in honour, without malice. You have his oath, his submission.'

Aristides knew the name. He felt his throat tighten in memory of another day, on the plain of Plataea, with dust swirling all around and death in the taste of it. He waved his hoplites across and they gained the other deck without violence, taking up positions there. Aristides eyed the small gap between the two decks with misgiving, but he joined them, looking for the speaker.

He found the man lying face down in obeisance. The translator was of no consequence, of course. Only the

Persian lord standing over him mattered. Artabazus was both short and very round compared to his countrymen. Aristides realised he really had seen him before, commanding others on that day.

'You are Artabazus?' he asked.

The translator repeated the words in Persian and the little man nodded. His eyes were dark, with grief or rage it was hard to say. Artabazus kept shaking his head, as if he could not believe what was happening. In comparison, Aristides felt rather expansive.

'My life will win you a fortune,' Artabazus said, 'but only if I am well treated.'

The translator never raised his head as he repeated the words of his master, so the voice was muffled. Aristides smiled. Artabazus had come with the Great King himself to Greece, with their Immortals, with their horsemen, with a host to make the Hellenes tremble. Aristides felt it like good wine in his stomach to see him so reduced.

'I accept your submission, Artabazus,' he said with some relish. 'You are my prisoner.'

Artabazus bowed deeply as the translator rendered the words into Persian. Aristides rubbed his chin in thought.

'You. Tell your master I would be interested in hearing his memories of Plataea.'

He waited while Artabazus listened and said something in reply, his surprise evident.

'You were there?' the translator said.

'I commanded the hoplites of Athens,' Aristides replied, his tone deliberately matter-of-fact. To his own surprise, Artabazus bowed again when he understood.

'You fought well,' the translator muttered, as if unsure of the words. 'Only the leader of the Spartans did more that day.'

Aristides felt his smile widening, showing his teeth as he thought of Pausanias.

'He too is here. I will introduce him to you, Artabazus.' He was rewarded with the man's mouth opening and closing like a fish and he chuckled. 'I imagine Pausanias will want to hear all you have to say.'

15

Pericles woke with the sun high in the sky and clean band-ages swaddling him around the neck and shoulder, right down to his ribs. It all itched unmercifully and he squirmed, drawing the attention of one he hoped was a physician. By his curled beard the man was a Persian, though he wore a robe that could easily have graced the Pnyx in Athens. Whatever he was, he approached as soon as he saw movement. Pericles leaned away from him, raising a hand as if in defence. The physician tutted to himself and slapped at it.

'Be at peace, Athenian,' he said.

'Pericles,' he muttered in reply. His fingers stung.

'A name that means . . . famous? Far-famed?'

Pericles flushed and nodded.

'My own name is Golshan,' the physician said, tapping himself on the chest. 'It means garden.'

A moment of silence passed while they looked at one another.

'I find you Greeks are much the same as real people, at least when it comes to cleaning a cut. Yours are stitched and bound with honey in the Egyptian style. Yes? It should all be cleaned and replaced every second day, to draw out water and corruption. The old honey should not be consumed. Do you understand?'

'Yes. You speak very well.'

The physician shrugged, though he looked pleased.

'I spent part of my youth in Cnidus, at your people's

school there. My father said a man who was good with wounds would never starve. He was correct in that.'

'Thank you,' Pericles said. He tried to ease the tightness of his bandages with a finger under the edge and the Persian slapped his hand away once again.

'Spartans don't scratch,' he said.

'I am not a Spartan,' Pericles replied.

Golshan smiled.

'I know. I intended to inspire you to a higher standard than your own. Spartans are beloved of physicians. Of all men, they complain least. Now, your injuries are light – you will have a scar along your collarbone and you will limp for a time. The leg should be rested for a month. After that, it will grow strong once more. I cannot speak for your personal habits. If you survive, I suggest you wash yourself a little more often. Do you understand?'

Pericles found himself flushing in embarrassment. There was a hoplite on guard at the door, no doubt set by Cimon to make sure the Persian didn't try to smother helpless charges. When Pericles raised himself on his elbows, it was with a grunt of pain, but it allowed him to see three others on low beds in that room. He thought he recognised one of them but could not bring the man's name to mind, so only nodded and raised his eyebrows in an awkward greeting. To his dismay, the fellow mimed scrubbing at his armpits and groin, clearly amused. Pericles looked away from him, suddenly furious. He did not see the man's expression fall.

'I cleaned you myself, with cloth and bucket,' Physician Golshan went on mercilessly. 'You must not let oil remain long enough to become rancid. Scrape it all away each day, bathe and then apply rosewater or a lighter oil than that of the olive. There is nothing wrong with clean sweat, but it goes sour. Yours, I must say, was particularly pungent.'

'Thank you for your advice,' Pericles said tightly. He hoped his gaze might set the man's hair aflame, but Golshan just shrugged.

'It is free, or in exchange for my life, as your officers explained it. Don't forget. Rosewater, or perhaps . . .'

'Yes. *Thank* you!' Pericles said.

The physician closed his mouth to a thin line. He rose, addressing the guard.

'Your master asked to be informed when this young man was awake.'

'I was told to stay here,' the man replied.

His words were met with a shrug.

'That is not my concern. I have done as I was asked.'

With a grimace, the hoplite left the room at a run. Pericles felt suddenly helpless as the physician sat on the edge of his bed and pressed a hand to his forehead. He wondered if he had the strength to fight back if the old bastard tried to strangle him. He hoped so.

'How long have I been here?' Pericles asked.

Golshan muttered something in his own tongue as he sat back.

'I made you drink poppy mixed with wine while I sewed your wounds. You were . . . talking and struggling for a time and you would not hold still. The cut near your neck was jagged and needed a steady hand. I would say return to me in six weeks and I will cut the threads, but who knows where we will both be then, eh? What? Oh, you came like thieves and pirates the night before last. This is your third day on Cypros.'

'And . . .' Pericles looked into black eyes, so dark as to have no sign of colour around the pupil. 'And we took the island? We hold the fortress?' He had the sudden awful thought that he might be a prisoner, that the garrison had rallied. No. The guard would have been one of theirs.

THE LION   149

With care, the physician leaned over and spat on the floor before he replied.

'You are the masters of Cypros,' Golshan said. 'For today. Until the Great King offers gold to your leader, enough to drown him in coins.'

He spoke with a sneer, which turned to confusion as Pericles began to laugh, wincing at the way it hurt.

'You think your king will offer gold to a Spartan?' he said. 'Ow. Oh, I can't laugh. It hurts to laugh. Please, please let him try. It will break my heart to see Pausanias load it all into a ship just so he can sink it, or whatever grand gesture he chooses. Please, amuse us with talk of ransoms.'

A clatter of studded sandals brought the hoplite back into the room. He looked around at the patients, visibly relieved the Persian had not run amok in his absence. The physician rolled his eyes.

'Up you get, son,' the hoplite said. 'Cimon asked for you.'

With a stifled groan, Pericles swung his legs over one by one and rose. Apart from the cloth wrapping his trunk and one leg, he was naked. The hoplite seemed to think nothing of it, but Pericles looked for something more and was pleased to see clean robes on a table, near a collection of shields and helmets. There was no sign of the kopis blade he had used in the corridor. Presumably, Cimon had taken it back. Pericles told himself he would have to get another one from the Spartans, though, as they didn't use coins of any kind, he wondered how he might do that.

'Help me dress,' he ordered.

Physician Golshan took a step forward without thought. He raised his eyebrows as the hoplite also responded, hearing a tone of command Pericles had learned from his father as much as the words. Between them, they wrapped Pericles in a single piece of pale blue linen, pinning it with a bronze clasp at his shoulder. Pericles relaxed as he stood up. He felt better, though his hand dropped to where a sword belt would usually be, tapping in frustration at his waist.

Pericles entered a hall that had a look more of a royal palace than any military stronghold. He was not sure what he had expected, but not floors of polished marble that reflected him so well it was as if he walked on the soles of his own feet. Not pillars capped in gold, or a ceiling that spread in stone rays, like a bird's wing. When he glanced up, he had a memory of dissecting a crow when he had been a boy, of holding the bones up to the light and wondering at the intricacy of them.

Hoplites kept guard on the edges of the room, but there was no sense of peace or stillness there. As Pericles made his way closer, a ringing sound could be heard, almost like a blacksmith beating an anvil. There was a great crowd at one end, perhaps two hundred or more all gathered. They were his people, at least. Pericles could tell that much with a glance. Yet from the moment he entered, he could see anger and the threat of violence in their midst. The air reeked of it. It was in the way they moved their heads, in jabbing fingers and the sharp tone of voices between the bell notes, long before he could make out actual words.

Pericles had to limp the length of the room to approach, denied his usual gait and confidence. He wished he had secured some sort of crutch, recalling the one Attikos had used on Scyros. Such a thing would have been a comfort as his leg began to ache, the pain growing sharper with each step. He found he was sweating by halfway and wondered if it would sour in the way Physician Golshan had said.

Pericles lowered his head in mulish memory. He hated doctors, especially battlefield ones. Pericles thought it did something to them, to see inside their fellows. No young soldier wanted to see those butchers creeping across the field after the fighting was over, finding them at their weakest point. Either way, he wished he had been sharper with the Persian and not thanked him like a damned fool. The man was his enemy, after all.

As he reached the closest edge of the crowd, Pericles saw Pausanias was there, wearing a red cloak. The Spartan and his guards stood on some sort of dais, raised one step above the rest. Pausanias was leaning on the arm of a gilded throne. His soothsayer, Tisamenus, stood alongside, filling a cup with wine and glaring, an expression quite unlike him. In fact, there seemed to be not much celebration at all in that place, as if the Greeks had lost a battle rather than won one. Pericles pushed through the outliers. His wound helped him then. Men stepped back when they saw his bandages, his unbound hair and pale, sweating skin.

Pericles caught sight of Cimon and Aristides before they noticed him. They were deep in conversation, their expressions as dark as that of Tisamenus, or more so. As he shoved his way through the crowd, Pericles followed their gaze. He paused then, seeing two very different groups at the heart. The bell note rang out again and at last he understood it.

A line of Persians knelt on the ground with their heads bowed. Hoplites in full armour with drawn swords stood over four men and two women in attitudes of unmistakable threat. Pericles felt memory stir as he recalled billowing curtains and a room of pale blue and gold. He had left his own blood in single footprints, he suddenly recalled. A wave of dizziness made him close his eyes. When he opened them, Cimon was there to take his arm and embrace him.

'I am glad to see you, Pericles. Are you recovering well? You were delirious for a while there.'

CONN IGGULDEN

'I will be fine,' Pericles said curtly.

Somehow, he was stung by the concern, though sweat trickled down his back and his calf felt as if it had been dipped in boiling water. He was not the only one who had taken wounds. Pericles resolved not to show any sign of it, no matter how bad the pain became. Aristides was there, a man who had known his father, who had stood with him at Marathon. He would not hiss or groan over a few stitches, not while others suffered. It seemed to be enough for Cimon. Without another word, he turned back to the scene in front of them.

Behind the line of kneeling Persians, a second group sprawled or stood. Eight men were there, filthy and matted, with chains around their ankles so they could not take a full step. Two of them were missing their right hand; another was blind, his eyes scorched out in great tears of scarring. Half of them had been freed of their shackles. Even as Pericles watched, hoplites with iron hammers were knocking pins out, one by one. The sound was the bell note he had heard.

He could smell them, he realised, an odour of rot, of death almost. No one stood too close to those unfortunates. In turn, the men glared around in confusion or rage. The blind one accepted a cup of wine in both hands. He sipped with a wince, as if it stung him.

'Who are those poor people?' Pericles asked.

'The ragged ones? Prisoners taken during the war,' Cimon said quietly. 'Two were keleustai officers. The blind one there was a trierarch at Salamis. Athenians, picked up in the waters where they clung to something and hoped for rescue. Instead, they were captured and put to torture.' His voice was a breath. 'There are only these eight now.'

'There are many more who did not survive,' Aristides

added. 'If we'd known they were here . . . They died waiting for us to come.'

'We found them in cells far below the fortress,' Cimon went on. 'Denied even light.' He shook his head, banishing some unpleasant memory as he went on. 'It is a hellish place, Pericles. Hundreds of tiny rooms. There are a lot of bones down there – and rats. They'd been forgotten in the end, or just left to die, we think. Some of the trierarchs would like to see the same punishment meted out to our own prisoners.'

'Those?' Pericles asked softly, inclining his head.

Cimon nodded.

'Those six and Artabazus – a cousin of the Great King who commanded a wing at Plataea. At the moment, he is under guard in one of the cells below our feet. Pausanias insisted on him having a taste of how Greeks have been treated.'

Cimon glanced at Aristides as he spoke, but nothing was said aloud. They had reached some private agreement that did not need to be said again. Pericles felt a pang of jealousy, wishing his wounds had not kept him apart while important decisions were being made. His father would not ask what they would do, he knew. Xanthippus would just tell them – and he would be right.

'Pausanias won't take a ransom,' Pericles said.

Aristides sighed.

'That appears to be true. I have argued the point with Spartans made suddenly deaf, as if even talk of wealth is somehow beneath them. Of course, they do not pay their rowers. Nor do they have as many ships as we do. Still, Pausanias is in command here. It will be his decision. Tisamenus has given him his second victory on Cypros, after Plataea. Who could deny the gods smile on the Spartan now? Whether that means Pausanias has the right to refuse even the possibility of

CONN IGGULDEN

ransoms is the heart of the discussion. I captured Artabazus, after all. Pausanias has no right to decide his fate.'

Again, Aristides and Cimon seemed to share some under-standing that did not include Pericles.

The final shackles fell away. The last of the freed Greeks began to stretch muscles they had not used in months or years. It was agony, that much was clear. Scars and sores were revealed beneath the iron. One of them wept, pressing his face into the crook of an arm. Others seemed almost delirious, hissing laughter in the gaps between teeth as they moved. The smell of them increased, so that everyone else breathed through their noses or sipped wine against polluted air.

The Spartans showed no sign of discomfort, Pericles noted. He renewed his efforts to resist the nagging of his wounds, though he found he had raised one heel to stand on bent toes, quite without deliberate thought.

The sound of marching feet brought an alertness to that crowd that had been missing before. Pericles turned with the rest as a troop of Spartans entered, just six of them with a bedraggled figure at their heart.

'Artabazus,' Aristides said to Cimon.

The Persian had been badly beaten, that was clear from the first moments. His features were horribly swollen and he held a hand curled against his chest in the classic pose of one sheltering a broken bone. He limped as badly as Pericles him-self and stared at the crowd from only one good eye. The other was either fully closed or gone, Pericles could not tell. The Spartans who jabbed him along with the butt of a spear had clearly been thorough. The very idea was disturbing, Pericles realised. Spartans were men who finished their child-hood training with a public whipping, endured in perfect silence to show the strength of their will. They would be merciless torturers.

THE LION

Artabazus was made to kneel with quick strikes to his calves. He raised his head in the presence of enemies, his will fed by the gleaming eyes watching him. Pericles saw his courage and wondered what Physician Golshan would say if he had been there. The idea brought a flicker of shame.

Pausanias came through the crowd, stepping down from the raised dais that held the throne. He stood before the Persian and used a thumb to wipe back the man's hair where it had fallen across his face. Pausanias looked into the glaring eye of the Persian general then. He smiled as he turned to face his own people.

'The oracle of Apollo at Delphi promised my soothsayer Tisamenus five great contests – five victories in his lifetime,' Pausanias said. His voice carried, though he hardly raised it. 'Plataea was the first, where I commanded all our forces – and broke the Persian host.'

The man at his feet spoke no Greek, but he was not a fool. He knew he was the subject of the speech. Slowly, Artabazus leaned over and spat on the polished floor.

'The island of Cypros was the second,' Pausanias went on unaware, pride radiating from him. 'Ours now, to hold. Who knows when the other three will come? Only the gods – gods who have given soft Persian generals into my hands, over and over.'

His smile dropped away then and he glowered at the crowd. The Spartans at his back stood in their red cloaks like an honour guard and Pericles recalled the man had been regent for a battle king. Pausanias had the manner well enough, one eyebrow raised as if they were fortunate just to stand in the same room as him.

'There are some of you here, senior men and strategoi, who have come to me and said we should ask for fortunes in return for these people – that this creature, Artabazus, is a cousin to the Great King. There are some who say wealth too is a form of war.'

His stern gaze seemed to seek out Aristides in the crowd and Pericles glanced across as well. The argument had the sound of something Aristides might have said. The archon of Athens stood perfectly still and did not look away.

Pausanias shook his head.

'I cannot say I understand those who see the world in such a way. It is fortunate that I retain command, or we might see our natural advantage sold like a birthright. We are not merchants, but leaders and soldiers! My interest lies in securing this island – a new garrison here, a permanent fleet in these waters, patrolling. These are my concerns, not the fate of prisoners!'

He looked around the gathered crowds, with contempt written across his face.

'The festival of Apollo Carneios begins in ten days, at the end of summer. They will be despatched then, sacrificed to the god whose oracle and blessing brought me victory at Plataea – and here on Cypros.'

Artabazus' translator had been taken away. He still had no idea what the Spartan was saying, but he had the sense it was not to his benefit. He met the eyes of Aristides as he looked over the room, one face he knew amidst the rest. Despite the beating he had taken, Artabazus had kept a sort of battered dignity. When he saw Aristides was watching, he smiled and jerked his head up in greeting. His good eye glittered and this time it was Aristides who looked away first.

16

The night was quiet. Hoplites patrolled the shore and at least part of the fleet remained alert, watching for reprisals from the mainland. Cypros had been settled first by Greeks on the western side, centuries before. When Persia grew in size and strength, those small settlements and fishing villages had been cast out, replaced by soldiers who worshipped Ahura Mazda and angels, who raised strange temples and built massive walls. The island was as old as the world and the air thick with the scent of ancient time.

Pericles felt goosebumps rise at the thought of being discovered. He stood in moonlight by a boat on the north side of the island. His eyes had adjusted to the darkness and he felt horribly exposed waiting there. Four fleet rowers sat in the boat with oars across their laps. They did not seem to feel the same tension and he wondered if they understood what they were doing, or had simply followed the orders of officers and cared nothing more. One of them even snored, until he was nudged with a foot.

Pericles felt his heart thumping in his chest. The Spartans were not fools. If Pausanias discovered them there, what would he say? Pericles had gone to the trouble of bringing two spools of fishing line, tormenting himself with a dozen scenarios of disaster. Night-fishing for squid seemed plausible, though he did not think Pausanias would believe it. What if Cimon or Aristides were caught? That could mean war – and if it began on Cypros, Pericles would be in mortal danger. The Spartan warriors were vastly outnumbered in that fleet, but if fighting began, they could never be discounted. The action at Thermopylae was still being discussed, spreading across Greece in wonder. Aspects of the tale worried Pericles when it came to dealing with the men of that city.

It seemed there had been three Spartans who survived the doomed stand by the sea at Thermopylae. One had been sent away right at the start, to carry the news. He hadn't made it back to the pass before the end and so hanged himself out of shame. When the fighting had become wave after wave of bloodshed and exhaustion, two more Spartiates had been sent away by King Leonidas. Grit had damaged the sight of both men, so they could see nothing but a blur. Pericles shuddered at the thought of that. One of them had decided he preferred death to being blind and staggered back to the pass, losing his life there. The other, as Pericles had heard it, was named Aristodemus. Despite his near-blindness, he actually made it home to Sparta. He was scorned there. No man gave him fire or food, or said a word to him. He was called a coward and spat upon. In reply, he demanded and was granted a spot in the front line at Plataea. Though blind, he had fought there like a madman, laughing all the while. Death had come for him, but he had regained his honour.

That was how the Spartans told it. Pericles wondered if he would ever truly understand them. It was not that they worshiped death, he knew that. Yet they threw lives away as if they were leaves on the wind.

He was not sure how he might react to every man calling him coward. He knew his father had earned respect and treated it lightly. Yet Xanthippus could still speak in anger of his banishment, when the people of Athens had turned against him. Pericles sometimes thought a reputation mattered more than anything – or not at all. It was hard to be sure which was true.

He froze, all idle thoughts shattering to pieces as something moved in the undergrowth. He had chosen a spot on the north shore, around the spit of land that was like a finger pointing east – far from any Spartan ships. Yet if one of Pausanias' people had spotted his small boat, he could be about to face armed Spartans hunting him down.

He swallowed, his hand touching the kopis knife in his belt. Cimon had returned it to him without a word when he'd asked about it, but it would not be much use against Spartans themselves. They had their own – and he imagined they were rather more skilled with them than he was. His wounds too were smarting. It had been impossible not to step into the shallows as the rowers had beached their little boat. The burn of salt in his calf remained and he thought the honey would have washed away. Physician Golshan would be appalled if they met again.

Pericles found he was breathing hard, waiting to see whether the shadows were hostile or not. He was grinning, he realised, a nervous thing that was no reflection of his mood. He hoped it gave him a wild look, though he doubted it.

An owl hooted somewhere over on his left. Pericles slumped in relief. Through cupped hands, he made the same sound. More voices spoke in reply, much too loud in the night. His people, it had to be. Spartans would have come in silence and all the more terrifying for it.

The little beach where he waited was barely a patch of sand, half-blocked by a driftwood branch as long as the boat and strands of kelp that had dried in the sun. Something rustled nearby and Pericles did not know if it was his people or some creature, perhaps a lizard or a turtle scurrying away. He waited, reaching down to tap his knuckles on the side of the boat as a signal to the rowers. They seemed alert, at least.

Cimon appeared out of the bushes, brushing hard at

CONN IGGULDEN

himself. Behind him came a bedraggled line of people, clumsy and weary-looking. The last of them was staggering badly, one arm around Aristides and the other curled up into his chest. Panting and exhausted, Artabazus collapsed, almost taking Aristides with him. The Athenian was not a young man and had to stand with his hands on his knees for a time, just breathing.

'That was . . . harder than I thought . . . it would be,' Cimon said in between breaths. 'I thought we'd . . . been turned around.' He shuddered, scraping at his face and hair. 'There were spiders in there! I seemed to keep walking into them. One of the things bit me, I'm sure. Unless it was a . . . thorn bush. I swear, that was worse than Scyros, Pericles. By the gods, I am delighted to see you! When I heard you return the owl call, I almost shouted in joy.'

Pericles felt his smile widen. With his bad leg, he had been no help at all when it came to getting the prisoners out. His role had been minor, though it was true someone had to pick the right spot and keep the oarsmen alert. Perhaps Cimon was just being kind, but he appreciated it.

'Did you have any trouble in the cells?'

Cimon leaned back, eyeing the moon as one who had to be finished before the sun rose. He was a careful man, Pericles realised, even before Cimon shook his head.

'Had to knock one of our own people out, but we smashed his lamp first. He didn't see anything. For all he knows, they escaped on their own. Come on. Artabazus is almost out on his feet. Help me get him into the boat with the others. I'll make better time without them.'

'Aren't you coming with us?' Pericles asked.

'No. Aristides and I need to be back on board our ships before the sun shows. If we're out of position by dawn, there will be too many questions. All we've done will be wasted.

That goes for you too, Pericles. If it takes too long, if the sun rises, you'll have to hide the boat and wait for nightfall. I'll say you're on one of the other ships, counting supplies. All right? Help me with him, would you?'

The two of them walked to where Artabazus was gently moaning to himself. Pericles muttered an apology in Persian, one of the few phrases he had picked up. The man shot a stream of words at him in reply, but he could only shrug and say it again.

With a muffled cry, they dragged Artabazus to his feet. Pericles and Cimon passed the Persian general into the hands of the rowers, then watched as he was wrapped in a blanket and left to his discomfort. Artabazus was followed on board by two men, one of whom glared at Pericles and held up his wrists as if in protest at remaining bound. Pericles reached for the kopis in his belt but Cimon touched him on the arm.

'Leave him tied. He was keen enough before and I don't trust him further than I could spit.'

Pericles remembered the man from the room they had stormed, standing with sword levelled. He nodded. Pericles did put out his hand to the women following, bowing his head as they smiled at him. The last was one he remembered from billowing curtains of blue and gold. In the moonlight, she was as beautiful as before.

'Are we go to be killed?' she said in Greek.

Cimon shook his head.

'Free. We will take you to the mainland and set you free.'

The woman leaned in quickly and kissed him before Cimon could pull away. He did not seem to be making any great effort, Pericles thought. In fact, his hand curled around her waist and made her arch, pulling her in. Pericles watched coldly, thinking of Thetis.

The Persian woman gasped as Cimon let her go, turning

her head shyly away as she stepped into the thwarts and took a seat by her brother. He seemed angrier than before, but he said nothing.

There was barely room for so many and Pericles hoped he would be able to push them off the beach into deeper water. His wound was going to get wet again, he realised with a sinking feeling. Not that it had dried much since the first time.

'Up to you now,' Cimon said. He raised one hand to his lips, as if she kissed him still. 'Remember – if there's any doubt at all, hide for a day and come over tomorrow night. No one says a word about anything – we are all blind and deaf about this, after it's done.'

Cimon spoke as much to the rowers as to Pericles. They all nodded solemnly, like owls themselves.

'Good.'

He reached down with Pericles and heaved at the prow, pushing the boat out through the shallows. Pericles scrambled on board, taking a sharp breath when his calf knocked the side of the boat.

'May Poseidon watch over fools like us,' Cimon said.

There was a smile in his voice and Pericles raised a hand as the rowers took over and the boat skimmed out to deeper waters.

Horns sounded across the bay, bringing the allied fleet to war readiness. Hoplites reached for kit and weapons, kneeling on decks with shields and spears. Rowers leaped down, leaving food behind as they took their seats and rattled oars out. Anchors were heaved up by teams of men and the ships began to move like hornets, alive and dangerous.

When no threat came, the mood settled slowly back from wild surmise. Pausanias tended not to drill his crews, but those who had sailed with Xanthippus knew the form. Yet the Spartan ships did not return to sleepy stillness. As the sun rose, Pausanias raised a black streamer from his stern, summoning senior officers to the flagship.

Aristides and Cimon saw the signal flag, each from a warship deck. They had an idea what it meant, at least. One by one, Athenian ships dropped anchors once again. Pausanias was within his rights as navarch. Boats were set down all over the fleet, bringing trierarchs and archons to the Spartan who had authority over them. Aristides felt his resolve firm. He did not like being summoned. Nor was he happy about being alone on a Spartan flagship. He had assumed he would be called to the cells on the island, to explain how a group of Persians could just vanish in the night. Standing on board a Spartan warship put him at a horrible disadvantage. None of the others would feel it, of course, but then they were not guilty of anything.

It was the work of a moment to heave in the little boat that bobbed behind his flagship. Pericles had not yet returned, Aristides knew that much. Would his absence be noted? The young Athenian had no senior rank, despite the esteem in which his father was held. Aristides had visions of the entire plan unravelling in a single hour. He clenched his jaw. No, it was begun. This was the crisis. There was simply no choice now but to think fast and see it through.

He saw Cimon alongside, on one knee in a second boat, already converging on the flagship. The Spartan vessels had clustered together with those of Corinth, Aristides noted. It seemed significant somehow, as if they no longer trusted the fleet around them.

Aristides felt old as his oarsmen swept him over to the Spartan ship. It loomed closer and closer, red-cloaked men visible on the deck. As they pulled in, Aristides looked up at wooden rungs. The sea was running a little high and the warship rose and fell in sickening swoops. Aristides was already soaked, of course – it seemed impossible to do anything at sea without getting wet. He ignored the raised hands of his own men and took hold of the guide rope, steadying himself as he climbed. He had to stop at one point as the flagship rolled towards him, but his grip held. When it swung back, he used the motion to stagger on board. His boat rowed clear and another took its place.

Aristides took in the presence of Spartan warriors on deck, armed and cloaked as if for war. They had their helmets resting back on clubs of hair, but that was the only concession to peaceful talk. Beyond that, they looked about ready to start a slaughter. Of course, they always did, Aristides reminded himself. Like mad dogs, they could go from apparent calm to snapping frenzy in a heartbeat.

Pausanias stood with Tisamenus, both watching Aristides as if trying to look inside his skull. The ship's wild roll did not seem to trouble either man. They adjusted to it without thought. The soothsayer cracked the knuckles of one hand in the other, his usual gentle manner gone. Pausanias had folded massive forearms. His glare was one of fury or betrayal – and rather more dangerous. Aristides saw Cimon just a few paces away on the deck, eyes wary. He resisted the urge to stand with his younger colleague, in case it was taken as some sign of guilt.

'Why have I been summoned?' Aristides said. 'Is there news from home?'

He raised one eyebrow to match Pausanias and stood in a relaxed position. Aristides had faced men like Themistocles in a hundred debates, he reminded himself. Pausanias was not likely to trap him.

'The prisoners are gone,' Pausanias replied. The bluntness was typically Spartan, but Aristides had expected it.

'You let them go?' he said in astonishment.

'I did *no such thing*,' Pausanias snapped.

To Aristides' interest, the Spartan glanced at his captains as he spoke. They were his people, but perhaps he did not trust them completely. Aristides hoped not. A great deal depended on it.

'You are in command here, Pausanias! If you chose to release the Persians, I would only say that I would have preferred you to discuss it first. I would have asked for a ransom, as I said before.'

Pausanias flushed darkly, his anger visible. Aristides tried not to show the fear that pinched at his bowels and shrank his stomach. Anyone who teased a mad dog deserved to be bitten, but he was not speaking to Pausanias, not really. Trusting to his authority and rank to save him, he was speaking to the other Spartans present – the trierarchs who might wonder about their leader.

'Artabazus was my prisoner, in particular,' Aristides went on, as if it had just occurred to him. 'Are you saying he has gone as well?'

Pausanias replied through gritted teeth.

'There is no sign of any of them,' he said.

Aristides could swear there was an actual growl to his voice. He felt his bladder tighten, a feeling he had not known since the morning of Plataea, with a Persian host advancing on his position. It was almost cruel to do this to the Spartan who had triumphed that day, but there was too much at stake.

'I see. That is . . . disappointing.'

'You are saying you know nothing about this?' Pausanias demanded.

Aristides shook his head.

'I have made my views clear from the start. A cousin to the Great King was worth a fortune – or perhaps some other advantage, I don't know. King Xerxes has been known to promise entire cities to those who please him, nations even. A satrapy would not have been beyond reach.' Aristides saw two of the Spartan officers exchange a quick glance, suspicion blooming in them. He made himself look reproving. 'I have to say, I am disappointed, Pausanias.'

'Will you submit to a search of your ships?' Pausanias said. 'To be sure they are not hiding in one?'

'A search of my . . . ? That is insulting from an ally, Navarch Pausanias. I have no doubts about any of my captains.' Aristides allowed himself to look offended as he went on. 'It seems to me that you are in command. The Persians were your prisoners, not mine. If Spartans care nothing for ransoms, perhaps they were allowed to escape in exchange for some other favour, I don't know! Persians promise much – and who is truly immune? You, Pausanias?'

Despite the danger, Aristides jabbed the air. He knew it was unlikely anyone had spoken to Pausanias in such a way since childhood. The Spartan had won the day at Plataea and yet he had to be destroyed.

'If you will not accept my oath,' Aristides went on, 'I'll let you search every ship, though it shames us both – and I'll send men to search each one of yours as well. Well, why not? If we cannot trust one another?'

'Aristides, please be calm . . .' Cimon said, the first words he had spoken.

Aristides waved a hand in disgust.

'*Why* should I be calm? I accepted your authority, Pausanias, did I not? At Plataea, when we had no hope?' It felt like blasphemy to name that day, but he made himself go on. 'I have shown you nothing but respect – for your authority and your position in the fleet. And you accuse me of this? You demand the right to search my ships? You shame us both. You know what is strange, Pausanias? I asked to ransom those prisoners – and you wanted to have them executed, or so you said. Then they escape. No ransoms now, to pay my rowers! No matter what happened, their loss is your responsibility. Not mine.'

He turned and gestured to the boat waiting for him some way from the ship. He had not moved a step since coming on board.

'Send your men, Pausanias,' Aristides said. 'Search the holds of your allies and show all our people you do not trust any of us. I wonder if this is all just dust in the air to make me blind. No matter what, I think you are responsible.'

Pausanias watched the older man climb down, never taking his eyes off him. He did not trust Aristides, nor any Athenian. After all, they had forced Sparta to the battlefield with lies and threats before. He despised them all.

Cimon left on the heels of the senior archon of Athens, looking coldly furious as if they were the ones wronged. One by one, the captains of other factions asked permission to leave and were dismissed back to their ships.

Pausanias was left on board with six Spartan trierarchs and Tisamenus. His friend looked worried and rubbed his jaw. Pausanias stood in silence as he considered. Aristides had turned it back on him. Pausanias had summoned them all to discern which of them had betrayed him, but somehow Aristides had cast doubt on his own account, even suspicion. Pausanias saw the way his captains looked at one another. He was filled with foreboding.

'The Athenians wanted gold for the Persians, navarch,' one of the Spartans said. 'If they are behind this, the prisoners must have been hidden, either on the island or on one of their ships. Perhaps we *should* look for them.'

Pausanias dipped his head in gratitude. Two more of his

captains nodded in support, but another would not meet his eye. Pausanias swallowed uncomfortably. The ephors of Sparta had wanted him to go far away. The young battle king could not have been clearer about his intentions. It made Pausanias weaker than anyone there knew. He shook his head. The ephors would never believe he had taken a bribe, surely? Unfortunately, he knew the answer. If it served to destroy him, they certainly would.

The sun was rising still. Pausanias had the whole day to find the prisoners and prove it was all some scheme of the Athenians. It would damage relations with every faction of the *symmachia*, the alliance, he realised. Perhaps that had been their plan all along. He set his jaw. He had no choice.

'Search the island,' he ordered. 'And the fleet.'

17

Aristides watched Spartan hoplites crashing around his ship, peering under every oar bench and kicking in the doors of storerooms. He could see anger growing in his men. He had given careful instructions to allow the search, even of their personal belongings. Even so, Athenian hoplites were seething. Only the presence of glowering senior officers kept violence from breaking out – and then only barely.

When Aristides looked up, he could see red cloaks on a dozen ships nearby. There were fewer than two hundred Spartiate warriors in that fleet, but most of them seemed to have been sent out. There weren't too many places to hide men or women on a warship, not really. Beyond a few cramped spaces near the stern, the entire deck and rowing benches were open and could be searched with a glance.

With sharp interest, Aristides saw two of Pausanias' ships rattle out their oars and begin to sweep around Cypros. It made sense to search the shore, though the island was huge. It would take Pausanias a month or more to be certain he had checked every cave or stand of trees. Aristides smiled at the thought, then resumed his glower as a Spartan officer came to report to him.

'We've found no one aboard, Archon Aristides,' the man said.

'That is not news to me,' Aristides snapped. 'Nor to Pausanias, I suspect. Whatever game your masters are playing, I do not have the prisoners. I swear it on Athena and Apollo, on Poseidon as I stand here in his realm.'

The Spartan flinched to hear such an oath, as if he expected Aristides to be struck down or storm clouds to appear. His suspicion changed to confusion as he turned away to climb down to a boat and go on to the next ship. He did not doubt an Athenian archon. The conclusion troubled him.

Aristides watched the Spartans row to another ship. He did not smile, though each time they boarded one of the alliance, it drove a wedge between them – not to the advantage of Sparta, either. He saw how they searched the ships of Corinth as well, sparing not even the vessels of the Peloponnese. Pausanias sowed anger wherever he went, but Aristides still hoped for more. Cimon knew the Spartans better than anyone. He was the one who had suggested Pausanias could be recalled by his own people, that if they found the right accusation, they could remove him without a drop of blood being spilled. The entire plan rested on Cimon's judgement of Spartan honour. Aristides chewed his lower lip as he stared over the sea.

In the distance, a Greek merchant ship rounded the tip of the land. One of the Spartan warships was escorting it in. Aristides sighed to himself. Carrion birds would come, of course. They followed armies and fleets alike, looking for scraps. There were certainly fortunes to be made on Cypros – the sale of slaves alone would bring some recompense. The Spartans may have scorned ransoms in good silver drachms, but Athens had twenty thousand rowers and they still had to be paid.

Pericles tried not to move as flies feasted on him. The day was hot and the back of his neck had already burned. He and the rowers had dragged the boat right out of the water in the darkness, sinking to their thighs in black muck that caked him still.

The Persian prisoners had not tarried too long on that shore, at least. They had slipped and fallen in the mud, but hadn't stopped to complain, not then. With one of the men supporting Artabazus, they'd scrambled away in the grey light of pre-dawn, looking back in fear as if they thought their new liberty might be snatched away. Pericles had watched them go until he was sure they had made it alive, but it was too late to head back by then.

The trip across from the island had taken a lot longer than he had expected. The rowers had exhausted themselves to make the crossing, but whether it was just further than they had known, or some current tugged at them, it had taken too many hours and brought dawn and utter collapse. Even as he waved off the flies that sucked his blood, the rowers snored, dead to the world. The sun had risen and Pericles had seen ships with red sails easing along the shore in the distance, looking for him. If they knew his name, he thought he might never be safe again. The Spartans were prickly when it came to matters of honour and he would surely be challenged. Yet there was nothing he could do. Though his stomach gnawed at him, though he feared discovery by locals, or even the freed prisoners bringing soldiers back to capture him, he still had to remain, sweating and itching through the long day.

The boat was covered in branches and sea-wrack, anything he could find. He'd done that much before the sky began to grow light. He knelt in thick grass, in the shadow of a twisted tree. Pericles winced as his leg cramped. He feared for the stitches in his calf. He'd felt something give as he'd heaved the boat higher, not even thinking to protect himself. He hadn't dared look under the wrappings since then.

Hours passed with interminable slowness. The sun rose, hurting his eyes when he looked at it. One of the rowers stirred and slapped himself to come alert. He saw Pericles was awake and nodded. In relief, Pericles let his head droop. He put his back against the tree and was asleep in moments, head leaning to one side to escape the sun's glare.

He drifted in and out of wakefulness as the oarsmen changed watch, but they did not trouble him again. He was the son of Xanthippus and they all knew his father, by reputation if they had not served at Salamis. When Pericles woke once more, the day had cooled and evening was coming. The sun was on the other side of the island, dipping behind mountains there. He was on the Ionian coast, Pericles reminded himself, standing to empty his bladder against the tree that had been his support. One of the rowers was gathering leaves to wipe himself and seemed pleased to have found a wild fig tree, though it was a small and straggling thing. Pericles looked around. He itched still from a thousand bites, his skin rough with them. His leg throbbed and seemed fat somehow, swollen with poison or pus. He was not certain what effect salt water and black mud would have on a stitched wound, but he imagined it was not good. He heard his stomach creak and pressed his fingers into it.

'Get the boat ready,' he called to the men. 'As soon as it's dark, we go – no lights, no sound.'

They were all Cimon's men and he had known them on Scyros. They nodded and set about collecting oars. One of them even tried a wizened green fig, but it was bitter and he spat out the pieces. They busied themselves as the sun sank.

Pericles watched the light change and the ships out beyond it. There were no red sails in view. He prayed to Poseidon to keep them safe in their little boat. In that moment, it seemed a fragile thing to carry them all.

When it was dark, he and the others heaved it into the water and clambered in. Pericles swore as he smacked his leg in exactly the same place, making one of the men chuckle.

They left the shore behind and Pericles felt his mood rise immediately. He had dropped the prisoners and whatever fate lay ahead for them, it was not his concern. Away from the land, he was already part of the fleet once more. His only worry was if they crossed paths with one of the Spartan ships in the dark. That would see the whole thing unravel.

The oarsmen laboured hard, heaving them along with no sound beyond the swish and gurgle of water under the narrow hull. They had made the journey in two stages before – around the island and then across the strait. On the return, they were trying to row right around the great finger of Cypros that pointed to the Persian coast. They did have all night, Pericles thought. Yet as the hours passed, it seemed he had lived his whole life on that boat, with his leg throbbing and starvation making him light-headed.

They stayed far offshore to pass around the headland. Pericles rose up as best he could, straining his eyes for the dark shapes of ships. He could not remember when he had last eaten and his lips were cracked and painful, though he ran his tongue over them.

In the distance, a single light showed, a point in the night that appeared and was lost with the movement of the sea.

'There,' Pericles said.

Relief filled him. For a time in the dark, it had felt like a dream, a night that would go on for eternity. The rowers took a sighting on the light, the single lamp Aristides had promised to hang for them. Home.

As the sun rose the next morning, the Spartan ships looked like someone had kicked a hive. Sails and cross-spars rose into the breeze, while oars swept others up and down the coast of Cypros. When Aristides put down a boat to ask what was going on, it was waved off by a Spartan trierarch who would not halt to receive him. The little craft was left in their wash.

Aristides could count, though. The rising sun had revealed five Spartan ships and not six, as there had been the night before. Aristides knew there was a chance one of them was just out of sight around the island. The manic activity in the others gave the lie to that. The Spartans were disturbed by something – and Aristides hoped it meant the plan had worked. He returned to the Athenian flagship and summoned Cimon to him.

He arrived in his own boat, Pericles alongside, both men under a visible strain as they struggled to show only polite concern. They knew better than to say a word of what they hoped was happening. Cimon helped Pericles climb aboard then talked of the most ordinary things – of water casks and supplies of dried beans and grain. The endless small labours of the fleet went on around them and the Spartans were even busier, sweeping around Cypros as they searched for their lost crew.

It was late in the afternoon by the time Aristides watched the Spartan flagship raise its anchor. A small boat appeared around its stern, just four rowers and one passenger easing through the waters.

Aristides had expected to be summoned to where Pausanias was strongest. It was a surprise to recognise the figure seated in that boat, red cloak gripped against the spray. The sea was calm enough, though Aristides suspected Pausanias was not. Aristides exchanged a glance with Cimon and Pericles, standing at his side.

'He is impressive,' Aristides muttered. 'Honestly, if you had seen him on the day of Plataea . . . For all his arrogance, having to do this breaks my heart.'

Neither Cimon nor Pericles replied. They were too aware

of the Spartan navarch making light work of their side steps, so that Pausanias landed on the deck like a great cat. It was unusual to see him alone, without his soothsayer. Tisamenus had become a talisman to him. That absence, more than anything, spoke of his defeat. Pausanias bore a short sword on his belt and a kopis in a scabbard, with a thong to keep the blade in place. Bare-armed, he stood still as the Athenians bowed to him. Though Aristides was both archon and strategos of Athens, Pausanias had been regent to a king – and he was still senior in that fleet.

'I know what you've done,' Pausanias said.

Aristides raised both his eyebrows.

'I'm sure I have no idea what you mean.'

Pausanias waved a hand as if the words were just air.

'I don't know the details, nor why you chose to move against me. Only that you did. Your reasons are not important, not really. I doubt I would understand them. I find I often can't understand the way Athenians think.'

Pausanias smiled, an ocean of bitterness in his eyes. He looked out to sea, to five Spartan ships where the day before there had been six.

'One of my captains has taken it upon himself to report what has happened here – the accusations made against me. I have lost another day I will not be able to make up, not now. So. He will tell the ephors of Sparta about Persians escaping, prisoners disappearing into the air. They will believe . . . Well, whatever they believe, you have your wish, Aristides. I must go home, to defend myself. You are the most senior man left. Is that what you wanted? Was this simply about who commands the fleet?'

It seemed to be a genuine question, though Pausanias was still as dangerous as a cobra on that deck. Aristides did not relax and instead frowned in puzzlement.

'What I want . . . ? I want nothing at all, Pausanias! The actions of lone Spartan captains are not my concern. Nor the politics of your home. Though as one who was once exiled from Athens, I must remind you, there is always hope of a return.'

'In Athens, perhaps,' Pausanias said bleakly.

Aristides shook his head.

'Wherever there are men, Pausanias. I do not believe our fates are written. They are in our hands and eyes and minds. You are a young man. You can come back from disaster – I have done so myself. Take hope from that. If you must go, I wish you only good fortune.'

Pausanias held his gaze for a long time, an age of awkwardness. At last, he shook his head, disgusted with them all.

'This thing,' he said, 'what do you call it? This "*symmachia*" – this league you began on Delos. Yes, of course I know of it. It will not stand, you do realise? It is a mistake to try and bind together such a varied group. There are a few strong cities like Sparta or Corinth – or Athens, Thebes, Argos, a few others. The rest are . . . weak. They can never be equals, not really. To pretend they are is a sort of insult to them, do you see?' At their blank stares, he cut the air with one hand. 'It is hard to put into words. If Athens has a fleet or great markets, no small city can dare tell you to leave. To call them equals is to force them to accept a lie, and smile as they obey. It is . . . a dishonesty that will eat away at men.'

Aristides blinked. He was reminded again that Pausanias was no fool. The Spartan had wielded great power and that brought insight, more than the Athenian had realised. Once again, he felt a pang to destroy a great man, but the truth was simple: Sparta was not part of their alliance. They had been asked, but refused. Sparta could not then be permitted to lead, as if nothing had changed.

'You may be right,' Aristides said gently.

Pausanias waited for more, but it did not come. In the end, his mouth twisted and he stood back, gesturing for his boat to approach.

'I do not know if we will meet again,' he said, including Cimon and Pericles in his glance. 'Perhaps it is better if we don't.'

He turned on his heel and climbed back down, stepping into his boat. He looked up at the Athenians as he took his seat and wrapped his cloak around himself. The three of them watched him grow smaller as he headed back to his own ship.

His captains had been ready for his return, it seemed. Sails rose on the masts of both Spartan and Corinthian ships. Almost as one, they caught the breeze and picked up speed, heading west for the Aegean and Sparta.

'He is quite wrong,' Aristides said after a time.

Pericles turned to him in question and Aristides shrugged.

'You are a young man of Acamantis tribe in Athens, like your father. Your deme is . . . ?'

'Cholargos,' Pericles said quickly.

Aristides nodded.

'You . . . sit with men of Acamantis in the theatre, you go to taverns in Cholargos – it is your home, your people. Yet you feel a greater loyalty, to men you do not know as well, to faces you cannot recognise. Is that not true?'

'To Athens? Yes, it is,' Pericles said.

'Good. A man can love his home street – and the city around it. I believe he can love the land just as well, in time. It will not be so hard, Pericles. We already have ties to bind us as one people – one culture. We all know the oracle at Delphi, or the Olympics on the Peloponnese. Any one of us can visit Eleusis for the rites of Demeter and Persephone.

CONN IGGULDEN

We know the names of the gods – and where they were born. Though the accents can be strange, we speak with one tongue, from Ionia to Macedon. No, Pausanias is wrong. A man can be Athenian first – and still love a greater people as his own.'

As Aristides spoke, red-sailed ships continued to dwindle into the distance. The day was coming to an end and the Spartans headed towards the setting sun, dark against its light.

'Will Pausanias be all right, do you think?' Pericles said. 'He seemed . . . defeated.'

'He is a decent enough man,' Cimon replied. 'As Spartans go. But your father understood. Sparta cannot lead at sea. The sea is ours. This way is better for Pausanias than just killing him.'

Pericles had seen despair in the Spartan's eyes. He was not sure that was true.

Another sail was heaved up on its mast, catching their attention. Closer in to the shore of Cypros, the ship that held it was a far cry from any of the triremes they knew. The sail alone was huge, bellying out in the breeze, held by ropes like threads that stretched right back to the stern. The merchant ship had no ram, but crested waves with sheets of lead and pitch tar at the prow, protecting the wood from rot. It sat higher in the water than any warship and so began to loom as it approached.

The trader had no oarsmen to ease passage, though the captain seemed to know the wind well enough. Pericles looked on the high sides and lead sheathing with awe. He had grown used to the idea that ships were fragile shells that could turn right over with a single rogue wave. This cog looked too sturdy, too solid for that. It rocked in the swell as it approached, coming dangerously close. Aristides found himself frowning up at a higher deck.

'Keep your distance, you fool!' his keleustes roared at their helmsman.

The fellow only shrugged, close enough to look down on the warship deck. The manoeuvre was well done and they seemed to have very few crew. Pericles supposed the wage bill would be a key part of their business, always kept to a minimum. He was fascinated by the strange ship.

As they watched, the merchant captain set down a boat on the far side, where there was no danger of the little shell being crushed between. He rowed it around himself and tied on to a rope by their own steps. The Athenian keleustes had two hoplites standing ready, but the merchant did not seem much of a threat as he rose to the level of the deck. He had a package tucked into his coat and dropped to one knee with a flourish to present it.

'Archon Aristides, I have brought letters from home. I'd like to discuss what cargo I can take back with me from Cypros. I understand you command the fleet.'

'I see. And who told you that?' Aristides said.

The man frowned, worried he had made a mistake.

'The Spartan, Pausanias. I went first to him.'

Aristides nodded. Pausanias had spoken to the merchant before coming to meet him. Once again, he felt a pang that Pausanias had stood in their way. He was an interesting man.

'Very well,' Aristides said. 'Pericles, take his letters from him.'

'Pericles?' the man said. His face fell. 'I am sorry about your father.'

Pericles felt blood drain from his face.

'My father? What about him?' he said, his voice just a breath.

The merchant captain shook his head.

'Ah. Then I am sorrier still to be the one to bring you the

news. Your father died a few days before I set out. Athens is in mourning.'

Pericles stared. It could not be true. He had no reason to think the man would lie to him. He was a stranger. No. Xanthippus could not be gone. He would go home and speak to him, one more time. He would tell him how much he meant . . .

Cimon reached out and touched him lightly on the arm.

'I'm sorry,' he said.

Pericles felt only irritation. His father could not be dead.

'You'll go home, of course,' Aristides said. 'I'll lend you a ship, or perhaps you can take a berth in the merchant. No, a warship will be faster. I wish I could come back with you, but there is much to do here, especially now. I cannot lay it aside.'

Pericles looked away. He would go home. He understood that much.

'Thank you,' he said to them both. His throat closed over words as he tried to speak. Both Aristides and Cimon had known Xanthippus longer than he had. They were Athenians and his friends. They understood, but they had known their own griefs. He would not weep in front of them. He stared out over the sea for a time, until he was ready to go on.

18

Pericles stepped out onto the docks of the Piraeus. The bustle was just as he remembered, but in that moment he felt like a stranger. When he had left Athens, it was his first day as a married man, with a fleet and battle ahead. His father had been alive and he had assumed ... Pericles shook his head. The journey back from Cypros had taken three weeks, stopping at half a dozen small islands for water or to wait out rough weather. The trireme's officers had left him alone for the most part. Whether that was in sympathy or because of the way he had rebuffed their attempts at conversation was not clear to him. Pericles had not spoken a word for days at a time. As he stood on the great port quays, he realised he would miss both the peace and the noise of waves.

Gulls wheeled overhead and perched on every post, watching fishing nets spread to dry. Braver ones strutted by Pericles as he stood there, shrieking for scraps. Sacks of grain were being unloaded along a gangplank, accompanied by shouts and curses. Each cart filled rattled away at a gallop across cobbles, pushed by a pair of young lads. People walked quickly everywhere, busy with trade and life. Pericles was home and it battered at him in the autumn sun.

After so long at sea, he had not expected anyone to greet him. Some part still hoped Thetis might have stayed like a sailor's wife, waiting for any glimpse of her beloved. That was a thought to raise his spirits, but she was not there. The merchant who had carried the news to Cypros had been at least a month at sea. The seasons had turned since the death of Xanthippus and there were no signs of mourning. His father's funeral had been long before. The body would be in the family tomb.

Pericles raised his head. That was where he would go. Cimon had been good enough to give him a pouch of drachms – his pay, though they had never agreed a rate. Still, he was grateful not to have to put new debts on the family or be dependent on the generosity of strangers. He thought he could probably buy a horse in those docks. It was said a man with a pouch of silver could buy almost anything there.

No, he would walk. The thought of stretching his legs was immediately right. He shifted his pack to his shoulder and set out, heading towards the city. The cemetery lay against the outer wall and he knew it was there he would find his father. Before he set off, Pericles raised a hand in farewell to the trireme captain and called thanks to him. The man acknowledged the son of Xanthippus by bowing deeply, one hand across his chest.

Pericles walked easily, feeling pleasure in the movement. The road into Athens was as busy as he had ever seen it. He recalled his father's stories of racing Themistocles from the port to the great wall – and losing to him, though he'd almost burst his heart trying. Without deliberate thought, Pericles began to run, adjusting his pack as he went. Those who saw him coming skittered out of his way, calling insults as he passed. Others were too lost in pulling a cart or a donkey, or in their own conversations. He darted around those, leaving them laughing in surprise or making crude gestures. His people! He found himself grinning as he ran, yet his vision blurred until he could hardly see at all.

He slowed at last, standing with hands on hips, heaving in great breaths. Time on board ship had made him unfit, he realised. His father would . . . There it was, that blow to his gut. It took the wind out of him every time he thought of Xanthippus' advice, or what he would say. Pericles hoped to see him again, on the other side of the river – but when he did, he did not want to be ashamed. He had his life to live, with all its mistakes and glories ahead. It could not equal his father's, who had stood at Marathon and Salamis, who had been part of a golden generation. They had done the impossible, defeating the empire that poured through the pass at Thermopylae, that had threatened all they loved.

The walls of the city had been rebuilt since the Persians had pulled them down. They stood even taller than Pericles remembered, looming as he approached. The great cemetery too had grown since the war. Many ancient tombs had been ruined beyond recovery, of course. Mass graves had replaced individual monuments. Themistocles had offended many when he'd used tombstones in a new gate. Pericles shuddered at the thought. His father had said any fresh grave could turn up an old finger bone or pelvis. They were collected with reverence and reinterred by groundsmen, each one a retired hoplite, grown old or wounded.

Pericles nodded to a pair of those men as they weeded between tombs. They bowed their heads in simple courtesy, though he did not think they knew him. He felt like a ghost coming back. He had been there last when his brother Ariphron had been brought home and reinterred under white stone. Pericles swallowed as he thought of that day, of blood that poured over his hands, brighter than the sun. In comparison, his father's death was . . . an absence. That was how he felt it. Not shock or tearing grief, as it had been with his brother. It was the knowledge that he would never hear the voice again, nor see his father laugh at some silly thing. He would never embrace the old man and see pride or exasperation in his eyes.

CONN IGGULDEN

Pericles slowed when he saw someone was already there, where he was heading. A man was crouched over a tomb of iron and marble – and for an instant Pericles felt alarm surging. He had Cimon's kopis blade in his belt and he touched the scabbard, moving faster. His hand dropped away when he recognised the figure.

'Epikleos,' he said. Xanthippus' friend and the closest thing Pericles had to a second father. The man had been there all his childhood – in the years of exile in particular.

Epikleos heard his name spoken and looked up. He was spare and slim, perhaps a little thin as he stood there. His hair was tousled and he was tanned, weathered by time and grief. There was dirt on his hands and he held a gardening tool. He looked up in dawning amazement as he recognised Pericles.

'Thank the gods!' he said. 'I'm so sorry, Per. I tried to get word to you at the end, but it was quick. He didn't suffer long.'

Pericles held his arms wide and they embraced, so tightly he could not breathe.

'Thank you. Of *course* you tend the grave,' Pericles said as they broke apart. He wiped at his eyes as he spoke. 'You looked after him all his life.'

'I did,' Epikleos said, with pride. 'And it was my honour. I can still hardly believe it's at an end.'

'Where are you living now?' Pericles asked. 'I haven't been home, not yet.'

'Oh, I have a little place, close to the Acropolis. I work at the theatre there. Unless I'm here. I come to speak to your father most days. Come, I'll walk with you.'

He handed Pericles his trowel and took a stoppered metal flask from his belt. Carefully, he poured a few drops onto the stone tomb. They reflected the sun and Epikleos saw Pericles hesitate. He flushed.

'I'm sorry. I'll leave you alone. Take as long as you need, of course. I'll wait by the road.'

He gathered up a few tools and carried them off. In the sudden silence, Pericles reached out and traced his father's name, then the curves cut for his brother. It was fine work, with panels in cream marble. His brother's part had only one scene – a host of Persian shields, his sole battle honour. Xanthippus had added both Marathon and Salamis – Athenian hoplites and a fleet of ships. The last was a simple scene from home. It was a good likeness of Xanthippus, Pericles thought. The carved figure was shaking hands with his family, saying goodbye. Pericles touched the polished face of his father and took comfort from it. His own image was not as good, but then he had not been there for the sculptor. Xanthippus and Ariphron had made him who he was, for better or worse.

'Thank you both,' Pericles said. 'For everything you did.'

He prayed for the souls of both men, head bowed. When he straightened, he felt lighter. He filled his lungs, tasting the air.

'I am the last of us,' he said. 'Watch me and keep me safe. I will not let you down.'

He patted the tomb. The sun was setting and he smiled as he turned away.

Pausanias frowned as he understood the ephors were not listening. He stood on the acropolis of Sparta, the sacred heart. The mountains that looked on around them were those of his childhood and all the generations before. He was at peace there, but also afraid. He knew how ruthless his people could be – how hard they had to be. They allowed no weakness, no failure. Athens sent failed men into exile; Sparta killed them. He knew that, as he had known from the moment he had heard his Persian prisoners had been allowed to escape.

CONN IGGULDEN

'If you censure me, if you hold me accountable for this, you are doing the work of the Athenians,' he said again. Why would they not understand? 'This is their plot – or they gave their blessing to it. None of the others would move without Aristides approving it. No, the Athenians made those Persians disappear. Perhaps they killed them and buried the bodies in the hills of Cypros; it does not matter. They knew suspicion would fall on me, that I would be forced to return home and speak in my defence. Even in the weeks I've been gone, the Athenians have had Cypros to themselves. An island won under my leadership, the second of the victories I was promised.'

The eldest of the ephors had campaigned in Ionia, retiring decades before. He had to have been eighty and it showed in the strange dark marks on his skin, the wattled throat, the sinews that made him seem as if he were built from wire, with skin stretched over all the rest. He wore a robe that left one shoulder bare and ended at his thighs. Only a pair of sandals protected his feet from stones. Axinos had fought for Sparta for forty years and knew more about the traditions and laws than anyone alive. The other ephors would follow his lead and so it was to him that Pausanias appealed. Axinos detested the Athenians as much as anyone. He had railed against them when they'd blackmailed Sparta into entering the war, threatening to give their fleet to the Great King. Spartans like Axinos did not forget that sort of wound, Pausanias knew. He depended on the old man's hate. He did not look away when Axinos turned and stared at him.

'Persians corrupt whatever they touch,' Axinos said. 'With their love of gold and pleasure. With soft flesh and promises. Did they turn you, Pausanias? Did they stuff your mouth with gold?'

'You were like a father to me, Axinos. You know they did not.'

'I know nothing of the kind. We gave you the fleet – and we told you to blunt the authority of Athens with it, to lead this alliance of theirs that makes sheep strong enough to scorn the wolf. Yet you stand before us, saying they have beaten you.'

Pausanias began to speak again and the ephor raised his flat palm, going on.

'Either you were corrupted by Persia and conspired to save the prisoners for some gain – power or wealth, nothing that matters. Or you did not see how they could be used against you. Either way, you have failed, Pausanias. You say there were five victories promised to you. That is a lie. They were promised to Tisamenus. Go from here and make ready. When it is time, we will send word.'

Pausanias knelt, knowing better than to speak again, though his stomach dropped away at the words. An ache began in his chest, some combination of rage and grief. Should he have run? Not returned to Sparta at all? The world was big enough to lose a man, surely? Yet he was the victor of Plataea! He had thought they would not throw that great victory on the fire. He shook his head as he came outside and saw Tisamenus waiting for him.

'They wouldn't listen,' Pausanias said, numb.

Tisamenus paled as he understood. He knew as well as most what it meant. Though he had not been born a Spartan, he had come to know them. He admired them above all peoples, but they were cold in a way he could still barely comprehend. One thing stood above all – obedience. If the ephors had turned against him, all the words in the world were just wind.

Pausanias walked as if in a daze, his life in rags. He had

gone up that hill to the meeting house of the ephors as one who had been regent to a king, as a veteran and leader. Men had greeted him with smiles as they recognised him, taking his hand if he let them. He came down as a shadow, abandoned by his people.

'Is there *nothing* that can be done?' Tisamenus said. 'Can't you appeal to the king?'

'I imagine he is delighted to be rid of me,' Pausanias said with some bitterness. 'He won't interfere, even if he could. No, the ephors have authority in this, in peacetime.'

'There has to be a chance! You saved them, every one of them. They can't just ignore that.'

Pausanias felt coldness settle on him. Tisamenus was his friend and companion, a Spartan citizen by adoption, with the rights of any man born there. Yet he was not one of them, not in the bone, where it mattered. He stopped, rather than stumble on.

'It was always a slim hope, Tisamenus. I knew that. The Athenians found the right knife to twist, that's all. They knew us well enough to find it – the constant suspicion here, the watching. Accusations ruin a man, my friend, especially in Sparta, where all men look to see who has grown weak. To be as we are requires that eternal vigilance, but it can be used against us . . . against me.'

'So they will throw away all you have done for them, for the city, because of an accusation?'

Pausanias nodded.

'I'd hoped . . . Yes, it seems that is exactly what they will do. They allow no weakness. Death cleans the slate. I'm sorry, Tisamenus.'

To his surprise, Tisamenus grabbed him by both arms, muttering urgently.

'Perhaps I have known too many Athenians,' Tisamenus

said. 'But if they are going to kill you, why not fight? Why not *run*?'

Pausanias broke his grip with some gentleness, touched by the other man's outrage on his behalf.

'If I do, they will have taken my honour as well. Can you understand? My life is nothing. I spent it at Plataea. My reputation remains. I have a son who has entered the agoge. How would he fare? My mother still lives! She would die of shame. I have cousins too who would spit every time they passed my grave – unmarked if I die in such a way.' He saw confusion still in Tisamenus and he sighed. 'They did not have to tell me not to run, because I would never run. If the ephors order me to take my life, I will do it. I am a Spartan, Tisamenus . . . and yet . . .' His voice fell to a whisper, barely sound at all. 'And yet, I confess I am afraid.'

Tisamenus could see Pausanias was trembling, in the grip of powerful emotions. He was like a wounded dog, his eyes wide. It was a kind of horror to see it in his friend.

'There are different ways to fight, Pausanias,' he said firmly. 'You cannot draw your sword, I understand that. But you cannot just go meekly to your death the moment they come for you! Can we delay the judgement? Appeal to King Pleistarchus or King Leotychides? Or some public vote?'

He saw Pausanias was listening. His heart beat faster.

'The ephors will not enter sacred ground,' Pausanias said, 'not if I claim sanctuary. No, don't look up like that! It is . . . madness, Tisamenus. It will not change their decision, only delay it. Yet . . . perhaps the kings might intervene then.'

'If there is a chance, no matter how small, they owe you that much. For Plataea.'

Pausanias shook his head like a twitch, his expression one of agony.

'You don't know what they will say. My blood is nothing, but my word, my obedience . . . you don't know!'

'There is a temple just there, Pausanias! Enter it and save your life.'

'At the expense of my honour,' Pausanias said bleakly. 'No. I can't do it.'

'Until we have tried everything there is to try,' Tisamenus said. 'Your life too has value, to me.'

Pausanias looked at him, feeling the world crashing around his ears. After an age, he nodded. The little building was barely twenty paces from where they stood. Pausanias remembered it was known as the Brazen House, a shrine to Athena.

The temple was small, as befitted a goddess not much honoured in Sparta. From one side to the other it was barely the length of two men. There was only one arch to enter and a single lamp within. Yet a boy stood gaping there, come to refill the oil. By his bearing and frame, he was a Spartan rather than a helot slave. Pausanias wondered what he had done wrong to be given that work.

'Kurios?' the boy said in confusion. The peace of his evening had been disturbed and he did not know what to say.

'I claim sanctuary,' Pausanias said. 'Leave us.'

The boy scuttled off, leaving his pot of oil behind. He would be whipped for that in the morning, Pausanias thought. He felt a weight settle on him as silence returned. Nothing would be the same again, he could feel it. Nothing. Yet there was one thing left to do.

'You must not be found here,' he said to Tisamenus.

'I am not accused! The law protects me still, if it means anything at all,' Tisamenus said.

Pausanias shook his head. On such a night, after all he had heard, he was not sure.

'Go quickly – perhaps you can find ears to hear you. I will remain here and I will pray. If nothing else, it will give me another day. Thank you for that.'

They embraced and Tisamenus rushed away into the gloom. Left alone, Pausanias looked around at the small temple, its golden panels so polished he could see himself in them. With a single step across its threshold, it had become his prison.

19

Pericles was dusty and a little tired by the time he reached his family home outside the city. He had to wait to be admitted, as the new wall was tall and well made. When the gate opened, he and Epikleos strode in, halting at the edge of a cloister that stretched along one entire side of the house like a porch. The red tiled roof was held up on carved columns in stone. Pericles was admiring the work when he heard a shriek within the house. He and Epikleos smiled as his mother came out. Epikleos in particular beamed, as if he had brought Pericles from the earth and air.

Pericles had expected grief – and there were signs of that in the dark robe his mother wore. His sister Eleni was at her own home inside the city wall. She had married a merchant with a fifth share in three ships and seemed happy. He nodded and smiled at his mother, as words and then tears poured out of her. He looked for some sign of Thetis, but he could not see her.

Manias came next out of the kitchens and took Pericles by the hand, embracing him.

'I'm sorry about your father. He was a great man,' Manias said. A crease appeared between his eyes as he looked Pericles over, seeing something that gave him pause. 'You've grown up. By the gods, lad, I remember playing the Minotaur for you and carrying you around the back field! To see you standing there so tall and scarred . . . I wish he could have seen it.'

Agariste looked again at the thin and dusty young man who had come home. Pericles waved away her worries.

'There was some fighting on Cypros. Just my calf – and a cut here, on my collarbone. I had a good physician. It's all mending well. I'll tell you about it.'

To his surprise, Manias patted him on the shoulder.

'I didn't mean wounds, though I'm glad they are healing. I meant . . . you're no longer a boy.'

'What choice did I have, as the seasons turn?' Pericles said lightly. He did not quite understand and so made a joke of it. In reply, Manias only smiled strangely and stood aside.

Thetis had appeared in the shadow of the cloister, her steps echoing on the wooden deck. She was looking flushed, a smear of grime on her forehead as she wiped the back of a hand. Her hair was piled high, drawn away from her neck and pinned erratically, so that strands flicked this way and that. She wore a short tunic of dark blue that ended above her knees, more suited to a man's style than a woman's. Still, she had good legs. Pericles felt himself smile, the expression quite beyond his control. He had imagined his triumphant return on more than a few occasions while at sea. Kissing her hard had featured in his dreaming, but not seeing her in the guise of a stable hand, bright with sweat and what looked like horse shit.

He and his wife looked at one another for a moment of breathless silence. He was only vaguely aware of his mother flushing and looking away from that intimacy – then glancing back, touched by memories and pain.

Thetis ran to him and for a moment, it was all as Pericles had imagined. His wife wept at his sudden appearance, pressing her lips to his jaw and throat. It was clear she had come from the stable, but he delighted in it, crushing her to him with new strength and making her gasp.

'Not too hard!' she whispered. 'You'll hurt the child.'

The world breathed out, set under glass. Even the air

became still as he leaned back and looked at a woman he did not know, but would be mother to his child. For an instant, a small voice deep in him wondered if it could be Cimon's, but the timing was wrong. The oath-taking on Delos had been at least a month before the marriage. No, the child was his – he'd sown his seed four times on the wedding night, after all.

Pericles realised he had been standing and staring for too long.

'Do they know?' he whispered.

She shook her head, pressing her lips to his neck.

'I waited to tell you first.'

That pleased him as much as the news. Thetis was his wife, loyal only to him. He needed to know she was on his side before all others, even his own mother. Wonderingly, he put his hand on her womb, feeling the slight swell there beneath the tunic.

'It looks like you will be a grandmother at last,' Pericles said to his mother. 'If it is a boy, I'll name him Xanthippus.'

Agariste stood as if struck, her eyes wide as she looked at the way his hand rested and back to her son's face. At forty years of age, the word did not seem to fit her. With a visible effort, she came forward to embrace her son.

'Your father would have loved to hear that,' she said. 'We'll throw a feast tonight, Pericles, to welcome you home. I'll invite all the neighbours, all our friends. To celebrate your safe return.'

Pericles noticed his mother had not congratulated Thetis and he found himself frowning.

'Perhaps it could be a marriage feast as well, mother. There was no time before.'

'That would be wonderful!' Thetis said.

Something in her voice seemed to snag his mother like a fish hook. Her eyes flickered and Pericles looked from one to the other, trying to understand what was happening. Thetis was older than him and had been married before, perhaps that was it. He realised there was more than a little tension between the two women, though they were both trying hard to hide it. That had to be a good thing, at least. If they both loved him, that was a bond of sorts. He could build from that.

'Of course,' his mother said after just a little too long. 'Thetis has been a blessing to the house. She has organised all our lives, Pericles – putting everything right that was wrong before.'

'I hope I have not overstepped,' Thetis said. 'I've just never had a home of my own.'

Pericles embraced her once more, leaving his mother's smile to freeze unseen.

'Well, you have now,' he told his wife. He took her hands in his and pressed her to him, cheek to cheek. 'You'll have our child here,' he murmured into her shoulder, 'with the best midwives in Athens in attendance. You are mistress of this estate, after all.'

'I thought so. It's like a dream,' Thetis said.

When she opened her eyes and found Agariste staring, Thetis smiled even wider.

'Come, there is a new bathing room I would like to show you,' Thetis said to her husband.

Her intent was unmistakable, as obvious as the flush of triumph on her cheeks. Pericles mumbled some excuse, smiling like an idiot as she took him by the hand and led him into his family house.

Agariste stood in silence, with Manias and Epikleos.

'Manias?' she said at last. 'Send runners out for tonight. It's short notice, but we'll want to make a show. I'm sure you can round up a few names in the city.'

As her servant bowed and left, Epikleos cleared his throat. Agariste was still a beautiful woman, much younger than the husband she had lost. She seemed to have grown tighter with age, as if time had sanded away spare flesh. At rest, she looked a dozen years younger than she was. Only when she smiled or frowned could the finest web of wrinkles be seen. Even so, she looked weary that afternoon. He wondered how much of that was from entertaining a younger woman in her house for months.

'I was going to take Pericles into the city, to the theatre this evening,' he said. 'There are some people I would like him to meet, who knew his father.'

He left it at that. Agariste knew him well enough to guess he wanted an invitation for them. She waved a hand.

'Ask them here, Epikleos. While we still can. Let us fill this house with light and life – and wine. I think, yes, wine would be a very good idea. My son is home!'

Lamps were lit all over the family estate. It looked very fine in the evening gloom. The destruction once wreaked by Persian soldiers was nowhere in evidence. Every burned beam and broken tile had been replaced, every fence remade. His mother had brought old wealth to her marriage to Xanthippus, tying an ancient name to one who was then a rising young Athenian. Their trust and hopes in that union had not been misplaced. Xanthippus had gone on to be the first name in Athens: archon, strategos – and a politician capable of conceiving the alliance of Delos.

Epikleos had intended to ask only four or five of those he knew best. That number had grown to thirty, then sixty, then two hundred over the course of an afternoon. He was forced to send messenger after messenger out to the estate to ask if another dozen or an extra thirty might possibly be made welcome. In those moments, Epikleos was pleased he was not in Agariste's presence to hear her response. All he actually received were polite words spoken in formal reply and given to the same messengers. As the day fled, their expressions retained something like amusement or awe, but still the numbers grew. Half the slaves of the house had been sent into the city to purchase food and wine, spreading the news even further as they gossiped and boasted. Epikleos was suddenly more popular than he had ever been as archons and strategoi of years past sent representatives to bribe him. By sunset, he had paid his rent two years ahead and secured his own personal supply of wine from the island of Thera – renowned for the quality of its vines and fine, volcanic earth.

By the time Epikleos himself arrived at the gate, the estate grounds were packed and music could be heard on the evening air. He blinked at the sheer number of people in view, worrying that he had been too generous with his promises. For himself, he stood in the company of two friends he wanted Pericles to meet – and one he could not refuse, who had asked to be introduced to the son of Xanthippus.

Epikleos and his little group were welcomed and directed along a lit path to a great open feast. No room in the house could have accommodated so many. Instead, Agariste had procured oak and marble tables in a huge array, along with every couch, cushion, blanket and chair from the rooms within. A thousand platters held meat and bread, olives, figs, honey cakes and sliced sausage, all while twin boars turned slowly over a firepit at each end of the field, tended and basted by her family staff. There was noise and laughter and some dancing – it looked like a joyous occasion.

Epikleos stared guiltily at all the guests, though it melted at the expressions of pleasure on their faces. The year may have been turning, but the breeze was gentle and the sky looked clear. The gods smiled on them, or perhaps their host.

Wine-bearers sought them out, moving like hunters through the crowd, appearing with clean cups in their hands, one held between each finger like a handful of tulips. With a flourish, they passed them out, filled them, bowed and moved on. 'One-in-three', Epikleos noted: a third red wine mixed with two-thirds spring water. As he took a deep swallow, Pericles himself came out of the crowd.

It was the simplest mark of respect that the host himself should greet favoured guests. It raised Epikleos in the eyes of his three companions, which brought a sense of relief.

'Kurios,' Epikleos said formally, 'I would like you meet my friends. This gentleman is Anaxagoras of Ionia, a visitor to our city, though I understand he has applied to become a citizen.'

Anaxagoras bowed deeply. He was both tall and very spare. His frame looked like poles draped with cloth as he folded and unfolded.

'You are welcome in my home, Anaxagoras,' Pericles said. 'The blessing of the gods on you.'

'It does seem likely,' Anaxagoras replied.

Pericles blinked at the odd response, but Epikleos was already pushing another forward.

'Zeno is another wild swan, Pericles. He found his way to Athens from Megale Hellas – one of our seed cities there.'

Zeno was around Pericles' own age, though he wore a strange robe gathered in great folds and belted. He looked Greek to Pericles, but with a prominent nose and slightly bulging eyes, as if he widened them to see everything. Even as Pericles spoke, Zeno was glancing around at the movements of the crowd, an expression of delight on his face.

'You are welcome in my home, Zeno,' Pericles said. 'I have not yet sailed to the new cities in the west. Were you close to Rome?'

Zeno stopped moving like a bird and focused completely on Pericles. Whatever he saw seemed to satisfy him, so that he nodded.

'I lived some way to the south, in the Nea Polis. Rome has thrown aside her kings and nobles, kurios, did you hear that? Our influence, I think. Perhaps they saw how we rejected our tyrants! They have begun a republic, where people elect those in power. Athens has taught much, though perhaps there is still as much to learn.'

He patted Pericles on the arm and swept past, raising his now empty cup to be refilled.

The last of the three men was the least strange, in some ways. Pericles had not overlooked him in the presence of such odd birds as Anaxagoras and Zeno. His single glance had told him he faced an Athenian of his own class, beard trimmed, curling hair receding, skin oiled and with a simple clasp of polished silver holding a chiton robe. Pericles had not missed the significance of the introductions, however. For all his pleasure in the pair of foreigners, Epikleos had kept this man to last.

Pericles was younger. On his own property, he might still have insisted on a guest bowing first. Instead, he picked up the signals Epikleos had given him and bowed deeply to the older man, giving him the honour.

'Pericles,' Epikleos said, 'it is my privilege to present Aeschylus, the master – the greatest playwright in Athens.'

'Epikleos is too generous. It is my honour,' Aeschylus said. There was something like awe shining in his eyes. 'I knew your father. I stood with Xanthippus at Marathon – and with Epikleos here, who held the line with me. We were certain

CONN IGGULDEN

we would not come home. I remember it as if it were yesterday! He must have mentioned it? Perhaps he saw my brother die. I never managed to speak to your father about it, but you knew the great man better than I. If you have time, I would love to hear anything you might recall.'

Epikleos cleared his throat.

'Now, now. Pericles is the host, Aeschylus. I'm sure he has a dozen places he must be . . .'

Pericles flicked a glance at his father's oldest friend, a man who had practically raised him for vital years of his youth. Once again, he looked past the words themselves and understood. He felt his throat tighten in inexplicable grief.

'No, I would like to talk of him,' Pericles said. The party was his responsibility, but it was early yet and his mother and Thetis had it in control.

'There are rooms free inside,' Pericles said after a moment's consideration. 'Dark for the moment, but let me fetch some lamps – and an amphora or two. Come, Aeschylus. I know my father loved your work. I went myself to see your *Niobe*. When she spoke, at last, having remained silent so long! I think we held our breath. It was . . . wonderful.'

'What lines did you like?' Aeschylus said.

Pericles looked aside for just a beat. When he raised his head and quoted aloud, Aeschylus staggered as if he had been struck.

'"A god makes fault to grow in mortals, when minded to ruin their estate. Men must abstain from rash words – and nurse what small happiness the gods allow."'

Pericles did not see Aeschylus whisper the last words along with him. He smiled, pleased to have been able to recall the lines, quite unaware of the effect on his audience.

'Come, gentlemen. You are welcome in my home. Let me repay some part of that day. In my father's honour, let us talk and drink, until we are blind and mute and helpless as children.'

Pausanias stood at the single entrance to the temple, the place his people called the Brazen House. It was nowhere near as large as the temple to Apollo, nor those of Zeus or Ares. Only the shrine to Dionysus was smaller, a god the Spartans accepted but could never love. Athena at least was a warrior – defender of home and hearth. Women came to whisper to her as they suffered pangs of childbirth. Few others did. Pausanias regretted the choice, though it had merely been chance which stone arch was closest when he made his decision to disobey.

Word had already spread. The hill of the acropolis was busier that morning than it might have been and he was certain he was the cause. No one actually spoke to him or called his name, but half of those who climbed the hill seemed to do so to stare at the one who had been regent to the battle king of Sparta, the victor of Plataea, now refusing the will of the ephors. In a single act, Pausanias knew he risked not only his life, but his reputation, his family honour. Every hour that passed brought home the appalling choice he had made. Obedience lay at the heart of the Spartan code! When the ephors had told him to go home and make ready, they had not sent soldiers to make sure he did. The idea that he might not accept their authority over him was simply impossible. Yet there he was.

Pausanias could only stand in the shadow of the stone arch, looking out in silence as he saw one of the ephors make the climb to confirm with his own eyes that it was true. The sun rose and spilled warmth across the hill. Pausanias thought of names of the past and knew they would all be frowning. Lycurgus, who had set the laws and said all men should eat together. Leonidas, who had held the pass at Thermopylae when no one else could – and sowed doubt in the heart of the Persian war machine.

The gawkers seemed to vanish for a time, as if they had been told to keep away. Pausanias felt his mouth grow dry as he waited. Tisamenus would have made his case, of course. He would have explained how the schemes of the Athenians had undermined him, not any flaw of his own. Pausanias prayed to Athena they would hear him. Though it seemed oddly blasphemous to stand in her place and whisper to another, he prayed to Apollo as well, his patron god, even to Ares, who had surely stood with him at Plataea and Cypros. It was a priestess of Apollo who had promised five victories to Tisamenus. Pausanias had brought two of them into the world, proving the god's will. Was he not due some recompense for that?

The sky was a blue he remembered from childhood. It might have been pleasant if his fate hadn't hung in a balance he could not see. When he heard footsteps, he almost forgot himself and stepped out of the Brazen House to see who it was. He halted in the last instant. He was safe only while he remained on sacred ground. If the ephors found him outside, they could snatch him up.

He folded his arms when he saw who it was. The battle king of Sparta had walked up from the city to see him. Pausanias swallowed painfully and folded his arms. The young man walked well, loping along like a leopard. Powerful of frame and lightly bearded, Pleistarchus was the son of Leonidas and it showed. The young king was second in Sparta that day – in peacetime. In war, Pleistarchus would be first and no man would gainsay his word. Still, he carried power with him and Pausanias knew his fate was being decided.

The king stopped at the archway into the temple, careful not to cross the threshold that gave Pausanias his sanctuary. For a beat, he merely looked into the eyes of the other man.

'I am sorry to see you so reduced,' Pleistarchus said. 'When your friend came to me, I could hardly believe it was true.'

Pausanias swallowed again, his mouth and lips dry enough to crack.

'It was all I could think to do,' he said. 'The ephors cared nothing for the injustice I have suffered, Majesty. I swear on my honour I have neither conspired with Persians, nor taken gold for the release of those prisoners.'

'You think honour is served by hiding in there?' Pleistarchus said. 'One of your own captains came home with tales of disaster. Whatever went on in Cypros . . .'

'Majesty, please!' Pausanias said, daring to interrupt though it shamed him. 'The Athenians . . .'

'The Athenians outwitted you!' Pleistarchus said. 'Or bought you, or betrayed you. I suppose we'll never know.'

'I swear . . .' Pausanias began in desperation.

The young king seemed suddenly weary as he raised a hand to halt the words. Yet his eyes glittered, in something like triumph.

'None of that matters now. The ephors made their judgement as one voice, in all their wisdom. As they did with me . . . when you took my army to Plataea and I remained behind.'

Pausanias heard the words with a hollow feeling, as if his legs could no longer hold him. He knew the young king resented him for that victory. Yet if he had not chosen sanctuary, he would already have been killed. His choice had won him a few hours, though if it was at the expense of his memory, his dignity . . . He made himself breathe. He had lost everything.

'Let me go into exile,' Pausanias said.

He waited, hope like a knife in his chest, until King Pleistarchus shook his head.

'I cannot. Not now. The ephors speak with the will of the

gods. You have insulted them. Even now, there are voices calling for you to be dragged out of this place and torn to pieces by the people. Only the wrath of Athena holds them back, Pausanias. No, if you have any honour left, I suggest you take a blade and put it into your heart. That is all that waits for you. Here, I will give you my own.'

Having the young king hold out his own kopis was a step too far for Pausanias. He felt anger kindle in him, though he took the blade.

'I don't think I will, Majesty, no. I see it would please you to have me gone. I may yet disappoint you.'

'Nothing you could do would disappoint me now, Pausanias. You are already dead.'

'I wonder,' Pausanias went on, growing heated in his anger. 'I have friends still, who served with me. Crews loyal to me. Spartans who formed the square with me. Perhaps I will ask them to come and bring me out.'

The young king stood still and Pausanias could see he trembled with great emotion. If Pleistarchus had kept a weapon, Pausanias wondered if he would have struck him with it. This was the son of Leonidas, who would never win a battle like Plataea. Still, Pausanias could have kicked himself for challenging the younger man. He could have bitten his tongue for saying such things aloud, but he could not take it back.

Pleistarchus nodded as if he had confirmed something to his satisfaction.

'The judgement of the ephors was clearly correct,' he said. 'At first, I worried some great error had been made. I see the gods still speak through them, in their wisdom. I do not think we will meet again, Pausanias.'

The king turned on his heel and walked back down the hill. Pausanias stared after him, left utterly alone. He was thirsty and hungry and sick with all that he had done.

20

Pericles groaned. Everything hurt. When he opened his eyes it felt like someone was stabbing him in the brain. Where was he? He had a vague memory of singing as he marched . . . marched? His head was throbbing in time to his heartbeat. Someone was groaning and he really hoped it wasn't him.

There was a wooden bench under him, polished and oiled. The end of it was carved like a dolphin. Pericles looked at the creature's cheerful expression for a time, running his hand over the shape. He knew where he had seen such a thing before, where he had seen a thousand benches of exactly that sort. It just didn't go with any of his memories.

The groan sounded again and this time he was sure it was someone else. Pericles raised his head as a pile of old robes unfolded and a man sat up. Anaxagoras. The name returned to him, along with a flood of memory. They had talked for hours with Zeno and Aeschylus – Pericles remembered enjoying the torrent of ideas. A prickling sense of worry stole over him as he looked around. He *was* in the theatre, with rows stretching around him in a vast arc and the Acropolis at his back. The sky was open and he felt very small and insignificant, lying there. Someone had been sick down his chiton robe. He had no memory of that. His left hand appeared to be fondling a wineskin that still gurgled as he held the leather. It smelled very sour, unless that was just his breath.

'I need to bathe,' Anaxagoras announced. 'Come. Zeno is in the fountain.'

CONN IGGULDEN

Pericles felt a jolt at that. His vision cleared and he rose to his feet, gripping the dolphin's head to keep himself steady.

'Has he drowned?' he demanded.

Anaxagoras peered over his shoulder. There was a stage there. On it, there was indeed a large fountain with a man draped inside. One leg pointed in the air and the other remained invisible inside the bowl.

'I don't think so,' Anaxagoras said. 'There is no water. It is all . . .' he waved a hand, 'a palace in Persia, not real. You know?'

Pericles blinked slowly. The world was steadying with every deep breath and he realised two things, that he stank horribly and that he was hungry. He touched his forehead and felt a bruise and swelling there.

'Was I . . . in a fight?' he said.

Anaxagoras shrugged, a gesture that looked like branches moving, as if he had more than the usual set of shoulders under his robe.

'Not real . . . You and Zeno used the blunt swords. You said something about showing the little bastard what Athenian training could do.'

There was merriment in Anaxagoras, and Pericles smiled and winced as he felt a split lip.

'I take it I did not win,' he said.

'Zeno is very fast. Like a viper. He fell off the stage, though, and he had to drink a whole skin of uncut wine as punishment. Hence, the fountain.'

'I remember that!' Pericles said in delight. 'Fetch him out, would you, Anaxagoras? The city wall is . . . over there, to the south. The river runs just outside and I am going to put my head in. There should be a tavern as well, close by the Itonian gate. My father used to favour it for its fried fish.'

He and Anaxagoras both heard his stomach rumble at the idea. Pericles grinned.

'They call to me, or my stomach to them, I don't know. Will it be open this early, do you think?'

'It is almost noon, so yes, I imagine it will be open,' Anaxagoras said.

They both turned at the sound of swearing and grunting from the fountain. Zeno managed to shove himself over the edge, though part of it came away in his grip. He stood in confusion, holding a great piece of painted wood that was clearly not a fountain at all.

'Where is Aeschylus?' Pericles said suddenly, looking around. 'And Epikleos?'

'Aeschylus went to his rooms to fetch his latest work,' Anaxagoras said. 'I remember that, as the sun came up. I must have dozed off afterwards. Epikleos prefers to sleep in his own bed. If he's not here, he'll be there – a street or two away.'

On the stage, Zeno looked around, a thoughtful expression on his face.

'Why am I in a fountain, Pericles? As a punishment, or reward?'

'Reward,' Pericles called firmly. A memory returned of marching into the city with wineskins and torches held aloft. There had been around a dozen of them, though the rest had slunk home in the morning light. Only Anaxagoras and Zeno remained, but he realised with pleasure that he thought of them as friends.

'We are going to put our heads in the river and then go for fried fish,' Anaxagoras said. 'In that order.'

Zeno rose to his full height, which impressed no one. With elaborate care, he placed the broken rim of the fountain into its bowl and backed away.

'Good. I need to walk, to clear my head. It has swollen twice its size since I slept.' Anaxagoras began to speak and he

CONN IGGULDEN

held up his hand. 'Don't try to tell me it isn't. I can feel the weight. I'm barely holding it up as it is. Come on, perhaps cold water will reduce it to the dimensions of men.'

As they left, Pericles looked back. From the viewpoint of the stage, the theatron seats rose, row upon row, with all the great Acropolis behind, a mountain of limestone with broken temples on its crest. There were some who wanted those sacred ruins left as a reminder of the Persian invasion. Yet nothing stood still in Athens. Teetering walls had to be pulled down with hooks and made safe, while loose stones were stolen and used in the city below. There would be workers sitting with a little meat and bread up there, enjoying a rest from their labours. Around him, he saw strange, painted ladders and racks of skene panels that could be drawn across to turn a simple stage into a meadow, or a fortress or a ship at sea.

Pericles had sat in those seats with his father and twelve thousand Athenians, the memory clear in his mind. He had never made his exit through the stage itself, out into the city beyond. He smiled. His father was gone and that was raw in him still, but he had found something he loved. He could feel it, a sort of wonder. He had never stood and looked *out* before. Athena loved her sons, without a doubt. He could feel the future, unless it was some effect of the wine and too much light. He was the son of an archon and strategos – and he had survived military service. To ever dream of leading the people of Athens, he had to be known to them. He smiled at the thought. He really was home.

The little group sat at a table in a room so packed and bustling they could hardly hear one another. With wet hair, Pericles felt more alert. One ear seemed to have blocked up with his dip in the river. At intervals, he tapped that side of his head with the heel of one hand.

The seats along the wall had come free all together when another group had stood to leave. Only the determination of Anaxagoras and Zeno had won the place over a group of dusty potters. They glowered nearby, forced to stand as they ate and drank.

The kapeleion by the city wall was thick with the smells of sweat, food and old wine. Flustered male and female servers shoved through the lunch rush, taking orders and carrying dishes in precarious structures, six or seven at a time. Pericles had already ordered the fried fish. Three platters had arrived in golden splendour, stacked high – along with a stoppered amphora, mixing bowls, two jugs and a collection of clay cups. Broken vessels much like them crunched underfoot.

As he had to lean away from a jabbing elbow in the crowd, Pericles was shoved right up against the wall. It was a long way from the music and polite laughter of a symposium. One heavy-set man just a pace away was describing a fight he'd had with a rival brickmaker. The fellow had a humorous style and spoke loudly and with a lot of laughter. It was hard not to be drawn in, so that half the customers in earshot chuckled as he described his opponent's impotent fury.

'He wasn't half my size, I swear. It would have been like hitting an angry boy . . .'

Zeno glowered at that, attending to his plate of food.

'. . . but then he came at me, all swinging arms – and he looked so red and puffed up, I started to laugh, so my strength just disappeared. It was all I could do to hold him off and the more I laughed, the angrier he got.' The man chuckled again in memory and half the crowd smiled.

Pericles was feeling better after his dip in the river and the fish. He chewed idly, wondering how to broach the idea he'd had – from earlier, or perhaps the night before, he was no longer certain.

CONN IGGULDEN

'*There* you are!' said a voice he knew.

Epikleos came through the crowd, Aeschylus close behind him. Epikleos was unaware of the brickmaker telling the story and oblivious to the way he'd eased right through the admiring audience and called out over the final line. He and Aeschylus turned their backs to the red-faced man as they pressed up against the table. Epikleos snatched up a piece of fried fish and chewed.

'You want to watch yourself,' the brickmaker growled.

Epikleos heard but ignored him. Aeschylus glanced back and took in the man's wide shoulders and heavy jaw. He shrugged.

'I have an offer for you, Pericles. Is there room to sit?'

As he spoke, Epikleos spotted a stool coming free and snagged it with his foot, pulling it over for the other man.

'I *said*, you should watch where you're going,' the stranger said a little louder.

Epikleos and Aeschylus turned around in the same beat of time. Pericles, Zeno and Anaxagoras rose as one, though they stood jammed up against the wall with a heavy table blocking them. Anaxagoras had to stand hunched over, his great head touching a beam.

Without hesitating, Epikleos jabbed the bigger man in the throat with two outstretched fingers. It was a nasty, painful little move, more scorn than anything. The brickmaker raised a hand to his neck and gaped at them. Before he could reply, Aeschylus suddenly reached out and gripped the man's beard in his left hand. With his right, he hammered a blow across the brickmaker's astonished face, knocking him down.

The noise of the crowd died away. Pericles waited to see if anyone else would move. The man who had fallen had friends, but it wasn't clear how many. One of them raised an open palm in soundless fury, grasping for Aeschylus. In reply,

Epikleos drew and laid a knife along the man's armpit. The arm remained outstretched and everyone froze.

'Why don't you take your friend outside for some air?' Epikleos said. His expression was pitiless as the man's gaze turned slowly to him.

The brickmaker had been stunned by the blow, but he was making angry noises and trying to rise to his feet. His friend glanced down and a nasty little smile crossed his face.

'You're brave when there's a crowd of you,' he said. 'Or punching a man who isn't expecting it. Let's see how you do when my mate gets up.'

The owner of the kapeleion was yelling for them all to get out. Conversations were starting up in the crowd as those with no interest tried to finish their food and drink and get back to earning a few coins for their families. Yet there were another three or four men alongside the one Epikleos held at bay. They were taking a keen interest in the developments and, like the one Aeschylus had knocked down, they were a crew of brickmakers, dusty and hard.

Pericles swallowed. Men had died for a lot less than this in Athens. He tapped his belt, but he didn't wear the kopis Cimon had given him. He hadn't taken a weapon of war with him into the city. In truth, a brawl that ended up with mortal wounds brought its own problems, even if he escaped without a scratch. A scandal like that could see an end to his career before it had truly begun. The thought brought words to his lips and he spoke.

'Shame on you for threatening veterans of Marathon and Salamis!' Pericles said.

The eyes of the crowd flickered to him and the builders frowned in sudden confusion.

'We came here to eat and talk business, not brawl!' Pericles went on. 'Aeschylus here stood at Marathon, in the line.

CONN IGGULDEN

Epikleos marched with him. Both of them walked a deck at Salamis and killed Persians. I saw it all, gentlemen. I was too young and I was left to guard my family. I watched a Persian fleet boarded and rammed and burned. That was war, lads. Not some pushing in a tavern. Put that knife away, Epikleos. Aeschylus – apologise to the man you struck.'

Pericles pointed his finger at the brickmaker. The man had made it back to his feet and stood like a bull, listening and swaying.

'I'll buy your wine, but that's all you'll get from us,' Pericles told him firmly. 'Go on your way, before good men lose their lives.'

He finished loudly enough to carry to all those present. There was a beat of silence and then pockets of laughter as tension broke. Pericles flushed, but Epikleos put away his knife.

'Who's the pup?' the builder said, rubbing his jaw where Aeschylus had struck him.

'The son of Xanthippus,' Epikleos said.

Silence spread across that part of the tavern once again, this time with all humour absent. The man stopped rubbing his chin and went pale. He stepped forward and Epikleos almost drew again before he understood no violence was being offered.

'Truly? You are his boy? Archon Xanthippus was a great man. If you are his son, I will take your hand and swear peace.'

'What is your name?' Pericles asked. He had seen the same light in the expressions of men who had served with his father, in Aeschylus himself. It made him uncomfortable and proud in equal parts, like strong wine.

'Talanas of Leontis, kurios. I was part of your father's fleet. I fought at Salamis.'

He put out his hand and Pericles took it. Even compared

to his own sword calluses, it was a great rough glove. The fingers closed over his own with casual strength.

The man eyed Aeschylus as he spoke.

'You too? You served with his father?'

'I did,' Aeschylus said.

'Then I'll count it an honour to have been knocked down by you. You are quick to anger, my friend. That makes more sense now.'

Aeschylus nodded, though he remained wary. The noise of the crowd had returned around them, with muttering and pointing fingers.

'There was, er . . . some talk of your buying our wine for us,' Talanas said.

Pericles sighed. His stomach had only just begun to settle. He raised his hand for a server to bring more cups.

Pausanias watched the sun touch mountains he had known all his life. The sight meant he was truly home. He had run those slopes a thousand times. He had made himself strong and lean and fast for all the years of training, the famous discipline that beat and hardened until flesh was oak and every bone was iron. More, he had learned to lead others, so that he had not failed at Plataea. Facing a great storm, he had not faltered. He was a Spartan. He breathed out, watching the way the sun smeared streamers of purple and gold across hills he loved.

Footsteps broke his reverie and he felt his heart beat faster when he saw it was Tisamenus striding up the path from the city. Was it good news or bad that they had allowed his friend to return? Pausanias could not decide. Tisamenus did not look happy and he felt his own mood darken as he read the future in his expression.

'I'm sorry,' Tisamenus said as he halted by the arch to the

Brazen House. 'The ephors have voted. They won't let you walk away. I asked both kings to intervene. The son of Leonidas is pleased it's come to this, I think. Pleistarchus could hardly hide his satisfaction. King Leotychides just said it was a matter for the ephors. He washed his hands in front of me.'

Pausanias nodded.

'Will they allow you to bring me water? Food? If I can survive a few weeks, I might yet appeal.'

As he spoke, it sounded hopeless, but he had no other choice. Even if Tisamenus had brought fast horses, there was still a wall across the isthmus, guarded by Spartan soldiers. No one could enter or leave the Peloponnese without permission, not that year. He wondered if he had a chance to reach the city of Argos. Surely there would be ships there that might take him away . . . ?

Tisamenus seemed to guess at his thoughts.

'They say no one is allowed to help you. Anyone who does will earn the same verdict. I . . . don't know what to say. It was like talking to a block, with all of them. As if they could not even hear me. I wanted to do something, to make them change their decision, but I . . . I couldn't.'

Pausanias reached out beyond the boundary of the little temple. Tisamenus took his hand, gripping hard.

'I've seen a few things, Tisamenus,' Pausanias said. 'I'm only sorry I didn't get to give you the rest of your victories.'

'Don't talk like that,' Tisamenus replied.

Pausanias shook his head.

'No, it's all right. I feel the peace of it, now I know there are no other choices.'

They stood, separated by the boundary of the temple, almost as life and death. Tisamenus opened his mouth and then closed it, unable to speak. They both turned as a second set of footsteps sounded. Pausanias squinted into the setting sun and then his eyes widened.

'Is that . . . ?' He smiled suddenly, his expression making him look like a boy again.

His mother was very old and she made hard going of the slope. Tisamenus went to help her, but she raised a hand to hold him off. He looked at her in confusion, but she had no eyes for him, only for Pausanias.

'Thank you for coming,' Pausanias said.

Of all those who lived, she meant the most to him. All his hurts and hopes had been spoken to her. Theano had known him as a child and when she looked on him, perhaps he was one still. Though her hair was white and she was bowed with age, the resemblance was clear. Tisamenus stepped back as Theano approached the temple. She reached into a bag at her waist and he wondered if she had dared the wrath of the ephors to give her son a little wine or bread.

Instead, the old woman drew out a single brick. With care, she laid it across the opening of the archway. Pausanias paled further, his skin like wax.

'Unworthy to be a Spartan . . .' she said, 'you are not my son.'

Behind her, a line of people were walking up the hill. Most carried stones; others stirred jars of lime mortar. A dozen Spartan soldiers walked alongside them. They were not men Pausanias knew, though he searched their faces. He thought they were the personal guard of Pleistarchus, men who had been left behind as he marched to Plataea.

One of them waved back the old woman and called up a group of builders with their trowels and aprons. They had come to complete the wall, to seal him in.

Pausanias crumpled, overcome.

'Go down, mother. Don't watch this.'

CONN IGGULDEN

Theano of Sparta turned, trembling, walking away from her son. Behind her, the builders set heavy stones in place, slopping mortar across each one. A thick wall rose, filling the arch and closing him up inside.

Tisamenus was forced to move back, though he kept his gaze on Pausanias as long as he could, until the stones rose and blocked his sight. When the wall was finished and the crowd began to make their way down, Tisamenus saw the soldiers would remain, standing guard. They had their eyes on him as they took positions, like statues before the temple. It took all his courage to step closer and put his ear to the wall.

'Pausanias?' he called. 'It seems to me the Athenians are responsible. They brought this about. Well, I'm owed three victories still. If the gods are kind, at least one of them will see Athens broken. Can you hear me? I swear it.'

There was no reply. After a time, he went down the hill.

2 1

A month had flown, bringing a week of rain and even a night of snow across Athens as winter deepened. Despite the frost, the theatre was busy as a hive. Four different playwrights had found choregoi patrons for the festival the following spring – sixteen plays between them. Each company demanded as many hours as they could get on the single stage. Musicians practised new tunes in discordant competition. Scenery painters found themselves negotiating with carpenters from another set. Different choruses came to blows as they fought for space to practise. The festival of Dionysus gave employment to a great number of Athenians. Perhaps some of them might even remember that and be grateful to their patrons for the rest of their lives.

High in the arc of wooden seats, Pericles looked down. He shook his head in awe as he tried to count the number of men working in that place. There had to be hundreds – and the vast sums Aeschylus said were needed made a little more sense. Pericles reminded himself it was an honour to be chosen as choregos for a playwright who had already won the great spring festival once. Only the famous Phrynichus had won it more often and he was approaching the end of his career, his honours all behind. Pericles was no longer sure whether it had been his idea or Aeschylus'. Either way, Aeschylus was the future and even an investment of four thousand drachms was surely not too much.

He tried not to think about it. Each day, new bills arrived at the estate. He had given his word to Aeschylus and so they

CONN IGGULDEN

had to be honoured. Neither his mother nor his wife seemed delighted to see so much silver flowing away from the family coffers. Thetis in particular insisted on checking every bill and sending runners to query the amounts. She didn't understand the damage it did, the embarrassment she caused him. Whenever he objected, Thetis just folded her arms and said they would rob him blind if she let them. Pericles bit his lip at the thought. The two women were very different, but in that one thing – that single, forbidding expression – he sometimes found it hard to tell them apart.

He cheered up at the thought of the child growing. Women changed when they were pregnant, as he understood it. Perhaps when the child was born, if all went well – he touched the wooden bench for luck – his wife would once more become the playful woman he had married.

He found he was chewing the inside of one lip as he thought. Thetis was already showing her pregnancy. She began most days heaving weakly into a bowl. Her feet had swollen and she complained about their hurting every time he saw her. One of the house slaves had the job of rubbing them at the end of each day, though it did not seem to improve her mood. She was always hot or irritated – and Pericles was the most common target of her wrath.

Though he would not have admitted it, Pericles was actually quite pleased to vanish into the city each morning, away from her complaints. For a woman who had known poverty, Thetis had certainly adjusted well to having slaves wait on her. Only Manias was immune as he had been freed and took a wage of his own. It did not stop her trying to order him about, however. The man himself had not said a word. No, it was Pericles' own mother who had intervened on his behalf – and that had led to another huge argument. Pericles was thankful Thetis had demanded a bedroom to herself, frankly.

There was a breeze off the Acropolis. Pericles rubbed a spot on his temple where an ache was developing. He was not unknown in Athens, he understood that much. Having Xanthippus for a father meant crowds stood in awe when they heard his name. At times, Pericles wondered if his father had even known how revered he was.

Pericles had wagered a good part of his family's wealth on the festival of Dionysus because Aeschylus too had known his father – and because it was his duty to do so. A noble son served Athens with a ship or a play, or service in war. It was true he had fought on Cypros, but that was far across the Aegean, where even sailors and fishing crews of Athens rarely ventured. When Pericles stood on the Pnyx hill and listened to the debates, or joined a jury to sit in judgement, he sensed he was still not yet a name, not as his father had been. No one whispered or pointed when he walked through the city. Winning the festival would put his name in every mouth, the victorious plays discussed for months or years after. Pericles was certain they were good, even great, but nothing was guaranteed, not against a man like Phrynichus. For all his arrogance and bulk, he was a master of the stage. In his cups, Aeschylus would admit he too wasn't sure they could beat him.

The playwright himself appeared down below, coming from the single-storey building of the back stage. With sheafs of papyrus crushed between arm and chest, Aeschylus was gesticulating, explaining something to a crew around him.

Pericles stood and walked down the aisle in the open air. Aeschylus went back inside for a moment, then appeared at the top of the ladder that led to the flat roof. There, gods could appear, lit with lamps from below so that their masks would gleam with eerie power. Aeschylus helped a stocky, bearded young man up to the platform then showed him how to stand, declaiming lines. He was to play the ghost of King Darius, Pericles recalled. The fellow's voice carried well, echoing across that vast space.

Pericles reached the bottom of the seats and stepped onto the stage itself, hearing his sandals click-clack on the wood. There was excitement there, he could feel it. In the bustle of scenery panels being carried past, in ropes and gilded armour – in the words themselves, as they rang out.

On either side of the stage, low buildings of tile, wood and canvas had been raised. Actors could appear and vanish into those wings, changing costumes and masks as the script demanded. Pericles heard them coming before he saw his friends appear. He grinned at the sight of Zeno holding forth, one finger raised as he described something to the others. Anaxagoras was already red, though with laughter or frustration, Pericles did not yet know.

Epikleos smiled as he caught sight of Pericles, seeming to understand instantly why he stood with a dreamlike expression, at peace in that place.

'Pericles! You have to hear the new pages!' Epikleos called. 'They are magnificent.'

They came together as a group on the stage, taking hands and offering wry comments in greeting. Aeschylus gave up his instruction when he understood his choregos was present. He bustled down the ladder of gods and joined them, searching in his sheaves for the pages he wanted.

'This, Pericles,' he said. 'I wrote it last night. What do you think?'

'Phrynichus will chew his own beard hearing it,' Epikleos added with a grin.

'You've read the new scenes?' Pericles said.

Epikleos nodded.

'They're good. You'll see. Aeschylus has to be favourite now.'

Pericles began to read the lines, murmuring them aloud to hear the rhythm and metre of each phrase. Aeschylus was good enough to have a chance at winning. His talent was a prodigy, but this . . . was like nothing Pericles had ever read. There had been only one play set in actual history performed at the Dionysus festival. The crowd had hated it and the judges had fined the playwright a whole talent of silver – a sum to beggar even a wealthy choregos.

'Xerxes: Cry out in response to my cries,' he read. 'The chorus wails aloud.'

'He is home, in rags,' Aeschylus said, his eyes gleaming with some inner light. 'He stands before the crowd a broken man. This is the climax, Pericles, the final lines! His father has come and gone as a ghost. Oh, you must read that part as well. His mother has been told of all her son has lost. I have named half of Persia and, at the end, he is finished . . . just the chorus left, and Xerxes, Great King of Persia, alone on stage. He begins a line and they answer him, as if he cannot finish it alone. Back and forth, back and forth. I tell you, that fat fool Phrynichus has nothing like this. Read on, read on . . .'

Pericles spoke the next lines aloud.

Chorus: Ai! We walk on sharp stones.
Xerxes: The triple-oared –
Chorus: – ships destroyed us!

Pericles paused, a sense of awe stealing over him. He was speaking with the voice of a Persian king. He knew an Athenian crowd would love every line. This was written for the victors of Salamis!

'And he *slumps*,' Aeschylus said in excitement, tapping the air with his fingers clenched to a point like a bird's beak. 'The

CONN IGGULDEN

actor shows defeat in every line as he says, "Escort me now to my palace." It should be delivered with despair. One by one, the lamps are extinguished . . . and darkness falls.'

Pericles looked up from the papyrus.

'It is wonderful. You're sure, though? Half the audience will have been at Salamis or Plataea. The benches are made from wrecked Persian ships! It's so recent. All the other plays are about gods and legends. I hear Phrynichus is working on some tale of the Fates.'

'If he is, he will not do it well,' Aeschylus said with a sneer. 'The man is a street-corner rhymer, not a playwright. This? This is all our lives, remade in this place. I swear, Pericles, the lines poured out like wine, like song, as if I had no say in them. I was guided by an unseen hand – and the crowd will be with us.'

'And the judges!' Anaxagoras added drily. 'The ones who actually award the prize? They are the ones you have to move, Aeschylus, not the crowd.'

Aeschylus smiled and shook his head.

'You are wrong, my friend. If I can speak to the crowd, if I can stop the breath in their throats and make their hearts beat just a little faster . . . If they care for the characters I write, if they love them . . . it does not matter what the judges think. Not to me.'

He spoke with rare passion and Pericles wondered if a set of plays could win the crowd and still lose the festival of Dionysus. It was not a pleasant thought.

'But we will *try* to win the judges as well, Aeschylus?'

The man had ink on his fingers, Pericles saw, deep-stained as if the marks might not ever be removed. He hoped there were no prints left behind when Aeschylus clapped him on the shoulders, on a new white chiton robe.

'We will. I've heard Phrynichus has some dry set. His

comedy is always well observed, but his legends and trage-dies are weak things – and he has *nothing* as good as this.' Aeschylus took back the precious sheet Pericles had read. 'I will spin a scene in a Persian court and it will be real.'

'What is reality, after all?' Zeno murmured.

Aeschylus nodded.

'Yes. Well, *yes*! Because there is no greater story than real life. Let fat Phrynichus try to match this!'

Beyond the theatre, a swell rose almost like the sound of the sea. Laughter ceased as they turned to it and it only grew. Cheering and song alike sounded to the south, louder every moment.

'What *is* that?' Anaxagoras asked the Athenians around him.

Pericles swallowed. Perhaps because he had been waiting for that moment for months, he knew immediately what the sound meant. He had left a great deal behind on Cypros – his innocence and some of his blood. Returning in a single ship to Athens had kept the worlds apart. Here, he was a chore-gos of the festival, heir to a noble family, son of an Athenian hero. Over there, where oarsmen and hoplites raised their voices in rhythm, he could almost smell the sea on the air. There, he was something else.

'It is the fleet,' Pericles said softly. The tall man glanced at him, wondering at his strange tone. 'The fleet has come home.'

It was the habit of local urchins to accept an obol coin for news when they had it. They raced through wealthier demes to carry news, relying on speed and energy to get there first. As the group left the theatre and went out into the street, Aeschylus spotted one of them. He whistled and raised an obol in his fingers. The boy came for it like a fish after a hook. To prevent him vanishing, Aeschylus took hold of his tunic in the same moment.

'Well?' Aeschylus said.

CONN IGGULDEN

The boy grinned at him, already trying to wriggle free.

'Ships in the Piraeus,' he said. '*Hundreds* of them.'

Aeschylus turned to Pericles, but the boy was not finished.

'Cimon has come home, kurios. Word is he's brought back the bones of Theseus, that anyone can touch them.'

Aeschylus let him go and the boy raced off, calling he had news to anyone willing to pay. The playwright might have spoken then, but they all heard a rattle of drums and a blare of horns coming closer along the street. That was a sound Aeschylus knew only too well and he closed his mouth on whatever he had been about to say, his expression tight.

Anaxagoras and Zeno groaned. Pericles looked past them, tapping one hand on his thigh. He wanted to go to the Agora and see Cimon. It was the right thing to do, if only to bask in the reflected light of that particular sun. He had earned his place at Cimon's right hand, after all. Instead, he watched the enormous figure of Phrynichus approach.

The playwright was surrounded by twenty or thirty men and women. Some of them carried little drums under one arm, rattling out rhythms to raise the pulse. Others made long metal tubes wail discordant notes. It stopped everything else going on in that street by the theatre. Passers-by gaped or smiled. Some waved their hats.

Phrynichus came to a halt like a warship snubbing on an anchor. He was a large man, standing a head taller than Pericles, though at least Anaxagoras could look down on him. Yet his bulk strained the seams of his robe, giving him the sort of weight that was hard to stop – and strange in Athens.

'Ah, Aeschylus,' Phrynichus said.

He leaned close, as if smelling the breath of anyone he addressed. Pericles wondered if his eyes were weak.

'Phrynichus,' Aeschylus responded. 'You know I have not yet used all my time. The theatre is mine for at least another hour. The city council will confirm, if you wish.'

'Oh, I don't mind waiting, dear fellow. My little troupe can amuse themselves watching your rehearsals, if you wish. All I ask is a quiet seat to write my lines. Honestly, I can make verse anywhere.'

Aeschylus glowered at the playwright. He had been intending to head over to the Agora to see Cimon come back, perhaps even to get a glimpse of the bones of Theseus. The noise was still rising nearby and half the city would be flooding over to see what was happening. Instead, Aeschylus found himself unwilling to quit the field to a competitor. It was childish and beneath him, but there was something about the smooth-cheeked playwright that rubbed him the wrong way.

'How are your plays coming, Aeschylus?' Phrynichus went on. 'I've made the most wonderful progress in the last few weeks. Two are finished – or abandoned, if you like.'

He laughed at his own joke and Pericles found himself smiling in embarrassment. The tension was thick in the air. Aeschylus had come out into the street to leave. Only his stubbornness kept him there.

'I have finished one,' Aeschylus said stiffly. 'I have the plot of another and a third in notes. My satyr comedy will come last, of course. I don't like to waste my time with those.'

'Yes, I've seen your work,' Phrynichus said lightly. There was a moment of chill in the street then. Phrynichus flushed, his colour deepening.

'I meant your strengths lie more in the noble emotions, Aeschylus – in fear and sorrow and rage. Yet comedy is as hard to write as love, I find, or even harder. Now, I see you gentlemen are dressed for the road. Are you leaving? I am happy to begin my rehearsal. I have my chorus with me.'

CONN IGGULDEN

Pericles wondered if the man had planned the encounter. Aeschylus said he paid spies to watch all the rehearsals and rewrites of his competitors. The stakes could not have been higher, after all. Reputations would be made or broken in the spring, both of the playwrights themselves – and whichever poor fools had produced the plays and spent a fortune doing it.

'Go on, Phrynichus,' Aeschylus said. 'I don't suppose an hour will make a difference by the spring. The stage is yours today.'

There was a glitter in the eyes of the other man, though Phrynichus bowed his thanks and swept past. His drummers began again as they entered the theatre and went through to the stage beyond, out into the light.

'Yours today, but mine for ever,' Aeschylus muttered.

Pericles found himself chuckling with the others as they joined the crowd heading to the Agora and the returning crews of the fleet.

22

As well as the great market, the Agora was where news was put up, nailed to boards attached to statues of the ten tribes. Laws could be read there – or a declaration of war. The council building too opened on to the heart of the city, with elected officials bustling about at all hours.

The Persians had burned Athens to the ground, but the city was made new, with oiled beams and dressed stones and bright tiles. There was something in the air, a beginning, a place of youth and ambition, supported by merchants and warships. No other city had a navy like theirs – nor the flood of silver to pay so many crews. Rowers spent their pay in Athens and, at the same time, trade deals were struck, bringing in fortunes and goods never seen before. At sea, Athenian warships established safe passage for alliance merchants right through the season. The results showed in new wealth and influence – in power.

Pericles was not prepared for the sheer noise that day. He and the others trotted around a corner onto the Agora and sound crashed over them like a wave. Athens alone had crews from two hundred ships – almost forty thousand men. The city was much quieter without them, but they did not sail in winter. It seemed Cimon had brought them all home, with their pay. The Agora was packed with singing or cheering sailors – and their women, come to greet them. Pericles glanced down an alley as he reached the rear of the crowd and looked away guiltily at what he saw going on down there. They had silver coins and they had been a long time at sea.

He could smell fried fish and fennel on the air, garlic, mint, a host of scents. Pericles imagined Athens would look like a different kind of storm had blown through in the morning.

When he looked behind, the road was filled with running people, all coming to see. Pericles saw Anaxagoras grab hold of Zeno before he was carried away with them, like a fish in a current.

'Come on,' Pericles said. He was the youngest there and the least worried about pressing into a vast crowd. He could smell the sea in that place, the healthy sweat of men and the damp reek of ships. It was in their clothes and beards, he realised, brought home with them.

With a laugh, he plunged in, winding his way through gaps, trusting the others to follow. The mood of those they passed was light enough at first, so that they gave way without too much shoving and only a few shouts falling behind. Pericles found himself grinning. Whether it was the odd rictus that plagued him at times of fear and strain or genuine humour, he was not quite certain, but it served to ease the hard looks directed at him. As he went further, more than one sly hand grabbed at his chiton, taking a grip on the cloth to hold him still. Pericles reacted with a twist and a yank, moving on before whoever it was could ready himself for violence.

The strangest part was to see so many women there. Perhaps it explained the simmering anger in the crowd, as men sought to protect loved ones or their whores. There were even children present, held high on the shoulders of fathers or brothers. Pericles found there was a knack to passing those. A quick tap on a shoulder made them turn, allowing him to dart through the gap.

He felt like a trout finding its way upstream, though he doubted any trout had ever had such a hard time of it. He was bruised by elbows and stamping feet, even a blow to the back of his head that was as much a cuff as a real attempt to hurt. It seemed to take an age to cross the Agora, but he found himself at last on the edge of the council building, the bouleuterion. It was the heart, where the crowd was so crammed together he could not see any gaps at all. Those he had passed still grumbled and heaved behind him, like a swell of the sea as they pushed forward or eased back. Zeno was blocked by two or three sunburned sailors, determined not to let anyone else get by. Anaxagoras and Epikleos were pulling at him, but the sailors just stared ahead, pretending not to see. There was no sign of Aeschylus. Pericles hoped he had not fallen underfoot. A crowd so packed in was a dangerous place.

Cimon stood on the raised section of new white stone, looking tanned and healthy. A dozen senior trierarchs were on either side of him, like an honour guard of captains. Pericles was pleased when Anaxagoras and Epikleos dragged Zeno through. A glance showed only furious faces behind, so that he pushed Zeno ahead and sheltered him.

There were hoplites too on the steps of the council building, their armour gleaming gold. Cimon wore a simple robe and Pericles wondered if he had considered how the crowd would see him. He felt a spike of envy at the sight of his friend smiling as he looked over the packed Agora. This was how reputations were made. Pericles did not know if it had been a consideration in displaying the bones of Theseus, but the results could be seen in the way the crowd craned their necks and chanted his name. Pericles frowned to himself. He too had been there to find the great Athenian king. He should be up with Cimon, accepting the acclaim of the people.

Aeschylus appeared at his side as if he had been spat out, looking even more tousled and battered than Zeno. The playwright's eye was swelling closed and he lifted part of his

CONN IGGULDEN

chiton where the seam had ripped, blinking at it. Pericles might have laughed at the state of him if he hadn't been comparing his lot with that of Cimon.

Cimon's father had also been a strategos and archon of Athens, leading men to victory at Marathon. More, Cimon was a successful battle leader in his own right. Cypros would be a jewel for Greece, a huge new island in a sea of smaller ones. Pericles shook his head. Being choregos for a play in the festival of Dionysus did not seem quite as grand as it had that morning, not in comparison. He wondered again if he had backed the right horse.

He had not stopped watching for opportunity. As the crowd moved on unseen tides, Pericles suddenly shoved Zeno through to the very front, where the crowd was held back by Scythian guards. Those men were clearly uncomfortable in the presence of that heaving mass, so that Pericles saw them resting hands on sword hilts. The foreign guards were not popular in Athens, though he supposed it was better than employing their own to control the rowdy Assembly. Scythians were the ones who gathered reluctant juries with a red rope dipped in paint, so that Athenians had to run ahead or be marked. They were a nomadic people, Pericles recalled, from somewhere far to the east. He wondered if they would be part of the Persian empire, if they had stayed at home instead of wandering. It was a strange thought.

'I *said* . . . where are the bones?' Aeschylus roared in his ear, making him flinch.

Pericles honestly hadn't heard him the first time. The crowd were all either chanting or singing and it merged into the sound of the sea.

'I don't *know*!' he yelled back.

He had begun to regret struggling across the Agora – for what? To watch Cimon made a hero? Yet when he was close enough to read his friend's expression, there was something sad or bitter in it. Pericles felt a fool. He remembered Cimon's father, Miltiades, coming home in triumph. Pericles had been just a child, but the early memory was seared into him. Cimon had seen his father cheered as a saviour of Athens, then destroyed.

The shadow of that showed on Cimon's face, Pericles was certain. Miltiades had gone out again and been ambushed by Persian forces. He'd lost all the goodwill he'd won, returning to Athens a wounded and broken man. Pericles' own father had stood as his accuser, forcing the family to pay a vast sum in recompense. The way Pericles heard it, half the fleet had been built with that fine.

Perhaps those memories explained why Cimon looked so dark, while others sang with the crowd, or directed a flow of wine into their mouths. Pericles stood very still, thinking of their fathers. It made him a knot in the ebb and flow and Cimon sensed it and glanced over, seeing him. Pericles saw him point, shouting into the ear of a hoplite so that the man went down the steps, gesturing briskly. The Scythians did not like it, of course, but they stood aside, bristling at the crowd in case anyone else dared take advantage.

Pericles slapped Epikleos on the shoulder and went up the steps. He stood in awed silence as he looked out over the heads of his people.

'You look well, my friend,' Cimon shouted. 'Marriage has been kind to you.'

The right words seemed to come effortlessly to him. Pericles only nodded. He felt like an awkward youth in Cimon's presence, but he was delighted to have been called up. He could see the crowd swirling in eddies of colour and noise. The great Acropolis was always there as the backdrop of the city, along with the Pnyx and the Areopagus – and the other hills of Athens. He remembered what Aristides had said about learning to love the alliance – all Hellenes, not just the crowds of home. In that moment, as they began to sing 'Athena', it seemed a very distant dream.

Hidden from the view of the crowd, a bier lay behind Cimon, deep in the shadow of the cloister and its columns. Pericles could guess which figure lay beneath the golden cloth from the length of it. A bronze helmet sat atop the figure, with a new crest and a deep polish so that it gleamed gold. Cimon saw his glance.

'Theseus,' he confirmed. 'You were there when I found him. You should share in this.'

Pericles smiled his thanks, though he felt a slight tightening around his eyes. It seemed it would be Cimon alone who had 'found' Theseus and brought him home. Anyone else had merely been present. He found he was not quite as delighted as before.

Pericles looked out over the people as Cimon raised his hands and silence began to come. It took a long time, but they stood at last in stillness, with only murmurs and laughter breaking out in places.

'I give thanks to Athena this day, for her blessings on her chosen people,' Cimon called across their heads. He waited until a great roar had died away before going on. 'I give thanks too for the *symmachia* – the alliance that brought Cypros back to us, for the fleet that patrols the sea and keeps us safe, and merchants honest.'

That last brought a ripple of laughter. Pericles looked at him in surprise. Cimon had come alive, somehow, speaking to the crowd as if to friends. Most men trembled and sweated when they were called to address others. Few enjoyed it, but it seemed Cimon was one of them. He tried to be pleased for his friend.

'You know we have been fortunate enough to find the

tomb of Theseus, king and founder of this city, friend of Heracles, Argonaut, slayer of the Minotaur – son of Poseidon. Sailor.'

The last word brought a great roar from half the crowd, making Pericles start. Cimon grinned.

'I present his bones to the people of Athens, asking only that they be honoured as a son of this city. We have come home. He has come home.'

There was no point speaking again for a time, not after that. Cimon patted the air, but they were in a fine mood. Some of them began to chant 'Archon' and he blushed. When the noise died down at last, he addressed them once more.

'My crews are home until spring. Our ships and our men are somewhat worn and they'll want to see their wives and their families. Those of you who wish to pay your respects to Theseus may enter after you are dismissed. Now, stand *straight*, Athenians!'

He said the last as a bark of sound, though he smiled. Pericles saw thousands of burly rowers in that crowd suddenly put their feet together and their arms by their sides, standing tall with their chests out at his order.

'Go in peace,' Cimon called over their heads. 'You are *dismissed*! See the dockmaster for winter work, or any pay outstanding.'

They waved hats and cheered again, even more lustily than before. The Scythians let the first ones through, allowing them to walk in awe past the bones of Theseus. Pericles saw them reach out and touch the cloth, patting what lay beneath. Part of the crowd pressed to be let through, with Scythians glowering at anyone who tarried too long. As many wandered away, the tension vanishing. Pericles could only stare. He'd thought they had come to see Cimon or the bones, but it seemed it had been a more formal dismissal. There were different kinds of theatre, he realised.

Aeschylus and Epikleos remained, with Anaxagoras and Zeno behind them. Pericles pointed them out to Cimon as they came through.

'Epikleos you know, of course,' Pericles said, summoning him forward.

Cimon seemed to understand how to speak to each man, gripping hands and saying a few words that brought forth smiles. Zeno and Anaxagoras were both included. Cimon staged a bow to Aeschylus when he heard the name.

'I know you, of course, kurios,' he said. 'I look forward to hearing your latest work. I hope Pericles here is as generous with his funds as he should be – "trierarchia" is a noble idea. Theatre and warships – what else is there?'

Aeschylus stammered and chuckled.

'Y-yes, I have said . . . I have said the same thing!'

Cimon laughed and clapped the older man on the shoulder. As far as Pericles could see, Aeschylus did not take the slightest offence.

'Come,' Cimon said. 'Let me show you a king.'

Their eyes widened as he gestured to the wrapped figure. The Scythians held back the crowd to give Cimon room with his guests.

Draped in cloth, the bones looked more like a man lying there than they had in the tomb, wound about by threadlike roots. Pericles could almost imagine the ancient Athenian leaping up from where he slept.

He and the others gathered around the bier, looking down. Cimon nodded to two hoplites standing guard. One took up the helmet and the other unwrapped the cloth with infinite care, revealing bones that had been cleaned and polished, the

THE LION

colour of old pine. Around them, a hundred voices sighed in awe.

'I have asked to be heard on the Pnyx tomorrow,' Cimon said. 'It would be fitting for the city to pay for a statue and a proper tomb, perhaps on the Acropolis, where Theseus had his palace. Your father, Pericles, said he would support such a thing. If not, I will pay for it myself.'

'They won't refuse you,' Epikleos said. 'I think you could ask just about anything of them today.'

'Perhaps,' Cimon said. His voice had tightened and Pericles wondered again if he was remembering old wounds. He shook himself and smiled when he saw Pericles was staring.

'Aristides has some feast planned for tonight. If your friends would like to come, I would be honoured to have them as my guests. The day is still young, though. I'd like to pay my respects at your father's tomb, Pericles, if that's all right with you.'

Pericles felt his mouth open in surprise. He had been thinking of Cimon as a rival. All that fell away in a moment.

'That is . . . kind of you. Thank you. I'd be honoured.'

The others seemed to understand it was time for them to leave. One by one, they took a final look at the bones of Theseus, then went down the steps. Aeschylus was the last to go.

'Reverence for parents is a noble thing,' he said. 'I am glad you have come home, strategos. If there is a vote to appoint you as archon, I will lend my support.'

Cimon bowed his head and the playwright turned away. Pericles watched him go. More than half the mob had drifted into the city. Some still waited to see the bones of Theseus, but not many. His people looked forward, not back. He followed Cimon out into the winter sunlight, shivering as a breeze found its way through the thinning crowd.

He frowned when he saw Epikleos returning, the older

CONN IGGULDEN

man trotting to the foot of the steps. The Scythians watched him come, ready to bar his way.

'Pericles!' Epikleos called. He looked relieved to see him still there. 'Your wife has come.'

Pericles felt a sour knot form in his gut, as if he had drunk too much wine or eaten too quickly. He was one man at home, another in the outer world. Or perhaps it was just that he knew men learned something about him when he was with his wife, something he might usually have guarded and kept private. It was a clash of worlds and he tried not to show dismay as he thanked Epikleos.

Thetis had not come alone, of course. Neither her new status as the wife of a noble family nor her particular condition would have allowed that. Women who married into the Eupatridae did not push through crowds of drunk sailors fresh from the fleet. No, she had brought a dozen slaves from the estate. Manias was white-haired and too old for the role she had given him, but a free man was needed in that retinue. Slaves would defend the mistress of the house, of course, but they could be knocked aside by any hoplite or guard.

Pericles looked on in silent fury as his wife made her way across the emptying Agora. Thetis had brought a horse with her, though she walked then. She knew very well what her duties were, as his wife and a member of her class. Regardless of her past, her life was at the estate, not parading herself around the city like a poor woman. He'd thought she understood. Her presence alone was a rebuke, a humiliation.

Cimon seemed to understand as he looked at him.

'You know . . . *my* wife didn't come into the city for me,' Cimon said.

Pericles smiled tightly, watching Thetis as she approached. The Scythians responded to some subtle sense and stepped aside so that she walked straight through. Cimon and Pericles went down the steps to her.

'It's good to see you so well,' Thetis said to Cimon. 'And you, husband.'

She kissed Pericles on both cheeks, then did the same with Cimon, raising a gloved hand to guide his chin back and forth. Her gaze lingered on him then, with a sort of fascination.

'Thetis,' Cimon said, in embarrassment. 'You know . . . we would not have found the bones without you. Would you, er . . . like to see them?'

A grimace flashed across her face. Pericles could see Thetis had not come to the Agora to look at old bones. He had the sinking feeling she had not risked the crowds for him either. Pericles had begun to pick up the pieces of their friendship, but a coldness began in his chest as he saw the way his wife looked on Cimon.

Her pregnancy was showing. Cimon paled visibly as his gaze drifted down and he understood. Pericles had to stand and simply wait while another man worked out if he was the father to a child in his wife's womb. Pericles saw Cimon relax and shook his head. The day was ruined and if he could not quite have explained his anger, it was there even so.

'You should go home, Thetis,' Pericles said. 'The city is not safe, not as you are.'

She turned her gaze on him and there was no joy in it.

'I walked the docks, Pericles, if you remember – when you were making the fleet ready. I am not a child, to be sent home.'

'I think . . .' Cimon began, visibly uncomfortable. 'I think I hear my name being called . . .'

He vanished, leaving Pericles and Thetis to hiss at one another. The Scythians could hear every word, he could see that in their carefully blank expressions.

'Go *home*,' Pericles snapped at her. 'If you don't care for your own safety, think of the child.'

'Why are you doing this?' she said. 'Is it to impress Cimon? I have Manias with me – and slaves from the house. I'm in no danger. Or would you make me a prisoner, Pericles? Is that it? Am I not to be allowed out except with your permission?'

'Well, why not?' he said furiously. 'Do you see Cimon's wife here?'

'I see some women,' Thetis said.

'Whores and market traders,' he replied, gesturing across the Agora. 'Those who have no slaves of their own.'

'I was free enough on Scyros,' she retorted. 'And before I married you.'

'Well, perhaps that is the price,' he said, clenching his jaw.

'Oh? For being raised up and made part of your precious family, was it? For having your mother sneer at me for my manners?'

'For being kept safe? For not starving or being forced to whore for other men?'

She tried to slap him, but he was too quick and knocked her hand away. He saw he had hurt her by the way she held it. Shame washed through him, mingling like acid with his anger. It corroded his certainties.

'Go home, Thetis,' he said again.

Her eyes were wide as she stared, then turned on her heel and walked off. He watched as she said a few words to Epikleos. He leaned away as if she had stung him, then rubbed his jaw. Pericles knew he would pay for it when he saw her again. He knew too that he had been harder on her than he'd meant to be. The way she'd looked at Cimon had hurt him and he did not think he would be telling her that. It had been as if only Cimon stood on that damned step, as if Pericles had not been there at all.

'Well, I'd rather be hated than ignored,' Pericles murmured to himself.

It was not a noble sentiment, but he was not in a noble mood. He looked at the bones of Theseus then and wondered what the ancient king would have done in his place. The bones were covered once more, but it was still a strange perspective. In a sudden impulse, he felt his mood turn. He resolved to apologise to his wife. Perhaps even to explain why he had felt jealous of Cimon.

He looked for the man himself, deliberately busy in conversation with one of his officers. They too had begun to head away, those who had no other duties. Pericles was known to a few of them and he acknowledged them as he approached.

'Are you . . . ready?' Cimon asked.

'Yes. I'm sorry about that.'

'I saw nothing, heard nothing,' Cimon said. 'Come, I have an amphora of wine from Cypros. I would pour some of it on your father's tomb, with your permission.'

Pericles smiled in genuine pleasure, touched by the gesture. He was not even sure where Cimon's father was buried, or if his tomb had survived the Persians and their hammers.

'I'm glad you are home,' he said. 'The city is too quiet without the fleet.'

Cimon laughed.

'As far as I'm concerned, winter months are to refit and resupply those ships, so that I can sail out in spring. I've found a way of life I love, Pericles. They'll have to kill me to take it away, I swear.'

'Even if they make you an archon?' Pericles asked. He could hear the acid in his voice, though Cimon didn't seem to.

'Even if they do. My place is at sea, my friend. Not here. I'll spend winter overseeing new keels and repairs, then I'm gone.'

CONN IGGULDEN

'Will you at least be here for the festival of Dionysus?' Pericles asked.

Cimon looked genuinely torn as he understood Pericles wanted him to see it.

'I will try, but if I'm called away . . . the alliance *works*, Pericles. It has made something new. Perhaps the Persians brought it about with their invasion, but your father had the vision. It might just be my life's work, truly.'

He saw disappointment in Pericles and gripped him on the neck.

'Come on. Show me the tomb of Xanthippus, so I can honour a great Athenian. Let me do that much. Tonight, we'll drink and eat, sing and tell stories. All right?'

Pericles nodded. Half the city would have leaped at such an invitation. He crushed down the pain and anger he felt and made himself smile. Cimon was an honourable man, he reminded himself. Perhaps it didn't matter if Thetis was in love with him.

23

The darkest day of the year was past. The mornings were still frosty before the sun rose, but there were occasional blue-skied days, promising spring. Pericles found it easier to use his father's house in Athens rather than head out to the estate each night. Beyond his duties with family holdings and the theatre, he also attended every jury and discussion in the Assembly he could. He was already well known there, with his contributions both concise and clear. He had been surprised at first that no one else made the points he thought were most useful, most relevant. Some men spoke a thousand words and said almost nothing, as if they had achieved their aim just by being heard. Pericles had begun to find satisfaction in an intense focus – in the right words and no more. It helped that he spent so many evenings arguing with Anaxagoras or Zeno. They mocked any loose thinking or ambiguity. Zeno in particular would pretend to faint if Pericles made a weak point.

That was how he explained his constant presence in the city. The others might even have believed him if they hadn't witnessed furious exchanges with his wife. Some women found the latter months of pregnancy a time of contentment and happiness. It seemed Thetis was not part of that blessed group. The morning vomiting had stopped months before, but she was always either too hot or too cold, while her back and feet ached at all hours of the day and night. Unlike a Spartan, she apparently saw no virtue in keeping that to herself. Both the estate staff and his own mother had

CONN IGGULDEN

developed a pinched look about their mouths as the pregnancy wore on.

Whatever his other concerns, Pericles threw himself into producing the set of plays that would make or break his reputation. The role of choregos was more than just a matter of paying bills. He had persuaded Aeschylus to develop the satyr comedy rather than consider it beneath him. Pericles smiled at the memory of a scene. At times, it embarrassed him how much he loved all of it – the wondrous masks that seemed so alive, even when left in heaps; the costumes that looked so real at a distance. Even the actors – the hypokritai – fascinated him. He had seen a man appear in rags as a poor messenger, vanishing into the wings to appear moments later with whitened face and pale Persian armour as the ghost of Darius, with a different voice and the stance of a king. Pericles had seen the transformation happen again and again, but it was still wondrous.

There was more, when he could admit it to himself in the quiet of the evenings. Cimon's return had shown him the importance of the festival of Dionysus. If Pericles and Aeschylus won, it would be a permanent silver coin on the scales of their lives. Men would praise Pericles for his judgement – and his name would be known across the city. He would be a discerning patron, a lucky man to have on your side. If he lost, he would be just another forgotten choregos who had backed the wrong horse.

Aeschylus was showing the strain as he struggled to write the final comedy of the set. Three serious works had come from him, plays Pericles thought were like nothing else that had ever graced a stage. The great gift had been a tale of Theseus – with an ending for the bones brought home. Aeschylus was a genius when it came to lines to move an audience to shock or tears. Making them laugh was a completely different task — and one that seemed quite beyond him. In desperation, he had asked Zeno and Anaxagoras to come up with lines. Working as a group had produced a lot of laughter, but the results were patchy to say the least.

Pericles watched the chorus sweep from one side of the stage to the other, practising the movement so they could make the audience think of spirits returned to haunt the night. In painted clay masks and black cloaks, they looked more like oil or crows than men. It was an eerie effect to have them chant a line as one, or just turn slowly to face the audience. Dark emotions came more easily than wandering about the stage with a huge phallus bobbing up and down. One of the satyrs had taken to hanging a drinking cup from his by its handle as he studied his script. That had actually made Pericles laugh and was now part of the play.

He had not lost track of the costs of the production. Both Thetis and his mother never wasted an opportunity to remind him of the pile of bills and accounts falling behind. The family fortunes had taken a battering from the years of invasion. No rents had been paid while Persians killed farmers and ate their flocks. It had taken a long time to find new tenants and let the crops come in to be sold in the city or taken out by ship. He had a new pottery style in the Ceramicus that was selling well — red on black, rather than the more traditional black on red. He had brought back a new breeding herd of ponies from the wild ones on Scyros as well. Those sold as fast as they could be weaned, to a city still desperate for pack animals.

The future looked bright enough for the generation to come, but in the meantime Pericles was forced to use silver that had been buried and hidden, the last of the family reserves. It had not helped that an entire set of clay masks had been broken. The cost of a guard would have saved

CONN IGGULDEN

them, but instead he had to employ a master potter at a huge price and short notice. Pericles suspected Phrynichus or one of his men was behind the damage, but there was no way to prove it. With a month still to go, Pericles even faced the possibility of having to visit a moneylender to bridge the gap in funds. He wondered how he could do it without half the city finding out.

He sighed as he sat and watched the satyr rehearsal. Aeschylus had not made clear that being a choregos meant keeping an entire theatre group all winter, in food and clothes and costumes and scenery, in paint and carpentry, in great riotous dinners that ended with them skidding on frozen streets or snoring in the gutter. Pericles smiled at some of the memories. It had cost him a fortune, but it had also kept him out of the house.

Phrynichus entered from the city side of the theatre, interrupting one of the satyrs as he declaimed lines. Pericles recognised the man by his bulk and was hurrying down to intercept him before Aeschylus noticed he was there. Since the destruction of the masks, the two playwrights were like rival cockerels whenever they met. A rehearsal day wasted was another one Pericles had to fund regardless. Four plays was madness, he thought, bounding down the rows of seats.

For once, it seemed Phrynichus was not there just to interfere or sneer at his competition. Pericles halted on the wooden stage as he saw Cimon too was present. The younger man strolled alongside Phrynichus, looking up at the Acropolis as they came out into the light.

'This is my stage,' Phrynichus was saying. 'Though others lay claim to it. I have a set of plays this year that are new — and extraordinary. In honour of your father, I would like to dedicate my first tragedy to him — to Miltiades of Marathon.'

Cimon said nothing, as if he had not heard. It confused the playwright, so that he frowned and bit his lip. In the same moment, Pericles came to a halt, enjoying the sight of Phrynichus fawning on a new-made archon of the city. Of course, the wealth of Cimon's family was well known. It made sense for Phrynichus to offer every courtesy to one who might be his choregos in later years.

'He would have liked that, I think,' Cimon said, after a silence that signalled no great enthusiasm. 'Ah, Pericles! I was wondering if you were free for dinner this evening. Your friend Zeno is an extraordinary fellow. Bring him along – and the tall one. We'll make a night of it.'

Pericles grinned, caught up by his friend's good cheer. He could see Phrynichus shifting from foot to foot, looking for some way to continue his part in the conversation. It made the boards creak. With a moment of pride at his own maturity, Pericles nodded to the playwright.

'I trust your rehearsals go well, Phrynichus?'

'As if the gods themselves are watching,' the man replied, instantly suspicious.

They all noticed Aeschylus spotting them at the same time, the man's sharp movement catching their attention. Phrynichus scowled. Unlike Aeschylus, he had never served as a soldier and the threat of violence brought out a furious spite in him. The approach of Aeschylus could be felt in their little group.

'Your satyr play is said to be very amusing,' Pericles went on, 'but your tragedies? I have heard they need a little work.'

'You heard . . . ? They need . . . ?' Phrynichus gaped, then turned to watch his rival approach across the stage. Without taking his eye off Aeschylus, he replied.

'They will shake the Acropolis! Master Aeschylus has nothing to match my new *Minotaur*, nor my *Narcissus*!'

CONN IGGULDEN

He turned to Cimon then, snatching an extra moment before Aeschylus reached them.

'I don't know if I have more than a year or two left in me, kurios. With the right funding ... but no, the honour is enough. Perhaps I could do more, if ...'

'Are you begging for coin?' Aeschylus demanded loudly. He actually took a grip on Phrynichus' arm and the other man yanked it away.

'I am doing *nothing* of the kind,' Phrynichus snapped, flushing as Cimon raised his eyebrows.

'If you are struggling, I could use your chorus in a few scenes,' Aeschylus went on, sticking in the knife. 'Or your satyr actors. I've heard their wooden phalluses are ... *especially* long this year. What a wonderful innovation.'

'You'll see,' Phrynichus said. 'One lucky year does not make a writer, Aeschylus. You'll understand that when the judges award me the prize.'

'No. You'll never win again,' Aeschylus said. He smiled almost in pity, though he detested the man. 'You have had your time, Phrynichus. And this rehearsal day is mine, so leave my stage.'

Phrynichus stood with his mouth open and Aeschylus waited for just a beat, before speaking again.

'No words? You had them once. My dear fellow, where did they go?'

Phrynichus spun and strode away, leaving Aeschylus to his triumph.

'What a very angry man,' he said.

'What if he does win, though?' Cimon asked seriously. 'Will he not remember what you said?'

Aeschylus shrugged.

'He won't. But if he does, I will be in mourning either way. Another blow can hardly hurt me more. And of course, if I win, my words today will be hot cinders poured on his head.' He looked embarrassed for a moment. 'I should not enjoy tweaking his nose the way I do, but there is something so very pompous about him. Oh, he has his followers. Both he and they believe he is better than he is. At times, it . . . irritates.'

Pericles saw the man's expression change as he considered whom he answered.

'Are you thinking of becoming a choregos, Archon Cimon? Perhaps next year, now that you have been elected to the Areopagus council. Pericles has learned more in these months than he could imagine. He said it has made a man of him.'

'I said nothing of the sort . . .' Pericles snorted, though Cimon only smiled.

'We serve the city in different ways. For now, my place is at sea. Archon and navarch of the alliance is more than I ever dreamed.'

Aeschylus seemed to understand that. He reached out and let Cimon take his hand in a soldier's grip. Pericles wondered how many of his friends would choose Cimon over him, or whether it was just his wife. His cheerful mood curdled at the thought.

'For now, the days are growing lighter,' Aeschylus announced, glancing at the stage and the setting sun, already falling behind the Acropolis. 'I have just enough time to go over the scene with my satyrs once more. Donkey ears! Yes, you! Where are your fucking donkey ears?'

He strode off, jabbing a finger at a hapless chorus member who had come on stage without them.

'He is better at tragedy,' Pericles observed.

Cimon laughed, amused at the antics of the satyrs on stage.

'For his sake, I hope so!'

'*Will* you be choregos to Phrynichus, do you think? He has a sponsor this year in Ephialtes, but it does not seem a happy arrangement.'

CONN IGGULDEN

Pericles found he was relieved when Cimon shook his head.

'Perhaps another time. I wanted to tell you . . .' He made a decision and went on. 'I won't be here for the festival. The fleet is refitted and packed with stores – and we need to be seen. The moment we get a run of good days, I'll be off again.' He reached out and touched a wooden beam to ward away ill luck. 'You'll be a father before I return.'

'I hope so . . . oh, you know what I mean.'

Pericles wondered if Cimon wanted him to come. The question seemed to hang in the air, but he did not say it aloud, for fear the answer might take him away. Cimon looked into the distance for a moment, as if something had taken the shine off his mood.

'Come on, Per. You don't have to watch every rehearsal, surely? Round up the others. The other night, Zeno said something about the great Achilles being unable to catch a tortoise in a foot race. Some glorious nonsense. I've been thinking about it – and I think I see the flaw. I would like to hear it again. With more wine this time, so I can understand it!'

Pericles laughed. He was one of very few who knew Cimon drank only one-in-six rather than anything stronger. Cimon had not been properly drunk since the year of his father's death, imposing an iron discipline on himself. It meant there was a serious core to him. His father's son, Pericles realised. Perhaps that was all they could ever be.

Zeno drained another cup of red wine and smiled, showing teeth that had been stained dark over the course of the evening. The little man did not have the capacity of one like Anaxagoras, who seemed able to drink and speak clearly all night, until a sudden collapse into sleep. In comparison, Zeno became drunk very quickly and lost himself in wild laughter somewhere near the bottom of a single amphora. It was still early in the evening and Pericles had gathered the group he was proud to call his friends. He noticed Aeschylus would occasionally lean under the table and scribble something with a piece of lead, but that was his way.

'Again?' Zeno said. 'Very well! Achilles sets off. Graciously, he has given our tortoise a head start, but he and the tortoise begin the race together. Perhaps with trumpets, if you can imagine it. Now, Achilles is a magnificent runner . . .'

'That is established,' Anaxagoras interrupted with a grin.

Zeno nodded.

'That . . . is *established*.'

'And the tortoise is very slow. That we all accept.'

They all nodded, a little blearily. Cimon was the sharpest there, with his well-watered wine. He was frowning.

'So . . . Achilles races away after the tortoise. In a short time, he has covered half the distance. The crowd gasps, but what is this? The tortoise has not remained still! It too has moved on. Achilles puts on a great spurt of speed. Sweat pours from his brow – and once more, he halves the distance between them. Yet once more, the tortoise has moved! You see?' Zeno looked around in triumph at the faces of the others. 'No matter how many times Achilles can halve the distance between them, he will never be able to reach that tortoise.'

'If that were true . . .' Cimon began. As he spoke, he drew curves on the tabletop in spilt wine.

'It *is* true!' Zeno said immediately.

Cimon shook his head.

'No one could catch *anyone* then! No runner could reach the one ahead, no army could advance against another and bring them to battle. There is something wrong with the way you describe it!'

'I don't think so. It's a simple fraction, when you think about it – an infinite series.'

CONN IGGULDEN

Zeno beamed at them all.

'Tell them the one about the arrow . . .' Epikleos said. 'No, the stadium! That one had me biting my own knuckles in frustration.'

He demonstrated, making Aeschylus laugh. Cimon fished a couple of beans out of a stew bowl and pushed one along the table, leaving a trail.

'Now look – if this bean is the tortoise . . .' he began.

The door to the tavern swung back, making a crowd of nearby drinkers grumble. The man who entered eyed the crowd, clearly looking for one in particular. He rushed further in when he saw the seated group, halting by Pericles and bowing to him.

'Kurios, I have been sent to say your wife is in labour. The midwife is with her.'

Pericles looked around at his friends, wide-eyed.

'Now?' he said faintly.

The man nodded, clearly impatient to be off.

'Yes, kurios.'

'You'd better go,' Cimon said with a smile. 'May the gods bless the birth, Pericles. Good luck.'

Slowly, Pericles rose to his feet. He could not quite hear the noise of the tavern. It was somehow muffled, while his thoughts came slowly. He knew he could run, which was all that mattered.

'Right then,' he said. They were all grinning, which was strange. 'I should, er . . .'

'Go! See your wife,' Aeschylus said.

As Pericles disappeared out of the door, Zeno raised his cup once more.

'Because none of us want to,' he said.

They had all met Thetis over the previous months. For a time, it seemed the funniest thing they had ever heard.

Aeschylus even wrote it down, though it would just make him frown in confusion the next morning.

Pericles was breathing hard by the time he reached the estate outside the city. He had begun to run in darkness, but grey dawn lightened the wall and gate. One of the house slaves was waiting there for him, so he did not have to bang his fist on the iron and rouse the whole household. It swung open and he hardly slowed as he went through.

From inside the building, Pericles heard a baby cry, a long wail that made him stop and pant, staring in awe. He took deep breaths, going into the house.

'Thetis?' he called.

'She is in here,' his mother replied, a great gentleness in her voice.

Pericles entered a room where Thetis lay on a bed with a child, wrapped and squalling. The midwife was there, a white-haired lady with great experience and one milk eye. She was collecting her things and putting them into a bag.

His wife's hair was tousled and damp. Pericles thought she looked a little bovine as he gazed on mother and child.

'Is it a boy?' he said.

The midwife nodded as she collected her things. The old woman patted him on the shoulder, then accepted two silver coins from his mother as she left, whispering her thanks. Thetis looked sour for some reason, as if his question had annoyed her. Yet he felt his heart lift.

'Thank Athena. Thank Hera. Thank you, Thetis! I'll name him Xanthippus – the pale horse. Look at his black hair!'

His mother, Agariste, dabbed at her eyes. For a moment, she embraced Pericles, though he stood like a post, unsure what to do next.

'Are you going to kiss your wife, then?' Agariste said, pushing him forward.

Pericles was startled into movement. He bent over Thetis, smelling blood and sweat, or the sourness of milk. He kissed her even so. The child quietened.

'The boy is well made,' his mother said. 'If the gods are kind, if he lives, he will be your heir – and mine. Heir to a long line, to archons and strategoi and advisers to kings.'

She spoke as if she wanted Thetis to understand. Whatever had passed between the two women over the course of the birth, it did not seem to have softened them. Pericles was grateful to have missed all the difficult hours.

'I thought the messenger was never going to find you,' Thetis said suddenly, her tone peevish. The baby fussed and murmured, eyes tight shut, tiny hands grasping at nothing. His son – his son!

'He did,' Pericles replied. 'I was, er . . . going through the accounts for the festival.'

'Yes, I can smell it on your breath. Was Cimon there? Did he come back with you?'

He knew she asked to hurt him, because he had not been there that night. For once, he felt no jealousy or anger. The sun had risen that spring morning and Pericles knew what that meant.

'No, Thetis. The fleet were ready to sail. Cimon has gone.'

Her expression was like a child denied honey or some sweet thing. He wondered if she would ever be slim again. He opened his mouth to ask the question, but caught himself. One barbed comment would lead to another, in spite and screeching rage. This was not the day for it. He had a son. Instead, he breathed deeply and kissed Thetis on the forehead. The infant began to wail then.

'Come, Thetis. Let me have the child. The wet nurse is waiting.'

His mother gestured and one of the house slaves entered, a Thracian woman Pericles knew had been purchased for this role. She was huge-breasted and her smock was marked in dark patches. He saw too that she was tattooed along her arms in intricate patterns of black or dark blue. The woman held out her hands, but Thetis did not pass the baby to her.

'I felt milk coming in. I can feed him,' she said.

'Ecra here can feed him,' Agariste said slowly, as if to a child. 'We'll bind your breasts and it will stop. You must run the estate, dear. *Your* estate, as you keep saying. Or do you think you can do that and feed a baby a dozen times a day? Ecra has nursed a score of children, haven't you?'

The slave nodded, flushing. The Thracian woman still stretched out her hands, somehow awkward in her need to hold the baby. The child had begun to scream again, an extraordinarily piercing sound that made Pericles wince.

'Come on, Thetis,' he said. 'Let me take him.'

Though she began to protest, he reached down and lifted the child away, feeling the weight and warmth of the dark little thing before handing his son to the slave. The Thracian took a seat in the corner of the room and lifted part of her smock up with her teeth. Pericles found he could not look away as an enormous breast flopped out, already dribbling milk. In the end, his mother stepped between them and shooed him from the room.

As he went to find something to eat, he thought he heard Thetis weeping and shook his head. Women were strange creatures, truly. To grow a child – and then actually produce *food* for a child, those were surely wonders of the earth. In the quiet of the dawn, as he chewed idly on a chicken leg he had found, he was glad his role was simpler.

24

Pericles was sitting on the lowest row of seats, reserved for archons and strategoi, as well as choregoi and the actual festival judges, each a volunteer from the tribes of the city. When shouting started backstage, he and Epikleos scrambled up and headed towards the noise of a scuffle. They had expected some sort of problem as Phrynichus and his company seemed to be in chaos. More than once, the man himself had appeared at the wrong part of the day, demanding to be allowed to rehearse and swearing vengeance on whoever was interfering with the schedule. Each time, he had been sent away with fury crackling in the air behind him. Their own rehearsals had been disrupted, and at times Pericles wondered if that had been the point. It did mean that the first sign of trouble had the whole crew converging on that spot, ready for a fight.

Anaxagoras had someone by the wrist, his free hand pushing a head right down so the man was practically bent over. Whoever it was struggled mightily until Epikleos jumped in and grabbed the other arm. The head came up then and Pericles could only stare.

He had not seen Attikos since sending him away to another ship, well-marked by a whip. He had watched every blow land with some satisfaction. Thetis had not been his then. In truth, she had not been anyone's. Yet the punishment was light for Attikos trying to force himself on a woman. On land, in peacetime, Attikos could have been tied to a board in the Agora and left to be stoned by passers-by, or until he died of thirst. Under war command, Cimon had chosen instead to flog and transfer him. It had been mercy of a sort. Pericles had not expected to see the wiry ape of a man again.

'Attikos! What are you doing here?' he asked.

Anaxagoras let go the moment he realised Pericles knew him. Epikleos held on, however, knowing rather more.

'I was turned off my ship, which I expect you knew,' Attikos said. 'Word spread I'd offended your family and no one wanted me then. Served as a rower for a while, just to live. No kind of work for a hoplite, was it? Captain turned against me and suddenly word was out and no one had a place, not for me.'

Pericles looked at the man and shrugged.

'What concern is that of mine? Oh, let him go, Epikleos. He is no threat – and he's not with Phrynichus.'

'What *concern* . . . ?' Attikos said, his lip curling. 'You *do* speak fine, don't you, son? Your father gave me work to keep you safe in the nasty old fleet, where men might try to make you their woman, or to stop foreign devils carving your liver like your brother. And I did that, didn't I? What do I get for all the care I took of his boy? Cast out, with a black mark against my name, so every man looks at me awry.'

'I *carried* you on Scyros,' Pericles snapped. 'I saved *your* life, Attikos. What did you do with it? You tried to force yourself on a woman. My wife, as she became.'

Anaxagoras turned sharply at that piece of information. Pericles waited for some sign of surprise in Attikos himself, but it did not come. Of course, he would have heard, along with the rest of the fleet.

'She wasn't your wife then – and I thought she was willing. She seemed to be. Look, that was my error, I never denied it. My stripes, on my back as well! But you took more than that

CONN IGGULDEN

from me. You took my name, my place – all I'd earned before. I'm turned out! No berth, no seat nowhere. Not even in the rowers. Turned onto the docks like a damned cripple, while Archon Cimon sails off without me. So, as you are responsible for my reduced condition, here I am.'

He looked around at the theatre building and the rows of seating beyond. Attikos sniffed and rubbed his nose.

'Looks like you have fallen on your feet, well enough. Rich as Croesus, while I starve. It seems to me you could honour your father and give me work – as a guard, perhaps. The streets are dangerous at night, everyone knows that. I'm not asking for much, just work. That's all!'

Attikos had somehow grown angrier as he spoke, so that he finished in what was almost a shout. Pericles wondered for a moment what his father would want him to do. He suspected Xanthippus would have been like a stone. He'd never had much sympathy with weaker men, or those who complained about their lot instead of just getting on and improving it. Yet he could see Attikos was very thin, more so than he remembered. He really was starving and there was a note of fear in him, beneath all the bluster. For one without family, without a good name, the city could be a hard place.

Aeschylus had come over to see what was holding up his rehearsal. Sensing the mood, he'd said nothing, but he was frowning, impatient.

'I could put him to work painting sets, or working the crane,' he said.

'No,' Pericles replied.

Aeschylus didn't know him the way he did. Attikos had not forgiven him and the man bore grudges for ever.

'There's always work in Athens,' Pericles said. 'With the potters, or carrying sand and ash on the docks, or building new homes.'

He had a tetradrachm tucked into an inner layer on his belt. With care, it would keep Attikos for a week while he looked for work. He fished it out and tossed it to him. Attikos caught it.

'That's it, is it?' Attikos said, holding up the coin. 'After all I've done for you? That's the price of your conscience? You can't even give me work? You little whoreson!'

'That's enough from you,' Anaxagoras said, dragging him off.

'Did she tell you I hadn't had my turn yet?' Attikos yelled. 'I had, though! She liked it too.'

Pericles knew it was meant to hurt. The trouble was, it did. Epikleos saw the blood drain from his face and nodded grimly, striding away. Zeno went with him. They took Attikos outside and when they returned, they were sweating, with bloody knuckles. Epikleos bore a new bruise over one eye, but he seemed cheerful. He tossed the same silver coin through the air and Pericles smiled with him, putting it back into his belt.

'*The Persians* – scene one!' Aeschylus said briskly. He pointed to one of his actors, staring at a sheet of papyrus. 'Put your mask on – and put down those notes! All lines should be learned by now. Three days before all these seats are filled – and I will not be shamed by your performance. Again, from the start!'

Pericles retired to his rooms in his father's old house, not far from the Pnyx hill. The entire street had been destroyed in the invasion, then rebuilt with all the speed and energy of his people. The new building was of oak, brick and plaster, airy and new, with a staff of six to prepare food and keep it safe from thieves while he was away.

He could not sleep. The angry visit from Attikos had stayed

with him and he'd refused the well-meaning invitations to visit a tavern with Aeschylus and the others. Epikleos in particular had been concerned at his dark mood, but Pericles needed to rest and think, more than company. Of course, he could also have returned to the estate, where his mother and wife were like two cats trapped in a sack and always yowling and scratching . . . No, he was happier in the town-house, staring at the ceiling in the dark.

The streets were very quiet in the small hours. At most, a group of drunken men might sing or laugh as they made their way home. The sound of running steps was different and it brought Pericles up to his elbows, listening intently. Attikos had not lied when he said the city could be dangerous, especially at night. The Scythian guards guaranteed the peace for cases in law or meetings of the Assembly. Beyond that, every man kept a hand on the hilt of a blade and an eye on those walking the same way. No wife or daughter went out at night without real risk. The brothels by the port plied their trade in the dark, but free women hurried home at sunset.

Pericles listened to at least two or three runners pelting down the road by his house. He tilted his head at what sounded like shouts in the distance. It was enough and he reached for a clean chiton and sandals by feel. The room was so dark he could not see his hands, but he dressed by memory, belting on a kopis blade with a grim expression. He could feel his scars as a ridge on his calf and a jagged line from his shoulder down his chest. Reminders of old pain.

Outside, more running steps could be heard. Something was happening and the slaves in his house were beginning to wake up in response. Light bloomed below and he went down the stairs. The staff looked to him to see off any threat and they opened the door to the darkness beyond, letting in the night's cold.

Pericles stepped out onto the cobbled street. In that moment, it seemed very quiet, though he could see lamps being lit in other houses nearby, spilling pools of light. He drew in a deep breath and smelled smoke.

'Athena keep us,' he whispered, looking for the source.

The city was made of wood and tile and mortar. Entire streets had become an inferno when the Persians set their fires. It had always been the fear since then, that some family would knock over a clay lamp and all their neighbours would die in their beds.

The Acropolis stood like a sentinel over the entire city, visible from all quarters. Pericles spun to face a possible threat in the dark as someone else came running. He drew his kopis and saw a man almost fall as he flinched.

'What is it?' Pericles demanded.

'Fire!' the man snapped, then swore at the one who had made him afraid.

Yet Pericles stood with his legs suddenly weak, the kopis forgotten. In looking past the retreating figure, he had seen a spark in the distance, at the foot of the great rock. Pericles had walked that road every day for months and he knew it as well as any other part of the city. The theatre. He began to run.

The city seemed to rouse around him as he closed on the strange light. From a distance, it was a living thing, moving and reflecting without a pattern. By the time he arrived, crowds were already busy all around him. They moved in panicky dashes, crying out in grief, or just standing with hands over their mouths.

Pericles went to the street entrance, where the people would be entering in just a few days to see the works of the festival, tragedies and satyr plays alike. He groaned – the fire was in the heart of the theatre building. He could see it spreading into the wings and he knew the masks were there, kept under guard. Where was the guard?

He lost his trance, knowing he would have to go in, though flames poured out and were still spreading. It was already a beast with tongues and claws, tearing up months of work. He felt hatred then, as he saw Epikleos hurry by.

'Pericles! Thank the gods. We're making a bucket chain to the river. If we can get two or three hundred of us in a line, we can bring a supply of water.'

'What about sand?' Pericles said. 'There is a builder's supply yard just over there.'

'Show me,' Epikleos said.

They pushed through the crowd and ran forty or fifty paces to a barred gate. A guard stood there with a spear, looking nervous.

'Stand back, son,' Epikleos said.

The guard tried to raise his spear, but Pericles shoved him out of the way and Epikleos kicked the gate open, breaking the main bar. Though the man cursed them, they ran in. Supplies were there, to make mortar. Pericles took up the handles of a small handcart, already heavy with a mixture of ash and damp sand.

'We need more men,' he said.

Epikleos vanished and began grabbing people on the street, directing them into the yard. In moments, they had half a dozen of the carts piled high, with a small crowd bearing shovels, anything they could find.

Pericles found himself wincing as he took a spade and flung dark stuff onto the flames by the theatre door. He was not completely sure how mortar was made, only that it used volcanic ash from the new city, where Zeno was from. He said a prayer as the stuff landed, then nodded as it smothered the flames. It had burned once; it could not burn again.

'More! Fling it on!' he yelled at the crowd.

They had a task at last and they picked up the coarse mix in their hands if they had nothing else. The little carts were empty and being rattled back for supplies in moments, with the owner appearing and threatening to bring them all before the council for theft. Pericles saw Aeschylus appear out of the darkness and speak in low tones to the man. There was silence after that.

The bucket line stretched away down the street to the river outside the walls. Pericles could imagine the water being brought in, hand to hand, but there was no sign of it then, just a line of Athenians, men and women alike, roused from their beds and doing their best to stop it spreading. He was touched by their courage, until he realised they did not want the fire to spread to their own homes. They had rebuilt before, more than once. They could not do it again.

The torrent of ash and sand thrown onto the flames meant Pericles could get in through the main entrance, over charred wood and smoke. He coughed, covering his mouth with one hand as the world swam. The fire was still burning ahead, he could see it, eating at canvas and wood in bright lines, pouring black smoke that moved like oil on water. All the masks were stored in the wings of the stage. The stage! He saw flames licking there and stamped on them, looking up to the Acropolis overhead. The rock would survive, but he could not let the fire reach the benches.

When he looked back, flame filled the entrance, cutting him off. He could retreat onto the stage itself, even up the rows of seating if he had to. The fire was spreading and he had cut himself off from the others by rushing in too soon. Where was the water?

He heard someone crying out in pain and he spun to face it. The flames gave light, so that he could see some parts of the wings, while others remained in the dark. He recognised the figure of Phrynichus by his bulk as the man flailed and shouted. Fire licked at him and the hem of his robe was already aflame.

Pericles rushed in without thought, beating at the man as Phrynichus wailed and tried to fight him off. The playwright landed a few blows, but he was sixty and soft in comparison to the one battering at him. When Phrynichus finally understood Pericles was trying to help, he was too exhausted to speak and let Pericles take part of his weight as he stepped out through charred beams onto the street beyond.

'Did you start the fire?' Pericles asked the man he held up.

Phrynichus looked at him in shock. He was wheezing and marked with soot, as miserable a creature as he had ever seen.

'No! I love . . . no. Why would . . . I?' he panted.

Pericles nodded, believing him. He had a suspicion how the fire had started. There had been enough spite in Attikos to burn them all.

As he stood there, he saw the line to the river was finally working. It had taken an age to get the first leather buckets back, but once they began, the ones at the front could throw them onto the fire and pass the empty ones away in their other hands. Pericles stood and watched as they soaked the entrance, making a slurry of ash and sand that would not catch fire again. The line moved further in then, throwing water on flames as they threatened to spread. It was tiring work, but if anyone faltered, others in the crowd took their places. It did not affect the speed of the buckets sloshing up. Those never slowed and it began to make a difference.

Pericles saw Zeno and Anaxagoras take spots in the line. He went in behind them, relieving a woman in a nightdress.

She kissed his hand and then he was heaving full buckets forward, over and over, surprised at the weight. Every house in the city had one or two of the deep things. Some had cracked and were lighter, while others shone with wax or oil and had a good strap handle. He stopped thinking for a time and just handed them on and on and on.

The wings were gone, that was clear. The water let others take ash or sand further in, scattering it over the stage. At least that would survive – and the seating beyond. Pericles gave thanks to every god he could name for that.

'Epikleos!' he called.

He could not leave his place in line, not then. Yet Epikleos heard. He appeared with his hair in spikes of soot and his face smudged with the stuff. He was grinning, his teeth showing white.

'Do you want me to take over?' Epikleos asked.

Pericles shook his head. He leaned closer, looking beyond his father's friend to the figure of Phrynichus.

'Chorus robes we can replace. Masks will be the problem. Can you run to the Ceramicus and place an order? Take Aeschylus with you. He knows what we need. If they can make a hundred masks in three days, we'll pay a bonus, whatever they ask.'

He thought of the few coins he had left in the lock chest at the estate. There was no alternative.

'Send a runner to a moneylender as well. At sunrise. Get me a meeting and I'll be there.'

'They ask too much interest!' Epikleos said. 'I have savings. Eighty in silver. It's not much, but it's yours.'

'We'll need much more than that,' Pericles said softly.

'Then the Assembly will have to vote funds to rebuild!'

'I'm sure they will. Epikleos? Arrange the meeting.'

Epikleos nodded and turned away. When he had gone,

CONN IGGULDEN

Pericles found he could not breathe well. His throat had tightened and he was not sure if it was strong emotion or smoke, or some combination of the two. He rasped each breath, but kept heaving buckets even so, moving the river water forward. The flames were almost out, and as dawn came he felt the light touch of rain on his face.

The crowd looked up as it fell and many of them cheered. The rain strengthened overhead so that the streets shone, washing black muck into central gutters and away. The bucket line could not see how to stop, so they kept going, though the charred wood was all drenched. They had been at it for hours and the results showed in their exhaustion and their embraces. In the end, families took the buckets they still held and just turned them over, walking back to their homes. The street cleared and the sun was rising. The rain kept coming as a light drizzle. Though he shivered and felt numb, it was the answer to prayers and Pericles turned his face up to it.

He could see through the wings of the theatre to the stage and the rows of seats beyond. If they had been stone, no fire could have threatened them. Perhaps one day they would be. In the meantime, he had three days and no money, but he would have to rebuild.

Aeschylus had gone with Epikleos. Pericles found himself wandering over to Phrynichus.

The big man still showed patches of brown char on his robe, where cloth fell away like paper. He was wincing and trying to judge the damage to his skin when he saw Pericles.

'We need carpenters and cloth,' Pericles said. 'We don't have to make new walls, just to hide what goes on inside from the crowd. We can nail cloth to a simple frame and do that.'

'The scenery is all gone,' Phrynichus said. 'Every painted piece. Each one . . .' He rubbed his eyes and held the bridge of his nose, looking suddenly like an exhausted old man. 'I have my masks and my people know the lines. All my copies are gone, but they still have it up here.' He tapped the side of his head. 'But without my scenery, how can I show the bank of a river? The maze of Crete?'

'We have three days . . .' Pericles said. There were only a few master scene-painters in Athens. Phrynichus seemed to have the same thought and he began to back away.

'Yes. I'll see what I can do . . .' He turned rather too quickly and hurried off.

Pericles started to laugh, then frown. He wondered if his potters could paint a scene as well as they did a vase. He thought they could. The sun was rising and he was filthy with soot and burned in odd places. Blisters swelled on his hands in fat yellow lines, though he had not even felt the touch of flames at the time. He was exhausted and nauseous, yet somehow made new.

CONN IGGULDEN

25

Spring had come in Athens, as if summoned by the festival. With the Acropolis at his back, Aristides found the place kept for him by one of the council, in recognition of his long service. On another day, he might have debated the rights and wrongs of such a thing. Granted, he was a senior archon and had served as strategos and polemarch – at Marathon, Salamis and Plataea. He had held every post Athens could offer, and known every honour except a statue on the Acropolis. He had refused that last, insisting that any funds the Assembly voted to that end should be used instead to repair the drains.

On this day, with his back aching, he was just happy he hadn't been made to wait in line with the crowds. He closed his eyes for a moment, enjoying the afternoon sun on his face. Facing south, the theatron seats seemed to trap warmth.

Aristides wished Xanthippus could have lived to see the way the city had responded to the fire. Even without the men of the fleet, every street for demes around the Acropolis had sent its young to help with the rebuild, thousands willing to fetch and carry, to nail and sweep. The theatre was not yet what it had been, but soot and dust had been cleared away and new structures of pine and linen hid the actors from the audience. Every board of the stage had been rubbed down and re-oiled. Aristides could smell it on the air, along with toasted sesame biscuits in honey. He opened his eyes and held up a bronze coin to one of the food sellers, securing a little parcel of them. The cloth they came in was a crude weave, but when he had unwrapped and eaten the contents, he tucked it away in his belt even so.

'Do you mind if I sit here, archon?' a voice said to one side.

Aristides looked up, shading his eyes against the sun. It was a man he did not know well, but he gestured to the empty seat even so.

'Ephialtes,' he said, in greeting.

Aristides knew the younger man was choregos for Phrynichus and a member of the Boule council that year, but little else. Round-faced and black-bearded, Ephialtes had reached the age of thirty and was well flavoured, a rising name in Athens. Aristides wondered if he would be an ally or a threat. It seemed a shame for Pericles to have such a burly competitor, before the son of Xanthippus had really found his path.

'Thank you,' Ephialtes said. 'I am glad to see you're not one of those who thinks seats are set by tribe alone. I never liked those artificial clans. What does it matter to me if you are of Acamantis, or Leontis? What, by the whim of old Cleisthenes? We are Athenians! That is all that matters.'

Aristides looked up into the bright eyes of a young man trying too hard to impress him. Ephialtes had the look of one in the presence of his hero, which made Aristides uncomfortable. He seemed to meet more and more of them as the years passed. Yet there was truth in all Ephialtes said, so he nodded.

'Or even more, with the *symmachia*,' Aristides added. 'I saw the great alliance begun on Delos, you know. I witnessed oaths sworn on ship irons and dropped into the sea. One language, one people. It was . . . it is, a glorious dream. You are young, Ephialtes. Perhaps men like you and Cimon will write that alliance in stone and not just water.'

A shadow seemed to cross the face of the burly young man.

CONN IGGULDEN

'Perhaps,' he said. 'Though Cimon accepted the position of archon, on the council of Areopagus. I . . . counselled him not to. I had hoped he would refuse. I thought better of him than that.'

Aristides sat straighter. The crowds were still coming in, finding their places. Most of them were indeed sitting in the sections reserved for the ten tribes – with two more for women and slaves. Those last were packed, with not enough space to fit a biscuit between the bodies. He remembered a meeting of the Assembly where Ephialtes had spoken against the council of archons, a year or two before. Aristides understood he was one of those who saw tradition as a chain rather than an embrace. There were always a few like that in every generation. For a moment, he gathered his thoughts. He felt old, suddenly. With more than sixty winters behind, he knew he could not have many more. Miltiades had gone, as well as Xanthippus and Themistocles. Aristides was about the last of the generation who had stood at Marathon and defied an empire – and won, he reminded himself. His greatest battles were memories; his greatest memories were battles. Yet perhaps he had time to debate with a young man who sneered as he said the word 'archon'.

'Archon is a word you hate?' Aristides said. 'You claim to be an Athenian, but reject our history and traditions? We are not *remade* anew each generation, with all the past overthrown. Those who went before hold us up! They bear us aloft – and we stand taller because of them. Oh, what did they know, those old men? They are not unlined and strong and new, like us! Yet they shed their blood for Athens. Our duty is simple enough – not to shame that sacrifice.'

'The council of archons has no place in a modern Athens,' Ephialtes replied. He was Athenian enough to warm to an argument, with half the crowd around them listening as they chewed sesame biscuits and nudged one another.

'You defined part of its role, when it honoured Cimon,' Aristides countered. 'As it honoured me with a place.' He waved a hand. 'Oh, there was power in it once, but Cleisthenes took away its sword and shield. We all know true power lies now in the Assembly, as it should. After all, the Assembly could vote to dissolve the council of the Areopagus. The opposite is not true.'

'No, it's more than just a shadow of the past,' Ephialtes said stubbornly. 'If men bend the knee to archons, if the calendar itself is named for men chosen from their number, so that they say, "This is the year of Aristides", or *Cimon*, then archons are raised above the rest of us!'

'Some men raise themselves,' Aristides said with a wry smile. 'So it is mere sense to honour them for their service. Unless you don't think Cimon deserved to be made archon, for his victories, for bringing Theseus home? For taking Cypros? Or perhaps you will say I did not deserve my place?'

He waited, but Ephialtes only chewed his lip, aware of all the listeners around them. Aristides nodded and went on before he could frame a reply.

'There was a time, Ephialtes, when Athens was ruled by tyrants. The archons were his battle lords then, his nobles. If that was still true today, I might agree with you. Yet what power do archons have, really, compared to the Boule council of the tribes, or the Assembly? We are not Spartans, Ephialtes – I suspect it does not hurt our influence and power to have a title with which to reward our most prominent young men. Yet in the end, archons only advise – after decades of experience. The Assembly of freeborn Athenians has the power. That is as it *should* be.'

An appreciative cheer sounded almost as an echo around

CONN IGGULDEN

him, as Aristides had known it would. From the beginning, he had pitched his answers to the crowd as much as to Ephialtes. Sitting next to him and sneering at archons! The young were always arrogant, though of course without that confidence, they'd never achieve all they needed to do. He understood it! If each generation was too much in awe of the ones that went before, they'd never get out of bed. It was the way of things.

The cheer built around where he sat. Aristides raised his eyebrows at Ephialtes, letting the people speak for him. Of course they approved! They *were* the Assembly! They were also waiting for the play to begin, so were bored and happy to join any distraction. The sound became a roar, spreading right around the arc of the seats. Ephialtes tried to speak over it before his point was lost.

'No common men sit as archons though, do they? Or is it just coincidence that Cimon is Eupatridae – a landowner, like his father, like all the rest.'

Aristides could have just cocked one hand behind his ear and pretended not to hear. The actors of the first chorus were coming on stage. Phrynichus swept through like a warship to take a seat right in the centre of the front row. The judges came in as well, flushed with excitement, one from each of the tribes Ephialtes claimed to disdain. The play was about to begin and the crowd was settling, but Aristides could not abandon the point. He too was Athenian, after all.

'I have no land,' he shouted over the noise, leaning over. 'I gave away all I owned.'

He rested his hand on a robe that was as tattered and old as he felt himself some mornings. He saw Ephialtes turn to face him once more out of the corner of his eye.

'That is why I thought you might understand,' Ephialtes replied. 'I thought you were a man of judgement, who might see the truth.'

He kept his voice low, but the crowd was settling at last, waiting for music to signal the opening scene.

'If you trust my judgement, accept my conclusion,' Aristides said coldly, stung. 'I have seen tyrants and ephors and kings, all raised above their fellow men. Our Assembly is a noble enterprise, with the Boule council to administer the city, all chosen by lot, with archons to advise. What matters most? It works.'

'It will,' Ephialtes said with a smile. 'When we raise no others above us. When all men are equal.'

'Men are *not* equal,' Aristides said too loudly, turning in surprise. Silence had fallen and frowns were being directed at their hissing conversation. 'Some are brave, some cowards! Some can save an entire people from destruction, while others only wail and weep and pull their hair. How will you recognise that, in your shining new city?'

'I don't need to,' Ephialtes said. Despite his pretence at cool disdain, he had grown flushed, in the grip of strong emotion. 'We are noble enough without a title, each and every one of us. I'm only sorry you can't see that. Your glories are past. You are a creature of the old world, clearly.'

Aristides turned to face the younger man in anger and wonder.

'I believe your seat *is* taken, choregos,' he said clearly. 'Find another place below, with Master Phrynichus. Quickly now. I have no more to say to you.'

Ephialtes did not heed the glares of those around, but rose even so, striding down the aisle to the front row, where it was true a seat had been kept for him. Aristides shook his head and tried to put the young man's anger aside. The sun was setting, for which he was grateful. The play was about to begin.

The tickets for the festival of Dionysus could have been exchanged for gold that year. The rivalry between Phrynichus

CONN IGGULDEN

and Aeschylus was already well known, but the fire at the theatre and the work to restore it had reminded the entire city of the wonders that would be performed within. They could have sold each seat a dozen times over and every performance was crammed tight as rowers, the streets around all silent. High on the Acropolis, thousands more gathered just to watch, morning and evening. Though they could not hear words, they could still see the costumes and masks, or catch strains of music and drums. It was the heart of Athens over ten days – four main competitors and sixteen plays.

The last time Pericles had slept had been the night he'd retired before the fire. He had snatched sleep since in crumbs, like a cup of wine or some morsel of food brought for the chorus. It did not satisfy, but it kept them all going.

Each new day was flung past in a sort of measured chaos, which made no sense at all and yet was completely true. Away from the main stage, Aeschylus was like a wild cat, rushing everywhere, gathering complaining actors like geese or children and pushing them on stage at the right time. The first two tragedies had gone down well, but Phrynichus too had enjoyed his share of applause. They were the two leaders at least, well ahead of lesser works. Yet it was too close. Aeschylus had hoped to be far ahead by that point. Only his *Persians* and his satyr play were still to go.

On stage, the company of Phrynichus reached a climax, some drowning scene of Narcissus that involved blue streamers being poured over him. Pericles thought it was a crude effect, but the audience seemed rapt and the applause and cheering that followed was real enough.

Pericles could look out from a gap between the linen walls that had replaced the burned beams. What he saw filled him with nerves. The judges were close enough to the stage for him to make out their expressions. Two of them were actually wiping their eyes. The rest were nodding and smiling. His stomach sank to see it. Phrynichus had won the festival four times before, Pericles reminded himself. It had always been a challenge to think they could beat him. He tried to tell himself that, but the truth was, he'd thought Aeschylus had been touched by the gods that year. The idea that they might suffer so much – spend so much – and *still* lose made Pericles feel physically ill. What would his father have said about beggaring the family for mere plays? He thought he knew the answer, unfortunately. Xanthippus would have said he should have funded a warship, that a good trireme kept the seas safe for Hellenes everywhere.

Yet he did not regret it, he realised. Whatever his father might have said, Pericles had seen something great in the plays and the company, something that made him feel alive. He wondered if he would feel quite the same if he had to watch Phrynichus raised up as the winner, cheered and lauded by the whole city.

'Where is Darius?' Aeschylus called from across the tented wing. 'No – *no one* is to leave now, I don't care what you've forgotten! There will be a short break to clear the stage and then we're on. Well, you'll have to go on without it then, won't you? Find me Darius!'

Pericles felt nervousness swell. He had not been so afraid when rushing towards Persian soldiers on Cypros, he thought with a wry smile. Perhaps the stakes had been lower then. He'd always felt he could throw his life away if he had to, if the moment required it. It was a different matter now he had a son, with his family fortune riding on the result.

The Assembly had voted funds to raise a makeshift theatre, though they'd appointed men of the council to oversee each coin spent. Even then, without hundreds of volunteers, the festival would never have opened. For new masks and costumes, Pericles had borrowed at a brutal rate, wasting a morning going from one moneylender to another. It was almost as if they smelled his desperation as well as the char on his skin. Or that they spoke to one another to set their rates.

He shook his head. He would recover. His potters had been forced to put aside their new designs for a while, but they would have their kilns up and firing again – and that would bring in silver. He'd clear his debts, in time, before they sat too heavily, like a great toad. He made a prayer to Hermes, god of merchants and traders everywhere.

The company of Phrynichus were coming back, bright-eyed and lifted by the approval of the crowd. They beamed as they saw their competitors waiting nervously in the gloom, exchanging cheerful insults and pleasantries as they passed through. Aeschylus snapped at one of them when the man dawdled too long, moving him along. In the seats, the crowd stood and stretched their legs, discussing what they had seen and heading to the clay troughs where urine would be collected for the dyers and leather-workers. Festival days were long days and half that crowd would visit a bathing pool at a gymnasium or perhaps the river to cool off and be clean at the end. The taverns would fill with light and life as they ate an evening meal and retired to sleep. The entire city celebrated the festival of Dionysus and they would all raise a cup of red wine to him, the stuff of blood and life. Pericles smiled at the thought. He had done that often enough himself in recent months. Few actual prayers were said however, not to the god of wine. The plays *were* prayers, the very act of putting them on a form of worship. In that way, the festival was a sacred thing.

It seemed an age passed before the crowd settled and were ready for the final play of the evening. Aeschylus and the other playwrights had drawn lots at the beginning for the order, then chosen which of their works would take each spot. It had been merest fortune Aeschylus had the last place. The satyrs would come on for the final day, with all their outlandish costumes. It meant his chorus would be the last that night to hold the attention of the judges – and all of Athens, rich and poor alike. The crowds on the Acropolis would see them lit by torches, an eye of gold.

By the time everything was ready, darkness had fallen. Aeschylus was ready to address his little troupe and Pericles stood with him as his choregos. He realised he knew each one of them by then. The actors had suffered through months of rehearsals and rewrites, as well as the fire and more drunken evenings than he cared to recall. Anaxagoras and Zeno had places in the chorus. Pericles had found friends there, where before he'd known only allies. They were smiling, he saw. They were ready.

'It comes to this,' Aeschylus said. The chorus wore their masks pushed up on their heads so they looked normal enough then. 'Phrynichus is slightly ahead, by my reckoning. Yet he has shown all he has to offer, whereas we have this last chance. The satyr plays tomorrow will change nothing. *This* is the climax, the moment we have worked towards. You know your lines. If it goes well, you will speak them to your children and grandchildren. So ... places. Chorus ready? Dionysus bless you all.'

He went out to the seats and Pericles walked with him, feeling all the eyes of Athens on them. Epikleos would remain to handle entrances and exits or any disasters. The playwright and his choregos would sit as members of the audience, alongside the judges. Pericles wondered if he would enjoy a single moment, or whether the prospect of financial disaster would ruin it for him.

The crowd saw them come through and settled into

silence. Only the crackling of torches could be heard, light spilling across the stage. Into that space the chorus came, masked in white, cloaked like crows. They slid across the stage as one and Pericles felt the hairs on the back of his neck stand up. Aeschylus had drilled them day after day until they moved in perfect unison. There was something eerie about the result. They flowed, a patch of night moving.

The musicians opened the scene, a tune in the Persian style, a strange thing in that place. The crowd whispered and smiled as they realised it was true. They would see the court of Persia on that stage, with Xerxes the king, a man who had stood on the shore at Piraeus, who had burned the city around them, not once but twice. They leaned forward in their seats, hands pressed to mouths.

As one, the chorus spoke, magnifying the lines so that they could be heard right across that vast, open space.

> Of the Persians, since departed,
> To the land of Greece . . .

In a single line, Aeschylus held the crowd in his hand. The Persians *were* gone, but not home! No, this was back, back to the time of the invasion. They had departed to attack Athens, with Thermopylae and Salamis and Plataea all ahead. Pericles found himself leaning forward, resting his chin on his clasped hands.

26

Pericles unrolled a vine leaf to reveal a flat cake of fried fish roe and breadcrumbs. He squeezed half a lemon over it, his mouth twinging at the prospect of bitterness. From the shore of the island of Salamis, he could see Piraeus across the strait. The great port of Athens was busier than ever, with dozens of ships in dock and two or three times that number at anchor, sending in boats to demand a berth before some part of their cargoes spoiled or missed its buyers. In comparison, Salamis was peaceful, though it had changed since the days of the Persian invasion. A new town had sprung up on the northern side, with farmers drawn to cheap land and fishermen to a sheltered coast. With their families, it had become a thriving community and at times it was hard to remember the days of fear, when Pericles had sat on those dunes with his brother, mother and sister, watching Persian warships killing their people.

He touched a hand to lips and heart. Salamis was a place for memories. Earlier, Pericles had walked to a little tomb on the shore, the name 'Conis' carved into it. His father's dog was buried there, drowned at sea when it had tried to swim after the great evacuation. Xanthippus himself had paid for the stone. For a man not much given to sentiment, it was a surprising thing to have done. Pericles always wandered down and patted the marker whenever he visited the island.

'This is delicious. You should try it,' he said to his wife.

Thetis nodded and accepted the leaf from his hands. Pericles tried not to show the spike of irritation that rose in him.

CONN IGGULDEN

Where was the woman he had married? He had thought for a time that Thetis might send his mother to an early grave. Instead, the two women had reached a state of armed truce, though it did not feel like a peaceful solution.

'It's very good,' she said.

She handed back the leaf and he tossed it onto the breeze. Did she think he wanted that part? He'd offered her a taste but she had taken it all. As it seemed impossible to leave sweet things anywhere in the house without her coming down at night and hunting them out. He bit his lip rather than say anything more, but she sensed criticism anyway. He could feel it in the way she glared at him, some subtle shift in her movements that spoke of anger and frustration rather than ease.

In a basket on the ground, his son suddenly woke and began to cry for food. Pericles said nothing – the boy did not call for him, after all.

'Can't you at least pick him up?' Thetis said peevishly. 'I'm still finishing my lunch.'

'Yes,' he said.

'What does that mean?' she demanded.

'It means "yes", Thetis. What else could it mean?'

'The tone – the *tone*, as you know very well.'

'In a single word? You are too sensitive.'

As he spoke, he reached out and gathered in the small boy. The child waved his fists, growing dark with anger. Pericles looked on him, holding him like a bundle.

'Are you ready, Thetis? I can hardly feed him myself. Of course, if you had not dismissed the Thracian . . .'

'Fine. Give him to me,' she snapped.

He handed over the child and stood up, brushing sand from his bare legs.

'I can see Epikleos and my mother coming back from the town,' he said.

THE LION

'Why don't you go to them, then?' Thetis replied.

She was pressing the child to her breast and yet looked unaccountably angry. He sighed.

'You should try to be calm,' he said. 'You'll sour the milk.'

She looked up at him with hot eyes, wanting to reply but trapped by the child feeding from her.

'Just go, would you?' she said.

'You're always so angry, Thetis! You said you wanted to get away from the house. Well, here we are! Can you not just enjoy the day? The sun is shining, the day is fine. We have food.'

'I thought we might be *alone*, Pericles,' she said. 'I wanted to talk to you, just the two of us. I didn't think you would invite Epikleos, nor your mother! With Manias as well, to keep an eye on me.'

'My mother has been in a low mood recently, as you know very well. Manias was on board ship during the battle of Salamis. He had never seen the actual island! And I could hardly leave Epikleos behind with the rest of us going off for a day at the beach.'

'You *could* have,' Thetis muttered. 'When do I get a moment away from *them*? You have the businesses in the city, your friends – what do I have? Where can I go? That house is like a prison, with *eyes on me all the time*.'

Pericles frowned as her voice rose to a shout. Fury in a man could be a terrifying thing, like a summer storm. Rage in a woman always seemed comical to him, or perhaps pitiful. He had learned not to laugh, so he spoke reprovingly to her, wanting her to be calm.

'Now, Thetis, you know as well as I do a child needs looking after. I bought you a wet nurse – and you insisted on feeding the boy yourself! Even now, you could pass the child to another and it would all dry up.'

CONN IGGULDEN

'Your mother says that, does she?'

'Yes. Given that she raised three children, I'd say she knows the subject well enough. Don't criticise my mother, Thetis. She has endured more than you know.'

'Unlike my own life of ease? Taken as a child, forced and made to play a man's wife? Made to run from his family? Abandoned on the docks of Athens, then married out of pity? Damn you, Pericles, for all your kindness.'

She began to weep and Pericles looked on her in simple frustration. Nothing he could do seemed to comfort her. He tried not to take to heart the things she said, but they hurt him and rankled for days after.

'Wipe your eyes,' he said roughly. 'I'll go and speak to my mother and Epikleos.'

He paused as he walked off, feeling sudden guilt. No matter how irritated he became in her presence, the moment he stepped away, his better nature returned. It was exhausting.

He came back and stood awkwardly as she nursed the child.

'He really should be on mashed vegetables by now anyway. When your milk dries, you'll be happier.'

'Just *go*,' she snapped.

Pericles walked away for a second time. He saw Epikleos across the dunes. The older man was shading his eyes, staring over the strait. Pericles followed his gaze, squinting into brightness.

'What do you see?' Pericles said as he drew closer.

Epikleos nodded to him, his gaze taking in the lone figure of Thetis left behind. There was sadness in his eyes then, but Pericles did not see it as he looked over the strait.

'A trireme . . . coming into port. Over there. One of ours – one of Cimon's, anyway.'

Pericles felt his heart beat faster when he spotted the ship.

Alliance triremes had been rare sights since spring, though they all heard reports and tales of the fleet, brought home in gossip and idle talk. Cimon was using the force he had been given to great effect, even without ships of Sparta or Corinth alongside. Trade was the result, as more and more merchants risked a sea free of pirates and Persians for the first time in generations.

Pericles thought back to his prayers to Hermes before the festival. The victory had surely been a gift of Dionysus, but the truth was, his fortunes had improved from the moment the judges announced Aeschylus as the winner. He still remembered the moment of sick horror when he'd thought it had all gone wrong. The last spoken line had died away. The actor playing Xerxes had vanished from the stage and the lights had been snuffed, one by one. The crowd had sat in darkness and complete silence for so long Pericles thought he would be physically sick. Yet it had been a sort of trance. They'd begun to cheer, stamping their feet, smacking their hands together and roaring at the top of their voices. It was a memory Pericles knew he would never forget.

Three of the older judges had chosen Phrynichus, but the rest had voted for Aeschylus. The god Hermes was a messenger as well – he brought good news and wealth.

The sight of a lone warship nagged at Pericles, as it did Epikleos. His mother looked from one to the other and sighed, seeing where this was going. Agariste did not enjoy the thought of an afternoon alone with Thetis. If the woman mentioned her cracked nipples just once more, Agariste thought she would probably strangle her. The boy should have been on mashed food by then anyway! It was not her fault Thetis had sent the wet nurse away in a temper when her breasts ached, they were so full of milk! Agariste had said nothing then, but it was hard to endure the months of complaints after that decision.

'Why don't you take the boat back to port and see what they're after?' Agariste said to her son.

He looked at her in wild surmise, caught between duty and curiosity.

'Are you sure?'

Agariste sighed dramatically.

'You'll be no good to me while you are distracted. Take Epikleos and cross over, then return for us. Manias is somewhere nearby, after his wild figs. Though he is rather deaf, we are in no danger.'

Epikleos smacked him on the arm and Pericles grinned. He looked back at Thetis, still seated and feeding his son.

'I'll let her know,' Agariste said. 'Give her peace for a little while. Who knows, it might improve her mood.'

Pericles hesitated as he turned away.

'You'll be good, won't you, mother? She is already annoyed with me.'

'I wouldn't do anything to upset that dear lady.'

Agariste spoke without any inflection, but Pericles still frowned. It did not help that his mother had a sort of wand-like grace to her still, an almost boyish frame compared to his wife. Thetis seemed to feel the comparison as a sort of constant rebuke. He sighed.

'Thank you. Come on, Epikleos.'

He and his friend trotted down the beach to where they had staked a small boat. They untied, clambered in and raised the sail with the ease of old ship hands. Epikleos pushed them off from the shallows and leaped aboard, turning the rudder so that the billowing cloth snapped taut.

By the time Pericles and Epikleos had negotiated a spot on the quays of the Piraeus, the warship too had found a berth, running a gangplank down to the dock. It was huge in comparison, a symbol of Athenian power that made Pericles grin to see. As importantly, three more triremes were under construction – the Athenian alliance contribution to the fleet that year. Pericles climbed up an iron ladder alongside one that was almost finished, stepping out to where he saw the trierarch gathering hoplites and sending them away.

It was the world he had known before returning to his father's estate and it touched him almost like pain to see it again. Each ship was its own little world, with all the men learning the strengths and weaknesses of their fellows. There was nowhere to hide on board a warship, but for those who loved the life, there was nowhere else like it either.

When he and Epikleos approached the captain, the man was studying a tally sheet of supplies and arranging to re-stock his ship. A gaggle of merchants waited on him and he glanced at the newcomers with a frown of disapproval. Pericles and Epikleos were sunburned from a day on the island, with hair worn loose and salt-stained tunics. Perhaps the man took them for dock workers, Pericles did not know. He stepped around the merchants and their men, though they crowded the dock.

'Good afternoon, Trierarch,' he called. 'Is there news of Navarch Cimon?'

'I cannot imagine it is any business of yours,' the man replied without looking up.

'Perhaps,' Pericles said without rancour. 'Though Cimon usually finds me when he comes in. You might let him know the bones of Theseus have been given a home on the Acropolis – a fine tomb and statue.'

The captain chewed the inside of his lip for a moment as he considered what he had heard.

'Ah. My apologies, kurios. I was distracted. I am Trierarch Philander of the ship *Horcos*. May I know your name?'

'Pericles of Acamantis tribe, Cholargos deme – son to Xanthippus, choregos to Aeschylus,' he replied with a smile.

To his surprise, the captain chuckled.

'You are the one I was told to see, kurios. I will have to call back the runners I've sent after you.'

He turned and did just that, ordering more of his men off at a trot along the road into Athens.

'What news have you brought?' Pericles said.

The captain looked pleased to have his work done for him. He smiled even wider.

'No news, kurios. Just three words. Navarch Cimon sent me to say, "Come and see."'

'That is all?' Pericles said, blinking. 'Nothing else?'

'Nothing he shared with me, kurios. "Come and see" is all.'

Pericles thought of his wife and mother, still on the island. There was a meeting on the Pnyx that evening, where the Assembly would debate and vote on the progress of colonies like the Nea Polis, south of Rome. That city was thriving, but there was another in Thrace not doing at all well, apparently. Ten thousand volunteers had been given tools and seed to start new lives there, in exchange for their labour. They were under constant attack, as Pericles had heard it. He'd intended to speak on the subject, voting to station a contingent of hoplites there for a few years, until they were established. Such things cost money and time, but he had expected to carry the debate . . .

He scratched his head. He could smell the sea, he realised. He had swum that morning on the island beach. Salt had dried on his skin and he felt its presence with every movement, like an itch of happier times. Yet Thetis would be expecting him back, and his mother would need him to step between them so their barbed comments did not become open warfare.

The trierarch was waiting for an answer. Pericles nodded, turning to his friend.

'Epikleos? If I take the boat back to the island, would you mind fetching Anaxagoras and Zeno down to the dock? I would like them to come with me.'

'What about me?' Epikleos said indignantly.

'I didn't want to assume,' Pericles said stiffly. 'You are no longer young and . . .'

'*Don't* leave without me,' Epikleos said over his shoulder, already running.

Pericles watched him go. Thetis and his mother were going to be furious, he suspected. If he told them before he landed once again at the Piraeus, it would be a very chilly trip. Somehow, the prospect did not dent the joy that rose in him at the thought of going to sea once more.

'"Come and see . . ."' he murmured to himself. A smile spread.

When Agariste sat down by Thetis, she found the younger woman holding her child and rocking, tears streaming from her. Thetis made very little noise, but her misery touched the woman she had driven almost mad with irritation and her demands.

'What is it, dear?' Agariste said.

Thetis shook her head, though she glanced around.

'Oh, Pericles has gone with Epikleos, to see what some boat is doing. They'll come back – or they won't and we'll take a fishing boat over to the Piraeus. My son is one for wild enthusiasms, I'm afraid. He does not always think them through . . .'

She realised Thetis might think she was talking about his marriage, so bit her lip. She could see Manias nearby, cutting blushed figs with his eating knife.

'Shall I take the child for a while?' Agariste said gently.

Thetis nodded and passed him over. Agariste rested the little boy on her shoulder, where he could belch and sleep in the sun.

'So . . . I saw you arguing with Pericles,' she said. 'He's very young, Thetis. A man and a husband, but . . . It was different with his father. Xanthippus was already a grown man when he married me, a strategos in his thirties, an archon. Pericles will be those things in time, but he is still a youth in some ways.'

'It's not his youth!' Thetis said sharply. 'I try to talk to him, but he doesn't listen.'

'Yes, well, he's not alone in that. Manias is not the only one, dear. All men go deaf when their wives talk to them, at least sometimes.'

Thetis smiled and wiped away tears, reddening her skin.

'I thought . . .' She gulped, as if trying to swallow. 'My mother told me if a woman kept breastfeeding . . . she could not get pregnant.'

Agariste's smile faded and she sat still, weighed down by her own memories.

'I believe it is harder,' she said in a breath, 'but if you are . . . intimate with a man, there is no true shield.'

'There were spots of blood last month, but nothing now. So I kept feeding him, though my nipples cracked, thinking it might help. But now I think I am!'

Her face crumpled as she said the last. Agariste gathered her in and held the baby between them, a warm knot that woke the child and caused it to wail in confusion and distress.

'If you are, it is good news!' Agariste said. 'Truly. Pericles will be delighted. I know he wants a brother for little Xanthippus, just as he had one. Or a daughter, like his sister Eleni.'

'I can't do it again,' Thetis said, sobbing.

Agariste patted the child with one hand and rubbed the younger woman's back with the other. At the same time, she raised her eyes to the heavens and any gods who happened to be watching.

'Of *course* you can,' Agariste said grimly. She would not be sharing her knowledge of certain herbs with the mother of her grandchildren, that was certain. 'So, have you been . . . with my son since the birth? I ask because some young women don't seem to understand.'

'I'm not *that* young,' Thetis replied, shaking her head. 'A few times, yes. We argue and sometimes days go by when he is cold to me, as if he doesn't care at all. Sharing a bed is the one thing we both . . . I think he regrets marrying me.'

She began to sob again and Agariste spoke to head her off.

'Well, I'm sure that's not true. Now, listen. You don't even know for sure. Your blood may not have come, but you know, feeding a child *does* hold it off, sometimes. This may be all in your mind. Or, it will be a brother or a sister for Xanthippus! That too is a good outcome! So wipe your eyes, my dear. Raise your chin and pinch your lips and cheeks when Pericles returns, to put a little colour in them. You are too pale. He will think you are ill.'

'He doesn't find me attractive any more,' Thetis said. 'Another child will ruin me.'

Agariste shook her head. Pericles needed half a dozen sons and heirs. It seemed he was still doing his duty at home, which was all that mattered. Her heart went out to Thetis, in memory of the young wife Agariste had once been. Yet she had survived those years. For that matter, she had survived her husband. That was not the sort of comfort she could offer to Thetis, but it was a woman's comfort nonetheless. Eventually, even beloved tyrants go to their graves – and their women are free.

CONN IGGULDEN

27

There had been moments over the previous days when his decision to drop everything and head back to sea had been tested almost to destruction. Pericles had endured a tearful conversation with his wife, which had then become a screaming match as Thetis accused him of making her pregnant and then abandoning her once more. His mother too seemed to regard the news of his departure as some sort of betrayal. In exasperation, Pericles had offered her the town-house while he was away. Agariste had grown thin-lipped at that, saying she would never give up her family home to Thetis, not while there was breath in her. He'd left the offer open, either way.

While the captain loaded stores, Pericles had at least been able to take part in the final debates on the Pnyx. His decision to argue for a permanent camp of hoplites on the Thracian coast had rather more urgency when he could take the decision and the funds for it himself. The Assembly had passed a vote of praise for him, though he noticed they also tallied and recorded every silver drachm sent down to the warship.

For all the quickness of his decision, it still took time to settle his affairs and appoint trusted men to act on his behalf. The next half-year payment on his debts would come due in four months. If Fate kept him away, it would be difficult or impossible for his mother and wife to meet it without him. He still fretted about that, but whatever Cimon wanted him to 'Come and see', it would surely not take much longer.

It was both an advantage and his private despair that the

warship had so little room for personal stores. Beyond the hoplite kit he had inherited from his father and brother, including a shield with a lion painted across its face, Pericles could add only cloaks and spare sandals, his razor and toilet stones, his kopis blade and a pouch of silver coins. The captain had agreed to mark him on the roster as a paid hoplite rather than a passenger, which helped. Of course, it also put him under the captain's authority, which was delicate. Epikleos too was added to the ship's roster, but Anaxagoras and Zeno were untrained and had to pay their way.

They left the docks of the Piraeus without great fanfare, though Thetis and his mother insisted on coming to the port to watch him leave. They stood with Manias and a young groom from the estate. Pericles raised his hand to them in farewell.

The ship turned slowly, one bank of oars sweeping its massive weight around. Pericles did not like to examine the feeling of relief that came over him in that moment. He was still worried he had made a mistake, but there was no doubt – some part of him thrilled to the beat of oars once again.

The captain sidled alongside, keeping an eye on his officers as they headed out to deep water.

'I, er . . . I hope I did not offend you with my manner on our first meeting, kurios,' the man said.

Pericles shook his head. He was still looking back at his wife and mother on the wharf, wondering idly whether he had to keep them in sight until they were lost to view, or whether he could turn away before then. While he decided, the captain leaned closer, murmuring into his ear.

'I took care of the other matter. You need have no concerns there.'

Pericles almost let it go. Zeno and Anaxagoras were on deck, delighted just to be on board an Athenian warship.

CONN IGGULDEN

Epikleos was in hoplite armour, looking stern and silver-haired. It was a moment of clear skies and joy, of heading back to the fleet – or at least away from his responsibilities. Yet the captain's words nagged at him.

'What other matter?' he said at last.

'I hope I wasn't meant to keep it quiet, kurios?' the captain replied. 'The one you wanted me to take on board? As a favour to you?' The captain saw only confusion in Pericles' face. 'Was that all right? He gave me to understand you wanted him on board, but in secret. I hope . . .'

Pericles knew then, with a sort of cold certainty. He strode across the deck, to the steps by the stern. He swung down to the hold where rowers were already at work, sweeping forward and back. Heads turned to see who intruded on their domain. He looked them over, searching.

The captain clambered down behind him, exchanging a worried glance with his keleustes. He was not certain what had gone wrong, only that he had made an error. A son of Xanthippus and friend to Cimon was not someone he wished to offend.

With no warning, one of the rowers suddenly swore. Pericles saw the man pull in a dripping length of oar with sharp and angry movements before standing up. He wore a cloth about his waist and nothing else. Pericles would have known him anywhere. He had carried that bony frame up a cliff face, after all.

'Attikos, come up on deck,' Pericles said.

'That was not the name he gave . . .' the captain began.

Pericles ignored him, heading back to the sun and air. His friends had gathered there, looking in question at him. In the hold, the captain ordered the rowers to cease pulling. The ship began to rock as speed fell away. It added to the sense of wrong-ness as Pericles faced the man climbing out of the gloom.

'I know him,' Anaxagoras said. 'From the theatre. Did he set the fire?'

'Did you, Attikos?' Pericles said.

'I did nothing,' Attikos said.

He was aware of the eyes of both hoplites and officers on him. Pericles practically saw him choose his manner to speak to those in power. Attikos kept his eyes downcast and his shoulders bent. He did not look like a threat to anyone.

'I came to you for work, kurios,' Attikos said. 'That's all I wanted. I begged you for a place as a guard, or a rower. In my poverty, you turned me away.'

'And the theatre was burned down,' Pericles said.

'Which was nothing to do with me, kurios, on my honour. A man has to work or starve. We don't all have fathers like yours, with houses and cedar trees and horses . . . all of that.'

Pericles felt coldness steal over him. There *were* cedar trees on the estate, planted by his mother after the Persians had gone. Was that a message to him? He knew Attikos was ruthless. If he was threatening Pericles' family, Attikos would discover he was not the only one.

Pericles smothered the anger that surged in him. He could pitch Attikos overboard. He doubted the captain would stop him. Of course, if the man drowned, it would be murder. Whatever ruse he had used to get on board, Attikos was one of the rowers on the ship. That protected him from rough justice of the sort that filled Pericles' imagination. Rowers sat on juries in Athens, and held positions in the council. They did not have to be good men, just strong ones.

He put aside thoughts of vengeance. Sons of archons could not take a high hand with a rower, not without ruining a career before it had truly begun. The Assembly would hear about it in the end and any trial could take a savage turn.

It was not too late to return to Athens, but he hesitated. If he put Attikos back on the docks, it would be like setting a rat free. Despite the presence of Manias and the slaves on the estate, a determined enemy could reach his wife or mother ... or his son. When Attikos glanced up, his gaze was utterly cold. Pericles made himself smile, though it was the hardest thing he had ever done. The captain was looking to him for a judgement, he realised, still aghast at having accepted a man under false pretences.

'Very well, Attikos,' he said seriously. 'I won't deny any man his living. I am a believer in second chances. Don't waste this one.'

The little ape of a man gestured as if to knuckle tears from his eyes then.

'That's kind of you, kurios, very kind. I knew you was a good man, I really did. I won't let you down, I swear it.'

'Thank you, kurios,' the captain said to Pericles. He bowed to him, though as he was one of the ship's hoplites, it was perhaps in error. The captain flushed as he rose.

'Tie this man to the mast,' he said, indicating Attikos.

Anaxagoras and Zeno were closest and they took hold even as Attikos began to splutter.

'Why take me up? Get your hands off! What's this now?'

'You gave a false name and lied to join my crew,' the captain said. 'That is my concern – and yours. No one else's.'

He said the last for Pericles, presumably in case he might object. It was hard for Pericles not to grin as he watched Attikos tied to the mast and his tunic cut away. The man's back was a mass of scars, bone and ink marks, tattooed into the skin.

Attikos looked around at those on deck, as if memorising faces. He embraced the mast, gripping with his arms and laying his cheek against the rough wood.

'Well, then. Watch this, boys,' he said, showing his teeth. 'It'll be a lesson for you.'

Pericles thought it was the first time they had seen the true man since finding him in the rowing benches. He saw the captain blink in surprise.

'Bring me a lash,' he ordered.

PART THREE

'The descent to hell is the same from every place.'

– Anaxagoras

28

Cimon was never still, Pericles realised. The cramped little dining room on his flagship was lit by a single lamp that barely touched the shadows in the corners. The man who commanded trierarchs of a dozen allies paced up and down its narrow length – four full steps and that a luxury. Anaxagoras seemed fascinated by the way Cimon ducked his head to miss a central spar, apparently without conscious thought. As the tallest of them, Anaxagoras was not well suited to meetings below. He had marks and lumps enough on his crown to show for it.

The man who addressed the group crammed into that small room was sweating, Pericles could see. Hesiodos was the king of Thasos and the oldest in that room by a few decades, with a white beard and dark teeth, those he still had. He stood alone there, without guards. He might have been nervous in the presence of Athenian sea power, or it might just have been the close room and the warmth of the night.

He had Cimon's attention while he spoke. The rest of them turned eyes or heads to watch Cimon pace, for all the world like a wolf in a cage.

'I am not asking to be released from my vow, just for a single year without paying the tribute,' Hesiodos said. 'We sell timber, marble and honey. This ship is probably made from wood grown on Thasos! Yet hard wood grows slowly. If I strip the forests again to make the payment for Delos, we will be starving next year. The market for marble has collapsed without Persia and our hives are still growing. We can't eat honey every day. Just one year without having to give every coin we earn to the alliance and we will recover. We might even be able to pay more next year, or the year after. That is in the hands of the gods, of course.'

Cimon stopped pacing, drawing every eye in that place to him. There was really no question of who held the authority in that room, nor the alliance. From the moment the Spartans had left, Athens was the power in the Aegean once more. Cimon was archon and strategos, navarch for the alliance, following in the steps of Xanthippus. Pericles had come to know him well over the previous year. He wondered if he'd ever command men the way Cimon did, the way his father had done. He was not sure if the manner came with age or even the titles of authority, though they played a part. Cimon allowed no weakness and he had become a master of his trade. In the end, perhaps that was all that mattered.

Pericles wondered how the king of Thasos saw them, the band of young captains and strategoi to whom he appealed that evening. The old man cast his gaze all around the cramped room, looking for any sign of support. Yet there was really only one voice that mattered. They all waited for it, though Pericles knew Cimon well enough by then to have spoken the words himself. In truth, Hesiodos of Thasos was not the first to have asked for special terms or help to pay. Pericles had witnessed half a dozen of the smaller states come to renegotiate the part they had agreed.

'You speak, Highness, as if it is a simple matter,' Cimon said in a low voice. The old man began to respond, but Cimon held up a hand. 'This fleet costs more than you can imagine to keep afloat. Have you any idea? Tens of thousands of men, who must all be paid. Food and wine to keep them strong. Then there are the repairs – the constant broken masts and spars and ropes. Why, we had a man put his foot

CONN IGGULDEN

through a rotten section of decking just this morning. It all has to be cut out – and replaced with timber dried for an entire year before it can be fished into place. So we must guard our stores on land, before all that good wood can be stolen. And we must guard our crops and our livestock. They too have to be paid, Highness. Can you conceive of it? A fleet like this is a nation afloat, or the right arm of one.'

The king spoke quickly, trying to head off his conclusion.

'A single year of rest and we might . . .'

Cimon shook his head.

'I have told you the need. This fleet keeps the sea safe for your timber and your marble and honey. Pirates no longer catch and burn your ships. Persians no longer land to steal your women or butcher your young men. What price would you put on their lives when you come here to bargain with us – we who watch the horizon for enemies so *you* can live in peace?'

He had grown angry, Pericles saw. Cimon was always short-tempered with merchants. For all he understood the need for them, they saw the world in terms of coins, whereas he saw something else. Pericles believed Cimon cared nothing for gold or silver, any more than Aristides at home. He cared for the fleet – and the influence of Athens. Nothing else mattered. Pericles wondered if he had ever had moneylenders knocking on his door in the small hours. He doubted it.

The king was clearly stung at being lectured so by a younger man.

'Archon Cimon,' he said formally, 'the people of Thasos are grateful for the fleet – though I remind you that we are not supplicants. We have paid our part, with every family taxed to make up our share. You don't see the families reduced to rags to make that payment. The young mothers weeping as they pass over their last coins!'

'Would they do better as Persian slaves, do you think?' Cimon replied. 'Would they weep then? When we had no fleet, these waters were not ours, not really. That is what I have learned, Highness. Trade and freedoms flourish when there are men like me ready to answer any threat. When the wolves come, we are here. Everything you value comes from that, everything. Because without that strength, it is just a throw of the dice whether all you love is taken from you.'

'These wolves, are they the ones anchored around Thasos? Or is it just alliance ships impounding my traders?' The king was red-faced, but he mastered himself with an effort. 'You have kept ships around Thasos for almost a year now. Nothing moves! If we are to starve, what does it matter who prevents grain from landing?'

Cimon began to pace again, as if he drew strength or calm from the act.

'You swore on gods and iron, Hesiodos, with all the rest. Ingots we stamped and dropped into the sea by Delos. Those are our oaths, enduring still until the end of the world. That if one of us is attacked, we all are. That we stand together and that we will give silver or ships or men each year to that end. Athens has three new ships in the water this year – and three more being built. We train our crews to risk war and disease and we do not complain. What of Thasos? Did you not have a gold mine once?'

The look Hesiodos flashed at the younger man was one of fury, quickly smothered. Pericles recalled Cimon's family had owned mines in the north, somewhere in Thrace, which sat off the coast of Thasos. From the king's reaction, that was not common knowledge.

'The mine failed,' he said at last. 'The gleanings of it are almost worthless.'

'"Almost" is a long way from worthless when a gold mine

is involved,' Cimon said. 'Your tribute was eight talents of silver each year. A talent of gold would clear your debt, Highness. You are a year overdue and you play with your oath as if we are bargaining in the market. Do you think I am a merchant?'

'No, of course . . .'

'Then stop treating me as one. Pay what you gave oath to pay. You see the results around you – and you will continue to see these ships in your waters until you honour your obligations. If I must, Highness, I will land ten thousand men and march them to your palace to claim the debt – from you, or your successor.'

'I am a member of the alliance,' Hesiodos said in shock. 'How is that not a threat of war? You would break the terms over a few talents?'

Cimon stepped very close to him, into the range where he might strike the other man. Hesiodos edged back, but Cimon pressed forward.

'You are the first to break the oath of Delos, Highness. I know your mines are not spent, but you would benefit from safe seas without paying for them. If Athens bears the costs, you can thrive, no? You would be a wise king to have made such a deal?'

'If you set foot on Thasos, every one of your allies will wonder when they will be next. It will destroy everything you have built.'

'No,' Cimon said. 'If I set foot on Thasos, it will be to make an example of those who break oaths before gods.'

There was a stillness in him and the king swallowed, the knob of his throat lifting up and down.

'I will give you three more months to raise two talents of gold – one this year and one for the next. After that, I will march on your palace.'

'You would not *dare*,' the king said. 'On my own land? I will destroy anyone who sets foot on Thasos without my permission.'

'Go from here, Hesiodos,' Cimon said. 'Do your duty and I'll take your hand as friend and ally.'

The king mouthed words in silence, as if tasting them. In the end, he shook his head. There was no give in Cimon, nor any of those who glared at him. Yet Pericles wondered if the old man really understood the threat. Cimon believed in the league of Delos – and the oaths they had sworn to create it. If he had to burn Thasos to the ground to secure its future, Pericles thought he would.

When Hesiodos turned stiffly to leave, Pericles went with him through the little door, closing it behind. At the steps to light and air above, Pericles put a hand out to steady the man's arm. It was shaken free as if his touch burned.

'I am a *king*,' Hesiodos snapped, climbing up. He was still trembling with anger or perhaps fear. 'Touch me not. I have borne enough insults for one day.'

'I heard none,' Pericles replied. 'Only concern for the alliance.'

The king turned a weight of scorn on him as he reached the deck. Out of the confines and gloom, it was easier to breathe.

'Your friend Cimon overreaches. He acts like a Persian or a king, not just the administrator of ships and trade. That's all he is! Tell him to watch his threats, the next time he meets a man of royal blood. Or someone will make him regret his every sly word.'

The king was poking the air with one finger, bolder on deck than he had dared to be below with Cimon watching him. The change was interesting, as if he was braver talking to those he thought beneath him.

CONN IGGULDEN

'Highness, there are a dozen calls on the fleet this year. We are spread too thin, more than you could know.'

'Persia is quiet, boy. When was the last time you even saw one of their ships? They have pulled in their horns. There is no *need* for such a huge fleet now, don't you see? We had to bear those costs during the war, but Persia licks her wounds, far from here. They won't be back. Should I beggar myself just to keep your crews fed when no one needs them? No.'

The man gestured to the boat that would take him back to shore. His two rowers moved immediately. More armed hoplites awaited their king on Thasos, not two hundred paces away. The king stood alone on the deck. He was brave enough, Pericles realised. Only his judgement was in doubt. He struggled to find words for one who treated his youth and status with contempt. Before he could speak, the old man went on as if his temper suddenly boiled over.

'Tell your friend to take his ships from my waters. If he has other calls on the fleet, he should answer them! I am a king of Thasos – an ally and a Hellene, not a prisoner. Not an enemy! The arrogance of Athenians! If Sparta had remained in command, they would not allow this injustice.' He turned to Pericles and his eyes blazed. 'Nor will I.'

Pericles could only shake his head as the old man climbed down to his boat and was rowed to shore. He knew Cimon would not change his mind, but it seemed neither would the king. The conclusion did not sit well with him. It was one thing to go to war against a Persian fortress. It was another to consider drawing a blade on his own people.

Cimon came up on deck a little later, with the tall figure of Anaxagoras seeming to take an age to climb out of the hold. The Ionian had been granted citizenship of Athens, sponsored by Aeschylus and Pericles himself. He had asked

Cimon to train him as a hoplite, so that he could be of some use in the event of battle.

The skills of war were never lightly given. Yet Cimon was generous and he had seen no harm in it. For an hour or two each evening, he had set up sword drills to be repeated over and over, the sort of thing a young warrior would be taught from the age of twelve or so. He had done something similar before with crews on Scyros, so it seemed natural enough when a dozen rowers asked to join in. Epikleos had taken a role as a trainer and Pericles made a fourth when Zeno joined them.

The hard labour of training helped Cimon lose the dark expression he wore most days, so that he laughed and relaxed. It was the only time he seemed to, Pericles thought. Anaxagoras was responsible for that. More, it had become a common sight for all the ships of the alliance fleet to see men drilling back and forth on deck, practising for the real thing each evening. There were wounds, of course, but that was always the case whenever large numbers gathered and held swords. Pericles was sure it had made them a more dangerous force. He only wondered if they would ever find an enemy worthy of the fight. If what Hesiodos had said was true, if Persia had really quit the field . . .

He took up a sword Epikleos threw to him, catching it easily. That was exactly the sort of brash move that resulted in a lost finger or an arm wrapped for a month. Yet he exulted in it.

'Guard for me, would you?' Epikleos said. 'I'll show them the first three combinations again.'

Each one was four moves long, a pattern of twelve in all that could be carried out at blistering speed by two men who trusted one another. Pericles nodded. The combinations created memory, so the body could react without thought. The difference between a trained man and an untrained one was the difference between life and death in battle, after all. He had his father to thank for a thousand hours of sparring, more, he realised. Yet he was gone, like the Persians . . . The thought nagged at him, something he could not quite bring into focus. Epikleos began the first sequence, ending with a shoulder barge that turned him, then a cut to his exposed neck. Epikleos shouted at the last, startling Pericles from his thoughts.

'Second variation,' Epikleos announced for those watching.

Zeno and Anaxagoras were soaking it all in, muscles twitching as they practised the moves in imagination before the real thing.

'And . . . one . . .' Epikleos chopped low, but Pericles did not move away. The older man almost fell as he pulled the blow before it cut him across the thigh.

'Pericles! Second variation! By the gods, I could have . . .'

'Sorry. Zeno, come and take my place, would you?' Pericles said. He turned away as Zeno darted in, quick as always. 'Cimon?'

The navarch of the fleet was explaining some move to one of the rowers, turning the blade slowly in the air to show an angle, moving his feet at the same time. He looked up as Pericles approached.

'What is it?'

'The king of Thasos said something odd when he was waiting for his boat.'

Cimon raised his eyes for a moment.

'He is an old fool. There is more than one gold mine on Thasos, as I heard it. The man is richer than half the members of the alliance. He could pay the alliance tithe for a hundred years, but still he holds back. Well, he will regret it.'

'He said . . . the Persians have pulled back – and that's true enough. We haven't seen a Persian ship, even a trader, for what, six months? More?'

'What of it? Which of them would dare enter the Aegean while we patrol?'

'Yes, I know, but . . . nothing? It doesn't strike you as odd that Persia is suddenly so quiet?'

Cimon shrugged, but he let his sword drift down as he thought.

'There was some movement around the Hellespont, re-member that? We picked up that fishing crew and they said Artabazus is governor there – no, satrap. Fat little bee, that man. I should have killed him on Cypros when I had the chance.'

'That's it, I think,' Pericles said slowly. 'They're busy in the north, around the coast of Byzantium. They trade there and we see their ships making their way along the coast. Yet no movement near Cypros? That too is a coast under Persian control. They have garrisons there, fishing villages, rivers and deep harbours, but we haven't had a report of a sail there since that time.'

'Are you agreeing with the king of Thasos, then? I have to say . . .'

'No, he's a fool, but it's been bothering me and there's something odd. We still see Phoenician traders around Thrace sometimes, with Persian goods. They stop to be searched and they pay their taxes and port fees, and why not? It benefits us all. But in the south? Not a sail. Not a single ship.'

He looked at Cimon and the same thought struck them both.

'It could be nothing . . .' Cimon said. He was already look-ing out over the island and redistributing forces in his mind. 'They never tried to take Cypros back. I wonder . . . what do you think they are hiding?'

CONN IGGULDEN

'I think there's a chance they don't want us patrolling there, looking there. If that's true, whatever it is, it has to be something we need to see.'

'I gave that old fool three months,' Cimon said of King Hesiodos. 'I can't take the fleet clear now or he'll think he has won.'

'Just a dozen ships, then,' Pericles said. 'The chances are, it's nothing. An absence is not proof. Zeno would love it. I am probably wrong. Just send a few to search the coast around Cypros. Perhaps it's just quiet because it's quiet.'

Cimon was still looking over the slopes of Thasos. He shook his head.

'No. I am no jailer, as old King Hesiodos would have me painted. I've given him my ultimatum – and I have allowed him to skirt his oath. Either he will satisfy his honour, or he won't. I will not watch him fail. Come, Pericles. Call my captains.'

'All of them?'

'Every one. I have half the holds full of the tithe to be taken to Delos for this year. We'll drop anchor there and if the weather holds, we can go further, on to Cypros.'

He saw Pericles frown and chuckled.

'What is it?'

'I'm worried I have persuaded you to send the fleet away from Thasos, all on a suspicion.'

Cimon smiled and shook his head.

'This is why the alliance exists, Pericles, why we have the fleet. Even if you're wrong, every small king that sees us pass will know the sea is ours. Come, let us see if your instincts are good.'

29

Xerxes wondered if the man at his side ever experienced the odd flutter in the stomach, the sense of dread that crept up on him and woke him, gasping, as the moon still rose. He saw no sign of nervousness in Artabazus – a professional veneer, or perhaps the numbness of opium and hashish. His general was said to indulge, though if it calmed his nerves, there was no harm to it. If anything, the little balls brought courage to the surface and made a man feel like a lion, at least for a time. Xerxes realised one of his own hands was trembling and gripped it in the other. He too would need to soothe his fears that evening.

It did not help that Artabazus could remember conversations with General Mardonius, who had failed at Plataea, or further back, General Datis, who had landed at Marathon and been butchered there. Xerxes shuddered at memories of childhood and his father. Persia had lost blood and gold on the shores of the west, more than could ever be weighed and counted.

The king stopped, and Artabazus halted immediately. He was used by then to the whims and enthusiasms of the man who ruled the empire. Some eighty guards and slaves followed the pair of them to answer his slightest need. They could raise a canopy and press cool drinks into his hand at a moment's notice.

Xerxes looked out over a river that snaked back and back into the mountains, miles from the coast, where no Greek eyes had ever come. In its widest parts, it was like the Hellespont in

CONN IGGULDEN

the north, where he had given Artabazus his satrapy. Every part of the river was filled with ships, stretching away into the haze of distance. In places, he could almost walk from one bank to the other on their decks, needing no bridge. His fleet, his imperial army. It raised his heart to see the sheer scale of it. In the morning breeze, he imagined he felt his father's spirit caressing him. That brought its own pain, but he raised his head.

'It has taken years to reach this point,' Xerxes said. 'Slaves have given their lives in joyous labour, by the thousand. They have drowned and been crushed in greater numbers than anyone can say. But we have dug mud flats into deep channels, where before there were none. We have cut down forests to make ships – and we have trained men to make war. Tell me . . .'

He could not say it, but Artabazus seemed to understand.

'We can win, Majesty,' he murmured. 'I swear it. I could pledge my life, but you know it is already yours, a thousand times over. We have learned from all that went before – from the cursed names.'

He would not mention Marathon or Plataea, not in the king's presence. Those were words unspoken, though they sat like weights on the king's shoulders, bearing him down.

Xerxes looked at the one he had chosen to lead the forces of the empire. Artabazus was still the same little tub of a man, though perhaps older around the eyes. He had known defeat and pain, but it had seasoned him, so Xerxes hoped. In knowing those things, he would be better placed to avoid them.

'The empire is vast, Artabazus. I do not think a man can conceive of its size. I am brought reports of riots or unrest, of garrisons forced out by great movements of my own people. Yet by the time it reaches me, it is all a memory, as if it had not happened at all. And yet . . .' He looked at his general, wondering how many of his fears he could share. The breeze fluttered his robe and he thought again of his father.

The throne was a lonely seat. Who else truly shared his responsibility? Not one of the thousands gathered in his name. Xerxes decided not to speak too freely in front of a man who might be made bold by his weakness. He needed Artabazus to take the fleet and his army to Greece, to spend years on campaign and to bring home the victory twice denied him.

'Trying again carries dangers, general,' he said after a long pause. 'For you . . . for stability in the empire. When you set sail, you will carry Persia with you.' The king reached out and tapped Artabazus over his heart. 'There . . . and there.'

He touched him between the eyes. Artabazus decided to prostrate himself, but Xerxes took him by the arm and held him up. It was an astonishing intimacy and said more of his trust in his general than any words.

'I will not fail, Majesty,' Artabazus said.

He was sweating, Xerxes saw, his skin shining in the sun.

'They knew we were coming, before. My father built the fleet on the Hellespont and the Greeks watched and reported our numbers, our route, everything. That is how they were ready for us, general. That will be our advantage now. How many ships do we have this year? How many men?'

He smiled as he said it. Xerxes liked to summon Artabazus and fire questions at him, testing his knowledge and comforting his own unease.

'Majesty, we have three hundred and eight ships, with thirty more under construction. I have rowing crews upriver, learning orders and skills. The new flag signals are a wonder. We will match the Greeks when we meet them again, I swear it on the lives of my children.'

CONN IGGULDEN

'And the training of men? How goes it now? Our Immortals beat the Spartans at Thermopylae, general. If I'd had fifty thousand of those, we would not have been turned back.'

Thermopylae was not one of the cursed words. It was the only bright spot in a doomed campaign and Xerxes brought it up at the slightest excuse, reliving the days of drama in the pass, and the fall of Leonidas.

'I would say thirty thousand trained to the level of Immortals – or Spartans, Majesty. Another sixty thousand who are approaching that level.'

Artabazus did not think the king would appreciate some of the stories of chaos he had witnessed. The truth was, it took more than just time and will to create a force like the Immortals. It took a belief in themselves. The vast army he had gathered from the furthest reaches of forty kingdoms did not yet have that belief. Yet he had given them fitness and it was true he had trained thousands to hold a sword and shield – with greaves and helmets. They truly had learned from the Greeks, and in the midst of his fear, he relished the chance to tear into the enemy one last time. Come victory or disaster, it would be the final act of his life, he was certain. If he won, Xerxes could hardly give him more than he had already. There really was only so much a man could consume and he was already too heavy and stiff in the hips. If he lost, he knew he would take his own life rather than be dragged into some Greek city, spat upon and abused. He smiled even so. It was the life he had chosen. In comparison, Persia was a far greater treasure and worth more than his single, beating heart.

'Train them until they bleed, Artabazus, until they cry out in pain and their breath is like the forge fire. Make them fit and fast and deadly, every one. They are to be my new

Immortals . . . or should I give them other names? Names of virtue or fearsome beasts? Tigers of India, say, or Leopards?'

Artabazus considered his reply for a moment, though it was not a suggestion when the Great King said such a thing. He suspected Xerxes had come to him that day just to pass on the idea. It was one reason the general dreaded the monthly appearances of the king on the river. Xerxes always had some new thought to improve training or the armour. It had been with the greatest reluctance that he had given up the idea of releasing tigers on the battlefield, as if they could be pointed at the enemy like an arrow. The escape of just one had led to two men ruined and one dead, with the animal finally vanishing into the hills.

'That is a fine thought, Majesty,' Artabazus said at last.

He had delayed until the king began to frown, but that was all he could do. It was not even a terrible idea, but he disliked having Xerxes interfere with the preparation of the army. It was clearly a source of worry for him. Artabazus could not recall a meeting without veiled hints of unrest in the empire or a treasury running low. The general was not sure if the Great King ever had to worry about his subjects in revolt. He was the chosen of Ahura Mazda, after all, his blood divine. Yet there were moments when Artabazus saw through to a frightened man, beneath the gold and jewels. Xerxes needed to win. He had thrown everything at a last chance against the Greeks. When it came, it would be a magnificent final chapter in the story, without a doubt. Artabazus touched his lips and heart in silent prayer.

'God be with us,' he said.

Ephialtes showed no sign of any emotion as the votes were counted and the decision announced. After the retirement of two ancients and the death of one he did not know, he

CONN IGGULDEN

had been elected as a strategos of Athens, one of ten. Seven were already with Cimon and the fleet. Ephialtes would head out in three new ships, training young crews in safe waters. In time of war, the title would have meant command of a wing or part of the fleet. Two of the other men elected that day would oversee the city garrison and the guards on the wall. Lesser posts, in peacetime.

In war, Ephialtes might have won glory enough to gild him as a name in the Assembly. As men like Aristides had done, or Xanthippus and Themistocles. Opportunities had poured upon them, he thought. His path would be harder without Persians attacking.

Still, it was a step. Ephialtes wished his parents could have been alive to see it. He had known poverty once, but no longer. It still astonished him how wealthy men courted rising stars of the Assembly, even those who claimed to disdain wealth. He had been offered part-shares in businesses, in a new silver mine and a stud farm. All without demands on him. When he had questioned the generosity, good men he admired had expressed surprise. What was the point of wealth if not to invest in a new generation? They believed in a fair society, after all.

Some of his patrons sat on benches above the meeting, come to see him appointed. It had not escaped his attention that they were all men who had raised themselves up after the war. His views on abolishing the council of archons were well known. He had no patrons from the Eupatridae or families like those of Pericles and Cimon. No, his people had worked for what they had – and were all the stronger for it.

He looked around, seeing Aristides waiting patiently to catch his eye. The old man too was there to observe. His voice no longer dominated debates on the Pnyx or in the council hall. It had become a piping thing. He still wore his habitual grubby robe, Ephialtes saw. The younger man had seen it once as a fine statement of honesty. Yet it seemed now like artifice to him, or mere show. His own robe was white and well made – and it changed nothing about him, though it was the best he had ever owned.

Aristides inclined his head and Ephialtes nodded back. He could afford to be gracious that morning. He had ships ready to take him out – and enough support in the council to appoint him as a leader of men. This was his day. He looked across to the others made strategoi, but they were mere placemen. Both of them were more experienced than he was, in war and in council or on the Pnyx. Yet he had matched them and he would exceed them in the days to come. He had read every speech published, every argument made. He had trained himself in body and mind – working on his birthday and feast days in the knowledge that not one of his competitors would work on theirs. Success could be beaten and subdued like metal on a forge or a wild horse. That had been his revelation and it had not failed him yet.

'Gentlemen, in my ship, I will take a part of Athens with me when I leave,' he began. Ephialtes smiled. A little humour made them love him. 'Though I am glad the captain has more experience than a new-made strategos.'

The council laughed, to the duration and volume he drew from them. He smiled in real pleasure.

'I welcome the honour, gentlemen. I will represent this council and the Assembly at sea, to the islands and the fleets of our allies. I give my oath to uphold our principles – of integrity, of courage and rule of the people. Those of you who know me can attest to my belief. I thank you for your vote today.'

They cheered as he stood back, and just for fun and spite, he held out a hand to one of the other two, forcing the man to stumble through a speech without preparation. It fell rather flat, but Ephialtes applauded him even so. The council broke for lunch and he went out into the Agora, where the officers of three triremes had gathered.

'Gentlemen, you are to convey me to the fleet, as strategos,' Ephialtes said.

30

Ephialtes fumed as he paced his own deck. He could *see* the damn island of Delos just off his bow as the trireme swung at anchor. He could also see the line of hoplites – Athenians! – who lined the quays and had refused to allow him to land, refused even to accept his authority as strategos. They had humiliated him in front of his crews, men who had taken to sea with a new-made strategos and would remember this for the rest of their lives.

For three weeks, he and his captains had swept or sailed from island to island, inspecting Athenian positions or members of the alliance. He had been treated like a visiting king, which was completely justified. As one of the strategoi, Ephialtes *was* the Assembly. In his person, he represented the power and reach of the entire city of Athens and every last man, woman and child within her walls. When they bowed to him, that was how he accepted it. Not on his own behalf, or out of vanity, but as the people themselves. He carried their honour with him, after all.

To be refused on the very docks of Delos was an insult of similar degree. He was not angry for himself, though the lochagos officer had shown no respect at all. The man had only shrugged and spat off the dock when Ephialtes told him his title and declared his right to set foot on the island.

That insult would not stand, could not be allowed to stand. Yet the Assembly had only granted him the bare minimum of crew and only a dozen hoplites of his own, all as fresh and green as he was as a strategos. Only one of the soldiers

CONN IGGULDEN

had war experience and that man had been made officer over the rest. Oh, they were fit enough and they looked as if they could handle spear and shield, but it did not change the reality: the hoplites left to guard Delos outnumbered his four to one. Ephialtes imagined too that the sort who might be left in charge of a vast treasury would be veterans. They looked like it, as he glared over them. Their shields and armour gleamed, but were a long way from new. It looked like kit a twenty-year man might have worn, each inherited piece polished to comfort.

Nor were they men he could surprise with a night landing. In the afternoon, he had watched in confusion as they lit a bonfire on a hill just inland from the docks. The result was a pair of fully crewed triremes that had come sweeping in from the other side of Delos. They had risked shattering his oars as they passed too close, judging what threat he posed. Ephialtes grew red-faced as he remembered the things they had called. Sailors were a crude lot, and though he told himself he loved the common men, he did not enjoy their wit when it was aimed at him.

There was no way he would be allowed to land, that much was clear. Ephialtes looked up at the setting sun as he had the thought and blanched at the sight of many more ships appearing over the horizon. Had they been summoned by the smoke as well? He could see the sails before the main part of them, as if the fleet climbed a hill. It was the same whenever a ship was sighted far away and he did not understand it. What mattered most was numbers, the sea power of a fleet – and the immediate conclusion. There was only one force at sea that year with so many ships. His initial panic at the thought of Persians was replaced by irritation. Cimon. Of course it would be Cimon behind the stubborn refusal of the hoplites on Delos, the aggressive trireme captains who darted like dragonflies over the water and made his crews look slow. It would be Cimon who was responsible for the humiliation of an officer of the Assembly duly appointed.

'As if summoned,' Ephialtes announced to any of his crew in hearing. 'When they arrive, I will certainly make my displeasure known to Cimon as a fellow strategos of Athens.'

He glanced around him, but his officers were all bustling about, aware of the impending presence of the fleet. They did not seem to have heard his grand comment. Ephialtes considered speaking again, but six of his hoplites clattered on deck then, standing at attention while the keleustes checked every part of the ship was worthy of inspection. They were all nervous, Ephialtes realised with a sneer. It was pitiful how men lowered themselves in the presence of others. If they did not, they could stand as equals, he was certain.

He stood with legs slightly apart and arms folded for a long time, while the sun began its slide into purples and grey and the alliance fleet rowed closer over deep waters. The smoke faded against the evening sky and there did not seem to be any great haste in their approach. There was just a slight breeze off the island as they took anchor around his ships and all that part of the coast.

Ephialtes watched, hiding his awe at the number of them. There had to be three hundred ships – and who knew how many tens of thousands in their crews! He had seen them last on the huge stone docks of the Piraeus at Athens, where many of them had been built and launched. The scale matched them well enough there. At anchor around the island of Delos, they seemed a far greater enterprise, a fleet of massive strength and sea power, a nation afloat.

Ephialtes unfolded his arms. His three ships had felt like swords at sea when he'd left Piraeus. He had watched the waves break into spray and the oars bite with a sort of savage joy, but it left him then. The fleet surrounded him and lost him in its midst. Wherever he looked, he could see men scrubbing decks, sluicing them with buckets of seawater drawn up on lines. He looked away from a few hanging very pale buttocks into the breeze. Even in his few weeks at sea, he'd learned most men emptied their bowels when the ships were moving. Their captains preferred not to be surrounded by bobbing turds when they lay at anchor. Yet there were always a few caught by some ailment. Ephialtes watched them, just one part in a thousand of an extraordinary bustle that seemed to overlook his presence completely. He felt a slow anger build. He was a strategos of Athens! At the very least, Cimon should have sent a boat for him.

Ephialtes could see his captain trying to catch his attention. He had no answers and avoided the gaze. With just a little luck, the man would see him as stern and distant, a figure to be admired as he waited to announce his presence. Where was the boat for him? Surely Cimon could not be unaware. Unless it was a deliberate insult. That would not surprise him, from a noble son. The Eupatridae were famous for contests of power and authority, often crueller to their own than those they considered lesser men. Ephialtes firmed his jaw at the thought, standing tall. If that was their game, he had one or two of his own.

Cimon sent a boat across as true dark came and the fleet lay at rest. He had been aware of the little group of ships by Delos from the first sighting, with all the interest of a guard dog spotting interlopers. The treasury of the alliance was there, after all. The smoke signal raised on the hill might have looked like a call for help, but it was almost the opposite. Cimon had two ships on station at Delos, as well as a large force on the island itself. A single line of smoke was merely to announce the presence of a stranger. Priests asked to visit the birthplace of Apollo and Artemis a dozen times a year and the smoke signalled their arrival. A second strand rising to the sky, separate from the first, would have meant a serious threat. Cimon would have driven the rowers to exhaustion then to bring him in.

The number and arrangement of the forces on Delos was one of a thousand tasks laid at his feet each month. Of course it was the reason a navarch promoted senior officers he could trust. Xanthippus had done it for Cimon when the Persians invaded, relying on him in the midst of battle. Cimon looked at the man's son and grinned to himself. Pericles was shaping up well and those shoulders could stand a little more weight. His own could certainly do with less.

Pericles had come across when his own ship was being scrubbed, sanded and set right. Wooden ships needed almost constant labour and each day brought new tasks round on rotation, from repairing a cracked mast to the endless oiling. The sun and sea seemed to strip oil out of a warship, so that every board and step had to be soaked anew.

Pericles was in quiet conversation with his companions when Cimon strolled across the deck, already smiling. Cimon enjoyed the company of Anaxagoras and Zeno in particular. Anaxagoras had wasted no time marrying an Athenian woman and getting her pregnant. He was like a dog with two tails about that. Cimon found Epikleos fair company, though the older man had gone a little deaf. Though it was no fault of his own, it was irritating to speak louder. There was also the slight sense that Epikleos had known Cimon's father, had walked with him at Marathon. Cimon had teased every memory of that day from him and valued adding them to his own store. Yet as a rule, he preferred those around his own

CONN IGGULDEN

age, without the awkward sense that one of them had brought his dad along.

When the boat returned, Cimon was already laughing with the others as they were given bowls of thick stew and a piece of bread. The food was terrible, but there were fruit trees and vegetables grown on Delos and they would do better in the morning, when they went ashore. The storerooms below the decks were filled with talents of silver given as tribute for the league, all under constant guard. The gods knew Cimon loved his people, but that did not mean he trusted them to ignore sacks of silver sitting all alone.

He looked up as the newcomer clambered to the deck, waving off the hand held out to him by a hoplite there. Cimon felt his heart sink as he recognised Ephialtes. He did not know the man well, but Ephialtes seemed to bristle in his presence whenever they met, as if Cimon had offended him in some way. He handed his bowl to the cook's boy and went to greet him.

'You are welcome, Ephialtes,' Cimon said. 'I was not told you had come. I would have sent for you sooner.'

The man bowed his head to a senior officer, though even that was somehow grudging, as if his neck only ever bent with a huge effort.

'I did wonder if I was being ignored, Archon Cimon,' Ephialtes replied. He would have gone on, but Cimon spoke immediately to interrupt him.

'It is "navarch" in this fleet, Ephialtes.'

Ephialtes smiled in triumph, delighted at the chance to reply in kind.

'Then it is "Strategos Ephialtes", navarch,' he said.

'Truly? Congratulations. Are your ships new additions to the fleet? They are very welcome.'

'I command them, yes,' Ephialtes went on. 'Under the authority of the Assembly of Athens.'

'Then you are all very welcome,' Cimon said lightly. He did not seem impressed by the new title and Ephialtes was growing red. 'I was just thinking I needed more officers . . .'

To his surprise, Ephialtes spoke over him, his voice taking on a brassy hardness.

'An authority which has been refused by your hoplites on shore, as well as the captains of two triremes in these waters. I am not concerned for my own dignity, but for that of the Assembly. For that reason alone, I must bring a complaint to you as senior officer.'

'I see.'

Cimon judged the man he faced once more. He did not like Ephialtes and so took a different tone.

'What form of punishment did you have in mind?' he asked.

Perhaps one who knew him better might have seen a warning in the sudden calm. Ephialtes did not, however. He gave the matter real consideration. He did not want to be seen as vengeful, but an insult had been received and the point had to be made.

'I would have thought . . . a whipping, perhaps. No more than that.'

Cimon looked at him for a long time and Ephialtes finally understood he had overreached. His colour deepened and he raised his head in defiance, refusing to look away.

Cimon nodded as if he had seen all he had to.

'Well, your complaint is denied, strategos. My crews have express orders not to let anyone land on Delos unless I am present, or in the event of my death, an equivalent officer of the alliance fleet. Do you understand? No mere captain or strategos may land. The League of Delos keeps its silver on the island, the very symbol of our alliance. So – there is no one at fault here. I will certainly not indulge your wounded pride in making it seem as if there is. Is that clear?'

'I . . . I d-don't think . . .'

'Is that clear, strategos?' Cimon repeated with more force.

Ephialtes nodded, his eyes glittering.

'Excellent,' Cimon said. 'With that decided, I hope you will eat with us. I have nothing fresh, but the cook makes a fine sour mash with barley, cheese and oxtail. You are welcome to join me as my guest. I know the men will certainly want to hear news of home.'

'Th-that . . .' Ephialtes continued to stammer, then took a grip on strong emotion and breathed deeply. Cimon had all the easy way of wealth and power, the sort of manner that took generations to create. If he was to be an enemy, it would not do to let him know. Yet Ephialtes did not think he could endure a meal with the man, not after a public humiliation. He made himself reply as if ice water ran in his veins.

'I wish I could remain, navarch, but I must see to my own ships. The Assembly sent me with barely enough crew. Can you spare me any men?'

He did not understand the quick expression that flashed across Cimon's face. It looked almost like regret as the navarch shook his head.

'It might be better if you let me select them for you, Ephialtes. We'll unload the tribute tomorrow, then sail for Cypros. That will be a couple of weeks by sail and oar. I can find you a good crew in that time, I'm sure. If you let my captains . . .'

'I need just sixty men,' Ephialtes snapped. 'Unless you seek to frustrate me, I remind you of my new rank. Am I not asking in the right way? Since the moment I arrived in these waters, I have been blocked and insulted. Well, that ends now! Whether you resent my appointment or not, we have spoken – and I have asked for sixty Athenians. Have them sent to my three ships by the end of the day tomorrow.'

Cimon looked coldly at him, then nodded.

'As you wish, strategos,' he replied.

Ephialtes turned on his heel and went back to the sea ladder and the boat waiting for him. Cimon looked over at the group of Pericles, Anaxagoras, Zeno and Epikleos. They were all watching in astonishment, of course. On the open deck, they could not even pretend they had not heard.

Cimon shook his head as he went back to them and took up his bowl. The mash had congealed and he worked a piece free and into his mouth, chewing hard.

'If you let your captains send anyone they like,' Pericles said, 'he will get the worst of them, the laziest thieves and bullies from the whole fleet.'

'Yes,' Cimon said. 'I tried to explain that. Our friend was in no mood to listen.'

31

Pericles wondered if there would ever be a time when the sight of the fleet under sail failed to raise his spirits. With a light wind, they soared south like geese, helmsmen keeping station in lines. Hoplites in polished bronze walked the decks. There was a joy and a speed to all of it that he loved.

Only the sight of the ships under Ephialtes could spoil his mood that morning, weeks south of Delos. The newly minted strategos of Athens had counted it a victory to receive sixty men to fill his benches and raise sail. Yet it had been as Pericles had guessed, with rather more knowledge of the fleet. Half the captains of the alliance had some crewman they disliked, some drunk troublemaker who riled up all the rest. They had been delighted to send their worst.

It had showed from the first day. The warships under Ephialtes had needed experienced men of the best quality to train green crews. Instead, they drifted to the rear of the fleet under sail, seemingly unable to match the pace or course of the rest. Worse, Ephialtes had appointed some of the new men as officers over the rest. Pericles had heard they turned out to be petty tyrants of the worst kind, kissing the sandals of the new strategos and tormenting those they commanded. There were said to be floggings on board every day, with half his crews bearing new stripes. It did not seem to have restored discipline.

Anaxagoras saw the direction of Pericles' grim stare as he came to stand alongside. The tall Ionian was always looking for a rail to lean upon, but of course there were none at the open deck. The great stern curved up and over, with a couple of steps set for a lookout to climb. The rest of the crew had to stand for the duty watches, until their feet ached. Anaxagoras felt the discomfort more than most, so that he rubbed the small of his back at intervals. He did so then, as he watched the three ships drifting far behind the rest. One of them cut its own path, losing ground all the time.

'Tell me again how that man was voted strategos,' Anaxagoras murmured.

Pericles flashed him a grin.

'The Assembly appoints ten every year. Some are kept, brought back again and again almost as a formality. My father was one; Aristides is another. Others fall away, if they fail to serve with any distinction. It is too early to judge how Ephialtes is doing.'

'Is it?' Anaxagoras said.

Pericles chuckled. It had been his delight to find Anaxagoras could be a very amusing man. It was easy to miss at first. Anaxagoras rarely laughed as Zeno did, until wine came out his nose. Anaxagoras may have married an Athenian, yet he was an outsider still, an observer. Coupled with an extraordinary mind, it lent him a fresh perspective. Zeno said there was no problem the tall man could not solve, given time and inclination. It was a rare compliment.

'It is astonishing how much discord he has sown in just a few short weeks,' Pericles said. 'He challenges Cimon as if it's personal, but lacks the knowledge to do it well. No, he is out of his element at sea, Anaxagoras. Sometimes the people vote a fool to power. The only comfort is that they can remove him. A tyrant would last rather longer.'

'Perhaps his crew will kill him first,' Zeno said, coming up behind.

The three of them stared out over the stern. Cimon was

CONN IGGULDEN

on his own flagship not two hundred paces away. They used the same breeze in their sails, a brotherhood of sorts. Even as Pericles had the thought, he saw Cimon stroll to his stern and glare at the ships falling further and further behind. There was no need to imagine his thoughts. Cimon had expressed them very clearly, though not before the other captains of the alliance.

'If a dog is tormented long enough, it will snap at its master,' Pericles said. 'Yet if they rebel, Cimon will have to put them ashore, to starve or beg passage home. And if there is violence, he will hang them. They are free men. They do not have to serve in the fleet.' He rubbed his jaw, feeling the bristles there. 'But I think Cimon will act before that happens. If he splits those with Ephialtes between a hundred ships, he might still save them. They'll learn what a good crew looks like – and what is expected of them.'

'On the theory that good apples turn bad apples good?' Anaxagoras said. 'Perhaps. Or they might ruin discipline across the entire fleet. One bad apple to each ship could play havoc, don't you think?'

'A bad apple won't get its teeth knocked out if it talks back to an experienced man,' Pericles said. He waved his hand. 'Either way, men are not apples.'

'No? Yet our friend the strategos does give me the pip,' Anaxagoras muttered.

At the other end of the warship, the lookout called 'Rising shallow!' at the top of his voice. He pointed with his left hand and the helmsmen adjusted their course, easing them away from possible threat. They were on a stretch between islands, making their way south and east as if they leaped between stepping stones. It was a path Pericles had travelled with his father and brother, and for a moment, memory choked him. Rhodes lay to the south and as they passed its northern tip, the horizon was simply Persia, vast and unknowable.

The thought reminded him of their purpose in having entered those waters. Ever since he'd noted the lack of Persian vessels, he'd hoped not to be made to look a fool. For all Cimon talked of the need for their fleet to be seen, Pericles did not want his judgement called into question. That too could be spent like coins, with nothing to show at the end.

He dragged his gaze away from the ailing ships wandering behind the fleet. That was Cimon's problem rather than his. Instead, Pericles shaded his eyes and looked for a single Persian craft of any kind. He squinted and turned, but the odd emptiness seemed to be holding. In that part of the south, there was not a sail to be seen. Not a fishing boat nor a merchant ship, never mind a ship of war.

Persia was a land empire, it was true. It was still strange to see empty ocean right along the coast of their southern heart. Pericles found his eyes tearing up from so long looking into the glare, but he was satisfied he had not wasted Cimon's time with a false warning. There was something peculiar in that absence. He could feel it like a storm coming.

As the fleet moved across the sea, the breeze died away to nothing. Almost in unison, sails were brought down and oars rattled out, sweeping them up to speed in good time, faster than before. Pericles could not help glancing at the ships under Ephialtes. They floundered as if they'd struck some unseen bank, wallowing in choppy waters. Oars appeared and then were pulled back in, for no reason he could discern. If that sort of chaos hadn't resulted in whipped crewmen each evening, it might have been amusing. As it was, Pericles clenched his fists.

At home on the Pnyx, Ephialtes spoke well and clearly, with a good sense of his beliefs. With the land under him, he

CONN IGGULDEN

was steady enough, but sea was different and unforgiving. Men stood revealed at sea. No doubt they would hear a dozen new complaints from Ephialtes when Cimon summoned the officers that evening.

Pericles shook his head as he turned away. There came a point when it was almost rude to watch. He noticed Zeno still seemed entranced, but Anaxagoras was staring in a new direction, his attention beyond the fleet.

On the Persian shore, a river mouth yawned, wider and wider as they crossed it. For an instant, Pericles thought he saw shapes at the edge of sight. He raised both hands to shade his eyes, but it had been like a bird's wing, a flicker that vanished in the haze. The sun was dipping low and he thought Cimon would soon give the order to head in to that shore and anchor for the night. Cypros lay to their south, but it would be a full day's sail to reach the coast he remembered.

'I wonder how far that river goes,' Anaxagoras said dreamily. 'When I lived in Ionia, some Persian merchants said the empire had no ending, that it just went on and on for ever. They described mountains and valleys, cities by the thousand, unknown to any of us.'

'Do you think they were telling you the truth?' Zeno asked.

Anaxagoras shrugged.

'Who can say? Yet we have sailed around their coast for days now. Did you see that river? Its mouth was as wide as the Hellespont, but I have never seen it on a map, nor heard its name. There is so much of the world I will never even see! It is a humbling thought. Even more so for you, Zeno.'

'Why for me?'

'Your height, my friend. You will never see as much of the world as I, because your viewpoint is so much lower.'

Zeno looked at him in apparent astonishment, though

Pericles had heard them argue in much the same way many times.

'You think a man on a ladder is wiser than one without?' Zeno began.

Pericles chuckled and left them to it. He walked back to the stern to empty his bladder downwind. The only ships he could see were of the League of Delos, the great fleet itself. His people.

The signal to heave to for the night came in plenty of time. Cimon always made the decision with sea room and light enough for his captains to reach shallow water and drop anchors without risking their hulls. His captains were adept at heading in at the slowest speed under oar, in waters so clear the boy on the prow could call depth by eye alone. The great fleet was quiet by the time evening came, with crews settling down to talk and eat and gamble or repair kit. Some told stories and others strummed an instrument they had made themselves, leading the rest in songs older than time. Before the light faded, a few oarsmen swam or took small boats to shore to look for fruit or set snares. They went armed, but there was no sign of herdsmen or villagers, not on those bare brown hills.

It was a time of rest and calm for those who rowed. The same was not true for their officers, however. After a day of watching the three ships with Ephialtes, Pericles was not exactly surprised to be summoned to the flagship. Not that he had senior rank in that fleet. Below the age of thirty, he could be neither strategos nor archon, epistates for the Assembly nor judge. He could vote on any matter, or sit on a jury. He could choose to defend or prosecute any case in law, if all sides agreed. Yet he was not trusted with the lives of others, not until he had learned *praotes* – the calm of a mature man.

CONN IGGULDEN

As a result, Pericles had not answered the first call for senior officers, until Cimon had sent a boat to fetch him. Since
then, he'd understood he enjoyed a confidence with his
friend that few others knew. Perhaps it was because Pericles
had shared experiences – he didn't like to think of some – or
just because their fathers had known one another. Pericles
didn't mind what it was. He'd come to realise Cimon was the
sort of man he needed to be. Pericles tried to deal with him
as an equal, sensing Cimon needed that from him. Yet the
truth was, he revered him. Cimon may have been young to
lead the League of Delos. Captains and archons accepted his
authority, as navarch of them all. Pericles frowned at the
thought. The irony was that only Ephialtes challenged that
authority, an Athenian-born.

In the last light of the day, Pericles could see Ephialtes hail
and approach, climbing up the rope and steps to the deck.
He sighed at the man's thunderous expression. Perhaps it
was the day spent in constant battle with his crews, but Ephialtes was clearly in a fine temper. He had brought a crewman
with him, one who adjusted the strategos' robe and cloak as
he stood there. Ephialtes glanced at Pericles and dismissed
him in the instant, his lip curling.

'Where is Navarch Cimon?' Ephialtes demanded from the
open deck.

He didn't look at Pericles as he spoke, so Pericles said
nothing. The strategos irritated him in a way he didn't trouble
to define. Some men were just fools. Pericles saw the crewman attendant step out of his master's shadow. He felt breath
catch in his throat.

Attikos, who nodded to him as their eyes met. The man
kept turning up like a curse. Pericles had not seen him for
weeks, though a few things made immediate sense. First, that
the captain who had brought Pericles out would have taken

the chance to rid himself of a man he'd already had to lash – and that Attikos would have risen under one like Ephialtes. The man looked a little nervous on that deck, as well he might. Pericles wondered how much Ephialtes had been told of their history. Cimon too would be interested to see him, though not pleased.

'I asked where Navarch Cimon was,' Ephialtes said again. 'Does he no longer greet his colleagues?'

This time, he spoke directly to Pericles. The younger man tore his gaze from Attikos to answer.

'The meeting has already begun, strategos.' He bit his lip for a moment, but he could not help adding, 'Some time ago. Navarch Cimon is in his meeting room below, with the strategoi and alliance officers. You are the last to arrive. He asked me to wait for you.'

Ephialtes flushed. He was late because his ships had laboured hours behind the rest. They hadn't reached safe anchorage before darkness, so that they risked both hulls and crews. Nor had they made any great speed in getting Ephialtes across to the flagship. Yet it seemed that that knowledge only deepened the man's sense of grievance.

'Then you are delaying me further,' Ephialtes snapped. 'Go!'

Pericles turned on his heel and led the man down steps to the hold. He could hear the murmur and quiet laughter of the fleet officers there, like the contented buzz of bees. That would surely change, he thought. He was bringing a wasp with him.

Pericles held the door and Ephialtes entered. Attikos stood back.

'I hope, kurios . . .' the wiry little man started to say.

Pericles closed the door on his words. It was a petty thing, but he still smiled as he turned to the room.

CONN IGGULDEN

The hum of conversation had halted. Most of the men had cups of wine and there was humour in the air that quieted as Ephialtes raised his chin and glared.

'I expected you some time ago,' Cimon said.

His tone was mild enough, but Ephialtes clearly took it as a rebuke.

'I was not sent word in time, Navarch Cimon.'

'Really? Well, it doesn't matter now. You are here. There are no serious issues left to discuss. In fact, gentlemen, I think we can raise a toast to a good day and send you back to a night's sleep and a meal.'

Cimon raised his own cup and all those crammed into the little room did the same. The mood was light and only Ephialtes stood like a rainstorm by the door. The gathered officers of the fleet made idle conversation as they began to leave, restoring the sound of contentment and friendship to the room.

'I would, er . . . Strategos Ephialtes?' Cimon said. 'I'd like to have a word, if I may.'

Ephialtes gave a sharp nod and waited as the others filed past. A number of them glanced at him, one or two with amusement. He only frowned, as serious as he could be.

Overhead, they could hear muffled calls to boats waiting and the steps of men walking across the open deck. That cramped room was just part of the hold at the stern. Pericles saw sacks of flour were stacked at one end where there had been none before. It was too small even for just the most senior men, but it still seemed to echo as they left Cimon and Pericles with a strategos of Athens.

Pericles bowed and stepped to the door to give the pair of them privacy. He had an idea of what Cimon would say and he was not sure he wanted to be a witness, perhaps one Ephialtes would recall later. He had it half-open when Cimon spoke.

'Stay please, would you, Pericles?' Cimon said. 'I would like you to confirm what passes here.'

His heart sank. Pericles could see Attikos in the open doorway, the man's expression confused. No doubt he would be listening, Pericles thought.

It seemed Ephialtes also sensed trouble in the air. His response was to go on the offensive and he spoke before Cimon could continue.

'What is the meaning of this? Sending men away and keeping me here? Calling me late and ending the meeting as I arrive! I ask only for the respect due my rank, navarch, nothing more.'

'If I relieve you of duty, Ephialtes, you will never be a name in Athens.'

Ephialtes narrowed his eyes.

'Without good grounds, Archon Cimon, I would force you to trial myself, if you dared try such a thing. Do you understand that? You are not beyond the law! I'm surprised I need to tell that to a son of Miltiades! If you seek to destroy my name out of spite or envy, you will not escape the damage.' Ephialtes glanced at Pericles, standing as if struck at what he was hearing. 'No matter who your friends are.'

Pericles watched Cimon. *Praotes* was a form of calm, but not among friends or on a sunny day. Men summoned *praotes* in the storm, when it mattered most. Those who had it prided themselves on treating disaster with a gentle smile. Cimon certainly used it then.

'I command the fleet, Ephialtes. No, allow me to reply. There is no peace declared with Persia. We remain at war-readiness, at least for the moment. So I will not attempt to persuade you to my side. Whatever the reason for your hostility, I don't share it. I too am an Athenian, but I am also navarch of a greater fleet and responsible for the discipline and conduct of all captains under my command. Men such as yourself, strategos. I could appoint more experienced captains to your ships – perhaps I should.'

Ephialtes began to speak again, but stopped when Cimon raised his hand. The submission seemed to wound Ephialtes, so that his colour only deepened to brick red.

'As navarch, I wish to maintain our sea power . . . and as an Athenian, I do not want to see one of my own senior men humiliated or ridiculed in the fleet! Therefore, you will return the worst of your men to their previous ships. I should have insisted on a better selection being sent across to you, not just the dregs.'

'So that is how it came about!' Ephialtes said. 'Was it in humour, or to teach me a lesson? I should have known . . .'

Cimon went on over him, as if he was not speaking.

'I will send four dozen of the best we have to be your crews. If you are still short, you'll have to make do. You will find the ones I send rather different quality from those you have now. We'll make the changes on Cypros, tomorrow evening as Poseidon wills.'

'I don't . . .'

'That is an order, Strategos Ephialtes. If you refuse it, no trial on the Pnyx will save you. As my father Miltiades discovered. It was Xanthippus who stood against him that day, did you know that? Pericles' father, who acted for Athens to censure a man who had overreached and cost the lives of many. So don't think for a moment that I am unaware of the consequences of failure or dishonour. I was there that day. I understand – and I welcome the responsibility of being navarch to this fleet even so. Understand *that*, Ephialtes – and we will be just fine.'

Pericles watched another man realise Cimon held himself to a higher standard than almost anyone. Ephialtes gaped like a fish in a net as he took it in. His face was very cold as he nodded.

'I suspect you will never understand the men in my crews, Navarch Cimon. They have not had your advantages. Nor have they learned to kneel to power, as some would prefer. Still, I accept your authority in front of your witness. You will not be able to say I did not. Am I dismissed?'

Cimon was hurt by the man's spite, Pericles could see that. The navarch dipped his head and turned away at the same time, so that he did not see Ephialtes leave. Pericles stood awkwardly for a moment, not sure if he should creep out as well, or whether he was still needed.

'I don't really need to win him round,' Cimon said at last. 'Only for him to keep his ships in line with the rest.' He smiled, but there was pain in it. 'He's probably right about being removed from command. I could do it, perhaps, though the Assembly might take all I value away from me.'

'Can they?' Pericles asked. 'The League is more than just Athens now. Perhaps you could remain as navarch.'

'Not if they appoint another in command of the Athenian fleet,' Cimon replied. 'If it was Ephialtes, for example . . .' He shook his head. 'No. I will tread carefully . . .'

He broke off as Pericles stepped to the door and opened it. Attikos was there, jumping up from where he had been listening.

'Just tying a strap on my sandal,' Attikos said, sly wit always close to the surface.

'Go back to your master,' Pericles said coldly.

The man bowed and vanished. Pericles closed the door and sighed.

'You could send Ephialtes up that river we passed. That would give him something to do for a few days. I thought I

CONN IGGULDEN

saw a sail there and Anaxagoras said we have no maps of the Persian coast.'

Cimon looked up in interest, though he was already shaking his head.

'I have never met a man more likely to suffer mutiny, or perhaps to wedge a ship in a mudbank. No, tempting as it is, I did not make the offer lightly. I'll give him first-rate crews – men I really trust. I would rather have his resentment, and gain three good warships, than have him content and lose them.'

Pericles saw it coming before the words could be spoken. He opened his mouth to object and then closed it, letting the blow fall.

'Men I trust . . . such as yourself, Pericles,' Cimon said.

He had the grace to look a little embarrassed. Months on board a ship with Ephialtes would be brutal, but that was the nature of service – and *praotes*. Pericles swallowed uncomfortably.

'I would like Anaxagoras, Zeno and Epikleos with me,' he said.

'Don't bargain, Pericles. I'll give you whatever you want. In six months, the fleet will be stronger for it – and our new strategos will have learned to love the sea.'

'I hope so.'

Cimon smiled, but then a frown changed his face entirely.

'You thought you saw a sail? Today?'

Pericles waved a hand.

'Probably not. It might have been a bird at that distance.'

'No one else reported any sightings.'

'Neither did I,' Pericles replied with a shrug.

Cimon nodded. He made a quick decision.

'Row back at dawn, would you? Before we raise sail. Scout to the first bend and then return.'

*

Artabazus waited in darkness. There were no fires on the banks of the Eurymedon river, not while the Greeks anchored along that coast. On deck and on land, his regiments ate cold food in silence. It was as if a leviathan swam nearby, hunting for prey. He felt sweat trickle down his cheek like a line drawn on his skin. He rubbed at it, feeling how stiff his muscles had become. When he was a boy, he had broken a plate his father loved and then had to wait for him to come home, dreading the strap and the anger for hours. It was worse than the actual punishment, he was certain. This felt like an echo of that fear, watching the daylight fade, waiting for the storm to rumble in, the indignation, the rising fury and the violence. He felt himself trembling and cursed his nerves. He had an army of Immortal regiments, a fleet greater than the Greeks! The king was with them, in a tent more like a palace than a soldier's bed. So why was he afraid? Surely Artabazus was his father, coming home, bearing his strap and his rage! That was a better way to think of it. He took a deep breath and reached for a sticky little ball. One more, to calm his nerves and help him sleep. The fleet would be gone in the morning.

He twitched at some noise in the darkness. He preferred torches to light the camp, but his own order forbade them. It had sounded like his father's step on the stair, the slow tread that terrified him. He had gone into Greece and burned Athens. In reply, they had followed him to Cypros. Now they had come again, hunting him always, tormenting him in his fears. Let me sleep, he prayed. I'll be good. Please, just let me sleep.

32

Pericles watched the folds of sail collapsing onto the deck, drawn in by a dozen willing hands. It was stiff with salt, marked in crystal whorls and a glittering sheen. He saw too the places where it had been patched. Cloth failed at sea, as did everything else. It was not part of his vision of a great fleet, but the reality was one of constant repair. On well-run ships, it would usually be before some vital part snapped or failed. For some League members, especially those with older ships, it seemed to be whenever the wind blew.

He grinned at the sight of Anaxagoras and Zeno heaving in the sail together. They had made themselves useful despite the lack of a formal position on the crew. Pericles suspected Anaxagoras could have drawn plans for a trireme warship from memory by then, he had spent so long inspecting the vessel. He had already suggested a new design of tiller, which Cimon had promised to build and test.

The oars made a great rumble as they were fed out below deck, length over length until they could be dipped down to the waters. In the past, single banks had heaved ships slowly along. Three rows of oarsmen, professionally trained, made the ships faster – and speed was power. They had proved that at Salamis.

With the sail rolled and tied and the oars sweeping, the mouth of the river seemed to open before them. Pericles had a sudden thought of being swallowed and chuckled nervously. Such things could be idle fancies, or messages from the gods. His mother had dreamed of a lion the night before he was born. He still carried that with him, as a symbol of his will. Whatever it meant, the simple knowledge gave him strength.

Pericles watched as the captain went to the prow. The ship's boy had climbed the mast like a little monkey, clinging on at the highest point. The entire crew was nervous in strange waters, Pericles could see that. Unknown currents could upset a trireme and of course the water hid rocks or the great banks of sand and shingle that could hold a boat as tight as a lover. With Cimon and the fleet waiting for them, that would just be a humiliation, but it was still one they wanted to avoid.

The river mouth was vast, Pericles realised, the shape of a fish-tail as it reached the sea. The waters were churned brown, thick with dust and silt drawn from mountains he would never know. He stared into the distance as the ship entered the fresh waters. The current could be felt immediately and the oarsmen began to work and sweat to maintain their pace. They went in, a single dart down the centre of the great channel.

The current seemed less fierce as they left the sea behind. On the river proper, the oars swept them along at a good pace, the first bend far off. Hills rose from the waters in what looked like red clay, with old trees and scrub clinging to life on tumbled slopes. Birds flew overhead, low to the water. There was life there.

The captain was making jerky little movements at the prow, Pericles could see, almost like a bird himself as he peered about. Pericles felt for him. The water was still full of silt; they might not even glimpse a rock before it ripped open their hull. With a moment of pride and memory, Pericles recalled something his father had once said. When nothing could be done, there was no point showing fear. When the crisis was past, men remembered those who had faced their deaths with calm. He stood tall on the deck, staring out at a different world from the one he knew.

They rowed towards the first great bend in the river. The banks were clear of anything but a few wild goats. They scattered as they sighted the single ship, which suggested they knew the shapes or sounds of men. Pericles frowned at that. The land was utterly deserted. He'd have to return to Cimon with an apology . . .

The boy on the mast shouted in warning. Pericles looked up at him and so was a beat late to see what had caught his attention. The captain too had been looking down at the churning waters. He gaped, while the keleustes called to be told what they saw. It was a moment of chaos and still Pericles could only stare.

Beyond the river's turn, a fleet waited, anchored on both banks. Persian regiments could be seen marching, vanishing into the haze. Even as Pericles breathed out in astonishment, the captain was roaring orders for them to get out. There were boats in the water, already darting at them like predators. Narrow little daggers, with six rowers. Pericles saw a cluster of them racing at extraordinary speed in their direction, their intention clear. He turned to fetch his shield and Epikleos was there, passing it to him. With a helmet resting on the club of his hair, Pericles took sword and spear as they too were handed over. The rest of the hoplites armed themselves and stood ready to defend the ship. They were a disciplined and experienced crew and they had long spears cocked before the first boats reached them.

Below decks, the keleustes roared new orders to the rowers. It was a difficult manoeuvre, but they had done it a thousand times in training. A long slow turn on rudders pushed right over would take them even further into enemy waters. Instead, on one side, all three banks of oars swept back hard, reversing their usual motion. The other side still heaved forward. It meant the ship could turn almost in its own length, but it was a dangerous move in unknown waters. The trireme shuddered and groaned as it turned, leaning horribly far.

Pericles stood on the open deck, watching the knife-boats slicing water to reach them. As well as rowers, they had warriors kneeling on some central spar, men in Persian armour he had not seen since Cypros. He felt coldness return to his stomach just at the sight of them. Men such as those had killed his brother, on a shore not very far from where they were. He would not turn his face away, he told himself, though they had filled his nightmares a hundred times.

Spears were thrown from the boats as they closed, rising like flickering shadows. Pericles raised his shield with the rest, overlapping the scales. He felt the impact rock him back like a punch. A dozen barbed things clattered to the deck, slipping and rolling underfoot. Without warning, Epikleos suddenly thumped a fist on his helmet, driving it down so that it scraped his nose. Yet Pericles was grateful. To look out on the world through that slit of bronze was a soldier's view. It returned him to a colder, more deadly version of himself, with all weakness smothered. He raised his right arm to bring the dory spear ready to throw, but did not release it. His task then was to defend the ship. The news of what they had seen had to be taken back to Cimon.

Though they had turned, there was still a breathless pause while the rowers readied themselves. In that time, the Persians had put a flotilla of the slender boats across their path, blocking their escape. More spears arced up at them from both sides, taking one hoplite in the back. He fell with a grunt and Pericles had no time to know if his armour had saved him as something else came whirring through the air and he had to duck under his shield. He almost threw his own spear in a blind rage, but the voice of the lochagos sounded then, calm and faintly exasperated.

'*Wait* for it . . . ! No one is to throw until I say so. Any spear lost in the sea will come out of your fucking pay.'

Pericles found himself grinning, his cheeks aching with it. Anaxagoras and Zeno had come alongside him, each bearing an old shield held together with what looked like wire and studded nails in the wood. They had practised a thousand hours on deck with sword and spear, but the reality of armed Persians intent on their deaths was something new. Pericles realised they were looking to him for instruction.

'Just be calm,' he said.

One or two of the hoplites heard and nodded. Panic was the enemy, more than the Persians. It was the first lesson they all learned and the one Pericles had remembered: panic killed men, more than plague, pox or jilted lovers put together. Pericles took a long, slow breath and felt able to smile at his friends.

'Our task is to get back to the fleet,' he said. 'Not to fight these little boats.'

As he spoke, the keleustes called for a faster time. The oars bit deep and men heaved in unison, forcing a greater pace. They were surrounded, with at least a dozen of the knife-boats whirring and clattering around them. Arrows flew, though good aim must have been almost impossible from one rocking dipping shell to another. Pericles thanked Poseidon for that, or perhaps Artemis for spoiling their aim.

Some of the attackers had reached the ship's sea steps and scrambled up, relying on speed to overwhelm the enemy. They were met with golden shields, run through by implacable hoplites. They fell back into the sea. Others grabbed at oars and tried to climb from them or just foul the stroke, it was hard to say. Pericles had the vision of a lion twitching and pawing at a host of stinging ants, with climbers suddenly everywhere.

Two men appeared over the side near him, rolling onto the open deck and coming to their feet. They were dripping wet and looked shattered, as if they had tried to ride an oar blade and been forced under a dozen times. Pericles punched his spear into the chest of the first, lunge-and-back, sending him over the side without even a cry of pain. The other was engaged by a hoplite. Three clashing blows sounded, but the contest was never in doubt and the man's blood splashed bright along the planking, dripping through to the hold below.

Ahead, a great cracking, grinding sound began. Pericles ducked behind his shield to have a look and saw the ends of one of the boats rising as the warship's ram crushed it. Terrified men leaped for the trireme's prow and missed. They fell into the water and were churned beneath the keel.

Pericles shuddered at that thought, imagining them tumbling back and back in those dark waters. Yet it meant the Athenian ship was free. The mouth of the river beckoned, with open sea ahead. The boats were being called back, Pericles realised. Some mournful horn sounded on shore and with curses and sharp gestures, they gave up the chase.

Panting, he watched Anaxagoras and Zeno help clear the ship of half a dozen bodies. Arrows and spears jutted from prow and deck, wrenched free and tossed overboard or kept as a trophy.

Epikleos was one of those gathering fallen kit before valuable items slid over the side. Pericles was not in the mood to help for once, though he clapped the older man on the shoulder as he went by. The violence had come out of nowhere, but it was what he had seen that stunned him. Pericles had watched a Persian fleet once before, from the shore of Salamis, with his mother and sister and brother at his side. It had meant the end of the world then, with Athens set aflame. He did not know what this meant, but it filled him with a cold anger that surprised him in its intensity.

Four of their hoplites had been killed. They were borne below, to be wrapped and treated with dignity. A dozen Persians were thrown into the sea, more than Pericles realised had reached the deck. It had been closer than he'd known. As he watched, the last of them was rolled without ceremony over the edge, falling onto the oars below.

The corpse seemed almost to dance there for a time, battered and tumbling, yet held up. As Pericles stared down from the deck, the man finally slipped through, head first into the deep.

The news spread through the fleet like sparks blown on the wind. League officers and senior captains came in as fast as they could be rowed over. They were sent back just as quickly with new orders, while the fleet prepared itself for war.

Cimon was grimly pleased, in his element at last. A thousand different things needed to be decided and hundreds of orders given. Satisfaction came off him like heat. For a while, Pericles wondered if he had been called to the flagship merely as witness. Then Cimon strode to him, resting a hand on his shoulder. The man had just dismissed a dozen captains with orders to land their hoplites on the shore and put them under the authority of the most senior man.

'You were right, then. Your instincts, Pericles! Now we have a chance to send our hunting pack against the old enemy.'

'We're going in?' Pericles asked.

Cimon nodded.

'Every hour lost is one more for them to prepare. I could spend a month planning an assault – and still fail.' He swallowed, his eyes suddenly bleak. 'Tell me again – how many do they have?'

'I caught only glimpses, but many thousands. More than us.'

'Then I have to land the crews as well. They've trained – and they are fit as dogs, every one. With swords, they'll fight, won't they?'

Pericles realised Cimon was seeking his approval for the decisions he was making. He could not blame him for feeling the weight of them. Cimon's father had rushed headlong against a Persian position and been overwhelmed. The strategos had returned to Athens a wounded and broken man, where, before, the city had chanted his name and thrown flowers at his feet. The thought of history repeating itself must have been terrifying, but Pericles agreed with his conclusion. It occurred to him that he should actually say so, that Cimon needed to hear it.

'They'll be delighted, yes. It's the right decision.'

He saw the slight flicker in Cimon's eyes that meant he had heard and understood. The answer was in the quick grip on his arm, the only thanks he would get.

'I can burn their ships when we've broken their army,' Cimon said. 'I'll send a few of ours down the river to keep them busy there – fire arrows will cause panic.'

'Remember those little boats. They'll have those ready.'

'Then our captains will have to fight them off, as you did. I can't do everything. Pass the word, Pericles. All crews to land – drive onto the banks at best speed.'

'We'll lose ships,' Pericles replied.

'We'll lose everything if we don't. Speed matters today. If I land my crews in good order, one by one, they'll be waiting – and we'll be slaughtered. Our best chance lies in a massed assault, all together and all at once. So: hoplites and crews in ship formations. Command by lochagoi, strategoi and League officers. My command is final. Watch for my messengers when you are in position. It will be chaos for a time, but . . .'

He broke off, snagging a runner as the man tried to slip past.

'You. All captains are to . . . What is the name of that blasted river, does anyone know?'

'I don't know, kurios. I'm sorry.'

'Don't worry about it. Just take word. I haven't seen Ephialtes yet. Take these orders to him – every ship to head upriver at best speed, to beach at speed. Form on shore and wait for orders. Crews to land both oarsmen and hoplites. Understood?'

The man nodded, then went back on his previous course, seeking out a boat to take him away. The fleet had come close to the mouth of the river as the news spread. They blocked the fish-tail and no one would be getting out, not until they had faced Persian forces once more.

Pericles found he was grinning again, though it had no humour in it and his mouth ached. He hated chaos, but Cimon was right. There were times when a good leader had to plan an action with care and time and consideration of terrain or supplies. There were others when it was better to just run in and smash an enemy in the face. Pericles rubbed his jaw. Of course, the tricky part was judging which was which.

The man Cimon had sent away was suddenly back.

'Eurymedon, kurios.'

Cimon looked at him in confusion.

'What?'

'The name of the river, kurios. I heard one of the other men say. You wanted to know.'

'Eurymedon river,' Cimon said.

The man nodded and vanished, while Cimon saw an entirely new group climb onto his deck. He went to meet them and Pericles gestured to the boat waiting off the prow.

He and his crew were going to face Persians once more. With the sun still rising, he would draw his sword in anger and wager his life. As he slipped past the contingent from Naxos, he found he was trembling. It irritated him, as if his body had chosen that moment to let him down. No, it was joy, he told himself, or excitement. His own father had stood at Marathon, while men like Aristides and Pausanias had thrown back the Persians at Plataea. If they had gathered in such numbers a third time, it could only be to invade once more. Just to be part of that filled him with determination. He had trained all his life for this.

He climbed down to the waiting boat and sat in the bow as it was rowed over to his own ship. His crew would be desperate for news by then, the only ones marked by battle in the whole fleet. He could see them on deck, shading their eyes to watch him approach. He made himself grip the hilt of the kopis in his belt until the trembling stopped.

As he reached his own deck, he had a brief vision of the theatre in Athens, of crowds moved to tears or laughter by words alone. If Cimon lost that day, all that would vanish from the world. Pericles reminded himself Aeschylus was more than just a playwright. The man had stood at Marathon. His own brother had been killed there.

Athens was the Pnyx and the people. It was also its stories and thoughts and invention. Yet it could all burn. All those things could be lost, without violent men willing to march towards an army much greater than their own.

33

Pericles shook his head, clearing away images of the past. He had landed once before on a hostile shore, carrying his brother's shield. His father had commanded then, as Cimon did that day.

By all the gods, it did not help that he was among the first to enter the river once again! He had passed Cimon's orders to Ephialtes and while he was still heading back, the man's three ships had rattled out their oars with more speed than he had yet seen. Pericles' little boat had rocked in their wash as they surged past – and the race was on. Whatever Ephialtes thought he would achieve by being first into battle, Pericles felt the urge to deny him. The strategos did not deserve any honour that might have gone to better men.

He had tied on his boat and scrambled up the sea steps, yelling for the crew to row for their lives. Everything at sea happened slowly, slowly – and then too damned fast, all of a sudden. Pericles had passed on the orders from Cimon while Epikleos brought his kit and helped him into it once more. The weight of bronze had been too dangerous to risk in a small boat, but the hoplites on deck had not removed their own. They'd stood grim-faced and ready as the warship surged after the three under Ephialtes.

It did not surprise Pericles to see the distance narrow as his crews began to overhaul the ones ahead. Cimon's intentions to replace the crew of troublemakers had all been lost in the news of a Persian fleet. The ones with Ephialtes were still the rejected. It showed in their chaotic movement, in the crowd milling on deck and fouled oars below. Yet they kept the barest lead as they reached the great river bend.

The difference between the first sighting that dawn and the results hours later was obvious as soon as the four ships came around the headland. The Persians had been quiet that morning, but Pericles had kicked their hive. Now they were everywhere, racing back and forth along the shore. Pericles swallowed at the sight of white-coated regiments forming into squares. He'd heard of those – the Immortals, who had faced a king of the Spartans at Thermopylae and cut him to pieces. They were the elite of the Persian army, present in greater numbers than anyone had known.

Pericles felt his bladder squeeze, suddenly full. He looked behind him, to where another dozen League ships were coming in. Beyond those, wave after wave rowed hard to the river mouth, fighting the current with every stroke. Cimon had entered the field. Yet Ephialtes would be first.

Pericles saw his captain peering over the prow as the warship bucked and dipped in broken waters, looking for the best place to land. There was no clear spot on either bank, but ships had been anchored stern to prow ahead. If they passed between those, they would only reach the shore over the teeming decks of the enemy.

It was the sort of decision that cost lives, and for once Pericles could only wait and watch. His father had loved to command; he understood it better then. It was not that authority came without crushing weight, just that the alternative was living at another's whim. As he stood and wiped sweat from his face, that was suddenly unbearable.

Ahead of them, Ephialtes had spotted some shallows. Pericles was close enough to hear him shout and see the man point. Ephialtes' helmsmen heaved the tillers over and his three ships rowed hard for the land. Pericles watched them

CONN IGGULDEN

shudder as they struck mud and shingle, slowing hard. The masts snapped on two of them, while the prows rose right out of the water, massive rams dripping black muck as they came to rest. Men began to pour over the bows, risking their lives in mud to get ashore.

Pericles heard his own captain swear. He saw the man point to a spot on shore that had no gentle slope to ease the massive weight of a warship. His landing place was a river bank fringed in grass, with trees hanging over their own reflections. Pericles swallowed as the ship made the turn and seemed to leap at the land.

'Brace yourselves!' the captain roared. 'Brace!'

The ship would not survive, Pericles was certain. He was not sure any of them would.

The arrival of Greek warships had not gone unnoticed. The entire army of Persia seemed to be racing towards their position, at least in the panicky glances Pericles could spare. The Persian generals would seek to prevent their landing, of course. Speed was to their advantage as well – and so the two sides would crash together in their desire to draw first blood.

The rowers below would have heard the captain's shout, but they could not know how close they were until they hit. Some of them could easily be killed in a hard impact. That was the result of the orders Cimon had given – and they were still the right ones. Pericles could see Ephialtes already on shore, legs black with river mud, just staring in what looked like horror at the sight of a warship racing to its destruction. Pericles clenched everything he had and began to pray.

Xerxes sat on a pad of ram's wool and silk, high above his guards on the back of a bull elephant. He had always loved animals and the enormous beasts in particular. They were the very symbol of royalty – kings of the forests. This particular animal had accompanied him with his father, to the coast of Ionia decades before. Xerxes wound his fingers into a tuft of hair along its spine, toying with it as he watched the Eurymedon river fill with Greek ships. They were like hornets, he thought, darting, trying to sting. Just one lone ship had found its way up the Eurymedon, as far as the first bend. His little boats had gone out to take it on, but it had escaped. It didn't matter, not really. Xerxes knew the Greeks well enough. They would have searched for a missing ship. They were curious people – and somehow they had found his army and fleet before he was ready.

The result could be seen in waves of ships coming in to waters his people had dredged. A year before, they could not even have navigated the river without fouling on a mudbank. They used his own labours, his own plans against him.

He showed his teeth, snarling at the thought of it, half-rising before settling back. His own land! It was an insult, a mark of their insolence. They needed to have that arrogance beaten out of them, born of luck and Spartans . . . He looked for red sails then and breathed out, forcing himself to calm. It was discomfiting to be attacked, but his army had worked hard and gathered in huge numbers. General Artabazus was experienced in his hatred for the Greeks. He was the one who had brought the Macedonian back into the fold, forgiving him his failures in the first campaign. King Alexander had not been able to persuade Athens to surrender when it was in their best interests, but he still commanded Macedonian troops, of good quality. Artabazus had been the one to see that.

The truth was, Xerxes had hoped for another six months, a year at most. He and his new Immortals would have gone out in the end, to force a battle. He could not face his father's shade if he had not.

Here, the Greeks had to give up their ships to step ashore. Here, his people knew the land, felt it under them. They walked their own earth, his jewelled empire. They knew too that he watched, king of kings – and that his ancestors stood with him. His father wound around and about his son, his breath in the wind.

Xerxes saw Artabazus riding to him, the general dismounting before the elephant and dropping to his stomach. The Great King held out his hand and the elephant reached up with its trunk, letting him step onto the length. With infinite care, the beast lowered him to the ground and he stepped off. Xerxes looked at the first Greek ships landing. They were coming to him.

'Rise up, Artabazus, in all ways,' he said. 'What do you need from me in this hour?'

'Only your blessing, Majesty,' Artabazus said.

His eyes were wide and dark and Xerxes wondered if he had been chewing the little black peas of resin that morning.

'You have it. This is the end, Artabazus, do you understand? What my father began at Marathon – a battle I avenged myself at Thermopylae. What poor Mardonius failed to complete at Plataea. We have won our battle honours, but had our losses too. End it for me now.'

The king looked around him, as if about to impart a secret. His guards stood impassively, deaf and blind.

'To the last man and last coin, spend it all, Artabazus. I cannot bear another loss. Do you understand? They put me in their plays, in Athens . . . with my father's ghost, speaking lines he never said. It is too much. Bring down my wrath on them, Artabazus. I will make you a king.'

The crew gripped anything they could. The great ship skimmed like a stone, almost in silence, until the prow struck.

The impact threw everyone from their feet. The mast broke cleanly at its base, falling back across the stern so that it crushed one of the helmsmen. He screamed and still they moved, on and on in a great rising groan that was too like a voice, like pain. Pericles staggered to his feet and watched in awe as the prow lifted like a whale breaching, higher and higher, the entire deck shuddering under him. It suddenly reminded him of riding a horse and he roared and raised his shield and spear in sheer joy. Some of the men looked at him as if he had lost his mind, but it was extraordinary and he grinned at them.

The ship cracked, that was the only word for it. Something suddenly gave way in the hold, perhaps the keel beam itself that held the warship together. It sounded as a vast, muffled thump and then a series of reports. Like a storm ending, the ship came to rest, but it would not be dragged back and put to sea again. Pericles could sense it, in a vessel he knew and loved. She had been broken, pushed too far.

Ahead, the rowing crew boiled out of the central trench, looking round in shock at the strange cant to the deck and the fallen mast. They had short swords drawn and many carried shields as well. It was a long way from the disciplined ranks of hoplites in greaves, helmets and chestplates, but neither was there hesitation in them. They had been rowers, but the ship was clearly dead. As soldiers, they poured out, leaping onto solid ground.

Pericles jumped down with them, looking back in awe. The bank itself had been driven apart, forced to rise like a frozen wave before their ram and prow. His ship's keel had indeed snapped in two places, her great heart torn out. It felt like an ending. He dropped to one knee and gathered a little of the dusty earth underfoot. His brother had died on a Persian shore. Perhaps some part of his spirit resided there still.

'Hello, brother,' Pericles whispered. 'I have returned.'

The men of his ship formed up behind rows of hoplites, joining two hundred or so to the six hundred with Ephialtes. There was security in numbers and the ships in the second line were still finding spots where they might risk a landing. Pericles saw Ephialtes stride across his front rank. His heart sank to see Attikos at his side, still a trusted man.

When Ephialtes came close, the strategos was looking into the distance, peering at the Persians rushing to engage them. He was red-faced and perspiring, opening and closing his hand on a sword hilt, still in its scabbard. As Pericles raised his head in greeting, it was Attikos who spoke, stretching his neck as lochagoi officers bullied hoplite ranks and rowers into shape.

'Like old times, isn't it, kurios?' he said. 'Remember Scyros? Where your wife is from?'

There was nothing to which he might object, not with Ephialtes close enough to hear. Yet Pericles felt the man's spite. He glanced at Ephialtes and found the man's usual arrogance missing. The strategos looked nervous and it suddenly made sense that he would keep Attikos close. Ephialtes wore the armour of a hoplite, with a fine crest to his helmet and a shiny new shield that gleamed gold. Yet he had not faced Persians in war, not as many others had. He would be afraid, of course. For once, Pericles had the advantage over him.

'If the Persians have any sense,' he said, 'they'll hit us fast and hard, with everything they have. We get stronger with every ship that lands, while they lose their advantage. They'll try to overwhelm us.'

He spoke to Ephialtes, thinking the man would appreciate a few words. Instead, the strategos jerked his head as if he had been stung, glaring at him.

'We are exposed here, without reinforcements. I wonder if that was Cimon's intention in sending me in first.'

Pericles only blinked at such an outrageous accusation. No one had forced Ephialtes to rush ahead of the rest. Someone had to land and hold the position. By the gods, it was thankless work, but . . .

Horns sounded ahead and Attikos murmured something to his new master. With a sharp nod, Ephialtes went into the first ranks, joining his shield in an armoured line of hoplites.

Ahead of them, Persian regiments came marching, the sound a sort of jingling rhythm. The air was clear and Pericles could see every detail of them, from their beards to their white panelled coats and shields. He could see their red mouths too, as they panted. They had run far, from a lookout on a hill across a valley to that spot. He hoped they were exhausted, though there was no sign of it. Archers swarmed with them on both wings. Pericles swallowed at the sight of those, offering his life to Ares and Athena.

There would be no halt to assess the enemy, that was obvious. The Persians came on fast, with a clear intention to sweep the Greeks into the river. In reply, the ranks under Ephialtes locked their shields. They would try to hold, to give time to those behind them.

Pericles glanced back once before he lowered his helmet. The next wave was fussing in the shallows rather than battering straight in. The Persians would be on them before they could be supported, he realised. In huge numbers. He looked left and right, seeing the strained faces of men he had brought to that place. Zeno was there, holding a shield Anaxagoras had made for him. Anaxagoras loomed over the line, his helmet a cast-off he had repaired himself with a line of lead. It shone silver, though it might yet crack

CONN IGGULDEN

with one good blow. Pericles swallowed nervously. Epikleos was there, in line, watching for him as he always had. They were good men, but they might all die there, just to hold a piece of river bank none of them had ever seen before that morning.

34

Pericles watched a regiment of Persian Immortals sweep towards him. A second square was coming over a hill in the hazy distance, like pale leaves carried on ants towards the Greeks. The Persians were hampered by the need to defend a vast stretch of river, perhaps even on both sides. Pericles knew he was the point of the spear – the ground where he stood was where they had to stand, no matter what.

They closed and closed at a good pace, while the eight hundred with Ephialtes and Pericles scraped the earth with their sandals and readied themselves. Pericles watched one hoplite with missing fingers bind his hand to a spear shaft so it could not be knocked from his grip.

At two hundred paces, the Immortals were a sea of heads and swinging legs, armour that seemed to ripple in the sunlight. It was hard to imagine anything being able to stop so many – and they were one small part of the whole. Pericles swallowed, his throat suddenly dry. On a battlefield, there would have been boys running through standing men, carrying skins of watered wine. The lack of them was a small irritation in the face of such an army, but he felt it even so.

Across the mass of Persian soldiers, voices called – and arrows rose from their walking lines, lifting gently, coming down like thorns. Accuracy clearly mattered little to them. Instead, they filled the air with shafts, whirring and whistling, rattling off Greek shields held aloft, or punching through and drawing out long cries of pain.

Not everyone in the crews had a shield. In a dozen places,

oarsmen had conspired with the carpenters to hold long shapes made from deck planking, nailed together. Men clustered in the shadows of those, five or six jammed in under each one as the whistling went on and on. The Persian archers clearly had full quivers from the way they spent shafts. They did not stint a single shot, pouring on as fast as they could draw, until they showed their teeth and panted like dogs, finally spent. Eighty paces.

In the foremost ranks, none of the hoplites with Ephialtes fell, though half a dozen of them had to snap arrows off and pull bloody shafts back through their outstretched arms. Six rows from the front, one burly oarsman had his arm nailed to his shield. He looked at the arrow in bemusement, not yet feeling the pain that would come. There was no place behind for wounded, not then. One of his mates tried to help, making him swear and laugh.

The Persian Immortals tramped closer, so the noise of armour and steps filled the day. There were so many. Pericles felt the nervousness of the crews around him, even in the stiff gait of lochagoi as they bustled and corrected, shouting at them to hold, to hold.

In other places that day, Pericles knew there would be League officers speaking to men of a dozen cities. There, in that moment, those near him were Athenian. He knew the ones from his own ship and they knew him. That was one secret of their line. Theirs was no vast and unknowing bureaucracy, brought together to fight for a distant empire. No, his people knew one another. They had raised sail and practised with sword and shield for months. They had broken bread and shared wine – and no man could run, not with his friends watching him. Pericles thought suddenly of the Spartans at Thermopylae, of the stories he had heard. Perhaps he understood a little better. Shame was worse than death.

A lochagos trotting along the line drew to a halt by him, perhaps seeing fear in the faces there. With the enemy so close, the man had only moments, but chose to spend a few of them in that spot. Arrows still thumped around him and he raised his shield so he stood in its shadow. With a grin, he clapped Pericles on the shoulder with his free hand, startling him.

'Remember, we are better men,' the lochagos shouted to those around them. 'Stand for your fathers and the gods – for Athena. She is all that matters in the end.'

He saw Pericles nod.

'And look after your friends,' he added in a lower voice, glancing to where Zeno and Anaxagoras stood.

Pericles dipped his head and the lochagos went on to the end of the rank, where he could observe half the men he'd helped train.

Ahead, horns sounded, blaring at extraordinary volume. At twenty paces, the Persians broke into a loping run, disciplined, beginning a roar that built in sound until it filled the air like dust. They rushed the last small gap between the armies, crashing against the Athenian shields. The sound was brutal, but the shield line held and the killing began in earnest. Pericles saw Persian front ranks spill right around, hacking at the wings.

Those were not veteran hoplites, not there. Instead, oarsmen jabbed spears and swords with desperate ferocity, untiring. Yet as they came face to face with a savage enemy, they forgot their training. Hoplites had one single truth battered into them from their earliest years – your shield protected the man on the left, not yourself. It took extraordinary discipline not to jerk it into the path of a swinging sword, instead trusting the man on your right to catch the blow.

CONN IGGULDEN

Despite hundreds of hours of sword drills, despite their unique fitness and extraordinary strength, oarsmen crumpled into chaos on the wings. Spears they did not use well were thrown in temper, swords drawn too early.

Pericles swore under his breath. With more men, Ephialtes might have widened the line or arced back the edges to prevent his wings being overwhelmed. As it was, he was being attacked on three sides and suffering. Pericles could see the strategos in the thick of the fighting, facing men intent on a quick victory on their own land. For a while, the Persian soldiers fought without fear or weariness. They were the best, and perhaps somewhere near, their king watched. Yet they were still only men. Against a good shield line, with spears licking out to tear flesh and slip between ribs, they would begin to fail. Arms would grow heavy, breath like hot spit in the mouth. The Athenians had broken as many at Marathon, with discipline and craft. Anger was not enough; courage was not enough.

At the front, Greek spears were taking a terrible toll, punching in and out, made red. As long as the front ranks stood firm against the flood, Pericles knew they could prevail.

The orders were brutally simple – hold: give the rest time to land and form up. Cimon would see what he needed to do, Pericles had no doubt. He would not abandon them. Pericles knew that as he knew the names of the gods. Yet as he waited, counting breaths, he saw a shift in the formation ahead.

The shield line wasn't holding. Pericles felt his stomach drop away at the sight. He suddenly remembered the men facing Persian Immortals were the worst of all the fleet, gathered under a strategos who seemed unable to take good advice. The officers were quiet up there where they should have roared, or ignored by the men they commanded. As

Pericles watched in horror, Ephialtes himself went down, knocked off his feet. He lurched up, red-faced and flailing, but Attikos was at his side, guiding him to safety through the ranks. There was blood on the strategos' face, Pericles saw. Perhaps Ephialtes was dazed from a blow to his head. He did not struggle as Attikos bore him back.

Pericles watched as something broke. When a shield line fails, it goes fast, each man suddenly alone and vulnerable. The Immortals sensed it coming and howled, a sound that chilled. These were the ones who had come to Greece to enslave and burn. These were men of empire, savage and without mercy.

The front crumpled, men dying every instant. The only chance to survive a retreat was to take each step back with shield held high, showing the enemy only the bronze slit helmet, shield and greaves, the sword or spear ready to stab. Yet the Persians pressed forward every pace, allowing them no room. Instead, they shoved and battered at them, losing lives to make them trip and fall, to make them turn, to make them run.

Pericles felt his stomach crawl up his gullet as lines peeled back. In the chaos, he had the sense his own crew was holding, appalled, but not ready to join any spreading panic. His lochagos was roaring something obscene at them, the insults oddly comforting. Pericles looked to his right and saw Zeno and Anaxagoras with Epikleos, all three a knot in the line, unwavering. They knew better than to run. It was not bravery exactly, just not blind panic. If it was their day, their moment, they could accept it. Veteran hoplites preferred to die on their feet, with their wounds all to the front. That was *kleos*, right there, or the hope of it, when all else had fled.

The lines Ephialtes should have been commanding gave up their last resistance. Persians came through in thunder, roaring and clashing weapons, red throats showing. Pericles

CONN IGGULDEN

was battered and turned by men shoving past, pouring with blood or driven mad by the rushing wings of their own death. Hoplite lines dissolved into chaos and disorder and they were driven as if before hounds, with the river close to their backs.

'Like old times, isn't it?' a voice yelled.

Pericles looked over and saw Attikos was there, grinning at him. Ephialtes was off to the left, still looking stunned as he adjusted his helmet. Pericles shook his head, suddenly angry. If he had to die, he did not want it to be with Attikos watching and commenting on it. The man had a well of spite in him, like a sour taste he could not wash away.

'Did you hear the prayers to Athena?' Attikos said, leaning in. 'There's another goddess I like more – Adrastia. She appeals to me, and men like me, men who feel the heel of the world on their throat. Your Athena might come to save a soldier, but not Adrastia. There is no mercy in her, son. She is a goddess of retribution.'

Pericles tore his gaze away from the wild glee he saw in Attikos. The Persian force was rolling Greek lines back in complete disorder. The crews Ephialtes had brought to that place were all ones their captains and lochagoi did not trust. Some were fighters, without a doubt, but others were thieves and liars, rapists or men who could not take authority. Without Ephialtes to rally them, they fouled lines that might have held, knocking men from their feet in their panic. Pericles was smacked aside by a man holding a shield before him, the whites of his eyes showing in his terror. Pericles saw Anaxagoras jerk aside rather than impale one of their own on a spearhead. The man hadn't even seen the danger.

'Back to the ships!' Ephialtes bellowed.

Heads turned to see who had given the order, but they hardly hesitated. As Pericles groaned, the retreat became a rout. His men were better trained, but they knew when the day was lost. If no one fought, the aim then became simple survival. The rush poured past him.

Men fell and were left or dragged up by their friends. Some were killed as they tried to retreat, crying out in agony as the Persians spitted them from behind. In the battering, heaving line, something flashed. Pericles saw a blur out of the corner of his eye, a hand swinging, something dark in it. He began to duck, but he was hit hard and dropped to the ground. Nothing made sense as he scrambled to rise. He thought he heard Anaxagoras calling his name, but darkness began to swallow him. Marching feet trampled past, though he could not understand why he lay at their level. Someone stabbed down then, a pain so great he could not bear it. The last Greek lines pulled back and Persian Immortals roared across the field in triumph, driving them towards the river.

Cimon had watched the first ships run hard against the shore. It was the oldest tactic they knew, sending armed men from sea to land at their best speed, even at the expense of the fleet itself. As a man of the sea, he hated to do it, but there was no choice. The Persians had a vast war host and every advantage of terrain and supply. He knew if he could not deploy his force quickly, they would swallow him up, like a snake taking a nest of birds one by one.

Being in command meant making decisions that would win or lose the day, his life and his people. He knew that when he directed his fleet into shallows closer to the river bend. It meant they lost fewer ships, but the men had to make their way inland on foot, loping along in squares. All the while, those first forces would come under terrible pressure.

As Cimon marched with the rest, he felt guilt rising like heat. He would never have abandoned Ephialtes, certainly not Pericles. He knew very well they would be looking for him, waiting for the main force, holding on, while all the time he had landed over an hour's march downriver. Yet they served as the candle that would draw Persian moths. The Persians had to defend that first spot beyond the river bend, never seeing the greater force coming at them from further back. It was good planning, but he bit his lip and tasted blood as he marched even so. Every decision was his; every responsibility his own. He wondered if his father had known the same sense of lonely awe and joy, and knew of course he had. There was nothing like the sweetness or the pain of it.

He craned his neck when he heard fighting ahead, dreading what he would see. There – the ships that had beached, visible once more. He could see an entire regiment of white-coated Immortals driving his people back. Greeks stood in the shallows there, some of them, fighting desperately for every pace they were made to retreat.

'In good order!' Cimon roared across his lines. The pace was picking up as he spoke. They wanted to fall on the unsuspecting enemy. 'Phalanx formation! Column to pha-*lanx*!'

They had trained for it over a thousand days of hard work and repetition. He did not need to look back to see the marching column jog into squares, lochagoi officers tending to neat lines and spears ready. Those long dory spears were terrifying in defence. They were even worse as a weapon of the charge.

On the river bank, the Persians had seen them coming. Their officers were trying to call them back from the triumph and the slaughter, to make themselves ready to face a new threat. Cimon frowned as he saw the way the enemy moved. Immortals were the best of the imperial Persian army, so it was said. In one of his quiet lectures back in the council building, Aristides had described the way they fought at

Plataea. Even the old man had been impressed by them, to a point. Yet these did not respond to orders with quick discipline. They did not turn fast and ready to face an enemy coming at their flank. Cimon showed his teeth. They may have worn the coats, but they were *not* Immortals.

'Spears and shields! League! *League! Engaage!*' he roared, his order repeated across the face of the marching lines.

Cimon watched spears bristle ahead of them, supported by the weight of flesh and bronze. They would punch a hole in the heaving Persian flank as it tried to turn. He would hold that spot for the main fleet to gather around him. No doubt the Persians would fling all they had at that part of the river bank.

He swallowed drily as he advanced with the rest. The Greek lines were disciplined, the finest in the world. He would swear to that. Yet they had not expected battle when they woke that day. No one had. Cimon sent a silent prayer to his patron gods and readied himself for butchery. There was light enough. This was bloody work and he knew it well.

35

Pericles felt himself being dragged, his heels snagging on something. The day had grown dark, with clouds covering the night sky. How long had he been out? He had a vision of Attikos standing nearby in the crush, then nothing. Had the little bastard hit him? Suspicion bloomed in his chest. He tried to struggle and discovered he was bound in ropes. He looked left and right and his heart sank. Persians. Even in the evening gloom, he would have known them by their oiled beards, curled and woven to a thick black mat. He tried to control the rising panic. There were stories of what happened to Athenians captured by the Persians. They had as much mercy as Spartans, which was to say none at all. He could only pray the details were exaggerated, as men will tell of ghosts and curses for the pleasure of frightening their friends.

After a nameless time, Pericles was thrown to the ground, or dropped, so that fresh pains sprang to life. He could see an encampment all around him, with tents and paths stretching into the distance on all sides. He had to be near the heart of it.

Around where he lay, half a dozen prisoners were trussed as he was. Some lay unmoving, while others groaned from the battering they had taken. As he stared, his guards were looping chains to some sort of iron post, their intentions clear. Despite his pain and the exhaustion that threatened to steal his wits, Pericles began inching away in the gloom, feeling like a snake shedding its skin.

He stopped when one of the guards strolled over and

kicked him hard in the ribs. New pain made him suck in a breath and the Persian chuckled. Pericles had been wounded, he realised at last, though he did not remember it happening. As the man strolled back to his labours, he felt anger rising like steam: at Attikos, at being abandoned by his own people, at whichever whoreson had battered him while he'd been help-less, even at the one who laughed and kicked a man who could not respond. It felt good, much better than fear. He let it burn through him, leaving him shaky and weak, but still less afraid.

One of the guards held a knife to his throat as they tied his hands to a slim slave chain, attaching it to the post. In his weakened state, it all seemed an unnecessary caution. All Pericles could do was draw his feet together and sit up, look-ing around at the camp of his enemy. After a time, he vomited, though there was nothing but yellow bile in his stomach. His head was splitting and he could see bright flashes as he gasped and closed his eyes.

'Did anyone see Cimon?' he muttered.

Two of the prisoners still slumped, unconscious. Another jerked at the voice, looking up.

'He came. Drove the Immortals right back. They took me up as they retreated. For information, no doubt. They're sav-ages, you know. It will be hot irons for us both.'

Pericles opened one eye to peer at the cheery soul chained alongside. He didn't feel braver than the other man, but something in that defeated tone sparked his scorn.

'Still, at least we'll be warm,' he said. 'There's that.'

He felt the other man staring. *Praotes* was calm in the face of death. The stranger chuckled to himself.

'My name is Laodes,' he said. 'Of the warship *Penelope*. Under Strategos . . .'

'Ephialtes, yes. I know it. I saw you land this morning – or crash. I felt our keel give way when we struck.'

'Be quiet over there!' a voice snapped.

Pericles looked up, surprised to hear Greek in the camp of his enemy.

'Make us,' he said.

'You *stupid* . . .' Laodes hissed. 'He's coming! Don't give them your real name.'

They watched as a man in hoplite armour walked over, peering down at the miserable specimens chained to the slave pole. By the accent, Pericles already knew he was a Macedonian. Straining against the restriction of the chain, he leaned over, trying to spit. It was impossible. His mouth was as dry as the earth around him.

'What's your name?' the Macedonian demanded.

'My name? Laodes,' Pericles said. He heard a strangled sound from his companion and grinned despite himself.

The soldier nudged him with his boot, hard enough to make clear it could be a lot worse.

'Well, Laodes, you'll be first when General Artabazus comes to question you. I suggest you tell him everything he asks. He might make it quick then.'

'What is it about you Macedonians?' Pericles said. 'That's right, isn't it? Your king came to Athens to beg us to surrender. To let Persia have our pride the way they took yours. We sent him away with nothing – and we went to meet the Persians at Plataea. Did you hear of that, in your northern forests?'

'You poor fool,' the man said, his voice dripping with scorn and anger. 'You think the future lies in your little city? I've seen an *empire*, vaster and stronger than anything you could imagine. I thought our great days were all behind, until we were made allies of Persia. My king felt the wind blowing, that's all.'

'No, he sold you,' Pericles said. 'He sold Macedon to sit at the feet of a foreign king.'

The man shook his head.

'I won't kill you, Laodes, if that's what you're after. I'll watch, though, as they put you to the question. It will be my pleasure.'

With an effort, the man made himself walk away. Pericles watched him go.

His companion strained his chain to turn towards him.

'What did you give him my name for?'

Pericles laughed wearily.

'It was the first one that came into my head.'

In the distance, Pericles could see the sky growing pale. He blinked at the dawn, understanding that he had lost a whole night in his stupor. A blow to the head was a nasty thing. He remembered leaping ashore, but the rest came and went in flashes.

On the opposite horizon, a different sort of light began to spread. Pericles turned east, then west to compare them, seeing movement that meant flames. In moments, the peace of the night shattered. Horns started to blow, warning of an attack.

'He's set their fleet on fire,' Laodes said in a delighted whisper. 'Look at the light! How far it goes! By Ares, he must be burning every ship.'

Pericles looked at the ropes that held his wrists together – and the iron links of the slave chain that wound through them. In the dawn light, he passed links between his fingers, feeling the roughness of the work. It was too strong for him to break, at least while he feared ripping open some wound. Yet Persians were rousing all across the huge camp. He did not think they would leave prisoners alive if they were forced to go out. Men boiled from every tent, shouting and pointing, rushing to don coats and grab weapons from where they had stacked them the night before.

'Cimon is coming,' Pericles said, with satisfaction.

He knew his friend. He edged closer to the pole itself, gripping it between his thighs. As Laodes watched, he began working his ropes back and forth against the rough iron, trying to make them fray.

The dawn light could not compete with the ships that burned along the river, not at first. By the time the sun showed above the horizon, Xerxes could see a line of fire rising as high again as the ships from the water. Men screamed in that furnace, he could hear them. Others jumped into the river by the thousand, swimming for the banks.

From the saddle of a warhorse, he looked in despair at the end of all his hopes. Artabazus was there on his own mount, his dark features made of wax as he contemplated the destruction. The Greeks, always the Greeks. Xerxes' horse tried to dip its head to the grasses by the river. In reply, he tightened his hands on the reins, but he had no words to convey his rage.

'Can we not strike back, general?' he asked. Even to his own ear, his voice sounded plaintive, weak. Xerxes cleared his throat and tried again. 'Just tell me where to march, Artabazus! If the men see me, I know they will rally. A fleet can be rebuilt.'

'Again? What would be the point?' he heard Artabazus mutter.

Xerxes blinked in surprise at him. The man was usually the model of a perfect officer, respectful and quiet. It seemed the sight of burning ships had spoiled his calm.

'What did you say to me, general?'

'I'm sorry, Majesty. I meant merely that they have been thorough. Ships on both sides of the river have been set on fire – and it has spread. Keels and ribs will block this river for years. There is no rebuilding this fleet, not now.'

Xerxes nodded as if he was receiving a commonplace report rather than the end of his hopes. He tried to hide the panic flaring in him. More than anyone, more even than Artabazus, he knew the nations of the empire would not allow another attempt. He had driven kings into poverty and worked thousands of slaves to death. The cost in gold and blood was beyond even his reckoning, but it had beggared Persia – from Marathon, to Thermopylae and Plataea, to this last great throw of the dice. The line of fire that contested the sun was an ending.

Xerxes cleared his throat, struggling to keep his voice steady. His hands were trembling, he realised.

'Can we see the enemy, general?'

Artabazus shook his head wearily.

'As their ships still swim, there is little we could accomplish even if we could.'

There it was again, that unaccustomed note. In another man, it might have been insolence. The Great King frowned to hear it, but Artabazus did not dismount to prostrate himself, as he might once have done. Xerxes could only blink in surprise. It would look weak for him to demand it, he thought.

Artabazus went on, waving his hand in disgust towards the river. The light of flames revealed Greek ships trying to make their way down the centre channel. Artabazus could see their crews heaving buckets up on ropes, dousing their own decks against the sparks that floated across, thick and gold in the morning air. Some of those ships would not survive the conflagration they had started, he did not doubt. It was a beggar's comfort.

Artabazus rubbed his chin with the back of one hand, looking more closely at the river.

'Majesty . . .' he began, 'we roused our regiments when the

CONN IGGULDEN

first ships were torched. I hoped then to save them. Yet there has been no massed landing here. It looks more like . . .'

Horns sounded in the distance and the general cursed and wrenched his horse around. Xerxes began to ask what was happening, but for once the general ignored him. Artabazus whistled to his officers and pointed to the main camp.

'This is a distraction!' he shouted. 'They are behind us.'

'What is happening? General!' Xerxes snapped.

Artabazus controlled himself with a visible effort.

'Majesty, the Greeks seek to draw us away by burning our ships. We need to get back to the camp. Every instant is one we cannot lose. Please, Majesty. Ride with me.'

Xerxes firmed his jaw and nodded once, sharply.

'Very well, Artabazus. Lead us in war.'

Pericles saw a shield line he knew as well as the face of his friend. Cimon had gathered all the hoplites of the fleet together for his assault on the main camp, that much was clear. Pericles watched in awe as some six thousand men of gold drove all before them. Spears glittered and in a sudden panic, he realised he was in danger of being spitted on them.

'Prisoners! Greeks!' he shouted, holding out empty hands. He had the experience of seeing grim faces in bronze helmets, over huge shields and gleaming greaves below, all while iron points faced him. They heard his words over the tramp of feet and the noise of armed resistance. The line parted and he stood as a stone in a river. Pericles called for a knife and one of the men paused at last as he understood. With quick slashes, he cut the bonds that still held Laodes. All the prisoners were awake by then, though one was still dazed and supported by another.

'Where is Cimon? Zeno? Anaxagoras? Epikleos?' Pericles shouted the names, though he was cursed and buffeted by his own people. They had settled into the mood for violence and were not pleased to find him in their path. In a short time, Pericles was cursed more often than he had been in his entire life. It was an education, he thought, and began to laugh.

'Pericles!' a voice shouted on his left. Cimon, marching with the best of the League. He was surrounded by a dozen messengers and Pericles saw Zeno was one of them. The little man had always been quick. They greeted one another in mutual delight.

'Here!' Pericles replied.

'The son of Xanthippus?' Laodes said at his side.

The man had risen to his feet and was rubbing his wrists. When Pericles nodded, he looked pleased.

'Your father was a good man. I am honoured.'

'All fathers are good men,' Pericles said lightly.

Laodes shook his head.

'You'd be surprised. Still, I am delighted to be free. If you could find me a shield and spear as well, I would be grateful.'

They could both hear fighting ahead, the hoplites streaming towards it. With apologies, they passed through the marching ranks against the flow, though it earned them more curses, some of which were of such a level of filth that Pericles was blushing as he reached Cimon.

'Here – and alive still,' Pericles said.

Cimon nodded to him.

'I fired their ships. If we can thin them here, we'll turn and face the rest.' The navarch eyed Pericles' wounded and filthy state and shook his head. 'You have no shield or armour, Peri. You should go back. Anaxagoras is on board ship, with Epikleos. They both took wounds yesterday.'

'Saving me?' Pericles asked.

Cimon shrugged.

'Trying to reach you. Either way, you can't stay with me.'

'Lend me your kopis blade,' Pericles said. 'I'll stand with you – as I did at Scyros and Cypros.'

Cimon bit the inside of his lip, but handed over the blade without any further protest. He saw the stranger who stood with Pericles.

'Didn't I see you lashed once?' Cimon said. 'For stealing? No – attacking an officer?'

Pericles glanced across and was surprised to see Laodes looking embarrassed as any boy in the presence of a man he revered.

'I believe . . . yes, kurios, that is possible. In my defence, he was a right bastard.'

Cimon reached over and took a blade from the belt of one of the men around him. The hoplite did not protest, though his eyes followed closely and marked who had it. Laodes bowed as he accepted the blade, marching along.

'Redeem yourself,' Cimon said.

He did not see the glitter of tears in Laodes before the man knuckled them away, rolling his shoulders and falling into line with the rest.

Artabazus marched his regiments as fast as he could back to the camp, though his heart sank with every step. They had neither slept nor rested in the sudden alarm and march to the river, only to turn and come straight back over rough ground. He hoped the Greeks had been as active in the night, exhausting themselves.

The morning had dawned cold and clear enough, so he could see a long way. The camp burned in places, with black trails lifting. As he came closer, he could imagine the slaughter within those boundaries. There was no fighting then, not while the Greeks could form up and wait for them. Artabazus swallowed hard. He remembered Plataea.

Only the red cloaks were missing to complete the scene. A line of shields glittered in the sun, with tens of thousands on either wing. He knew that golden stone, as he knew the ones his king insisted on calling Immortals, though they possessed neither the quality nor the fitness of the Persian elite. Dressing soldiers in the uniform of better men does nothing for them, he thought, except to give them a false view of themselves. He'd seen them strutting around in their white coats, unearned.

Artabazus drew in deep breaths of cold air. There was a hill nearby and he sent messengers to direct Xerxes to head for it, with his private guard surrounding him. The king could not be risked where stray arrows or spears flew. His life was the only one that mattered. Artabazus felt resentment rise in him and smothered it ruthlessly. He had a task to complete and the numbers to do it. For all their Greek manoeuvres, for all the slaughter in the camp, he still had an army twice the size of the one he faced.

Artabazus watched as Xerxes rode with his men to the hill. He wondered if the king would let him live, even in victory. The loss of the fleet was a wound to them all and Artabazus knew he might bear the cost of it, no matter what happened. It split his attention as he marched towards the burning camp and the Greeks arrayed for battle before it.

CONN IGGULDEN

36

'League! *League!*' Cimon called. He lengthened the sound, so that it went on and on, like a wolf's howl. When he had every eye on him, he cast his voice across the standing ranks.

'My father stood at Marathon,' Cimon called.

The remains of the Persian camp smouldered at his back and, in that moment, he could have been one of that blessed generation. Cimon looked across all those who had rowed or sailed to that place. He realised he knew at last what it meant to plant his feet and stand, with brothers and men of his city, with the whole world as the stake. Athens . . . No, he caught himself. They were more than that. He had been searching for the right words. They came suddenly, as water from a cup, as a Persian army advancing like a wall.

'Some of you here today stood with him. With Miltiades and Xanthippus and Aristides and Themistocles – men like us. They fought on the fennel field, against a huge army, until they cast Persia back into the sea. The empire came to demand that we bow, that we kneel. We said *no* . . . and raised spear and shield against them.'

He looked around at ranks of bronze-clad hoplites, at the many thousands more on the wings. They were utterly still as they waited, straining to hear every word. And all the while, Persians tramped and tramped closer.

'It was the greatest moment of my father's life,' Cimon went on, his chest swelling to reach them all. 'So he told me. When he came home, his people carried him on their shoulders and pressed amaranth flowers into his hands. They said Miltiades would be immortal. His memory is.'

Some of those present nodded, right across the lines. Young men understood, as older men failed to understand. Pericles felt his throat tighten with strong emotion. He had not heard Cimon speak like this before. The navarch held them rapt and silent, and words poured from him.

'I fought at Salamis when they came,' Cimon went on. 'They brought an army greater than the remnant you see today, greater than cities. We rowed and boarded and burned all that day, until we were exhausted. Yet we broke them – at sea, on land. I was Athenian.'

He looked around at them.

'Today, I am more. I see Athenians here, as on the day at Marathon, but I see too men of many cities, of kingdoms as far as Ionia. All bound as one – in our great league, our alliance. My friends! Marathon and Plataea are the past. *This* is our day, our time, our year. This is the day of sons. This place, by the river. They came to us . . . now we have come to them. This is where we will stop them. Look to those around you – to faces you know. The Persians will break against us as the sea against a rock.'

He let a beat pass, intending to signal to the lochagoi to take over the discipline of the lines, to resume the bullying and threats that would distract the men from an enemy closing on them. In that silence, they began to cheer, without words, in simple defiance of the Persians coming. If Cimon had intended to say anything else, it was lost in that inchoate roar, that voice swelling until the ground trembled. Unless it was the march of Persia making it shake.

Pericles saw white-coated regiments join into a single front. They looked strong, a heart of empire – and so many. In the distance, he saw a small group ride clear of that advancing mass, heading to a hill where few trees grew. It could only be their king, come to watch as he had once sat on the shore down by the Piraeus, with a white pavilion billowing and snapping above his head.

Pericles called every curse he knew down on Xerxes. He preferred him as Aeschylus had written his lines: in despair, led by the chorus into shadows. This could not be his victory! Persia had brought a host to Greece to force them to kneel. Cimon had lost his father to them; Pericles had lost his brother. For decades, Persian gold and blood had washed them all and changed them. Pericles shuddered at the thought. He and Cimon still tumbled on that red shore, with the great wave breaking.

Artabazus hid any sign of fear as he rode along the wing. He had too many memories of Plataea ever to look with calm again on a hoplite line. Yet they did not have the Spartans! The red cloaks were missing from their battle ranks. Artabazus had made sure that that news spread through his regiments. Yet the Athenians too had stood at Plataea. He remembered those as well. They had not broken then.

He felt despair nag at him. Why did some men refuse to look away, while others ran? The Greeks were not stronger than his soldiers, nor braver. He was certain of that. The Hellenes were skilled and ruthless warriors, but so were his. Artabazus had trained his men harder than they had ever known, in fitness and drills. If he found the sight of Immortal insignia uncomfortable, the men seemed to love them. How could the Greeks not run from so many? The gods they followed were just echoes, thoughts in the mind of Ahura Mazda, Lord of Wisdom.

Artabazus set his jaw, determined. Plataea was far off, left behind in time and place. Its shadow could not stretch so far, he was certain. His feet walked on Persian dust, watered by the blood of his ancestors for ten thousand years. It had known civilisation when the Greeks still lived in caves and feared every passing storm.

He remembered a phrase from years before, like a whisper. He and his men *were* the storm. They had rolled down from the hills and they would scatter Greeks in a great gale. He prayed for it, as Xerxes and his personal guard trotted clear, heading for the hill Artabazus had chosen.

Those royal eyes would watch a generation redeemed, Artabazus promised himself. He swallowed, though his throat was dry as dust. He could taste it on his tongue, as if he was still at Plataea. He shook his head, refusing to be afraid.

'Ready archers!' he called.

They would strike first, as they had at Thermopylae, making men flinch and duck like children. That was the first thunder, the first blood.

'Regiments! Immortals! Make ready!' Artabazus roared.

His voice could not carry to so many. It was repeated up and down the line, the words overlapping like poetry. He shivered, feeling flesh rise on his bare arms. The morning was cold, he told himself, with a breeze from the direction of the river. It was not that he rode to his own death.

The pace was increasing, so that he had to make his horse trot to keep his position. That was a good sign. His men had trained for this, though they'd expected to meet the Greeks in a different land and a different year. Yet perhaps they felt the same outrage at hoplites on their own soil, at the ships that still burned along the river, or the lines of smoke rising from the camp. In a day and a night, the Greeks had come as terrible destroyers. This was the answer he had brought. Artabazus realised he was muttering to himself and bit his lip.

CONN IGGULDEN

He felt faces turn to him. Arrows flew only at his word and he had wasted a dozen paces staring at the enemy as they became so clear, so close!

'Archers! Send them the storm!' he bellowed over their heads.

Ten thousand bows bent and were released. The swarm kicked, the air moving like a breeze. Greek lines rippled as they raised shields. Artabazus could feel their fear, on a strange land.

'Engage! For King Xerxes!' he called again.

His voice was lost in the tramp of feet and the snap of bows, but it was repeated down the line, across the face of regiments and into their hearts. They heard and they responded with a guttural roar, pressing in hard.

Artabazus went with them, holding position in his third row. He saw the faces of Greeks as they held shields overhead, battered to their knees by arrows. Many would be struck down under that hail, he was certain. He could not see their lines waver, but men vanished between the shimmer of scales, as if plucked out. He smiled, then dismounted, sending his horse running with a slap to its haunch.

Artabazus saw a few of his men grinning, responding to his own wild expression. He felt his heart soar as the massed front lines crashed together, willing the Greeks to just break, to run.

He heard Persian voices rise in anger as spears found them, punching through armour and coming back red, over and over. The first charge was hard against those locked shields. The archers had better luck against the wings and Artabazus saw more men fall there. Yet the centre held, though the Greeks were rushed and overwhelmed.

He felt the first worm of doubt enter when that great charge faltered. Men could gather speed only where there was room to do it. As the front ranks compressed against Greek spears and shields, all those behind could do was heave forward, hardly able to take a single pace. Yet the savagery only intensified and men died in hundreds. Away from the centre, Artabazus could see Greeks without the golden armour he knew from his nightmares. They carried spears and swords like the rest, but their shields were just wood and rope and they wore no helmets.

He sent new orders to press the wings and felt the response as they began to bow back. Artabazus roared then, letting his men see him, exulting with each step he could take forward against the press. He gave them heart. Yet the centre held like the tip of a wedge and all the forces he had brought could not drive it back. Instead, he saw his new Immortals ground down on iron and bronze.

One of the enemy officers saw the wings driven back and shouted orders in their tongue. At his shout, the entire Greek force suddenly withdrew twenty paces. The Persian soldiers shouted as they ran into the space, falling over themselves. Artabazus waved his arms, yelling, fearing a ruse.

True Immortals would have advanced in good order, not abandoned their lines. These merely wore the coats of better men. They went in as a rabble, just as the shield line locked and reformed.

Once again, spears jabbed out, a host of the things that filled the view of every Persian advancing against them. Two or three razor points hit each man rushing that line. Artabazus could hear the dull orders of their captains calling each blow in and out – and in and back. It was ugly and workmanlike, but it tore the heart out of his people. No matter how brave they were, how strong, they were met with spears low and high. Though they tried to knock them aside, there were more, striking past to tear and gash thighs, arms, necks and shoulders, until they fell weakly back, panting, dying.

Artabazus felt despair spread. Good men could see no way past those thorns. The Greeks had killed hundreds, thousands, and lost only a few. Yet they still stood, spears raised and shields overlapping. All Artabazus could see was the shadowed helmet slits, the greaves beneath and painted faces on the shields, laughing at him.

Once again, his regiments pushed the wings back – and forced the entire line to retreat. Artabazus realised he was trampling through burned remnants of the camp, across scraps of tents and dead men, all crushed into the soft ground. Perhaps he could drive them to the river and overwhelm the wings then. They could not reform with rushing waters at their back – and he would have them at last. He nodded. Xerxes watched. He would whittle them down.

Artabazus filled his lungs to give new orders and one of the Greeks beat him to it, bellowing commands. Artabazus was close enough to the front to turn his head. He gaped, recognising Cimon from Cypros. And the one at his side . . . he had not learned his name, but he had commanded the little boat the Greeks had rowed ashore, letting Artabazus escape. He hesitated and in that moment, the Greek shield lines pushed back. They had held against an overwhelming force, but they too saw the danger of the river getting closer. To win themselves room, the entire line rushed forward at the same time, pulling back spears, using shields themselves as weapons, bashing them into faces all along the Persian ranks. It won them only a few paces, but then Artabazus saw something that tore the heart from him.

In the centre, perhaps a dozen of his men turned from that sudden advance. Artabazus could not know if they were exhausted, needing just to get back a few paces and regroup, or whether they thought they were about to be killed. Whatever it was, they buckled and turned to flee, pushing back into their own. Fear spread like fire across grassland.

The Greeks did not rush forward as his men had, Artabazus saw. Yet their officers were alive to the sudden advantage and snapped new commands. The spears were withdrawn once more and the entire shield line battered forward in another rush, hitting first with shields, then slamming spears through every gap – into the sides and faces of men still reeling. The Persian centre fell back again and Artabazus could see a great cup beginning to form as his line bowed and strained. In the crush, his men could not respond. They felt utterly helpless, and panic entered among them.

'Hold! Hold the centre! For the king!' Artabazus roared across them.

Some heard, but over the crash of sound, many did not. All they knew was that their rank was retreating from an enemy suddenly pressing forward.

Many tried to hold, for honour or the name Immortal. Yet each man faced death on his own. Whether it came or not, they turned from the implacable face of it, from spears that punched and jabbed and spattered blood over golden shields.

'Hold!' Artabazus cried in desperation, but they could not. They broke and the slaughter was terrible.

Xerxes watched in horror as a golden wedge drove through the heart of his regiments, itself a spear. His people could not hold and he wondered if his was a life cursed. He had come so close to victory, only to have it snatched from him.

He raised one leg to mount, his weight coming down on the outstretched hands of a personal slave. He swung his leg over and looked back at the battle still going on. Bitterness touched him.

CONN IGGULDEN

'That is enough,' he said. 'Mount your horses and take me from here. Quickly, before they come.'

His guards were still staring, he saw. They stood, patting idly at the necks of their mounts, shading their eyes to see. Anger rose in him, at failure and all their bovine stupidity.

'The battle is lost!' Xerxes shouted. 'Mount up! Or would you have your king captured as well?'

His tone seemed to call them back to awareness. Of the forty men he had brought to that place, a few flushed and cleared their throats as they mounted around him. Even then, he saw them following the progress of the slaughter in glances as they wheeled their mounts. Xerxes shook his head. Battles were fought by men – and men grew like weeds in scores of cities. He would come again, rebuild again.

The commander of his personal guard was a man who had served his father. In truth, Hafez was a little old for the role, more ceremonial than anything. His beard was grey and tightly curled, with skin like leather. Xerxes had known him since childhood and when the old man cleared his throat, the king looked up.

'Majesty, you should dismount,' Hafez said. His voice was gentle, as if he spoke to a child.

'What do you mean "should"?' Xerxes snapped. Had the old fool lost his wits? He could see Greeks roaming beyond the battlefield now, picking at corpses while others loped after his regiments. His Immortals were as dead as any other men, he saw.

One of the guards put his hand on the king's reins, holding the animal in place. Xerxes blinked. In a spasm of temper, he dug in his heels, hoping to see his horse scatter them. Yet the guard turned the horse's head, forcing it around while it whinnied and snorted. Xerxes reached for a jewelled sword at his waist and felt his arm held, actually held. They dared to touch him!

The slaves who trotted behind were prostrate, unmoving. The gaze of his guards was hard. Xerxes trembled, his voice shaking.

'Let me pass, Hafez,' he said. 'You would not break your oath. To me, to my father.'

'Dismount, Majesty,' Hafez said more firmly.

In a daze, Xerxes did so. He shuddered as they laid hands on him.

'Ride on, all of you,' Hafez ordered, his voice like a whip. 'This is not your concern. Go home. Find peace.'

'I will give a city to any of you willing to kill this man,' Xerxes said clearly.

He looked up, but no one returned his gaze. One by one, guards and slaves went away, leaving him behind.

In the end, Xerxes stood with just Hafez and one other. The man's son, he realised.

'Let me go,' Xerxes said. 'Please. I can raise another army, another fleet.'

'No,' Hafez said with regret. 'No, you can't.'

The sound of a horse approaching brought a new and different tension to the little hill. Xerxes looked up in hope, his eyes widening as he recognised the rider.

'Artabazus! Save me from these traitors. Honour your oath to me!'

The young king watched in hope as Artabazus turned his horse in place, looking back at the slaughter of the battlefield. The man did not smile as he looked at his king. Instead, he shook his head and rode on.

Xerxes slumped. He had withdrawn a dagger as Artabazus distracted the two men. He lunged with it then. Hafez jerked aside, so that it scraped his armour and did not draw blood.

CONN IGGULDEN

The old man took the blade from his hand and shook the king roughly.

'My father trusted you,' Xerxes said in fear. 'He watches you now.'

'Then I am sorry,' Hafez said.

He drove the dagger up under the king's ribs, working the blade back and forth until he was sure. Xerxes gasped and all the strength went out of him. Slowly, gently, his guard lowered him down and let him rest against a tree.

Hafez and his son looked at one another in grief. Their horses cropped the scrub grass of the hill and the sun was setting at last, turning the river gold. On the field of blood, Greeks were marching towards their position, interested in the men waiting on that hill.

'It is done,' Hafez murmured. He bent down and examined the young king he had loved all his life. 'He is dead. The empire mourns from this moment. Come, we must take his body home.'

37

Ephialtes walked through a field littered with dead men and fallen weapons. It was not a quiet place, not when Persian soldiers could be looted for amulets, coins, even beads woven into their beards, often in gold or jade. The rowers were busy there, sectioning off the field by ship's crew and bristling at anyone walking by, defending their territory as they stripped the dead.

Ephialtes shuddered at half a dozen sights as he made his way to Cimon. Attikos loped at his side like a tame wolf and Ephialtes was glad of his presence. It had been Attikos who'd kept him alive in the crush of men and flashing metal. The wound Ephialtes had taken was no more than a gash under his hairline, but it had spilled dark blood right down his face, and for a time he'd thought it might be mortal. A ship's carpenter had stitched it for him, but Attikos had kept him alive and he was grateful.

Ephialtes eyed the smaller man walking at his side, glaring at anyone who came too close. Attikos was a walking knuckle, ill-fed and scarred. Ephialtes knew by then that there was some enmity between him and Cimon, as well as Pericles. He did not know all the details, but it was hard to miss the way they looked on him. As the strategos approached Cimon, Ephialtes knew he should really send Attikos away, perhaps to the boats, already busy on the river. They needed willing hands – the labour getting that fleet afloat once more would be a week of work. Cimon had literally thrown everything at the banks of the Eurymedon. Many of his ships would have to be scavenged for the rest, with just keels and beams left to rot in the soft Persian mud. Every deck would be crammed with men on their return, Ephialtes thought – a return in triumph.

Cimon had become a man of influence. Without the Spartans, he had broken a huge fleet and army, on land and sea. The wrecks of Persian ambition still smouldered on the river, hissing as they collapsed into the muddy waters.

Ephialtes saw Cimon was talking to one of the enemy, a man who stood in subtly different armour, with his hands bound. It was typical of him, playing the noble archon while men still slipped from life.

Ephialtes waved a guard aside as the man sought to challenge him. Cimon looked over at that and smiled, no doubt secure in his victory. Ephialtes returned the expression, though something curdled in him. Cimon bore no wound, after all. Like all his class, he had sat back and let working men fight for him. No doubt he would not shrink from the cheers, or the adoration of crowds back at home.

'Strategos Ephialtes,' Cimon said in greeting. 'I am glad to see you on your feet. It looked a nasty wound.'

Ephialtes blinked. For a moment, he was touched by the concern, but he caught himself. That was just one of their tricks, the way they noticed little things and made a man think he was important to them. Archons and the sons of archons. The Eupatridae were taught such things from the cradle, he was certain.

Ephialtes bowed his head, acknowledging the comment.

'I've had a few stitches. You escaped any hurt?'

'Yes, thank the gods,' Cimon said.

'I see,' Ephialtes said drily.

To his pleasure, Attikos made a snorting sound of humour. Cimon frowned in recognition.

THE LION

'The man with you is a troublemaker, strategos. Attikos has been flogged at least twice – and that was lenient, considering all he has done.'

Ephialtes leaned back to look down his nose at Cimon.

'Is he? I have found him loyal enough. Perhaps I judge a man as I find him, not on his past.'

'Dangerous,' Cimon replied. 'The past can be a teacher – or a warning.'

He caught himself then, biting the inside of his lip before going on. While Ephialtes considered a stinging rejoinder, Cimon gestured to the man in bonds, still watching them.

'May I introduce His Majesty King Alexander of Macedon, our prisoner this day.'

The king bowed to them both, though to Ephialtes' eye, he too seemed to have some indefinable air of superiority, as if Cimon and the Macedonian shared the same joke. Amusement was part of it, even as one stood as prisoner to the other.

'A traitor to Greece,' Ephialtes said.

The king looked up sharply at that, but did not reply. Cimon sighed, suddenly weary. He was filthy with dust, sweat and bruises. He had not eaten all that day, nor slept the night before, that he could recall. The shine of battle was seeping from him, leaving him leaden.

'His Majesty is not Greek, of course,' Cimon said.

He made a gesture for Alexander to turn around and the king did so, trusting him. With a sawing motion, Cimon cut the ropes. Alexander of Macedon turned back and rubbed one wrist on the other, his eyes questioning.

'Take the rest of your men and go home,' Cimon said. 'I've made my decision.'

'You're letting him go?' Ephialtes demanded.

Cimon paled in anger then. He rounded on Ephialtes, fast

CONN IGGULDEN

enough to make Attikos drop a hand to his sword hilt in clear warning.

'I am the senior officer in the field, Ephialtes. I am navarch and archon of Athens. You think you can join my fleet in these last days, ruin ships and crews and then question my judgement in the field of war? You reach too far – and Attikos, *if you draw that sword another finger's-width, I will make you eat it.*'

Ephialtes mouthed in silence. The Macedonian king cleared his throat and Cimon looked back at him.

'Give me your word, Majesty. Never again to take the field against any force of the League, to call us friend and hon-oured ally from this day on.'

'My oath on it,' Alexander said with slow force.

Cimon jerked his head and the king left as quickly as he could, whistling to a group of his men who waited without arms or armour, hardly even under guard. Ephialtes watched in sullen anger. It seemed Cimon was rather friendly with men who had fought for a foreign king just that day, men who spoke Greek. Their crimes cried out to heaven and Ephialtes was honestly surprised not to see them all beheaded, or herded onto a ship and set afire. That would have been a fitting end, not just left to wander home.

From the moment the battle ended, Ephialtes had known he had some ground to make up with Cimon. He had fought – and taken a wound. With the great victory, they could surely put aside any small differences and begin again. Yet from the first, he had been greeted with cutting com-ments and scorn for his personal guard. Ephialtes gathered his wits, though his cheeks were hot with indignation.

'It is your decision, of course,' Ephialtes said. 'I just hope the Assembly agrees when we return.'

There. Let him worry about that! Ephialtes kept his ex-pression stern as Cimon glanced at him.

'Is that a threat, strategos?'

'Not at all . . . unless you would deny the Assembly their role? When we return to Athens, the people will decide honours and censure, will they not? As after Salamis? There will be an inquiry, with witnesses called to tell all they have seen. I imagine some will wonder why you released key prisoners, but that can wait till then. The campaign is not even over, after all.'

Ephialtes made himself finish on a more positive note, realising suddenly that it would be better in that moment if Cimon didn't think of him as an enemy. Armies lost men every day, on sea or land. Injuries brought fever and death, never mind desertion, fights – there were a hundred ways for a man not to come home. That was how Ephialtes would have handled the situation if their positions had been reversed. He suspected he would have to be careful from that moment – and he would certainly keep Attikos close. There was one he didn't have to worry about. Attikos knew his best chance was at his side, after all.

Cimon looked at Ephialtes strangely. He began to reply, but then saw Pericles and Epikleos approaching. Ephialtes felt a pang almost of jealousy as the man's attention turned from him, as if he didn't even matter.

Both newcomers looked exhausted, but Epikleos more so. He stood with hooded eyes, half asleep and swaying where he stood. He was the oldest among them and yet he too found the energy to glare when he recognised Attikos.

'You again?' Epikleos muttered.

Attikos winked at him, pleased to be known and feared.

'How is that theatre? All rebuilt?' Attikos replied.

Epikleos' mouth twisted as if he'd tasted something foul. He looked away rather than respond.

Pericles too had noticed Attikos. His smile faded and he

stood with his jaw slightly out, his expression hostile. Ephialtes shook his head.

'We did win the day, didn't we?' he said loudly. 'With so many glowering faces, I might wonder! Be assured, gentlemen, when I testify to the Assembly, I will speak well of all of you.'

Ephialtes smiled at that, delighted at his cleverness. Cimon and Pericles shared a glance of resignation.

'How many ships still swim?' Cimon asked the younger man.

'We've lost around a dozen beyond repair. Another twenty can still be saved in a good port with a dry dock. They can probably be patched and towed home, so Anaxagoras says. He is a fine judge of such things, Cimon. I trust his word on it. If we load those crews onto sound ships and avoid bad weather, we should be able to get them home. Just a couple of men on the tillers to steer and a lookout. The lighter the better, I think.'

'That's good – more than I'd hoped,' Cimon said. 'Very well. There isn't enough light now to begin boarding. Pass my order on for the men to make camp as best they can. There's little or no food, but they have the river to wash in and drink from. That will have to hold them until we're on board again tomorrow.'

'Wait . . . we're not going on?' Ephialtes interrupted. 'Half the enemy are still streaming away from this place! Will you let them go too?'

Cimon set his jaw and replied carefully, aware his words might one day be repeated before the Assembly of Athens.

'We have burned their fleet and broken their army, but I have neither men nor supplies for a prolonged campaign into the heart of Persia. My task here, strategos, was to break, burn and destroy the strength they gathered in this place.

That is accomplished. After all, I have no orders from the Assembly or the League to launch an invasion of the empire – unplanned.'

'It seems rash to simply abandon this position, however,' Ephialtes said, warming to his theme. 'Why not go a day inland, at least? Who knows what awaits us there?'

'You are welcome to, strategos,' Cimon said coldly. 'But I will not spend one more life without good reason. As navarch of the alliance, my orders are to head back to sea. Oh, and Strategos Ephialtes, I will be replacing the crew on your ship with better men. Yours are poorly trained and disciplined. You fall behind in every manoeuvre.'

'I believe I led the river landing, however,' Ephialtes snapped.

Once again, Attikos made his snorting noise.

'Though you were routed,' Pericles said.

Ephialtes looked to him. Yes, of course he would support Cimon. They were of the same social class. Just as Cimon had freed a king of Macedon with a wink and a smile. That was how their world worked.

'Against overwhelming odds, my crew made a good showing, I believe. I'd rather keep them. If they are taken from me, it will be against my will and I will be forced to make an official complaint when we get home. In addition to the rest of my testimony.'

The strategos scratched a thumbnail on his lower lip as if in deep thought.

'I wonder, though . . . I pray it is not true. Is it that your nerve has deserted you, Cimon? Perhaps . . .'

He broke off when Cimon gave a short, sharp bark of laughter, caught by surprise. To Pericles at least, it looked like he was in pain.

'My father stood at Marathon – and when he sought to punish the Persians, he took a wound that would kill him. I served at Salamis and saw more men drowned than I knew lived. So many, Ephialtes! All tumbling together, Persian and Greek. I have seen Cypros come over to us and been navarch to the alliance. This river, Eurymedon, runs red and black with char, with ash. No, we're finished here. Go where you want; I've seen enough of death today.'

Ephialtes could only stare at the raw emotion. He hated Cimon in that moment. He needed the noble class to be as facile and weak and pointless as he believed them to be. Not this. He looked for some other way to hurt this noble son of Athens.

'And yet . . .' he said, 'when you let a king of Macedon walk free from the field, I did not realise you would be withdrawing the army and fleet at the very moment of our triumph. Did he offer you something, Archon Cimon? You were talking to him as I came up, weren't you? What did that king and ally of the Persians promise you?'

'You faithless, ungrateful whoreson,' Epikleos growled at him.

He began to draw the sword at his waist and Attikos went for his own. Ephialtes gripped his man's wrist, knowing they were outmatched.

'There is no need for violence here, not among us,' Ephialtes said.

He had recovered his smile and if this was not where he had intended to end up, he could still make it work. He had Cimon, he was certain. No protection of his class would save him, any more than it had his father.

'When we return home,' Ephialtes went on, 'I believe it is my duty to call for a case in law – for a jury of our people to judge the actions I have witnessed here. Justice will be discerned then, not here, on a foreign field.'

The accusation would be enough, he was certain, just as it

had been for Pausanias of Sparta. Ephialtes could see that hard realisation bloom in Cimon's eyes. Of all men, he knew how far a conquering hero could fall. Cimon had been at his father's trial, brought merely for failure in battle. The Assembly was fickle and they punished the slightest taint of dishonour. If a strategos of Athens was the accuser, Cimon was done . . .

'I will prosecute him,' Pericles said suddenly. 'As my father brought the case against his father.'

'What?' Ephialtes said, off-balance.

Pericles shrugged.

'It is my right, as a free Athenian. You have called the matter, but I will make the case against.'

'I had thought I would do that myself . . .'

'Oh, I am sorry,' Pericles said. 'You should have said. Still, I will not withdraw now. I have spoken and it is my right. As my father before me, I would see justice done, swiftly and without mercy.'

Cimon turned a look of utter betrayal on the younger man. Ephialtes saw and nodded to himself. They were like cockerels, he realised. With just a little nudge, those noble sons would turn on one another and use their claws until blood flowed. It was even better coming from Pericles, though it made Ephialtes consider Pericles in a new light. If he could be so ruthless with those he had called friend, he would be a man to watch.

'Be about your duties, all of you,' Cimon said roughly. His voice was hoarse and he turned away from them. 'Tend the wounded and collect weapons and armour. We leave this place tomorrow.'

38

The king of Thasos stirred, woken in darkness. He sat up when his servant cleared his throat. The sun was rising and yet he had slept badly and yawned. He'd risen twice in the night to pee in the pot under his bed. As he swung his legs over, he felt the coldness of it against his heel.

'Majesty, I bear grave news,' the servant said.

He bowed his head while Hesiodos blinked at him. The king's bare legs were withered, the skin sagging almost like cloth. It still surprised him to see them sometimes, where once they had been powerful. He had leaped over walls as a young man, seeking out enemies or occasionally their daughters. His own wife had been a capture, carried on his shoulder while her husband and brothers beat the bushes for him. He rubbed one eye, feeling himself grow alert. Those had been better days. It had not escaped his notice that she'd been dressed for travel, nor that her brothers never came close to searching in the right place. It had still been exhilarating.

In memory, he reached across without looking, patting the place where she had lain for many years. Gone now. He missed her still.

Slowly, as all things were slow in the mornings, Hesiodos rose and stepped into his bathing room, where vats of water were heated before dawn for him. His slaves prepared a bath that took twenty years from his joints and brought him fully awake. He glanced over – the servant still waited. Hesiodos sighed as he was dried down. He slapped hands away as he dressed himself. He was not that old! His wife had needed help at the end, he recalled, when her face had sagged on the one side. That had been the strangest thing, but he had escaped her weakness, at least to that point.

By the time he put on a robe and sandals, the presence of the servant was beginning to annoy the king.

'Very well! What news has you hovering there like a fly? Before I have even eaten?'

The young man spoke in a rush then, desperately relieved to be able to pass on the news that bore him down.

'The League fleet has returned, Majesty. They have surrounded Thasos. Your admiral asks for your orders.'

King Hesiodos rose to his full height, his shoulders almost straight. He had been a warrior once and he remembered the arrogance of the Athenians only too well.

Leaving the room, he trotted down a long cloister to where steps rose to the highest point of the island, the tower of his palace. His legs were aching by the time he reached the top. Eighty steps brought flashing lights to his vision and he wondered if he too would be struck down.

If he had not been panting so hard, his breath might have caught at the sight that greeted him. The day was warm and the winds gentle, but he stood as if struck, sweat appearing on his brow.

Hundreds of ships had indeed surrounded Thasos. He knew the shape and type of them, as well as their purpose in his waters. His own fleet had been out of port when Cimon had come before, which had suited him well. It was easier to argue he could not afford a tithe or a ship for the alliance when he didn't have half a dozen in his personal dock.

Hesiodos rubbed his chin, resting one elbow on the stone parapet. He felt alert, he realised. The run up the steps had done him some good. Yet he could see boats coming in to land – without his permission. Hoplites of Thasos were

CONN IGGULDEN

down on the docks and there would surely be bloodshed if he did not take command. The king swore and began to trudge down the steps once again. At the bottom, he paused, calling for a messenger. There was more than one way to win a war.

Cimon brought his flagship alongside one he did not know, a fine vessel that had not been in port on his last visit. It grated on him that King Hesiodos could just have handed over two of those fine warships and there would have been no dispute. The fleet needed gold and men – but ships most of all. Cimon had lost enough of them at Eurymedon.

A dozen men in hoplite armour paraded on the docks, for all the world as if they would prevent him landing. Cimon's helmsmen were skilled enough to bring him in close and he chose to address them aloud. For once, it was without the staring eyes of Ephialtes, far out at the edge of the fleet with his poor crew. Cimon did not smile at the thought of Ephialtes raging. The man had made himself a threat – and one as yet unresolved.

It was a good part of the reason Cimon had returned to Thasos. If the inquiry in Athens went badly, he could be banished or executed. Even if they dismissed most of the accusations, Cimon knew he might still lose command of the fleet – and with it the chance to make an example of Hesiodos and Thasos.

He clenched his jaw as the king himself appeared on horseback, dismounting with a flourish like a man half his age. The king's guards all carried bows, Cimon noticed, as did some of the crews on his warships in dock, watching balefully.

Cimon dipped his head like a bull facing an enemy. If this was to be his last act as navarch to the fleet, there was no mercy left in him. He glowered as Hesiodos came close, seeing the king's resentment as he had to look up to an Athenian.

'You've had time to consider your answer to the League,' Cimon called to him. 'Will you honour the oath you swore at Delos? Or break it before the gods and doom all your people – and your line?'

'News of your victory reached me here weeks ago,' Hesiodos replied, his voice straining to match Cimon's volume. 'What fleet does Persia have now? Thasos is an island, Cimon. Only a fleet can attack us by sea.' Perhaps because he stood on his own land, on a dock he knew, he spoke with confidence, a smile twitching at his mouth. 'Let there be an ending made here. I release the League from your responsibilities to Thasos; release me from mine. Let that be enough.'

Cimon sighed. He had not expected anything else, though fine warships sat in dock and the gold mines on Thasos could pay their part of the tithe a dozen times over. He knew he could argue fairness or unfairness until he was blue in the face and it would make no difference. Still, he had not returned to Thasos to argue.

'As navarch of the League of Delos, I order your capture and immediate trial. Take him up.'

Hesiodos gaped, looking around in astonishment at Cimon's words. His own small guard braced for attack, while those on board his closest ships began to march down to the docks. Hesiodos was sweating in the morning sun, aware that his position was terrible. The League had no authority beyond what he granted to it, but they were all around Thasos and he . . .

Hesiodos saw that those coming off the ships were not forming up to protect him, but had surrounded his guards. There were scuffles and then bright blood splashed across the cobbles. The king shrank from the sudden presence of violence, but Cimon's men bound his arms behind his back and held him ready.

Cimon walked down a bouncing wooden gate from ship side to the dock. He did not smile and Hesiodos swallowed as he saw a darkness in the younger man that he had not observed on their first meeting. War changed a man, Hesiodos realised. It was not a pleasant thought. He had threatened and blustered – and been caught out. The realisation spread like a sickness in him.

'There is no need for any more killing!' Hesiodos said. 'What have you done? Where are my men?'

'Most are bound in the holds of your ships,' Cimon said as he came closer. 'Though a few fought last night. Poor leadership, Hesiodos. I don't like to punish slaves and followers. Not when I can stand before the man himself.'

'I will pay the tribute, Athenian,' Hesiodos said. 'Take one of my warships – with its hold full of silver. I will double the amount this year!'

Cimon looked around at the island stretching away from him. From the moment he had entered those waters, he had intended to make an example of the king. Hesiodos seemed to understand his life hung in the balance and sweat trickled down his cheeks like a tear. With his hands bound, he could not wipe it away.

Cimon rubbed his chin, considering whether an execution would weaken or strengthen the League. He remembered what Pericles had said of his father, when Xanthippus had run mad for a time. The Athenian had burned a dozen Persian towns after the death of his son. That loss of control still shamed their family, in both the fury and the telling of it.

It did not matter that Cimon could no longer trust Pericles. They had not spoken a word since the younger man had volunteered to stand for Ephialtes on their return. Cimon thought of his own father – and made his decision. Perhaps it would be one more stone for Ephialtes to throw when they returned, but no, he would not murder an old man.

'You will do more than that, Hesiodos. I see six ships in your dock. I will take those to help replace the ones we lost against Persians this year.'

'That is too much . . .' Hesiodos began to splutter.

Cimon went on, ignoring him.

'You will escort my men to your treasury and you will open it. Whatever lies within now belongs to the League. Now, we can leave it there . . .'

'This is piracy! How dare . . .'

'More! We will pull down the walls of your capital . . .'

'You have no right! I am a king!'

'More?' Cimon went on implacably. 'Very well! We will reduce your palace to rubble. Speak *again*, Majesty, and I will sack your capital. You call me Athenian? Remember then that I know what seeing a city burned means. You have broken your oath of Delos. I offer you penance be-fore the gods to redeem it – or destruction. Choose which it will be.'

Hesiodos glared. Cimon saw the man's mind working, yet the king did not seem bowed. There was a glitter of bright anger, even triumph in his eyes.

'Very well,' Hesiodos said at last.

'Good. Lead me in, Hesiodos. I would see this famous treasury of yours. Every piece must be counted.'

Hesiodos chose not to speak again. Deep in thought, the king looked down at the ground as they pushed him on, making him stumble. He'd known from the first sighting of ships that they would land. He was not yet sure they would let him live, but he had planned for their return, ever since Cimon had threatened him, his Athenian arrogance in every glance and turn of his head.

On foot, Hesiodos led them into his capital, seeing fearful families crowding back at the sight of strange soldiers. Some of them dared to call out to him, asking if he was all right. He felt the sting of humiliation then. His advisers had warned him Cimon would not forget his refusal. For a time, the king had thought he had been vindicated, that Cimon was too busy fighting a huge battle on some river so far to the east he did not even know its name. Then the League fleet had returned and all his hopes were dashed.

Hesiodos had made a mistake, thinking they would never dare to attack a member. Yet the Persians had lost their strength! From Marathon to Thermopylae and Plataea, then to their last roll of the dice at the river. There was no reason for the alliance to exist, not any longer. Men like Xanthippus passed from the world. So did oaths.

In the palace, Hesiodos saw hundreds of Cimon's League hoplites were already there, no doubt making sure his people were not hiding fortunes. He could not watch as they began to pull down the walls, using spears tied with hooks and ropes as well as great hammers. It was a deliberate cruelty and he saw no regret in Cimon as the man looked across.

Hesiodos nodded. They thought to make an example of him. They called themselves a league, but there was only one city at the heart of it. That was the truth, whether they admitted it or not. Athens was the great power, as shown in the presence of Cimon in his royal palace.

Only one city had the strength to stop them. As Hesiodos saw his treasure rooms opened and the first sacks carried into the light, he thought of the young messenger he had entrusted before going out. When it was dark, the boy would take his little coracle and row across to the mainland. He would make his way to allies – and the words of a king would wing across the land. It could not be stopped then. His cry for help would reach the kings of Sparta – and they would act.

Epilogue

The Spartan king stared through long grass at the man he would kill. Pleistarchus crouched in land more like a garden than a field of war. Dark reeds protected his men from any chance of being seen and a river ran through that part of the Peloponnese. It was all a far cry from the dust around Sparta, where water and food had to be fought for. Arcadia was a verdant place, of drooping fruit and gentle pastures. Pleistarchus could see the results in the young king who rode with so little caution, convinced he was the hunter and not the prey.

Pleistarchus sensed the man at his side might rise. He reached out and gripped his forearm hard enough to hurt. Tisamenus grunted, trying to pull away and failing. Water rippled under them in the marshy ground and something moved, splashing nearby. Pleistarchus held the man still harder. Tisamenus might have been made a Spartan citizen, but he had not been born one. Whatever the god Apollo had promised the soothsayer, Pleistarchus did not trust him.

'Let me go!' Tisamenus hissed, pale with pain.

'And see my luck walk away with you? No. Be silent.' Pleistarchus said.

He released him, knowing the order would be enough. Tisamenus glared then, real anger showing in his eyes. Pleistarchus did not look away and merely waited until the other man remembered he was as helpless as a child to any of the Spartans present. If Pleistarchus ordered his death, Tisamenus would not be able to save himself, not against the least of them. Even if he betrayed them all, Tisamenus would not survive.

A hundred paces away, the young king of Dipaea raised a hand to shade his eyes. He and his hunters had tracked four men from where they had been spotted near the walls of his city, following them all day to this place at the edge of his territory. His men were fit and they knew this land well. Though he'd forced them to a good pace, somehow the ones they followed had stayed ahead, glimpsed only in the distance as they crossed hills and ridges. King Anais did not know which of a dozen territories of the Peloponnese they called home, only that they loped along river banks and the middle of grassy meadows, leaving a trail a child could follow. The king was renowned as a hunter. Powerful of frame, Anais wore the skin of a lion he had brought down himself across his shoulders.

It had been a good plan and it had begun perfectly well. The young king who tried to band together all the peoples of the Peloponnese as a union had ridden out with flags and horns when strangers had been sighted and run from his guards. With a fine, clear trail to follow, Anais and his personal guard should have run straight into the arms of the Spartan force waiting for them.

Pleistarchus glanced back at the eighty Spartiate warriors he had brought to that place. Every one of them was over thirty and had fathered a son. They were the elite of his city – men renowned for their skill. Every single one was a name in Sparta. Yet they knelt in slippery muck and waited for the son of Leonidas to order them up.

The towns and small cities of the north were only a few days march from Sparta. He'd planned a quick campaign to put down the seeds of their little rebellion before it truly began. The Arcadians had their figurehead in Anais. They had their inspiration in the Athenians, with their alliance,

CONN IGGULDEN

their league. That was the heart of it, of course. Sheep who taught themselves not to fear the wolf.

Pleistarchus parted the fronds that hid him. By all accounts, this Anais spoke well. He talked of a new generation, of youth and strength. In another time, he and Pleistarchus might have been friends. Yet he had put himself on a path that led to his destruction. There would be no union of small states to challenge Sparta. Not on sacred ground. Instead, a leader would be killed, his head raised on a spear and planted before his own walls. The idea would be stillborn and forgotten in a generation. Sparta ruled. There would be no more challenges.

Pleistarchus had feared no small force the king could have brought with him. His four men had led a hunting party of no more than a hundred to the place Pleistarchus waited. The difficulty came from the much larger force approaching their position from over the nearest hill. Pleistarchus still didn't know if they were from the city of Mantinea, nearby, or somewhere further. He waited, judging their strength, feeling leeches or frogs slipping across his thighs in the silence.

The king hadn't moved and every time he turned to stare out over the marshy ground, Pleistarchus could believe he had been seen. There was something in the manner of the young man that made him think the sun had flashed on a shield. His men had smeared them with mud against such a thing, but it was not easy to hide eighty Spartans in a marsh, not when a few of the hunters were on horseback. One of them said something to the king and the man laughed.

'Will you withdraw?' Tisamenus whispered.

Six hundred men had come to that place – and whether they had been summoned by some unseen signal or were simply training in the area, they had certainly foiled the plan to kill Anais.

Pleistarchus looked at him in fury just for voicing the idea. Tisamenus was no ally, Pleistarchus reminded himself. The man was only present because he had been promised five successful contests. Plataea had been one – and presumably Cypros, as the Athenians called it a victory. Three more lay for the taking, Pleistarchus believed. He closed his eyes for a moment, dedicating his life to Apollo and Ares, then asking his father for a blessing.

'Up, lads,' Pleistarchus said. 'Destroy these laughing whoresons.'

The Spartans rose from the marsh as one. They had removed their helmets but they shoved them back on, raising spears and shields that were streaked in black mud. The king gaped at the sight as they lurched into view. Tisamenus found himself rushing forward with them rather than be trampled. He saw the young king yank on his reins and the horse's eyes wide and white-rimmed as the Spartans rushed them.

Anais never had a chance. Spears thrust at him rather than his horse. The Spartans knew better than to wound an animal that might drag its rider out of range. They made sure of the king and he slipped from the saddle as the animal kicked out and bolted too late.

His guards had come to that marsh to hunt criminals, not face armed Spartans intent on murder. They rallied quickly as Anais went down, no doubt raised on wings of outrage. It did not help them. The first dozen to engage met men who casually knocked their swords aside or punched them from their feet with the bosses of shields.

Tisamenus had to keep going, staying close to the son of Leonidas as he stalked a suddenly nervous enemy. The word of who they were flew ahead of them and he could see the

CONN IGGULDEN

name of Sparta was worth a regiment. Those they faced outnumbered them, but Pleistarchus drove his eighty Spartans straight into the heart of their lines. Spears stabbed out and men fell back into their fellows.

They formed a shield line, their own spears raised. The Spartan guards grunted as they battered those away. It was not weapons that won wars, but the skill of those who wielded them. Every man with Pleistarchus had learned to break a shield line for as many hours as he had devoted to maintaining one. They went through the front ranks of hoplites like men faced with boys.

When the spears broke or were lost, they drew not swords but the terrifying kopis blades that chopped and hacked with tireless horror amidst the lines. Each Spartiate advancing was a wall of bronze and a blurred kopis hacking at fingers, shins, shouting mouths. They tore through in blood and the slaughter was brutal.

Roaring anger was drowned in screams and when they broke, it was almost in relief. The Spartans did not pursue them, though Pleistarchus did not order them to hold. They knew they were still outnumbered, though half the Arcadians lay dead or groaning on the soft grass, bleeding into the earth.

Pleistarchus found he was breathing heavily. He knew he had killed a man, but he could not find the body in all the limbs and blood. He still held his kopis and he almost killed Tisamenus when the soothsayer moved on the edge of his vision. Tisamenus held up his hands, pale at the savagery he saw in the Spartan battle king.

With an effort of will, Pleistarchus controlled his fighting rage. He wiped his kopis clean and checked it for cracks or chips along the edge. It would have to be re-sharpened, of course. Piece by piece, he assessed his kit, removing his helmet and inspecting the nose-piece. It was a soothing ritual from childhood and it calmed him.

'A good day,' Pleistarchus said.

Tisamenus stood a little out of reach, watching the man go back to his usual quiet watchfulness.

'That is my third contest,' Tisamenus said grimly.

'And if there is another rebellion against Spartan rule, I will call you to my side once again,' Pleistarchus said.

'You will waste what I was promised!' Tisamenus replied.

'I will use it,' Pleistarchus said with a shrug. 'For the glory of Sparta. Perhaps we could have won without you today, or not. Who knows? I will not scorn a promise of Apollo.'

'I have other plans . . .' Tisamenus said.

Pleistarchus looked at him in genuine surprise.

'You have been adopted as a Spartiate, Tisamenus. I cannot undo that, but it puts you under my discipline, as it did with Pausanias, before. And if I choose to use your gift for two more battles, then send you away, that is what I will do. Or I will have you killed.' The king shrugged. 'Obey or disobey, Tisamenus. You are a man – the choice is your own.'

'Then I ask a favour,' Tisamenus said.

'I cannot say I will grant it. Ask.'

'If I remain at your side for one more victory, my fourth, I ask only that the last is held back . . . until you or I face Athenians on the field of battle. I made an oath to Pausanias and I would honour it.'

Pleistarchus chuckled. The day was gentle and the breeze was warm on his face. He nodded.

'I am willing, soothsayer. Very well. My word on it.'

CONN IGGULDEN

Historical Note

Cimon's story is surely one of the great lives of ancient Greece. Son to Miltiades who commanded at Marathon, Cimon was a young drunk who took hold of himself and rose to become a strategos of Athens during the Persian invasion. The part he played afterwards is well attested. He and hand-picked crews burned out Persian strongholds on islands like Eion and pirates on Scyros, where he also found the bones of Theseus and returned them to Athens. Cimon captured Cyprus, destroyed a secret Persian fleet on the Eurymedon river – and landed to break an army that would have invaded a third time. In that way, Cimon brought down Xerxes, the king killed by his own guards. Cimon became the greatest strategos of Athens, the lion of a new generation.

The lack of information for key years between the Persian wars and the conflict with Sparta is a great shame. The details of Xanthippus' passing have been lost, for example, though it was around 478 BC – just after the Delian League was formed. In many ways, that is the foundation event for modern Greece and so has especial significance. Men like Aristides and Xanthippus gathered leaders to Delos and secured an eternal oath. Iron ingots were dropped into the sea as a physical demonstration as well as a metaphor. The treasury was stored on Delos for years.

Below the age of thirty, Pericles too is often missing from the record. Given his father's active involvement in the fleet, the overwhelming likelihood is that he was with Cimon for the key events of this book, but there is no way to be certain. In later life, he led military forces at sea and on land. His early training can only have been undertaken here, in these years.

I have used licence to put the Persian general Artabazus on Cyprus at the time of the Greek attack. Artabazus did survive Plataea – the only senior officer to do so. Through a combination of bribery, persuasion, force and sheer lies, Artabazus brought around twenty thousand Persians out, across Macedonia and modern-day Bulgaria (Thrace) and all the way home. There is a striking comparison to be made with Xenophon's Ten Thousand (as told in *Falcon of Sparta*) – but one lesson might be: whether or not the victors write history, *someone* has to. Without a Xenophon to record that epic return, the details are lost for ever. Artabazus was welcomed by Xerxes and given a satrapy by the Hellespont as reward for his service. I put him at the battle of Eurymedon river, though that is unknown. His military career continued long afterwards, however.

Pericles returned home to Athens after the death of his father. For the great festival of Dionysus that took place in Athens each spring, he was indeed the 'choregos' (producer) for Aeschylus' set, including *The Persians*, the earliest surviving tragedy. The description of Greek theatre is as accurate as I can make it. Drama itself seems to have been the worship of Dionysus – putting it on and going to see plays. Each playwright was judged by ten judges chosen at random from the tribes of Athens. The playwright and choregos put on a set of four – three tragedies and a 'satyr' play.

(Note: the satyr plays were a sort of tragi-comedy produced with three more serious works. The satyrs in question did wear huge erect phalluses and donkey ears, so they are

CONN IGGULDEN

unlikely to have been too subtle. Unfortunately, only one by Euripides survives – with a few fragments of others. It is hard to describe an entire genre from that. It is also a matter of scholarly dispute whether the seating in Athens was arranged by tribe and whether women and slaves had sections to themselves.)

At this point, drama tended to be very serious indeed and often consisted of re-enactments of legends and myths. To set a play in recent years with characters who still lived was extraordinary and daring. I hope I've represented fifth century BC theatre with some of the original energy. Though a little later, I recommend the plays of Aristophanes. He was a mad genius and could be very funny.

Sponsoring a play was a well-established route to becoming a name in Athenian politics. In supporting Aeschylus, Pericles backed a man who had actually stood alongside his father on the field of Marathon. Together, Pericles and Aeschylus would win the great competition of Dionysus, but in addition, Pericles seems to have collected an extraordinary group of dangerous thinkers during this decade. He learned argument from Zeno and natural science from Anaxagoras. They were misfits and outsiders, but became his great friends – and they were key influences during this crucial time. The man he is here is not the man he will become, not yet.

Note: the names of Pericles' two sons were Xanthippus, named for Pericles' father, and Paralus, after an Athenian hero. Gaps in the record are always interesting to writers, such as much of his first marriage. As a matter of interest, the Greeks avoided giving authority to men in their twenties, as it was considered the most dangerous decade. They were certainly adult and full of life and strength, but inexperienced and therefore capable of tremendous error. As such, they had to be kept away from serious decision-making. They could not be strategoi or magistrates or stand for the council until the age of thirty.

I've told the end of Pausanias as it was written by Thucydides. Events are one thing, motivation can be harder to discern. There *were* some accusations of Persian prisoners going missing, with the accompanying suspicion of bribery, but the manner of his death is still surprising. I imagine the young King Pleistarchus – and of course his ephors – might have been pleased to have the victor of Plataea brought low.

Pausanias did take refuge in a small temple of Athena known as the Brazen House – or Bronze House in modern translations. He could not be taken out of that sanctuary and so his own mother, Theano, set a brick in the doorway, denying him as her son. He was then walled in and died of thirst. He deserved rather better, I think. As King Pleistarchus died without an heir, the line of Pausanias rose once more. His son would become king, which might explain why statues to Pausanias were raised in that place.

After the battle of Eurymedon river, the threat of Persia under Xerxes had vanished. Cimon had played a crucial role and, as leader of Delian League forces after Pausanias' destruction, perhaps it is not so surprising that he reacted badly to a minor rebellion by the island of Thasos. The Thasians made the not-unreasonable point that the huge sum they paid each year to the treasury at Delos was no longer needed. In reply, Cimon besieged them for two years, destroyed their small navy and surrounded their capital. The people of Thasos were appalled – and they sent messengers to Sparta, the only military force in Greece capable of taking on Athens, asking them for justice.

CONN IGGULDEN

Life is linear in one sense – events do follow one another. They also happen in clusters and sometimes all at once. It is tempting to impose a clean narrative on events: Scyros, Cyprus, Eurymedon, Thasos. History is always more complex, however. At the distance of over two thousand years, events can sometimes seem inevitable. The reality is that individuals made the best choices they could, for good or ill – and sometimes all they valued would be swept away by forces they could neither control nor predict. For those who wish to learn more of this extraordinary period, I recommend *Pericles: A Biography in Context* by Thomas R. Martin.

Finally, it has always been my preference to cut out years where little happened, though it does sometimes leave me with characters who are too young. I have compressed some of the lesser years of Pericles in his twenties. The ancient world moved slowly and fleets were slower still. It's my feeling that plots should be faster.

The final book of the series brings us to the great years of Pericles, my intention from the very beginning. It will also bring war with Sparta.

Conn Iggulden, London, 2021